Jackie FRENCH

The Lily
in the Snow

Angus&Robertson
An imprint of HarperCollins*Publishers*

Angus&Robertson
An imprint of HarperCollins*Publishers*, Australia

First published in Australia in 2019
This edition published in 2020
by HarperCollins*Publishers* Australia Pty Limited
ABN 36 009 913 517
harpercollins.com.au

HarperCollins*Publishers*
Level 13, 201 Elizabeth Street, Sydney NSW 2000, Australia
Unit D1, 63 Apollo Drive, Rosedale, Auckland 0632, New Zealand
A 53, Sector 57, Noida, UP, India
1 London Bridge Street, London SE1 9GF, United Kingdom
2 Bloor Street East, 20th floor, Toronto, Ontario M4W 1A8, Canada
195 Broadway, New York NY 10007, USA

A catalogue record for this book is available
from the National Library of Australia

ISBN 978 1 4607 5385 9 (paperback)
ISBN 978 1 4607 0838 5 (ebook)

Cover design by Lisa White
Cover images: Woman © Ildiko Neer / Trevillion Images;
all other images by istockphoto.com
Author photograph by Kelly Sturgiss
Typeset in Sabon LT by Kirby Jones
Printed and bound by CPI Group (UK) Ltd, Croydon, CR0 4YY

To Lisa and Cristina,
who changed a single book that worked
a little too well into a quite different series,
and to Eve and Angela,
who helped make it happen

AUTHOR'S WARNING

Two passages in this book contain the verbatim words firstly of HRH Edward, Prince of Wales, and later the words and beliefs of Adolf Hitler. The sentiments expressed by both are vile, inaccurate in every way, and abhorrent. Including them in this book was necessary, however, as the beliefs of those men led to so much tragedy. If we are to understand how the horrors of World War II happened, as well as the perversion of the philosophies of men like Nietzsche into the fascist belief that continues today, we need to know not just what those men stated, publicly and privately, but what they urged and, in Hitler's case, forced or coerced their citizens to do. As both men are now distant in history, and yet gaining defenders in a world that has not personally seen the horror they unleashed, it is important that the men, and their ideas, be accurately portrayed.

Chapter 1

There is an art to feeding a man so he is no longer hungry, and yet longs for more.

Miss Lily, 1913

LONDON, 20 DECEMBER 1928

VIOLETTE

Rats scampered, frozen footed, across the snowdrifts in the alley next to Worthy's Teahouse in Mayfair. The child stood singing by the doorway, angelic in her plain white dress, paler than the grey slush of London, her curls blonde, her face and fingers tinged with blue. Her voice soared, high and pure.

In front of her, fashionable London hurried home dressed in fur coats, fur-lined gloves or fur-collared overcoats, arms loaded with Christmas presents, or with footmen to carry the parcels walking behind.

Only those who paused to listen noticed that, though the words of the Christmas carols were English, the accent was French, perhaps, or Belgian. Others might wonder if the child's thinness disguised her true age, closer to thirteen, maybe, than ten. None saw the calculation in her eyes. She made very sure that they did not.

An elderly gentleman pushed open the teahouse door, then paused to drop a shilling in the cloche hat at the girl's feet. Such small feet, stockingless, in shoes slightly too large. 'Are you hungry, my dear?'

'I am always hungry, monsieur,' she said, presenting him with a smile that might have been worn by the angels in the battered convent, years before.

He gestured to the doorway. 'If you would like …'

'Thank you, monsieur,' she said demurely. She bent to pick up her hat with cold stiff fingers, wrapping it around its coins.

He followed the girl inside. This would never do at the Savoy, of course, nor even at Simpson's. But taking a shabby child into the warmth of Worthy's for a cup of tea was so obviously a charity.

The room smelled of toasting teacakes and damp shoes. He sat across from her and watched her read the menu, her hat and its coins on her lap, the snowflakes melting in her blonde curls. It was not easy coiling naturally straight hair in rags each night to ensure ringlets, but the effect was worth it.

'Hot chocolate, monsieur?' the girl asked shyly, glancing up with wide blue eyes.

'Of course, my dear.'

'And may I perhaps have buns?'

He smiled expansively. 'Anything you wish.'

'Buns *and* cheese on toast? Oh, thank you, monsieur!'

He gestured to the waitress.

Worthy's service was efficient. The cocoa and buns were brought immediately. The kind gentleman waited till she had sipped her hot drink and eaten half a bun quickly but delicately. 'What is your name, my dear?'

'Violette, monsieur.' The girl finished the first bun, and began on the next.

'It's a miserable day for a child all alone in a big city,' he suggested.

She raised blue eyes to him. 'Oh, yes, Monsieur.' The answer might have been an admission that she *was* alone, or simply agreement. She finished the second bun, then smiled as the toasted cheese was placed in front of her.

'You are French?'

'Belgian, monsieur,' she said shyly, as if she did not like to correct such a knowledgeable man.

'A refugee?' he asked, sympathetically. The Great War had been over for a decade but some, at least, had not returned home, their villages destroyed or haunted by the atrocities they had suffered.

'No, monsieur. I have come to England to find my mother. Her name is Lily Shillings. She came from a village called Shillings too, but I cannot find it on a map.'

She offered the information, as she always did, in the hope that it might elicit information, an 'Ah, I know the family well' or 'You mean Shillings in Yorkshire?' But the man showed no sign that he knew the name.

'How did you lose her?' The kind words did not quite disguise his, still unspoken, quiet planning. 'During the war?'

Almost every family across the British Empire had been fractured by the war, but those countries where it had been fought had suffered worst, homes turned to rubble, farmland to blood and mud, families running in the night.

'Yes, monsieur.'

The gentleman didn't query how a Belgian child had an English mother. Violette was used to that. This conversation was simply to establish that she was, indeed, unprotected, and to suggest that he, a nice man, grandfatherly — though of course he would think of himself as virile, an elder, not really old — might help. He touched her thin bare hand briefly with his gloved one. 'What will you do when you find your mother, my dear?'

Violette finished her cocoa before she answered. Usually she gave an answer the gentlemen would like — 'I will never leave her side' or 'I wish so much to be loved' — before quickly pocketing whatever tip they left on the table then escaping into the crowd before he offered her a warm, safe ... and, presumably, discreet ... place to stay.

But this was the third teahouse and friendly gentleman today. Violette was no longer hungry and the money in the hat would pay for her lodging. And so she smiled at him, her first genuine smile of the day. 'When I find her I will kill her, monsieur.'

She took the last slice of toasted cheese with her as she left.

Chapter 2

Middle-class girls dream of being wives and mothers. Girls of the upper echelons know that others will care for their children, their meals, their clothes. They dream of alliances, and their families plan them. Those alliances bring power.

Miss Lily, 1913

SHILLINGS, 18 JANUARY 1929

SOPHIE

'Pardon the intrusion so early, your ladyship, but the Prince of Wales is in the breakfast room.'

Sophie opened her eyes. She had been dreaming: gold grass that crackled underfoot and white-trunked trees; a green-eyed man with sun-kissed skin, bare chested as he sat on a stump of wood and carved his crosses.

She blinked at the small, nervous maid in the doorway. Beside her Nigel woke and yawned. The room smelled of the apple-wood flames twisting up the fireplace, her own perfume and the bay rum Nigel used after shaving. Outside the wind stroked the old stones of Shillings Hall. 'Did you say the Prince of Wales, Amy?'

'Yes, your ladyship. In the breakfast room, your ladyship. Sorry, your ladyship.' Amy bobbed a curtsey.

Well, thought Sophie, today at least would not be boring.

Three years earlier she had flown across the world to save the man yawning beside her. Her reward: a husband she loved, twins she adored, an estate run by the excellent agent she had appointed, a household that ran perfectly.

4

She was beginning to realise that a happy ending might be a slightly dull one.

Though, of course, she now had a title too, and a prince who felt free to inhabit their breakfast room.

'Did His Royal Highness say what he wanted?' asked Nigel sleepily. Presumably not breakfast, thought Sophie. The Prince of Wales rarely ate breakfast or luncheon, convinced, despite his acute thinness, that he was chubby.

'His Royal Highness said he was due to launch a ship at Southampton this morning, your lordship.'

'Which is probably why David has vanished in the other direction,' murmured Nigel. The heir to the throne's habit of not appearing at official functions was legendary to those who knew him, though of course never mentioned in the press. The public wanted a prince charming, and should have one.

'Tell His Royal Highness we will be there immediately.' Nigel swung his legs out of bed.

'Nonsense. Stop pandering to him,' said Sophie. 'You need to shave and Green needs to do my hair properly. James and Hannelore are coming to lunch, remember?' She turned back to Amy. 'Please tell His Royal Highness he has to have a cup of coffee and a bowl of porridge before I get there. Tell him he's as thin as a match with the wood shaved off and that I will be seriously annoyed if I don't see a nearly empty bowl in front of him.'

Amy looked even more terrified.

'Just tell him we will be there as soon as we can,' Nigel assured her. 'Would you mind seeing that his guards get breakfast too? In the library, I think. His Royal Highness always forgets they need to be fed.'

Nigel turned to Sophie as Amy shut the door. 'Darling, he *is* the Prince of Wales.'

'And I am an ignorant colonial and so I don't know one is not supposed to order a prince to eat his porridge. Besides, David likes women ordering him around.'

Nigel paused, his hand on his brocade dressing grown. 'Has David made a pass at you?'

5

'Of course, darling. It would have been rude of him not to. David does like married women. How do the Americans put it? Married women never tell, rarely swell, and are grateful as hell. But he was sweet when I said no.'

'You should have told me.' It was impossible to interpret Nigel's emotions from his words.

Sophie hesitated. Intercourse had become an impossibility for Nigel since the surgery shortly after their wedding. Nigel, of all people, knew that did not mean the end of physical satisfaction for Sophie, and nor had it. But Sophie knew that even a touch anywhere abdominal could mean agony for Nigel. Although managing well, he still had days when pain from what the surgeon diagnosed as growing adhesions — places where the scar tissue was growing into other organs — made it difficult to leave his bed. The condition was not usually dangerous, but that did not lessen the pain, or the exhaustion pain brought with it.

Sophie suspected that sexual desire might lead to pain too. She was the one now who subtly warded off Nigel's even subtler sexual overtures.

Was this a mistake? They had never discussed his limitations or desires. They should have, Sophie realised, just as she should speak of the man who was as likely as Nigel to have fathered the twins who were now probably spitting out their own porridge in the nursery down the hall.

Sophie had slept with John just once, a night of desperation and joy in his hut at Thuringa, before her wild flight across the world to be with Nigel before the operation that might have killed him. That extraordinary man with dark green eyes, so different from the dapper Prince of Wales. And from Nigel, whom she loved ...

'You will never need to reassure me,' said Nigel quietly. 'If you wish to have an affair —'

'I don't.'

Nigel reached for his dressing gown, rather than ring for Brooks, his valet. 'You will one day.' He spoke with the confidence of a man who knew women well.

6

Sophie thrust away the memory of the scent of gum leaves and fresh sweat. This was not the day to discuss the complications of sex, not with a prince of the realm hopefully now scoffing porridge below. 'Well, if I do have an affair,' she said lightly, 'it wouldn't be with David. I am far too outspoken to be a prince's mistress.'

'You'd demand Home Rule for Ireland and legal contraception instead of a diamond bracelet?'

'At the very least.' She smiled at him, this darling man she would never regret marrying, despite her longing for deep blue sky and blue-hazed hills — and the occasional slow burn of a body that longed for love. Sweat and twisting limbs, not discreet, soft loving touches in the night, the call of a mopoke as if it were laughing at them, the thud of a wallaby startled by the sounds of human passion ...

She thrust the memory away again. Nigel had always known Rose and Danny might not be his. He knew she had loved the man who had called himself John to honour his twin brother, dead in the Great War. Some had called 'John' a saint. Sophie knew that he was not, or not if sainthood demanded celibacy.

Sophie had loved Nigel for years; she had loved Miss Lily even longer. But she had not married him when he had first asked her, after the war, but almost a decade later when he had needed her to save his life, and Shillings. She loved Shillings too, the isolated estate wrapped in its ancient hedges and stone-walled fields. But this cold grey morning she longed for the scent of the billy boiling on a campfire of eucalypt branches, of summer sweat, and for the uninhibited yelling of cicadas.

'Homesick?' Nigel asked.

Darling Nigel. He always understood her. 'A little. It's the long winter days.'

'You used to love snow.'

'That was before I got chilblains in makeshift hospitals in France and Belgium,' she said drily.

The door opened. A good lady's maid never knocked. Green was the perfect lady's maid. She was also one of Nigel's oldest friends, almost as close as Jones, who had once been the Shillings butler and was now Nigel's secretary, godfather to the twins and, since Green's return from Australia, once again her lover. Green was entirely happy for others to have husbands. She merely did not want one for herself.

Green placed the tea tray on the side table. Three teacups, not two. A maid who was a friend drank tea with you. 'The Prince of Wales —'

'Is in the breakfast room. I know,' said Sophie, pouring the tea, smoky and fragrant and imported from Japan, then handed Nigel and Green their cups. She took a Bath Oliver and nibbled.

Green sipped her tea. 'Actually he's up in the nursery playing horsey with the twins.'

Sophie grinned. David was impossible. Moody, demanding, irresponsible, but how could you not like a prince who appeared at dawn to play horsey with your twins?

'With a bit of luck Nanny will order him to eat up his porridge too.' Nanny had once had her own name, but had been shocked when Sophie had used it. Sophie had not made that mistake again. 'The green wool dress and jacket?' she added to Green, as Nigel crossed the room to the door that connected to his dressing room, where Brooks would be waiting, today's tweeds warming by the fire.

'The claret silk dress with the ruby beading,' said Green firmly. 'After all, he is the Prince of Wales. You might not get a chance to change for lunch either and the prinzessin always dresses beautifully.'

'Royal poise. Hannelore would make a hessian sack look stunning.' Sophie gazed out at the snow. 'Motorcars,' she muttered. 'I liked it better when it took most of a day to get here by train. Now people can invite themselves whenever they like.'

'You could have said no,' said Green mildly, sipping her tea.

'Hannelore is my oldest friend, even if she keeps inviting me to Germany to meet this miracle politician of hers. I am never going to Germany again, and she should know why. And James ...'

Sophie took another biscuit. James Lorrimer, public servant in the most literal sense, spymaster and confidant, had once asked her to marry him. Through most of the Great War they had both assumed that she would. Now he too was a friend. 'James will want something too.'

'He hopes you'll open the London house again so you can keep an eye on upper-class bolshevism,' said Green.

Sophie sighed. 'I have attended six extremely cold and very boring meetings with Lady Mary, and given James my report. The British communists are good hearted, ineffectual and carefully ignorant of what is really happening in the Soviet Union. As far as I am concerned Nigel and I have done our duties to our countries, and more.'

'Nigel would say that one's duty continues till one dies,' said Green.

'And what would Miss Lily say?'

'The same,' said Green, who had known Nigel and Miss Lily for far longer than Sophie had, a fact Sophie only sometimes resented. 'Noblesse oblige.'

'I am not noble, even if Nigel has given me his title. I am an Australian of working-class stock and my factories feed the Empire. I've done enough duty for one lifetime.'

Green eyed her shrewdly. 'But you are bored.'

'Oh, dear. Greenie, darling, do I show it?'

'I don't think Nigel has noticed, or Jones. Jones is happy with a quiet life at last. And Nigel ...'

Green grew silent. Both women knew Nigel had hoped to win political influence when he finally took up his seat in the House of Lords after the war. But while Miss Lily had quietly commanded the respect of most of the most influential women — and some of the men — of the great houses of Europe, Nigel was ... unremarkable. Not a bad speaker; a sound man, but not compelling.

Nigel had not been sorry when increasing illness had forced an end to an unspectacular career. He showed no signs of wanting to resume it. Perhaps he had accepted he had neither the charisma nor the connections to influence government policy. Perhaps he simply no longer had the stamina.

Did he wish for more? Sophie had never asked him. Nor had he asked her.

'I can tell because I'm bored too,' said Green, her blue eyes frank and friendly under her bobbed hair. As a lady's maid, Green did not wear a maid's cap, just a black dress — a subtly more glamorous one than other ladies' maids, created by a Paris fashion house to be unobtrusive, but fit her still most excellent body in the most flattering way possible.

Green had been Miss Lily's maid and companion in adventure for decades, often in the service of their country. She had left only when Miss Lily had been forced to vanish during the war, but returned to Shillings at Jones's request to support Sophie's rescue of Hannelore from the rebels after the war. Green had shared Sophie's life in Australia as her maid there too, as Sophie tripled the vast business empire her father had left her then campaigned for her 'almost' success in the election.

'Back at Thuringa you'd have seduced a handsome young stockman.'

'I can't do that here,' said Green regretfully. Like nearly all the Shillings servants and tenants, except for Jones, she had been born on the estate, and was related to almost every household. 'I'm not even sure I'd want a young stockman any more.' She hesitated. 'I miss Lily. I thought I wanted routine after the war. But life with Lily was ... eventful. I miss that too.'

'But Miss Lily has gone,' said Sophie softly, trying to ignore her own pang of loss for the woman she loved. So Green was bored too. 'We both know why.' She put down her teacup. 'At least we have a royal prince to entertain us this morning. That will be diverting, at least. And I will wear the claret silk.'

'With pearls,' said Green. 'The long ones, in a double drape.'

'And pearls. Or maybe I will call Ethel's nephew and have him whisk us off to Paris or Istanbul in his aircraft.'

'Not in a snowstorm,' said Green practically.

'Bother the snow,' said Sophie.

Twenty minutes later, clad in the low-waisted claret silk and looped pearls, her hair shining, her make-up light and perfect, Sophie emerged into the corridor just as the Prince of Wales, on all fours, thudded past with her not quite two-and-a-half-year-old daughter on his back, followed by Jones bearing Danny.

'Gee-gee!' yelled Rose, who had not yet achieved much intelligible vocabulary, one hand clinging to his shoulders, the other waving in triumph as she and the prince reached the end of the corridor first. A Ming vase threatened to topple off its console table.

'We racing, Mama!' announced Danny.

Sophie steadied the still rocking vase. She smiled at the prince, a slow meeting of eyes, an even slower moistening of her lips, just as Miss Lily had taught her all those years back, so that for three long seconds the prince knew he was the only person in her world. 'Should I curtsey, Your Royal Highness, or present you with a rosette and a nosebag of hay?' Sophie offered her cheek for a kiss, swan-like, graceful. Impossible after Miss Lily's lessons to be less.

The prince smelled of something spicy. His lips were cool. 'Coffee?'

'I think we can manage that. Rose, darling, go with Nanny now.'

Rose met her mother's eyes. 'More gee-gee!' she demanded.

'Breakfast.'

'Gee-gee!'

Sophie's hazel eyes met her daughter's defiant green ones. Gum-tree green. Danny had already obediently taken Nanny's hand. 'Breakfast,' stated Sophie.

Rose accepted the inevitable. 'Bye-bye.' She patted the prince's immaculately trousered leg and toddled after her brother, carefully ignoring her mother.

'She'll have forgiven me by mid-morning,' said Sophie, taking the prince's arm. 'Breakfast for you, too.'

'I'm banting.'

'You are doing no such thing. You are positively skinny, David. Stop all this too fat business immediately.'

'Yes, Sophie.'

'And don't "Yes, Sophie" me like that. I'm serious.'

'Yes, Sophie.'

Sophie grinned at him, then sobered. 'What's wrong? Nigel said you were supposed to be launching something or other this morning.'

'A useless job for a useless prince.'

'David —' She stopped at the sudden despair in his voice.

'You know it's true. My father only allowed me to even see cabinet documents last year because the doctors told him he was dying. Now I am useful for display purposes only.'

'And you want more?'

'By Jove I do. I *need* more. The country needs more. Sophie, last month, up in Wales, seeing those families starving — men working twelve-hour days in the pits and yet their families can't buy enough bread to eat. I cried,' he said simply. 'Twelve years ago I saw men like that die for their country in a stupid, useless war. Now the warmongers rise again and my people starve and I can do nothing.'

It was true. She had no comfort to give him. 'I'm sorry, David. One day ...' It was scarcely tactful to say his life would change when his father died. That might be forty years away, now that the king had recovered. And how much power could a king wield these days?

'Yes,' David said quietly. 'One day. But by then there may be no monarchy to inherit. My grandfather once told me that kings are no doubt important people, but they can all too easily lose their thrones. And they are too apt to think of themselves and not other people.'

'Your grandfather was wise man.'

'A wise king, though my mother did all she could to stop our chats in case he gave me ideas about being a truly *effective* king one day. I am supposed to be a puppet prince, good for opening bazaars and mouthing platitudes. But the old man was right. The people shot my godfather, the tsar of all the Russias. It could happen here. Remember the English soviets proclaimed by the troops during the ceasefire?'

'The English soviets only lasted a few days before the men all went home. The people love you, David. The newspapers adore you.' And you should still do your duty and launch that thingummy, she thought.

But just now it was more important that he eat, and be comforted with all the charm a student of Miss Lily could provide. Hereward appeared to open the breakfast-room door for them, just as the footmen carried in the silver chafing dishes of kedgeree, devilled kidneys, bacon on fried bread, eggs coddled and eggs scrambled with smoked salmon, the silver porringer, and set them on the sideboard next to the ham, the cold game pie, the piles of apples, tangerines, grapes.

'David, old chap,' said Nigel, appearing in sombre tweed. 'So good to see you, sir.'

The day had formally begun.

Chapter 3

Duty is such a simple word. You will meet it often, I hope, if your lives are to be rich ones. And each time it will have a different meaning.

Miss Lily, 1913

David ate his porridge almost without noticing, as Sophie told him yet another story from her wild impossible flight across Australia and north to India. 'Miss Morrison was extraordinary. Her face had been burned off when she rescued a pilot from wreckage at the Somme, but she flew her aircraft like an eagle.'

David absent-mindedly took a bite of the parsley-dotted scrambled eggs Sophie had placed in front of him. 'I think I will learn to fly.'

'They'll tell you it's too dangerous,' warned Nigel, forking kedgeree.

David shrugged. 'My father still has two other sons.'

One of whom was addicted to morphine, fast women, the occasional fast man, and even faster cars, and the other crippled by shyness and a stammer, thought Sophie. 'Toast?'

'Far too fattening.'

'David, for the fiftieth time, you are not fat. Eat up your toast and marmalade then we can go for a nice fitness-enhancing walk. Unless of course you intend to go to your launch.'

'Terribly bad manners to be late,' the prince said lightly. 'Best not go at all. What have you to show me? A fascinating new enterprise to breed zebras?'

Sophie laughed. 'Only a few new pigsties. But a walk in the snow will be ... bracing.'

'I'd rather ride.'

It was a command from a man used to his every wish being granted, except the ones that mattered most. It hurt Nigel to ride these days, but nonetheless Sophie rang for Hereward to ask Billson to bring the horses round.

The good sweet smell of hot horse droppings on fresh snow almost reconciled Sophie to the English winter. She and David raced along the road to the cottages. Nigel would follow sedately in the car, thus allowing the prince an illusion of flirtation. David won the race by leaping the stone wall — foolhardy when one didn't know what might be behind it — but one could not say that to a prince, especially one who needed reassurance.

They slowed the horses to a walk after that. Word of the prince's arrival had flowed from manor house to estate cottages. The doorways were crammed with women curtseying, girls trying to look both demure and enticing in what was obviously their Sunday best, hair hurriedly loosened from plaits, or adorned with ribands for those who had dared their parents and 'bobbed'. One of the men called out, 'God save His Highness!' The cry echoed along the line of houses, each with its post-war tiled roof, modern plumbing — water piped to a tap indoors, with another pipe to remove it — and new plaster. Each had its vegetable gardens of cabbages and leeks poking green heads out of the snow, and brambles that would be roses come summer.

'A model estate,' remarked the prince, as Nigel parked the Rolls and joined them. And an extremely damp one, thought Sophie as the horses walked slowly past the last cottage, Nigel at her side. If the grey sky was any lower she'd be able to poke a hole in it with her umbrella.

'We do our best, sir.' Nigel looked at a crop of winter wheat with satisfaction. 'Sophie found the perfect estate agent after the war. It's a pity he's at a sale today — he'll be wrecked at missing the Prince of Wales. The estate runs like clockwork. Or better.' Nigel grinned at her. 'It doesn't need winding up every eight days.'

'No,' said Sophie slightly regretfully. 'It doesn't need much managing at all.'

'If only England was as well run and prosperous,' said David lightly.

This was her cue to say, 'It will be when you are king, sir.' Sophie was silent. As a successful businesswoman, as well as a graduate of Miss Lily's teaching, which encompassed as much politics as charm, she knew how fragile the peace was with Germany. That country was still suffering under the unjust reparations France had suddenly imposed once the German army had been disbanded in good faith.

The stock market boom in the United States worried Sophie too. Too many fools were making fortunes in what was essentially no more than a gamble that stock prices would keep rising. Her father used to say to be wary when fools could make fortunes ...

Her horse tossed its head as two cars proceeded carefully down the snowy Shillings driveway, breaking her from her thoughts.

'Oh, dear. David, I'm so sorry, I forgot. The Prinzessin von Arnenberg and James Lorrimer are coming to luncheon.' She smiled at him. 'And I need to change out of my riding clothes. It is all your fault, David darling. You make me forget everything else.'

'Except, I hope your husband,' said Nigel.

'I never lunch,' said the prince. 'And I would prefer not to meet Lorrimer. Always talking about duty — and you know about his first wife?'

Sophie shook her head.

'Jewish,' the prince said shortly. 'Wealthy, of course, like all that kind, but a good thing for Lorrimer's career that she died.'

Sophie stared, speechless, as the Prince of Wales turned his horse's head for the stables.

Too late. The second of the cars stopped. A furred and elegant hand waved. David sighed audibly and reined in his horse as the chauffeur opened the rear door.

Two perfect shoes, clear stockings on the best legs of European royalty, glimpsed beneath a coat of pure white Arctic fox. A sparkle of diamonds at her throat and at the edge of the neat fur hat — Sophie might wear pearls, but diamonds were suitable for royalty at any time of day.

Sophie wasn't sure how Hannelore afforded dresses and gems now that her and Dolphie's estates were in Bolshevik hands, but today she was fairy princess meets Theda Bara. Sophie tried to remember how one presented royalty to royalty, especially now Germany had abolished royal titles. Luckily the chore was taken from her.

'Cousin Hanne!' The prince's tones were truly warm. 'It has been far too long.'

Hannelore paused before she spoke, the 'Miss Lily pause' that made the audience focus on whatever was said next. 'But you did not come to Sandringham when my Uncle Dolphie and I were there,' said Hannelore, reproachfully, slowly letting her eyes rise to meet his and hold his gaze. 'We missed you so.'

Queen Mary had invited her German relatives to visit again as soon as the war ended. They were there often now, although of course these meetings were never mentioned in court circulars.

David dismounted, removed his riding gloves, then lifted Hannelore's hand to his lips. 'My mother had you on my list of brides before the war. I should have spoken then.'

Hannelore laughed. 'And now it is impossible. The handsome English prince must wed one of his subjects: your father says so.' She kept her hand in his. 'But perhaps instead of marriage you might ... come to tea?' The words and tone were almost innocent.

'I would love to come to ... tea.' The prince kissed her hand again.

Hannelore is gathering him in as her protégé, thought Sophie. It might be good for the Prince of Wales to learn more of real politics than just weeping when he visited a mining village and saying, 'Something must be done.' Hannelore would be an excellent teacher, despite her foible about her almost-known German political protégé.

But Hannelore would not marry David. An English prince must not marry a former enemy. Nor would Hannelore become his lover. Hannelore would never have a lover now.

A hurried half-hour later, Green had removed Sophie's riding dress and boots, quickly restyled her hair, carefully fastened yet another dress, this one with panels of green lace between panels of gold silk, hooked the pearls back around her neck, and reapplied the powder and lipstick. Green was a miracle. Sophie descended the stairs.

'Hannelore, darling, you look beautiful. James, it is so good to see you.' She presented her cheek to James to be kissed, and kissed Hannelore's cold skin in turn. 'Where is His Highness?'

'David has departed already,' said Hannelore. 'He says he will adore you forever, and left two very large stuffed toy zebras for Rose and Danny. I must see your twins too, Sophie.'

'Of course.' Hannelore looked tired now that she was no longer charming the Prince of Wales, and far older than when they had been students of Miss Lily's. 'Though I hope they have had their lunch already,' Sophie added, 'and are down for their nap. But we can peer in at them.'

Sophie smiled at James. Step one, Miss Lily had taught her, back in those magic months before the war. Smile, and almost everyone will smile with you. 'James, do excuse my tardiness. You know what it's like with HRH. One has to drop everything! You'd love a brandy snifter, wouldn't you, after that cold drive? Or do you think whisky is a better warmer?'

Ask a question to which they will answer 'yes' to forge a link between you. Ask questions to which they know the answer.

Hannelore, Nigel and James knew exactly what she was doing. Charm was as automatic to her now as the swan-like glide, the slight pause on entering a room, the grace with which she moved her hands. Nonetheless, James smiled as expected.

'Whisky,' he said. 'The Shillings whisky is superb.'

Nigel laughed. 'I can't take any credit. My father put down the barrels before I was born.'

The two men moved towards the library. Sophie had a sudden nostalgic pang for the quiet winter days in Miss Lily's private drawing room along the corridor, toasting crumpets by the fire with Hannelore, Emily and dearest Mouse, laughing as they dripped butter and honey.

Mouse had died in childbirth; Emily was Mrs Colonel Sevenoaks, corpulent and envious of Sophie's more prestigious — and far happier — marriage. Hannelore had lost her estates to the Russians in the war and had been captured and tortured by Munich revolutionaries, but she now seemed to be re-established in society, though Sophie had seen little of her since she'd returned to England, wary of meeting the uncle Hannelore regarded as a brother, who had tried just a little too forcibly to convince Sophie to marry him.

Such long journeys we have all made, she thought, as she led the way upstairs, except for Mouse, her travels through life so tragically cut short.

'Sophie.' Hannelore paused on the stairs. 'I must speak with you.'

'Speak away, darling.' But I am not coming to Germany, she thought. Too many memories and none of them good. Nor am I going to write a cheque for your fiery little politician, no matter how good his intentions.

'I must see Miss Lily. It is urgent. Truly urgent.'

Sophie stopped, schooled her face, then turned around to face her on the staircase. 'Hannelore, you know Miss Lily vanished at the start of the war. Her ... friendships with ... those who became our enemies made her suspect. She has retired. Even Nigel ... only rarely hears from her.' Which was true, if not the whole truth.

'But Miss Lily wished for peace. As we wish for peace. It is the Bolsheviks who are our enemies now.'

'Fighting for peace?'

'You of all people must know that sometimes one must fight. It is who we fight that matters. Our common enemy is to the north, in Russia.'

Hmmm. 'Perhaps. What a mistake it was for your Kaiser to arrange for Mr Lenin to return to Russia during the war. If it hadn't been for that piece of treachery, the revolution might not have happened.'

'Is that analysis from Miss Lily?'

'No, it is my own, and from an editorial in *The Times*. Truly, Hannelore, I can't arrange a meeting with Miss Lily.'

'Nigel must know how to contact her! Miss Lily is his —' Hannelore stopped. Miss Lily had never exactly explained her relationship to the Earl of Shillings, nor why he allowed her to use Shillings for three months each year to school her chosen girls.

Neither *Burke's Peerage* nor Debrett's gave any clue, either, for there was no Lillian Vaile there. When they had first met Sophie had wondered if Miss Lily were possibly an illegitimate child of the late earl, and thus Nigel's half-sister. She wondered if Hannelore was too tactful to put forward the same theory now.

'Why do you need to see her so badly?' she asked instead.

'Because Miss Lily would understand. She of all people would accept that England and Germany must be allies. Her network of friends across Europe and the world, all those girls who are now women, in so many royal houses and families of power ...'

A network gathered for British influence and knowledge, not for a would-be German politician. 'You think Miss Lily would convince those influential friends to support Herr Hitler?'

'Of course. If she could only meet him she'd understand how much good he could do with the right connections. Sophie, you cannot know how bad it is in Germany now. The communists in Berlin have their own army. They battle on the street with any who do not support their cause. The desperation, the ... the decadence, as if no one can bear to look at reality and so seeks any escape. The heart of Germany is dying, Sophie. I cannot see my country die.'

'Hannelore.' Sophie shook her head helplessly. 'I wish I could help. But I can't take you to Miss Lily. Nor can I support Herr Hitler, either in person or with my money. I'm sympathetic to the need for a peaceful Europe, of course I am sympathetic. But my own country needs me too. Needs my factories, my energy.'

Actually her factories were running perfectly without her now, managed by the Slithersoles, father and son, and Cousin Oswald, except for a few hours' guidance by mail or telegram each week. She did in fact have both the money and the energy to devote to Hannelore's Herr Hitler, if he was as miraculous as Hannelore believed. The nasty taste in her mouth, however, legacy of both her rescue mission to brutish post-war Germany and the little Nigel had shared with her of the man Hitler's manifesto, meant she doubted she would spend either on him.

'And of course you have a family now, as well,' said Hannelore softly.

Which Hannelore would never have, after the injuries inflicted on her in the revolution.

'I'm sorry,' said Sophie. It seemed cruel to take Hannelore to see the twins now. How could anyone see Rose and Danny and not long for children too?

'Please,' said Hannelore quietly. 'Please, help me to see Miss Lily. It is more urgent than you can know.'

'I can't,' said Sophie softly. She added, with perfect truth, 'I wish we could all be together again. I wish it far more than you could know.'

Chapter 4

*Dinners are long because of the necessary progression of many
courses. But if a luncheon takes three hours it is because the diners
enjoy the company as much as the food.*

Miss Lily, 1913

HANNELORE

Luncheon was perfect, Hannelore thought, sipping her Moselle,
watching the firelight glint on the crystal wine glass. Of course
it was perfect. Miss Lily might be gone, but she had instructed
Nigel Vaile's household well.

Lucky Sophie, to have married not just an ancient name, but
a house organised to perfection, furnished with the treasures the
Vailes had collected over the centuries.

Hannelore doubted her friend truly appreciated the heritage
of Shillings. After all, she had abandoned it, and Nigel's offer of
marriage too, to build her business empire in Australia. Doubly
lucky Sophie, to have got all this anyway, and so effortlessly: a
home, a husband, children, and money, a name and intelligence
to lend to whichever cause she wished.

Once, Hannelore's home too had been furnished with heritage
and money, her great-grandmother's embroidery table, medieval
storage chests, smelling of woodruff, the tapestry coverings on
the chairs wrought by so many great-aunts, the carpet from the
North West Frontier, a gift from Queen Victoria. Now — if they
had not been burned — all were possessed by the Bolsheviks.

Hannelore spooned up her cock-a-leekie soup, tweaked from a

Scottish peasant soup to a clear bowl of rich consommé flecked with prune. Miss Lily had learned the art of balancing food with each season in her years in Japan. This meal sang both of winter and of warmth.

Hannelore smiled her appreciation and laughed despite her tiredness at James Lorrimer's anecdote about his straight-laced Great-Aunt Euphemia, who would never have had a dish with such a ... suggestive ... name in her home, nor coq au vin either. She charmed him with gentle touches on his wrist and a slow smile at everything he said, as if she alone appreciated it.

What did James think of Mussolini's treaty with the Vatican, making it an independent state, in return, presumably, for the Church's tactful silence about the Italian dictator's ruthless control over the country? Or the coming British 'flapper' elections, the first in which all women over twenty-one could vote?

And James smiled back at her, with laughter crinkles at his eyes, as if he knew quite well he was being charmed, but enjoyed it nonetheless.

Hereward proffered quenelles of pike, balancing the tray superbly on his right hand, his handless left arm discreetly tucked into his butler's jacket. Quenelles were by far the best way to deal with that troublesome fish, with the lightest of champagne sauces.

Hannelore turned to Nigel for this next course, as formality required. Had Nigel read the new book, *All Quiet on the Western Front*? A book that reminded a generation now trying to forget the anguish of little more than a decade ago, preferring dance clubs and rouged knees to facing the problems left by war.

She knew Nigel had read it — Sophie had mentioned it — but Hannelore too still obeyed Miss Lily's rules of charm. A man like Nigel would know he was being flattered. He would still enjoy it.

'A hard book to read,' said Nigel. He looked out the window. 'Even harder memories.'

'A necessary book,' said Sophie firmly. 'Society is trying too hard to forget. Or to remember only convenient sections, like heroism and memorials. They forget the agony. And the women.

Sometimes the women ambulance crews almost outnumbered the living men on the front line.'

The table was silent. 'I will always feel guilty that I never saw active service there,' said James.

'You served your country the best way you could,' said Nigel. 'The Empire's resources were stretched to breaking point. If the United States hadn't entered the war we might now be only a few ragged starving troops still fighting for a yard or two of mud.'

Nigel glanced at Hannelore. She knew the moment he realised there was no tactful way for her to enter this conversation: she had never seen fighting on the front line, but, once the Russians had taken her estates, she had spent the war in the household of her uncle, the Kaiser, before his exile.

Nor had the German army lost the war, and all at this table knew it, even if most of the general public and the newly written history books liked to pretend it had. Germany had agreed to fair terms in the 1918 Armistice, when continuing would have meant even greater starvation and anguish in the occupied countries, as well as the increasing risk of Bolshevik revolution in Germany, and even in France and England.

The agreed upon ceasefire had also been a convenient way to oust a Kaiser who was at best incapable as a leader, as well as mentally unbalanced. Germany had been betrayed by France's trickery, by England agreeing to the change in terms, and United States President Wilson stepping away from any involvement in the deeply unfair Treaty of Versailles in 1919.

Hannelore knew that some felt she was ... overzealous ... in her hatred of bolshevism. But few of those in England or Germany who regarded bolshevism as hope for equality, ending the privileges that condemned so many to poverty, had seen communism in practice. She had lost her estates to Bolshevik troops, and been abducted and tortured under the Bavarian soviet army before it was ruthlessly supressed.

Hannelore looked carefully at her plate. Sophie had undoubtedly told Nigel and probably James, too, of Hannelore's injuries and escape, as well as her post-war poverty, alleviated by the Higgs' cheque that had established her factory and refurbished the estate Dolphie's uncle had left him. But none of that was fit luncheon conversation at an English manor house, even if she could bear to talk about it.

'What do you think of the American stock market rise, James?' Nigel asked, breaking the silence before it stretched uncomfortably. 'Sophie thinks it can't last.' One did not talk money at a formal meal, even when one's hostess was successful in business; nor did one speak across the table. The master of the house was defining this luncheon as a gathering of friends where society's rules need not be followed.

It was also kind, thought Hannelore. Nigel was always kind. This was the compassion Miss Lily had tried to teach them: understanding how another felt. There was so much of Miss Lily in Nigel, not just his empathy, but the colour of his eyes, even the shape of his face, though Nigel's hair was dark to Miss Lily's blonde. Once again Hannelore wondered if Miss Lily was Nigel's half-sister. Whatever the relationship, it must be genetically close. Ah, how good it was to know of genes now, and how eugenics affected the world ...

'The United States' industry and farmlands make it the wealthiest country in the world,' objected James. 'It's too big to fail.'

'You spent much of the war there, did you not?' asked Hannelore. She smiled, to remove all past enmity from her words. 'Cajoling the United States to sell the Allies armaments, to lend them money and finally to dispatch troops to Europe?'

Sophie shook her head. 'Its very size now is what makes American economic influences dangerous. The American market rules the world only because it is enormous. But many of the American stocks are overvalued — there is no clear relationship between the real value of many American companies and their stock prices. Greed is setting those now, not output or profits.'

'Clever Sophie,' said Hannelore lightly. 'You understand more of the world than a hundred politicians.'

And you will not help, Hannelore thought. You sit here in quiet comfort with your children and your earl and your factories even as the world lurches towards another war, as bolshevism sweeps across the Continent. What will you do when your factories are nationalised? When Rose and Danny are killed by a firing squad just as poor Tsar Nicholas's family and so many of her other friends and family had been?

Only one man had the vision to save Europe now. She had met him at a luncheon much like this and ignored him too, the bourgeois little Korporal who Dolphie had so surprisingly invited.

That was the luncheon at which Prince Waldi — widowed, fat, fifty and flatulent — had tried to seduce her, for surely every unmarried woman must be desperate for a husband, or at least a lover. Waldi had fetched her coffee after luncheon, clicking his heels as he bowed and handed her the coffee cup. 'I would bring you stars and unicorns,' he whispered in what was meant to be a lecherous whisper but sounded more as if he had the grippe. 'But all I have to offer is this coffee.'

'Sugar?' she asked, to get rid of him.

Waldi clicked his heels again and departed towards the coffee tray.

Hannelore was suddenly aware of another man behind her. 'I cannot offer you stars or unicorns.' The voice was a hilarious mimicry of the prince's tones. 'But I can perhaps protect you from his attentions for an hour.'

She turned. Blue eyes that saw her properly, in a kind, intelligent face. 'How can you do that? Herr Hitler, is it not?'

He inclined his head instead of giving the conventional bow. His accent was good, despite his lower middle-class origins. 'We could talk politics, Your Highness. The prince is allergic to politics. I hear he comes out in a rash.'

Hannelore laughed. A clever man. A funny man, with no pomposity. Suddenly she liked him enormously. 'You are the president of the National Socialist Party, I believe? I think they call you Der Führer?'

'I am simply a man who loves his country, Your Highness. That above all. A man who will give his life to saving us from bolshevism, from the creeping decadence of Judaism, from the

Treaty of Versailles that not only cripples our economy but saps our very will.'

It was as if reality had suddenly flowed into the empty elegance of this room. Herr Hitler's bright blue eyes met hers again. And suddenly she was his — not as a lover but as a follower. She, who had been lost ever since the outbreak of the war, had found a will again, a purpose and a life ...

Hannelore realised Hereward was behind her, offering yet another salver. Medallions of venison with juniper and port wine sauce. She smiled at him, accepted two medallions and a helping of winter apple, walnuts and chicory from the footman who followed him. The conversation flowed about her. 'Even Jones has bought shares,' said Sophie.

'A butler with a share portfolio!' said Hannelore.

Nigel smiled. A lovely smile. 'Jones is my secretary now. A private secretary with a portfolio is entirely respectable.'

Hannelore looked up, startled. There was something in the way he said, 'entirely respectable' that was familiar. So very familiar. 'I did not think that Miss Lily would ever spare him. Jones was devoted to her,' she ventured.

'It was the war,' said Sophie lightly. 'Even the most magnificent of butlers must be spared in wartime.'

'Of course,' said Hannelore.

Over the next few hours she ate a savoury of a single oyster in a froth of batter; brought glasses of wine to her lips, but did not drink; consumed her portion of lemon soufflé, more taste than substance; and nibbled cheese and walnuts. She watched, she laughed, she listened as finally the long conventions of a formal lunch wound to a close.

Sophie glanced at the windows. Already the short winter day had dulled. 'If this was Australia I'd suggest a walk in the sunshine. But since I have not yet found a way to can sunshine and bring it to Europe, coffee for all in the library? Or do you men wish for port and cigars before you join us?' She stood.

'If you don't mind,' said James, 'I might head back to London before the snow makes the roads impassable.' Ah, thought

Hannelore, whatever you hoped to gain from this luncheon, you have achieved already, in your talk with Nigel in the library.

'I should leave too,' said Hannelore, who had gained nothing except further frustration, not at all compensated by the pleasure of good company at lunch. 'If you would have my car sent round?'

Nigel rose in one smooth movement, despite his age and what must be crippling scars from his surgery. Hannelore's own scars often made it difficult to rise with the grace expected of Miss Lily's ladies, especially after sitting for several hours. But Nigel had managed it perfectly, just as Miss Lily would have done ...

She did not stare at him. She very carefully did not let her gaze linger nor her expression change as she kissed Sophie.

But when Nigel kissed her hand as she departed she felt the shape of his fingers in hers: small hands for a man, slightly large for a woman, as Miss Lily's hands had been just slightly too big for classic beauty, always carefully disguised with ruffles at the cuffs, and gloves. There was a scent too, oddly familiar under the fragrance of bay rum.

Her chauffeur drove at a cautious ten miles an hour through the slush, following James's vehicle, whose slips and slides warned of icy patches. The cars slowly drew apart. James evidently had more need for speed than she did. There was no function at the embassy tonight, nor did Dolphie need her as his hostess.

She had disregarded the fleeting coincidence of resemblance between Nigel and Miss Lily as soon as she had thought of it. But now, in the snow-muffled silence, broken only by the Mercedes purr, it came again.

Dolphie's role at the embassy was officially Cultural Attaché. Unofficially, it was to gather gossip, to try to mend the royal alliances between Germany and England that were still close personally, but not acknowledged publicly.

Yet Dolphie had heard no gossip about the Earl of Shillings, except for his mediocre political career after the war, and his illness and marriage. Miss Lily herself was never mentioned, which was exactly what she had asked of each of her 'lovely ladies', the girls she had trained to make the most of every asset a woman might use, especially those ignored by finishing schools.

Every 'lovely lady' knew that gossip about the Shillings 'school' might make her subject to gossip too. The pact had held, so well that Hannelore only knew of Sophie and Emily, and her own grandmother — and that there had been far, far more.

Miss Lily did not appear in *Burke's Peerage* or Debrett's. Which meant, thought Hannelore, that she was probably illegitimate, as she had long assumed. But the relationship must still be a close one. One did not give a relative the freedom of one's home and estate for three or more months each year without both trust and liking. Surely Nigel must know where Miss Lily was now. And if she had been killed in the war, or now lived permanently abroad, why not say so?

Mist rose from the ice-tipped fields. By the time they reached London's outskirts the white fog had turned yellow, its threads had become cat's tails and finally the classic pea souper, though Hannelore had never known a pea the colour of dirty soap. English humour, calling something so yellow after something green?

The house Dolphie had rented for himself and his niece was several streets from the embassy. The fog was even thicker there, the street jammed with carts and carriages as well as cars. It would be quicker to walk. She knocked on the window between the back seat and the driver, instructed him to park when he could, then slipped out the door and onto the footpath.

The fog was no clearer on the footpath, but at least it was easier to make one's way next to the shop windows, nor, in this haven of Mayfair, was there risk of being accosted by unwanted attentions. A breath of warm and toasted teacake emerged from a Worthy's Teahouse and then she heard the high, pure song of a girl.

It was a Flemish lullaby. One of the maids at her uncle's had sung it sometimes, to amuse the children at nursery tea. Hannelore smiled at the memory, then looked at the almost empty hat lying on the footpath in front of the girl. Such a young girl, in such a thin dress, so cold, so hungry.

For two years, in the war, she had been hungry. For months after she had starved.

But she had no money to give this girl. A prinzessin did not carry money. But she smiled at the girl and received a blue-eyed smile in return.

She would send Albert the footman with money for the girl, five shillings perhaps. But Hannelore also knew too well what might happen to money given to a young girl — a father waiting nearby who would take it for beer with a gin chaser at the nearest pub, perhaps, or a pimp who would not just take the money but blacken her eye if there wasn't enough.

No, far better to instruct Albert to take the poor child into Worthy's, to buy her cocoa and corned-beef sandwiches — possibly made with beef corned from Sophie's far-off Australian cattle. No one could steal a meal the child had already eaten.

My act of compassion for today, she thought. Miss Lily had advised that everyone needed to commit one act of individual compassion each day, to inhibit self-obsession. Love for humanity or one's country was not enough. The hand and heart must help another person personally, or at least via Albert.

Yes, Miss Lily would approve. Miss Lily, who had the network that the Führer so badly needed if the party was to make any major impression now that conditions had improved under the Weimar Republic. Miss Lily, who was so very similar to Nigel …

Chapter 5

Love is indeed the most satisfying meal of all, my dears. But never think it will satisfy you as dessert or entrée too.

Miss Lily, 1913

SOPHIE

Sophie helped Nanny and Alice, the nursing maid, feed Danny and Rose their suppers. Danny spooned up his bread and milk and then his stewed apple neatly and politely, as if already aware it was his duty as the next earl to take his nourishment.

'Gleek!' announced Rose, spitting apple and custard onto the window.

Nanny glanced at Sophie, wondering which of them should administer discipline and obviously hoping it would be Sophie. It was already apparent that the toddler's strength of will was only matched by her mother's.

'No,' said Sophie calmly to her daughter.

Rose reached out a sticky finger and ran it down the glass, making a pattern in the mess. Sophie wiped it up with a napkin, then met her daughter's eyes as Rose held up another spoonful. 'No,' Sophie said again.

'Glarrark!'

'No.'

Rose drooped, looking reproachfully through her eyelashes at Sophie. Sophie laughed. 'It is still no.'

Rose sighed and ate her spoonful of stewed apple.

'See?' said Sophie. 'No spanking necessary.'

'Only for you, your ladyship,' said Nanny.

'Children want to please adults.' That had been one of Miss Lily's maxims. 'You just need to show them firmly how to do it.'

Nanny set her lips, so obviously not saying, 'That is easy for you to say, your ladyship.'

Sophie pressed a kiss onto Rose's curls and Danny's straight dark hair. Her bath would be ready, perfumed with French salts. Green would have laid out her dinner dress. The fire would crackle with apple wood; the man she loved, who loved her, waited in the library with her two close friends, while her children would sleep, safe and beautiful, in this nursery. Life was blissful.

If only it was not predictable as well.

The four of them ate informally in the library most nights, the dishes placed under covers on the sideboard by Hereward the butler. A lady's maid like Green could not eat in the dining room, but a meal in the library with the earl and countess was ... possible. Especially where servants in this house always came from the estate, as their parents had before them, and even more so now that so much unemployment meant fewer jobs beyond the estate. The Shillings servants would tolerate behaviour that their peers in other great houses would most firmly object to in the strict class order of the servants' hall.

Cars and telephones might now link Shillings more closely to the world, but it was still a world where the master protected the tenants and the tenants were loyal. Shillings had been rich in secrets for the past thirty years — many far more scandalous than a maid dining with her employers.

Nigel helped himself to hare, casseroled in cider with carrots and parsnips. 'What did Hannelore want?'

'Miss Lily,' said Sophie shortly.

The fire snickered in the silence. Each in that room longed for Miss Lily too. Each also knew that, except for the briefest of appearances, Miss Lily had gone. Sometimes Sophie wondered which of them missed her more. 'And James?' Sophie added.

It had been interesting that James had wanted to speak to Nigel, not her. While Nigel had worked with James — or possibly for him, as an agent of the Crown — it had been Sophie who James had approached two years earlier to gather intelligence about the Bolshevik tendencies among the aristocracy.

'Nothing political. He wants me to help identify a hospitalised man whom I met briefly when he was a staff officer,' said Nigel slowly. 'He'd hoped I'd known him better than I had, but I think we only met three or four times, and only one of those informally. An Australian, as a matter of fact, acting as liaison with the French. A Major John McDonald.'

Sophie flinched. But John was the most common name in the English-speaking world. There was no reason to think there was any connection with the man she had left behind. The 'John' she had known in his hut by the Thuringa gate claimed he had assumed the name of his dead twin brother. But James had found no record of a lost twin named John, nor even any enlisted twins with other names who might fit the story she'd been given back in those days of gold and sensuality in Australia. It had been a fiction, or possibly a hallucination of a man traumatised by deep war damage. Sophie had even met two other men in her hospitals who claimed to be their own brothers — and those other 'brothers' of the men who had seen what they could not bear to have witnessed.

'He wants you to go to Australia? Surely there's someone there who can identify him,' said Jones.

Nigel shook his head. 'The man in question is in a hospital outside Paris.'

'Why still in France?' asked Sophie.

'Possibly because no one knew who he might be so no country has claimed him. Or he may simply have been overlooked. It happens.'

'Another lost memory case?' asked Green. It was not uncommon, due to widespread shock and head wounds. Men posted as missing or even killed during the war did still occasionally turn up even now — as did those who had deliberately assumed the identity of a dead comrade to evade wives, debts or police, or occasionally to gain an inheritance.

'Possibly. The poor chap had a bad dose of mustard gas, as well as other wounds. He can neither speak nor make out anything except the vaguest of shapes, and his face is too scarred to be able to see what he looked like before his injuries. The scars on his hands have grafted them together so he cannot write. He can walk, but not for long periods, I gather. John McDonald was declared dead, but no body was recovered. His wife, or widow, employed an investigation firm after the war, to try to find out what had happened to her husband.

'It seems no one witnessed Major McDonald's death or, at least,' Nigel amended, 'no one who survived. The agency has also been checking hospitals, of course. Finally they found a man of roughly the right age and height.'

'Surely they could have found him before this!' said Green angrily.

'They probably focused on returned servicemen in Australia and in England, as well as hospital records here in Britain — this is where most of the patients with major injuries were sent initially. But for some reason this man stayed in a hospital in France, and there are enough similarities for Mrs McDonald to travel there to see him. James says she is sure the man the agency located is her husband. But although he can hear, he has made no sign of recognition.'

'Memory loss, I suppose, or truly bad shell shock, if indeed he really is her husband. Poor woman. And poor man,' said Sophie. 'The most obvious reason for him to still be in France is that he IS French.'

'But one who understands fluent English,' said Nigel. 'That's what alerted the investigator. But now he won't respond at all to any questions.'

'A man of integrity,' said Jones. 'If Mrs McDonald is mistaken it would be better for whomever he is to let her think he is her husband, and be cared for by her in a home and not a hospital. I presume she is well-off, to have come all this way?'

'The family seems comfortable.'

'Would you recognise him?' asked Sophie.

'I doubt it. Not after twelve years, even without his injuries,' said Nigel. 'But the officers he served with are of course back in Australia.' He shrugged. 'It's possible that if this is McDonald, he might recognise me and make some sign. That's what James hopes.'

'I remember McDonald, I think, though I saw him only once,' said Jones. 'Big fellow, if he's the one I'm thinking of. Good at rugby. Remember that match outside Pozières? He scored the winning try.'

'I doubt he plays rugby now,' said Sophie. 'No useful birthmarks?'

'If there were, the question of identity would presumably have been solved.' Nigel glanced at Jones, who nodded. 'We'll go, of course. A vain hope at best, but one can't ignore this kind of thing.'

His unspoken words whispered though the library: there is no essential work, either political or on the estate, that I am needed for here.

'May I go with you?' asked Sophie. Suddenly Shillings' neat damp fields and soggy forests had closed in on her.

'We could all go. Paris! Hats!' said Green dreamily. 'And Coco Chanel has some fascinating new designs. Evening trousers in the most divine velvet —'

'I was thinking more of discussions with my Paris agent about the new line in canned baby food,' said Sophie drily. Although technically Australia could only trade with Britain, Sophie had circumvented the restriction with a company based in England that employed agents across Europe and the United States.

'I should have known,' said Jones. 'But won't you miss the children?'

'We can take them with us. And Nanny. I am sure the Ritz can cope with a pair of toddlers.'

Jones blinked, but made no comment. Sophie realised that in the days when he, Nigel and Green travelled before the war, they probably moved swiftly, unencumbered by children, a nanny, and all the paraphernalia that went with them. Well, times had changed.

Sophie glanced at Green. 'Greenie and I might even be of some help to Mrs McDonald. No matter what the outcome, she will probably be glad of women to support her.' Miss Lily had also taught her that a man would more easily confess weakness to a woman, not another man. Sophie might be able to convince the scarred man in the hospital bed to communicate when a man could not. But that possibility need not be spoken.

Jones looked at Nigel, who nodded in his turn. 'I'll make the arrangements,' said Jones. 'As soon as possible, I suppose.'

'Yes. The least we can do is give Mrs McDonald the feeling that she has not been abandoned in the search for her husband,' said Nigel. He hesitated. 'Did Hannelore say why it was so urgent that Miss Lily meet her German firebrand?'

Sophie shook her head. 'I assumed it was just for general support. But you're right. She did imply it was urgent.'

'Write to James,' suggested Nigel. 'He may know more.' He smiled. 'At the very least a German prinzessin's urgency may be another piece in his jigsaw of the Empire.'

Sophie pulled the bell for Hereward to take the plates away.

Chapter 6

A woman's greatest power comes from the refusal of so many
men to admit that she has any, much less long-term, plans and a
strategy for achieving them. Strategy will nearly always win against
the assumption that chance will solve life for you.

Miss Lily, 1913

HANNELORE

Hannelore dipped the nib of her pen in the inkwell. Even Dolphie used a fountain pen now, but one could not write a truly individual hand with a mass-produced pen.

My most dear Adolf,
*   It was so good to hear that you are happy with your new home.*
The mountain air will refresh you, as you must need after such
campaigning.

She applied the blotting paper, then thought how to express herself before she continued.

I have not yet had the success here that I wished for. I am still sure,
however, that the British aristocracy must see that Russia is our
true enemy and that only a Germany united under a strong leader
can act as a bulwark against bolshevism …

Dolphie's official position was Cultural Attaché. His real job was to persuade their English royal relations to support Germany's cause and lessen the burden of reparations. But the war was still too close. Germany continued to be seen as an enemy, not an ally against bolshevism and the growing strength of the Soviet Union, nor did her generation want to think of war, or even politics, just jazz and motorcars, dance clubs and cocktails.

Or domesticity, like Sophie and Nigel. Hannelore put down her pen and walked to the window, gazing out at the yellow London fog, so thick one could almost slice it.

She could not concentrate, not even on a letter to the Führer. The news this morning had been ... disturbing. But surely it meant nothing.

Albert had given a meal to the strange child singing outside the teahouse. But a few days later Albert had told Welsh, her maid, about the child's strange claim. Welsh had mentioned the story to Hannelore, as she brushed Hannelore's hair this morning, complaining about the new housemaid as she brushed.

'That's young people today, madam! Thinking they are too good for honest work. It's like that girl you told Albert to take to the tearooms. Do you know what that little minx told him?'

Hannelore shook her head slightly under the ministrations of the hairbrush.

'She said she is really an English aristocrat! Whatever will these girls think of next?'

Hannelore smiled. 'A lost princess?'

'The daughter of an earl's sister. What was his name? Something to do with halfpennies. No, shillings, that was it. The Earl of Shillings.'

Hannelore lifted her hand to halt the hair brushing. 'The Earl of Shillings doesn't have a sister.' If Miss Lily was an illegitimate half-sister, thought Hannelore, she had never been acknowledged.

'Of course it is ridiculous,' Welsh had said. 'A street urchin could never be related to an earl. But Albert said the girl insisted. Her mother was Lily Shillings, and she was going to find her.'

Hannelore's first thought was triumph. She might use the girl's claim — true or not — to make Nigel admit where Miss Lily was now. Then reality changed the dream. Miss Lily, of all people, would never abandon a daughter, even an illegitimate one.

Yet Hannelore still thought about the claim all through her breakfast, the milk coffee and a fresh roll with butter, which was all she ate in the mornings, from a tray in her room. The claim was impossible, just as Welsh had said. And a sister of Nigel's, legitimate or not, would be Lily Vaile, not Shillings. Unless of course Miss Lily was not entitled to either surname, but had assumed the name of Shillings. For after all, no surname had ever been mentioned in those magic months before the war.

Miss Lily had been in her forties, at least, though with her grace and charm none of the girls had been able to agree about her age. Was she still young enough to have had a child during the war years?

An illegitimate child of an illegitimate sister? Was that why Nigel and Sophie no longer received Miss Lily? But she could not think that of them. They were kind. Like Miss Lily, they would never abandon a child, or her mother. It was just the name that had caught her attention when she was so eager to find Miss Lily. A coincidence, no more.

And yet.

'I hope I'm not interrupting?'

Hannelore came back to the present as Dolphie entered. He spoke English, as they almost always did in England. Their role there was to appear as innocuous as possible, and they wouldn't be innocuous speaking German. He was immaculate in a white tie: Dolphie refused to adopt the new habit of dinner jackets, declaring it an American decadence. He dropped a kiss on Hannelore's hair. 'Who are you writing to?'

'Herr Hitler.'

'Ah. You have news for him?'

'Much less than I had hoped. Where do you dine tonight?' Hannelore acted as his hostess, but rarely accompanied him elsewhere. One day — preferably soon — Dolphie would find a wife who was socially acceptable, extremely wealthy and, as importantly, whose money was available to her husband, not in a trust fund or controlled by her father.

That she would probably be American was a pity, but had to be accepted. Europe had too few heiresses and too many aristocrats who needed fortunes. Once Hannelore had hoped, even assumed, that Sophie would be that heiress, and theirs a marriage not only of convenience but of love.

Dolphie had never spoken of Sophie, though he must know that Hannelore had met her several times since their return to England. That was significant. Sophie had not just injured Dolphie's pride, but his heart.

'A dinner at the embassy. Please give the Führer my sincere regards.' Dolphie had joined the Party three years before, though that was not yet public knowledge. Nor would it be till they had achieved power, something that seemed as far off now as it had in 1925. Only one seat in the last elections, when they had hoped for at least ten …

'I will.' Hannelore paused. 'Dolphie, I … I think I would like to make an enquiry. A delicate one. Complicated perhaps.'

'May I ask what it is?'

She smiled at him. 'No. Nieces are entitled to their secrets. But I might tell you if it comes to anything. Can you suggest anyone who might help? A woman, preferably.'

'I think I can. The embassy employs her sometimes. Intelligent and discreet, and sometimes most inventive at getting the information we need.'

'She sounds perfect.'

'I'll contact her tomorrow. Are you free in the afternoon if she calls?'

'I can be. Thank you, Dolphie.'

He shrugged. 'It is just a telephone call.'

'Thank you for not insisting on knowing why I want her. Thank you for … for everything.' Giving me a home, a social role, for introducing me to Adolf Hitler. For my life …

'You are the closest family I have left. Do give Adolf my regards.'

'I will.'

She turned to her letter again.

Chapter 7

Travel is always an adventure, especially when it involves a journey of the spirit, as well as place.

Miss Lily, 1913

SOPHIE

Shillings
31 January 1929
My dear James,

Thank you for your kind note. It was delightful to see you again at Shillings. Nigel always enjoys your company so much, and you know how much I value not just your presence and friendship, but your perceptions of the world.

This letter is partly to let you know that we — an entourage of Nigel, Jones, the two children, Green and Nanny, Nanny's assistant and me — embark tomorrow morning for Paris en route to the hospital you mentioned. I profoundly hope we can be of help to Mrs McDonald. It is such a tragic duty for her. At the least, perhaps, we can help her feel that others, too, care about the fate of her husband.

I also wished to tell you of a conversation I had with the Prinzessin von Arnenberg on the afternoon of our luncheon. She urgently wishes me to put her into contact with Miss Lily whom, she believes, would support the desire for peace between our nations espoused by Herr Hitler. Like you, I am not so certain that a man as angry as he appears to be, and whose followers so violently attack their political opponents, truly envisages a long-term friendship with

Britain, despite his speeches about our common enemy and how Germany will look to regain its lost territories in the north, rather than west towards Belgium, France and England again.

I told Hannelore, truthfully, that Miss Lily is no longer available. On reflection, however, both Nigel and I wonder if there was something more to Hannelore's request than a general wish for Miss Lily to convince her many powerful friends to support the National Socialists.

I am, therefore, making you a gift of the knowledge as the person best able to establish whether Herr Hitler and his peculiar brand of socialism do intend a major escalation of their efforts soon, as Germany remains such a flammable nation, despite its growing stability. I now feel entirely relieved that it is in your hands.

Truly, James, and all joking aside, I am deeply glad that a man of your ability and integrity works with such determination for the good of our Empire. I remain yours with love and admiration always.

Sophie, Countess of Shillings

Green's choice of acceptable travelling wear for the Countess of Shillings involved heather tweed trimmed with dark mink, a sealskin coat with caped mink collar and a cloche hat trimmed with the same fur. Green herself wore a maid's black — but of silk, beautifully if conservatively tailored, and her stockings were silk, not lisle.

Nigel had decided that Brooks, his valet, would not accompany them. Sophie wondered if just possibly this might mean Miss Lily would appear — although Brooks had been trained by Jones, he had not met Miss Lily, except briefly as a child when Brooks was a farmer's son on the estate. It would be discreet to ensure he never did.

Brooks seemed content with his holiday. He and Jones had convinced Nigel to adopt the modern dress at last: the new fashion of wide woollen trousers with deep cuffs and a subtle pattern to the weave, pleated fronts and the new slash pockets as well as a double-breasted coat and waistcoat.

'You look handsome,' she said, kissing him on the landing before their entourage moved off.

Nigel shrugged.

He is missing Lily again, thought Sophie. Sometimes she too longed for Lily with an intensity that shocked her. If she craved her, what must Nigel feel?

Two motorcars — the luggage had been sent on ahead — Jones chauffeuring the first, a new Silver Ghost, chosen by himself and adored by him immoderately, with Green at his side and Sophie and Nigel in the back. Nanny, the twins and Amy were in the second car.

The nursery maid, Alice's sister, was married to one of the tractor drivers on the estate, the result of Sophie's ruthless modernisation of farm life after the war. Peace had brought a severe shortage of labour, with so many farm workers lying in the soil of France and Flanders. Alice's sister was expecting her third child any day now and Alice had willingly relinquished her place to Amy, who had never been to Paris or anywhere further than Doustdene, twenty miles and a world away from the Shillings estate.

They motored to Dover, where they took possession of adjoining staterooms overnight in first class.

The Ritz in Paris remembered Mademoiselle Sophie Higgs, heroine of the Great War, and was duly impressed by the earl's title. Five adjoining suites waited for them there too. The Ritz, at least, had few class distinctions: if a client could pay then even nursery maids were acceptable in their most expensive suites.

Sophie gazed around the gilt and marble foyer; it reverberated with brittle English voices, for few French would ever stay at so parvenu a hotel as the Paris Ritz.

'He lost the entire fortune in one night at the tables at Biarritz. And hers too, of course. All they have now is the title ...'

'A simply fabulous party ...'

'Oh my dear, she looked divine! And that necklace ... Dodo bought it from a Russian refugee. Used to be a princess. So many of them in Paris these days — fabulous bargains. Pickles has promised to find me a Fabergé egg ...'

'... so Mother and I are going to put flowers on his grave. We always do on their anniversary. The commission has put up proper crosses now ...'

'Bertie ruptured his truss swinging on the chandelier. Daddy is going to be livid when he gets the bill ... no, for the chandelier, darling, do keep up ... and then we all went swimming in the Seine ...'

'The Brazilian Bond Scheme is the investment of a lifetime, old chap. You'll double your money in two months ...'

You'll lose it in four months, maximum, thought Sophie, but she refrained from telling him so. It would cause a scene; nor would he believe a woman, or anyone, perhaps, in these heady days.

It felt strangely good to be *doing* something. Sophie had been *doing* ever since she was sixteen, but a mother of two children had a duty not to risk herself on transcontinental monsoon flights in a plane made mostly of plywood and glue, nor accompany Ethel on a motorbike ride across the Pyrenees, nor accept Anne's invitation to join their archaeological dig in Mesopotamia.

Neither was this the time for further expansion of the global business empire she had spent almost a decade building. She preferred to wait and see what the American economy did. If it proved as unstable as she suspected it would there would need to be changes, but she could not yet predict what they might need to be.

Bored, she thought again, and once again thrust the thought away. What right had she, who had so much, to regret all she had been given? Including Paris ...

A morning in the Tuileries Garden with Danny and Rose, as they chased pigeons who strutted just slightly faster than they could toddle; an afternoon viewing the most delightful hats and gowns, and having her measurements taken once again as they had changed slightly since her pregnancy. Though none of them spoke of it, this also gave Nigel a chance to rest before meeting the unknown man at the hospital.

The Silver Ghost waited for them the next day.

So much was familiar, even now this land of war had been returned to peace: the black-clad peasant women with bulging leg veins, loads of firewood on their backs; farm women who looked normal until you saw they lacked an arm, an eye or a leg, or had the hollow eyes left by nightly dream battles.

Yet there was life now too: children everywhere, laughing, playing with hoops or skipping. Dogs trotted carelessly along the streets, no longer fated to end up in a starving refugee's pot or captured as a messenger dog for the army. Cats clothed almost every windowsill, the perfect spot for soaking in the winter sun.

Sophie did not know where cats went during wartime. Perhaps, being wiser than humanity, they were simply not there, and flashed into a separate universe until it was comfortable to return.

Green looked at the map. 'Turn next left. No, not that one, I'm sure it's just a farm track. The next road left.'

'When does a farm track become a road?' enquired Jones equably.

'When it is big enough to appear on a map. There it is! Turn now!'

'I'm turning. How far now?'

'About a mile,' calculated Green. She peered through the windscreen. 'That must be it there.'

'That's a hotel. The hospital must be here somewhere.'

'I'll stop and ask the landlord,' said Jones. 'I said we should have turned onto the other road ...'

They're heading for another quarrel, thought Sophie, gazing out at fields of turnips, possibly one that might break up their three-year reconciliation. Greenie had flirted with the waiter last night, a man half her age but obviously interested in blonde hair (far more blonde and less grey than three years before) and a well-preserved bosom. Green was beautiful when she let the lady's maid's cloak of insignificance slip off her shoulders.

Eventually they returned to the farm track. The hospital, it seemed, had once been a farm house and was more nursing home than hospital. 'For incurables, according to the barman,' said Jones as he slid back into the driver's seat.

More turnips, rows and rows of them; pigs rooting in frost-hardened furrows for the stumps of (probably) cabbages; dull green hedges of a plant Sophie didn't recognise and then a slate-roofed building, one grey stone wall roughly repaired and outbuildings that had once housed hens, sheep or cattle over winter but were now the refuge of men.

A man in a dressing gown faded to drabness limped about the cobbled courtyard on two wooden stumps and two crutches. As they drew closer Sophie saw his eyes and mouth had been lost to a vast ripple of shining scar tissue, with only a slit created for him to eat or drink.

At least he had working hands, she thought, unlike John McDonald.

Jones drew to a stop next to a newish Ford with the indefinable look of a hired car. Sophie waited for Jones to open the door for her — one must, after all, obey proprieties in public — then walked side by side with Nigel up the stairs, Green and Jones behind them. Jones pulled the bell. It clanked somewhere within the stone walls.

They waited.

The door opened. A very small nun looked out — white wimple, black robes — twenty years old perhaps but the size of a twelve-year-old. She looked up at them enquiringly.

Please don't let this be a silent order, thought Sophie. Hard enough for men closeted away from the world, without the additional loss of voices too. 'Bonjour, ma soeur,' she began, as another robed figure appeared behind the first one.

'Your ladyship?' The accent was unmistakeably Australian, the face within the wimple weathered not just by sunlight but in a way Sophie was familiar with from the war — unrelenting days of heat and cold, frostbite, infections and wind. 'I must apologise,' the robed woman added, 'I don't know the right way to address an earl and his wife. I am Mother Antill.'

'If you don't mind informality,' said Sophie. 'I am Sophie and this is Nigel.'

'Lord and Lady Shillings,' corrected Jones quietly. 'I am Huw Jones, his lordship's secretary, and this is Miss Green.' He didn't try to explain Green's presence. Even a countess did not need to bring her maid to a hospital.

'Thank you, Mr Jones. Please come in.' Mother Antill stood back. 'Excuse Sister Emmanuelle.' She smiled at the small nun. 'She has not spoken since the war. But she does not need a voice to speak to God, or act for Him.'

'You are Australian,' stated Sophie.

'I am. Or was. Do follow me.' Mother Antill led the way through a small freezing anteroom to an equally cold corridor smelling strongly of turnips, its walls brightly replastered in places, its well-scrubbed floor cracked concrete, then into another room, only large enough for six straight-backed chairs, a battered desk and, to Sophie's relief, a small but adequate fire. 'Please sit. Sister Emmanuelle, will you bring tea?'

Mother Antill grinned at Sophie as she sat behind her desk. 'I have given my life to God, but not my morning cup of tea. My niece sends me packages from Australia and I am weak enough to indulge in her kindness. You have come about Matthew? The man who might be Major McDonald?' she amended. 'We name all our unknown soldiers here.'

'Do you have many?' asked Green quietly.

'Eighteen. Once there were fifty-six, but time and families have reduced their numbers.'

'And none can tell you who they are?'

'They all have identities now, except for Matthew. The rest simply have nowhere else to go, or no wish to return to pity in Australia. Yes,' to Sophie's look of enquiry, 'they are all Australian. I founded this place as a hospital during the war, funded by the township of Gunamurra, and ran it as a civilian. I have heard of your hospitals too, Lady Shillings. When my husband was killed,' Mother Antill's calm look rejected the automatic gestures of sympathy, 'I joined this order, and after my novitiate I came back here. We are more a nursing home than a hospital these days. The people of Gunamurra still send us money, and we make brooms to sell too. You may have noticed our broom hedges outside. It is enough.'

But barely, thought Sophie, looking at the roughly repaired walls.

'What can you tell us about Matthew?' asked Nigel.

'Very little that can help identify him. The hospital he was originally in was bombed in early 1918. Its records were destroyed, and all who knew him there were killed. From Matthew's mustard gas injuries we estimate he was first a casualty in the latter part of 1917. I gather that Major McDonald went missing on 22 October 1917, but then so did so many others near that time.'

'And he is unable to speak or write?' asked Sophie.

Mother Antill hesitated. 'We are not sure. The scarring is severe, but he is able to make brooms and to feed himself holding a spoon in both stumps. But if he is given a pen or pencil, he lets it fall. It is possible that the nerve damage is too severe for him to use a pen, but still manage less subtle tasks. He can see vague shapes, but not read, nor probably recognise faces. As for speaking, he cries out at night, but hasn't spoken by day.'

This was unexpected. 'Does he cry out words?'

'Sometimes,' admitted Mother Antill. 'And, yes, they are in English. The accent is educated, but still, I think, Australian. Ah, thank you,' she added to Sister Emmanuelle, bringing in the tea tray. Five cups, one teapot, no milk, sugar, nor other refreshment. Sophie doubted even Mother Antill could conjure cake or biscuits from turnips.

Mother Antill poured. The tea was weak and tasted stewed — the leaves must have been dried and used again.

'Why do you take him for an Australian?' asked Jones, sipping. 'Just his accent?'

'No. Matthew dragged another man from the hospital rubble after it was bombed, a Lieutenant Grierson. The lieutenant said Matthew was a fellow Australian, but he just called him "my mate". I'm afraid the poor man died before he could tell us more.'

'Matthew can hear?' asked Green.

'Yes. Matthew understands English, French, even some Latin.'

'Is he happy?' asked Sophie quietly. She shook her head as Green began to object. 'You are happy here, helping others, and Sister Emmanuelle too.' She thought of the other John, in his hut by the gate. 'It is possible to be happy with a simple life after so many years of anguish.'

Mother Antill nodded. 'You are correct. I am happy. A life of service to others can give extraordinary fulfilment. Matthew is a good man. Unlike most of the men here, he can walk, though it's painful for him to do so — both knees were crushed when the hospital was bombed. He can even push a wheelchair if someone tells him which way to go, and he also supports some of the others in a daily walk around the courtyard, when weather permits. But happy?' She shook her head. 'No. I wish with all my heart that we could give him joy. We can't.'

She put her teacup down and stood. 'Will you see him now?' It was not really a question. 'Mrs McDonald is with him, and her brother-in-law.'

'Her brother-in-law?' echoed Sophie. 'You mean Major McDonald's brother?'

'Stepbrother, I gather. They have different names.' Once again Mother Antill hesitated. 'Mrs McDonald is sure that Matthew is her husband. Dr Greenman, her brother-in-law, is not. Matthew shows no sign that he recognises either of them.'

'A head injury might mean he has lost his memory,' Sophie pointed out.

'Yes, of course. But it's more than that.' Once again Mother Antill paused, clearly troubled. 'Matthew does respond when other patients speak to him, and also to us. But he doesn't even seem to hear Mrs McDonald or Dr Greenman.'

'And that troubles you?' asked Nigel quietly.

'Yes,' said Mother Antill. 'If you follow me, I will take you to him.'

The corridor again and an even stronger scent of turnips, with a hint of what might be bacon and potato. The next door opened to the cobbled courtyard, and a smell of live pig, instead of meat.

The perambulating legless man had vanished. Mother Antill hesitated. 'It will look less dreary in a few months. The broom bushes flower in spring, and in summer we can take the men on walks down the lane.'

'What would make it less dreary now?' asked Sophie.

Another grin, more suited to Australian paddocks than a convent. 'A lot more money,' said Mother Antill. She led them across the mud and into what must be the ward for men who needed less intensive care.

The building had been stables. Now each of the four stalls held a narrow wooden bed, a curtained cupboard, a chamber pot, a man. One looked up from a newspaper that was propped up on a kind of cage so his fingerless hands could turn the pages. Another, seemingly intact, watched the ceiling, not even registering their movement as they passed. A mumble of voices came from the cubicle at the far end.

Sophie's skin prickled. For some reason it was hard to breathe.

It was impossible. Not here, not now. It could not be ... *he* could not be ... She forced herself into a state of calmness. I am a swan, she thought. I am a swan, gliding on the water ...

The man in the cubicle raised white eyes towards them as he heard their footsteps. Sophie made herself look only at him. Too many must already have instinctively looked away. And watching him gave her an excuse not to meet the eyes of the man beside him.

Matthew's scars were bad, though Sophie had seen worse. He did have eyes, even if they were grey-white within the shiny redness of what was left of his face. No nose, but someone had ensured he kept his nostrils. His ears were stubs, the left almost entirely gone, but evidently he could hear. No hair, except a patch of brown and grey on one side of his skull, though Sophie thought that scarring looked different from his facial scars, from a fire after the hospital was bombed, perhaps. His forearms were covered by the white sheet, topped with a much-darned patchwork quilt. Sophie imagined the sisters spending their nights mending, patching ...

It was ... more peaceful ... to imagine that, than to face today. She took a breath, created a smile, was aware that both Nigel and Green knew of her distress, even if they did not know why.

She let her gaze turn at last to the two figures sitting on hard-backed chairs beside the bed. The first was a woman, thirty-five perhaps. Sophie had expected the hopeful Mrs McDonald would be wearing sensible grey serge or flannel. Instead she wore a wool dress of a blue that suited her blonde hair. Her matching open coat was trimmed with gold embroidery. Silk stockings, good pearls and matching earrings.

Why? Mrs McDonald must know the man on the bed could not see her clothes. Had she dressed for her brother-in-law, or because today she would meet an earl and a countess? And yet she hardly acknowledged their approach, her gaze intent upon the patient lying in the bed. She had dressed for him, Sophie realised. She wishes to look beautiful for the man she loves, even if he cannot see her clothes.

She turned reluctantly to the other man, who had been sitting on the chair next to his sister-in-law.

He had stood at their approach. He carefully did not gaze at Sophie nor even show surprise. But of course Mother Antill must have told him that the Earl and Countess of Shillings would arrive today. He'd had more than a week, or even longer, to prepare for this.

'Lord Shillings, Lady Shillings, Miss Green and Mr Jones, this is Mrs McDonald and Dr Greenman, and this of course, is Matthew. Matthew, Lord Shillings has come to help see if we can find out who you are.'

The man on the bed remained motionless, as if he hadn't heard.

'Good morning, Mrs McDonald,' said Sophie, wondering at the steadiness of her voice. 'I so very much hope that we can help in some way. Good morning, Matthew. Please excuse our interrupting you. It is with the best of intentions.' She forced her gaze once again to Dr Greenman. 'Good morning, John,' she said.

Mrs McDonald looked at them in surprise. 'John?'

'That was the name I used for a while up in New South Wales. Good morning, Sophie. Congratulations on your marriage.' Dr Greenman's voice was casual, as if they had met briefly, once or twice, for afternoon tea perhaps. And yet it was the same voice that had spoken with comfort and compassion to so many at Thuringa. It was the voice that had once whispered passion, even love.

'Thank you for coming. Thank you, too, your lordship.'

Nigel held out a hand to Dr Greenman, who shook it.

He was still John, despite a touch of grey — less tanned perhaps, his face closed where two years ago it had been open. A tweed suit, a good coordinated tweed coat, his hat and leather gloves on the small cupboard by the bed. She was shocked how little difference the formal clothes, the haircut made. This was still John, in every way that counted. She could feel it, as if a telephone cable connected them.

'You know each other?' asked Green, then stopped abruptly. Sophie could sense the moment she made the connection.

'We last met when Dr Greenman occupied a hut on Thuringa. Yes, we know each other,' said Sophie.

Chapter 8

VIOLETTE

The room the pennies allowed her to sleep in stank of rats, damp cloth and urine. Fungi grew from the walls. Five other women slept there, their ages ranging from (possibly) ten to (possibly) one hundred and four, though poverty, filth and starvation made it difficult to tell. All had to huddle on three small mattresses that were little better than rags. But the room provided safety from men, blizzards and the fog that was so thick you could almost slice it.

It did not protect you from the thefts of the other women, but the cold made it necessary to sleep in all her clothes anyway, and Violette kept the coins and her few pound notes between the layers of her clothing. She also kept her knife in its leather holder carefully anchored to her body with her knicker elastic, and made sure she let the other women see her use it, carefully peeling an apple with its sharpness.

The knife meant Violette slept undisturbed except for the scampering of rats and the occasional grey drip from the sagging ceiling. That night, however, she would not need to sleep with rats. She most probably would not even need her knife.

Violette's second meal of the day had been provided by a woman. This was not unusual — London, like all cities, had its 'kind ladies' eager to give a girl from the country a bed — and employment in that bed. This woman was different.

53

Violette had found her watching her with an almost hungry stare. Forty years old, perhaps, which was very old, and dressed sensibly but not fashionably in a blue cloche hat and well-darned gloves. The woman had listened to two songs — no longer Christmas carols and so less lucrative — before dropping a sixpence in the hat.

'I wonder,' she had asked tentatively, 'if you would like to have tea with me?' The woman gestured to the teashop behind, a Lyon's Corner House this time, not a Worthy's.

'Thank you, madame.'

'You are Belgian?'

'Yes, madame,' said Violette, surprised. 'How do you know?'

'I ... I recognised the song you sang. A Belgian family stayed with us during the war. The Maillots. Do you know them?' The woman shook her head, answering her own question and smiling. 'But Belgium is a big place.'

'I am desolate, madame. I do not know them.' Violette waited till they had sat down and her companion had ordered cocoa and a selection of sandwiches before asking, 'You were fond of that family, madame?'

'I married their son,' she said. 'I am Mrs Philippe Maillot. He and his father and brother died at the Somme, and our daughter and Philippe's mother of the influenza.'

'Madame, I am so sorry.'

Mrs Maillot dabbed her eyes — the handkerchief was embroidered with flowers, but mended too — and smiled. 'You remind me of Daisy, a little. She would be about your age. Her voice was sweet too,' she added awkwardly. 'My dear, you are very young and it is very cold. Are you ... have you anywhere safe to go?'

'A room. But I am searching for my mother.'

For the first time the look of enquiry was genuine. 'You were separated in the war?'

Violette nodded. 'Her name was Lily Shillings. I have rung many Shillingses, but no one knows of a Lily.'

'Hmm. You could place an advertisement in the newspaper,' suggested Mrs Maillot. 'Ah, cocoa, lovely.' She offered Violette the sandwiches, then bit into a corned beef and pickle one. 'Perhaps say *Mrs L Shillings: please correspond care of this publication. Your daughter wishes to contact you.*'

'It is Miss Shillings,' said Violette evenly.

'Ah.' Mrs Maillot put down her sandwich. 'How did you part?'

'She left me, madame. I was only a baby. I do not remember her.'

Mrs Maillot took a sip of cocoa before she spoke again. 'My dear ... what is your name?

'Violette, madame.' She lifted her chin. 'Violette Shillings.'

'Violette, you must know ... if your mother wasn't married perhaps she had no choice but to leave you in Belgium. The life of an unwed mother ...' Mrs Maillot shook her head. 'It is not easy, for her or the child. She may have thought you were better off with a family. Did she make provision for you? Leave money?' she added, when she saw Violette didn't understand.

'I do not know. My grandmère — I called her Grandmère even though she was not my grandmother — rented a cottage. We were happy until she died.' Violette did not add that Grandmère had taught her adopted granddaughter a range of skills, from embroidery to how to dispatch those who had collaborated with the hated Boche. But practising both had made them happy.

'And then?' asked Mrs Maillot sympathetically.

Violette's look hardened. 'An orphanage. The Sisters sent me to be a servant, but it was not as a servant that the house they sent me to wanted.'

'So many orphans after the war,' said Mrs Maillot apologetically. 'I don't suppose the Sisters could check each request.'

'No?' Violette shrugged. 'I escaped. I lived. And then I thought —' She stopped.

'That your mother might offer you a home?'

'Perhaps, madame.' Violette did not want to lie to this good woman.

Mrs Maillot bit into a cheese and tomato sandwich energetically. 'Well, the first thing we must do is find her. What do you know of her?'

Violette hesitated. 'Grandmère said that she was beautiful. Her dress was beautiful too.'

Mrs Maillot smiled. 'That is good, but not much help in locating her.'

'Grandmère said she came from a village called Shillings too. But I can find no Shillings on a map.'

'It is too small, perhaps, or it may be an estate or even a big house. But there may be a Shillings telephone exchange. We could call the operator and ask.'

Violette grew still. This was ... useful. She had never considered telephone exchanges. She nodded and helped herself to a sandwich.

'And churches. There might be a Shillings church. Or trains, perhaps.' Mrs Maillot was increasingly enthusiastic. She opened a practical handbag and pulled out a train timetable. 'Shillings Station!' she said triumphantly after a brief pause. 'It will be on the phone, perhaps. If it is, the stationmaster will be able to tell us if Shillings is a village, or just the name of the area.'

Violette blinked. After all these years, it seemed that her mother might be only a train journey away. 'My mother was an aristocrat, too, madame, a sister of the Earl of Shillings.'

Mrs Maillot stared at her. 'An earl is easy to find. He would be in Debrett's.'

'I do not know this book, madame.'

'But surely your grandmother would.'

Violette clenched her hands under the table. 'Grandmère wrote to the earl, just after the war. He did not reply, only the man who called himself his agent. The agent said that there was no Miss Lily Shillings in the family.'

Mrs Maillot looked at Violette with sympathy. 'Possibly the family did not want the scandal of a child born out of wedlock. It happens, my dear. A wealthy family makes provision for a child, and then has no more to do with them. Your grandmother didn't suggest you join your mother after the war?'

'No, madame. Never.'

'I see. Violette ...' The voice was awkward again. 'This room you have I ... I would be so very pleased if you would stay with me. Just until we have found your family, of course.' Though Mrs Maillot's hopeful tone made it clear she doubted that a mother who had given up her baby would want that baby to join her now in whatever life she had since made for herself.

For the first time since Grandmère died, Violette allowed herself tears. 'I ... I would like to stay a little time with you, madame, until I find this Shillings.'

But no more, she thought sadly. Mrs Maillot was so obviously longing to replace her daughter, the child with the sweet voice and, undoubtedly, with a nature as sweet as her mother's. Mrs Maillot did not deserve a daughter who had helped kill collaborators, who had, perhaps, killed a 'kind old gentleman' back in Brussels (she had not waited to find out his fate) and who planned to kill again.

For half a minute she allowed herself the fantasy of becoming Violette Maillot, daughter of a widow of limited means, but with enough money to order cocoa and sandwiches. They would go to church on Sundays and Violette would make madeleines for tea, and a tisane for her mother when she had a headache, just as she had done for Grandmère ...

But she was not that girl and never would be. But perhaps she would let herself pretend. Just for a while.

Chapter 9

Children belong to no one but themselves. We only borrow them.

Miss Lily, 1913

Sophie tried frantically to dredge up chatter to cut the silence, but already Nigel was breaking it. He put his hand on the pyjamaed wrist of the man in the bed.

'Major McDonald? Colonel Vaile here. You might remember Jones too. He was my batman back then. He played forward in the rugger match.'

The man on the bed looked straight ahead, as if he didn't hear. Yet he heard us approach, thought Sophie.

She couldn't stay there, and not just because of John's ... Dr Greenman's ... proximity. Neither she nor Greenie could help identify this man. All they could do at this stage was clutter up a 'do you remember?' masculine conversation.

As would Mrs McDonald and Mother Antill. There might well be things neither Nigel nor Jones nor even Dr Greenman would want to say in women's company. 'Remember the brothel in Egypt, old chap? That girl who did the act with the python?' Not that Nigel or Jones would ever have visited a brothel ...

Perhaps.

She smiled at Mrs McDonald and held out her hand, gloved and elegant, the kid skin hiding her own red scar tissue, the honour badge of the tens of thousands of women who had volunteered, unofficially and never counted, in the war. Hands that touched infected wounds, hands that must be washed repeatedly in cold water and lye-based soap that cracked in the cold and became infected too. Mother Antill's hands were marked with that badge too. The hand Mrs McDonald put in hers was not marked by wartime nursing, but neither was it soft and white. The woman worked, and her hands showed it.

'Mrs McDonald, we have a hamper in the car. Mother Antill might possibly share her tea with us again?'

Mrs McDonald glanced longingly at the man on the bed, even as she stood at Sophie's urging. 'I would rather stay here.'

Mother Antill understood. 'Miss Green, perhaps you would help me with the tea while her ladyship and Mrs McDonald fetch the hamper?' It was a voice used to gently command.

And suddenly Sophie and Mrs McDonald were outside in the courtyard, where two men from another ward walked slowly, one with a stick in his hand, the other gazing at the cobbles as he muttered under his breath. 'My mother is a pineapple, pineapple, pineapple. My father is an orange ...' The mumbler did not glance up as they passed, though the man with the stick gave a polite greeting to Mother Antill.

Sophie led the way to the car. She opened the back door then hesitated. 'Mrs McDonald, would you mind if we talked in the car? It will be more private.'

The woman stopped, suddenly suspicious. 'Why do we need privacy?'

'So I can ask questions that might embarrass any listeners. Like whether your husband was circumcised,' said Sophie frankly. 'Mother Antill has been married, but the other sisters ...'

'Ah, I see.' Mrs McDonald slid into the back seat next to her and accepted the travelling rug Sophie placed over their knees. Their breath flowered in small white clouds, even there in the car.

'Coffee?' Sophie unscrewed the top of a Thermos. She smiled encouragingly. 'I don't think Mother Antill's tea has enough strength left to revive a mouse.'

'Thank you. No, nothing to eat, thank you.' Mrs McDonald sipped, then looked at the black coffee, not Sophie, when she replied. 'Uncircumcised.'

'You know the word,' Sophie remarked.

Mrs McDonald flushed. 'My brother-in-law mentioned it. He ... I ... They, the sisters, wouldn't allow me to see John unclothed. I suppose that is reasonable, if he were not my husband. But a doctor is different.'

'Did Dr Greenman,' it was so much easier to use the unfamiliar name, as if there was no relationship to the man she had loved in every sense of the word, 'find any identifying marks?'

She shook her head. 'John doesn't have any useful moles or something like an appendix scar. He did have a scar on his left hand, but of course that is gone now.'

'Mrs McDonald, excuse my frankness, but all you have is a man who has brown hair, and who is roughly the right age and the same height as your husband.'

'He is shorter now, from his injury and being bedridden for so long.'

So 'Matthew' was not even the same height as John McDonald, thought Sophie. Surely this woman was deluding herself. 'Why are you so sure he is your husband?' she asked bluntly.

Mrs McDonald hesitated. 'I know this will seem idiotic, but it's his smell. Yes, there's disinfectant and carbolic soap and illness but, under it all, it's John. Faces change, your ladyship. I didn't even *know* I remembered what John smelled like. But as soon as I grew close to him I knew it. There are a hundred other things too — the way he moves his head, the set of his shoulders. It's nothing anyone but me would understand. Except his brother, perhaps.'

But only a wife, or long-term lover, would know the essential scent of a man, thought Sophie. She would always know Nigel's. 'Dr Greenman isn't as sure as you are?'

'He says he might be John. I think he thinks he *is* John, but for some reason he won't give a definite opinion.'

Or he thinks he isn't, and doesn't want to hurt you, thought Sophie. 'What is the legal situation?' she asked.

'Quite clear. If John can be positively identified, then I'm his next of kin. I'll take him home. Even if I didn't have the means to do so, the Australian government would repatriate him once they knew who he was, at the request of the French government, unless he had family who would contribute to his support here in France. But if he refuses to admit we are his family …'

Ah, thought Sophie, so a man who cannot speak or write and may have brain injuries has few rights. He must do as his next of kin and his country order.

'But until he's identified there is no way to prove he's even Australian,' continued Mrs McDonald bleakly. 'So he stays here.'

'Your word isn't enough to convince the authorities?'

'I don't know — probably not, unless his brother adds his weight to the identification. But that isn't the point.'

Mrs McDonald looked down at her gloveless hands, the nails short, the calluses on her fingers those of a woman who had been in the saddle much of her life, a gold wedding ring, an engagement ring with sapphires and diamonds. 'Mother Antill says that he has the moral right to choose whether to go or to stay here, to be John McDonald or Matthew, even if he doesn't have legal rights. I … I agree with her.'

Ah, a woman with intelligence and sensitivity, not possessiveness, thought Sophie, as Mrs McDonald fumbled for a handkerchief. Sophie passed her one of her own. Mrs McDonald wiped the tears, then blew her nose. 'He has almost nothing now, you see,' she said quietly. 'Just the choice — to be Matthew or to be John. I can't take that from him.'

'Even though you're sure he is your husband?'

'Especially because I am so very sure. I love him,' Mrs McDonald added. 'I didn't know if I still would, after all this time. But I do, even if he won't accept me.'

'I see.' Sophie took a smoked salmon sandwich, and then a sip of coffee. She needed sustenance. 'Do you think he has lost his memory?'

'No. Or at least he remembers enough to know me.' Despair edged her voice. 'Why would he respond to the sisters, but not to me, if he didn't recognise me? He won't even take a spoonful of soup from me, but I've seen Sister Emmanuelle hold a cup for him.'

'I suspect Mother Antill thinks he has some memory too, and possibly even some voice. But surely life would be so much better for him at home than here? The sisters do their best, but ...' She gestured at the frozen turnip fields, the cabbage stumps, the mud, the inadequate puffs of smoke from only two of the farm house chimneys.

'I know. I don't understand it either. Even if John doesn't ... doesn't love me any more, he would have warmth and care at home, far better than the sisters can give him here.'

'Home is where?'

'Burrawinga in the Western District. Sheep country. Stone walls and far horizons. John loved it. The boys enlisted together. Their father died in 1917, a few weeks after John was declared missing.'

'You've managed it since then?'

'There's a manager, Mr Hamilton, for the day-to-day decisions, but, yes, I have looked after the station since my father-in-law died. Legally it became mine when John was declared dead,' she added, 'with a quarter of the income to Daniel — my brother-in-law,' she added for clarification. 'Dr Greenman.'

'What will you do if Matthew doesn't acknowledge you?'

'Go home.'

Sophie stared at her. She hadn't thought this woman would give up easily. Mrs McDonald smiled. 'I'd have no choice. Daniel won't leave me here, and I'm not going to condemn him to a life attending me in France. It hasn't been ... easy ... for him coming back here, though he hasn't admitted it. It isn't fair to put him through even more. No, I'll go home and then come back with a companion. I'll volunteer here, not as a nun — I have no vocation and, even if I did, my family would have a pink fit. They are very, very Presbyterian,' added Mrs McDonald drily.

'I see,' said Sophie slowly. And she did see. A life of devotion, emptiness or rejection every day from the man she loved who refused any gesture of recognition. Pain upon pain.

And for the man in that bed in the cold stone ward? If he were John McDonald he would have to be on his guard forever, unable to make close friendships or learn to speak again in case he gave himself away to the woman who was always there, and would always consider herself his wife. Every day he would have to face that she was sacrificing her life for him, when she could be comfortable at home or even marry again, now that more than seven years had passed and he could legally be declared dead.

And if he were not John McDonald?

Perhaps then, one day, out of pity or pain, he would pretend he was. And that might be even worse.

She opened the car door as Nigel, Green and Jones came towards the car. Dr Greenman lingered at the doorway with Mother Antill, who seemed to have accepted her tea leaves would not need to be reused again today. Sophie was glad. A day could contain only so much emotion.

Sophie sat in silence next to Nigel in the back seat of the car as the conversation flowed around her. She would have liked to huddle, but Miss Lily's training held. Even her neck remained graceful as she stared out at the fields. Brussels sprouts this time ...

'It's possible he's McDonald,' Jones was saying. 'He may be thin now, but the width of the shoulders could belong to a rugby player.'

'And possibly half the British and Australian officers played rugby,' said Green wryly. 'I think it might be contagious.'

'Well, what do you think?' demanded Jones.

'A woman knows her husband,' stated Green.

'Really? You know so much about husbands.' Green flushed. 'It must be fourteen years since she's seen him,' argued Jones. 'Fourteen empty years of continuing to search for him, instead of going on with her life. She's been living a fantasy. This could be part of it.'

'We have no reason to think her life back in Australia wasn't rich and fulfilled, even while the search for him continued,' said Nigel. It was the first time he had spoken. His hand moved discreetly to hold Sophie's. She turned and gave him the hint of a smile. 'Mrs McDonald looks like a woman of sense and determination. Women like that rarely lead empty lives.'

'So why has she come across the world on a wild goose chase?' demanded Jones.

'Duty?' suggested Green. 'Hers is not the only family that's employed enquiry agents, even if it is just to know where their men's bodies lie.'

'Love,' said Sophie softly. 'She looks at him with love.'

The car rattled on the rutted road. 'Yes,' said Nigel at last. 'There is love.'

'Turn right,' said Green, looking at the map again.

The car swept into a road of houses, neatly gardened rows of vines, vegetables or flowerless geraniums. They would be in the city soon.

'Do you really think it will help if we go back tomorrow?' asked Green.

'It will help Mrs McDonald,' said Sophie. She did not try to analyse her feelings about John, or this new version of him, Dr Greenman. Later, she thought. This must be examined later. 'It isn't fair to leave her alone.'

Jones nodded. He glanced at Nigel. 'We have a duty to help McDonald's widow. And McDonald, of course, if that man is him.'

'If you don't mind,' said Nigel slowly. 'Only Sophie and I will go tomorrow. I can drive,' he added. 'Sophie can navigate.'

Sophie's mind lurched back twelve years to her last attempt at navigating: driving through the smoke-filled darkness near the front lines; the smell of sulphur, mud and blood; knowing she must reach her destination or tens of thousands would die or be left scarred, desperate, in agony ...

She had failed to stop the use of mustard gas. Matthew, whoever he had been, had been mutilated because of her failure.

'Yes,' she said briefly. 'I'll navigate.'

The others must have heard something in her tone. The rest of the drive was silent, apart from Green's directions.

Chapter 10

You can tell so much about a woman by how she wears her gloves.
A good maid ensures that each finger is eased off, so there are
never any wrinkles. A woman without a maid — or an impatient
one — may even use her teeth to pull her gloves off. Look for teeth
marks, my dears.

Miss Lily, 1913

VIOLETTE

The house was four long, slush-covered streets from the train
station: a bungalow, needing paint, separated from its neighbours
by a patch of winter-brown grass, and a row of dormant roses,
neatly pruned. Mrs Maillot unlocked the front door.

The house smelled of cold and, faintly, of a coal fire. 'The
kitchen will be warmer,' apologised Mrs Maillot.

'It is a palace for me, madame,' said Violette truthfully.

The hall led past three other doors, all shut, to the kitchen
door at the back of the house. The kitchen windows had clean,
though mended, lace curtains, and looked out on another square
of grass, a vegetable bed, a leafless tree and a washhouse.

Half the kitchen table was covered with a white cloth,
embroidered at the edges. The other half had been kept clear for
food preparation. It held a butter dish and a salt cellar. A dresser
displayed willow pattern china. The stove had been skilfully
banked up. This was clearly where most of the small life in this
house was lived. Mrs Maillot opened the air vent then added
more coal. The fire flared.

Mrs Maillot then reached into the larder, a thin cupboard with a few cans, a half-empty pot of jam, a bread bin and a large brown pottery dish with a lid. A vegetable rack sat on the floor, containing three potatoes, a carrot and a parsnip. Mrs Maillot removed the brown dish.

'I made soup last night. Pea and ham, and there is bread and jam for afters. I'm sorry I have nothing better to offer — I don't cook much for myself. I'll just go and light the fire in your room and air the sheets ...'

The daughter's room, thought Violette with sudden pain, ready for sheets to be put on the bed even though she would never sleep there again.

'Madame, please, do not trouble yourself ...'

'It is no trouble.'

The voice was painfully eager.

It was strange to have someone care for her; to have nothing to do except sit and breathe warm air. She looked at the photographs on the dresser as Mrs Maillot bustled about the room next to the kitchen. A man in a suit who looked kind. The husband? A much older couple, in pre-war clothes, possibly the parents. Four photos of a girl, as baby, toddler, and one when she was perhaps fifteen, a studio portrait. Violette had assumed Daisy Maillot had died in the early epidemic, but of course each winter still had deaths from influenza, even if it seemed to have lost its post-war virulence.

A pretty girl, Violette decided, but not remarkable. But then she had no need to be, for she had been loved.

Mrs Maillot hurried back. 'I left a nightdress warming for you too. I think Daisy's dresses might fit you, a little big perhaps, if you do not mind another's clothes.'

'It is an honour, madame.'

The soup was ... adequate. As Mrs Maillot had said it was pea and ham, and lacking any depth of herbs or seasoning. But Violette ate three bowls full. Her hostess ate none.

'Truly those sandwiches were all I needed at luncheon. You are far too thin,' said Mrs Maillot worriedly. 'We'll visit the butcher tomorrow. A small joint of beef, perhaps, and Yorkshire pudding. And scones … you know, it has been years since I made scones. I must put a note out for the milkman — milk and cream, I think. You'll need cocoa in the morning. He delivers eggs too. And a fresh loaf from the baker.'

The room still felt curiously lived in, even though the fire glowing in the bedroom fireplace had only recently been lit. A doll in a frilled dress sat on a cushioned chair. The nightdress was only a little too large, the bed warmed not just by the fire, but by a hot brick wrapped in flannel. A framed tapestry above the bed said *God Watch Thy Rest*.

'Sleep as late as you like,' said Mrs Maillot from the door. 'It … it has been such a hard time for you. You need rest and building up. We'll get more soup bones tomorrow too.'

And perhaps I will make the soup, thought Violette. She had seen leeks out in the garden, and there were those carrots and potatoes in the vegetable bin. There might even be a bay tree on the walk to the butcher's.

Mrs Maillot hesitated, then crossed the room. She bent and kissed Violette's cheek. 'Sleep well, my dear,' she said. She turned the gas light off as she shut the door.

Violette waited till her footsteps had vanished to the kitchen again, then checked the door was unlocked. The front door was locked, but only with a bolt on the inside.

She was not a prisoner then. She had not thought she was, but Violette Shillings would not have survived so long if she had not been cautious.

She lay back in the soft warm bed, under the comforting weight of blankets and a quilt, then she felt under the pillow to check her knife was still there. Satisfied, she slept.

Chapter 11

Men have moustaches and beards. Women do not. Except, of course, they do as they grow older. It is an unadmitted fact that men and women both become more androgenous as they age. Your tweezers will be your best friend, my dear, with the first hairs of your goat's beard, but I will also show you a useful thin toffee you may apply that will remove the smaller hairs on cheeks, forearms and legs. Hairlessness in women is associated with youth, and youth with beauty. I advise reading a good book propped up on a cushion while plucking, to pass the time.

Miss Lily, 1913

To Sophie's surprise Nigel excused himself as soon as they returned to the Ritz — he was usually sensitive to her moods and she needed him now. She sat in the living room of their suite, staring at the snickering fire. Flickering, eating the logs. Apple wood, she thought by its scent, hoping the Shillings people were all settling in safely for the evening. The Ritz did not subject its guests to the scent of coal.

But she could smell eucalypt smoke again, see the flames rise in John's campfire, the billy coming to the boil as he made tea for her. The night she had gone to him in desperation ...

She could not think of that. She must not think of that. What should she do? What should she say to him, to Nigel? Her mind and emotions felt like they had melted together —

She stood and walked over to the window, then turned as the door opened.

'I have brought crumpets,' said Miss Lily gently, standing back to let the waiter carry in the tray.

The waiter placed the tray on the table and set out the teapot — silver, naturally — the silver hot water pot, the milk jug and sugar basin, each with the crest of the Ritz. The English might be barbarians who drank tea instead of coffee, but the Ritz did not allow its employees even the ghost of a Gallic sneer.

The crumpets were accompanied by butter, honey and a toasting fork. The waiter laid them by the fire.

'How ... I mean why ...?' stammered Sophie, as the waiter left the room.

'Sit,' said Miss Lily. She gestured to the two armchairs, then poured tea. She handed Sophie a cup then bent, each movement a symphony of grace, placed a crumpet on the toasting fork and held it by the fire.

Sophie shut her eyes. She was back at Shillings, in that magic winter before the year of war, Hannelore laughing as her crumpet fell off the fork, and darling Mouse ...

She felt tears warm on her cheeks, knew that was exactly what Miss Lily intended: tears for all she had lost. Tears for Mouse and valiant Dodders. Tears for her father, tears for John.

Because the John she'd known was just as lost as her beloved friends. That golden man in his ragged shirt who washed in a gully and sang 'Danny Boy'. That simple, sunlit man who spent his days carving crosses for every dead man he'd watched charge into battle, or quietly counselling the returned servicemen of the district, who would journey to his hut by the gate for understanding or simply a cup of tea, the song of lyrebirds and of peace ...

She had thought, after that night together, that he had fled — but he'd only gone to find coffee for her breakfast. She had arrived home to the telegram announcing Nigel's surgery; had flown to him in England, never thinking of pregnancy till weeks later.

John had said he lived each day for his twin who had died; he had taken his name, too. She had asked James Lorrimer to search for him with what information she had, but James had found no twins who fitted their ages and names among the Australian forces. Why had John claimed his stepbrother as his twin?

The John she had loved had vanished, like so many who were precious to her. He had become the well-dressed, silent Dr Greenman. This was why she cried — and it had taken Miss Lily and the scent of crumpets for her to find her grief.

'Here.' Miss Lily handed her a crumpet dripping honey and butter. Sophie ate. Reality seeped back. She licked the butter from her fingers, as she had so many years before.

'Thank you for being here,' she said.

Miss Lily smiled. 'A husband is not the right person to talk to about a lost love. Miss Lily may be, perhaps.' She looked back at the fire. 'I asked Green to bring my things to Paris with us.'

'Ah,' said Sophie. 'Things' presumably meant the wig, the clothes, the make-up, the undergarments that subtly changed Nigel's thinness into the figure of a slender woman. There was perfume too: a touch of rose and oakmoss under the scent of toasting crumpets. Miss Lily had taught all her girls to choose a signature scent, one that would speak of comfort, beauty and charm, each time another smelled it.

'I loved him,' Sophie said simply.

'Yes. And now he seems to be gone. Though Dr Greenman must also be a compassionate man if he has chosen to support his sister-in-law through this.'

Could John and Dr Greenman really be two entirely different people? Sophie did not believe it, even if perhaps Dr Greenman did. They were aspects of each other, as Nigel and Lily were aspects of the one person too.

And she loved both Lily and Nigel, mourned that at any one time the person she loved could only show part of their personality. Was that because society could not accept a person born a man, who wished to be a woman? But Sophie did not believe that was entirely true of Nigel. The Earl of Shillings could have conveniently remained 'in the East' while Miss Lily appeared at his estates often enough to ensure they were well run.

But although she suspected that the person she loved was more comfortable — and certainly more effective as an espionage agent — as Miss Lily, Nigel Vaile had returned regularly to his estate, and even remained at Shillings and entered the House of Lords after the war, nor had he vanished when his hoped-for political career did not blossom.

And sexually? Sophie was not attracted to women; had not been sexually attracted to Miss Lily until she had known the other part of her persona. But she'd felt a sexual tension in her love for Lily after her marriage. Was it because she did desire Nigel? She didn't know. Nor did it matter.

And Miss Lily's feelings? Miss Lily had only known Sophie a few months before she had hoped Sophie might marry Nigel, even if it would be years before Miss Lily would make the proposal again. Had Miss Lily desired Sophie?

No, that did not matter either.

She gazed at the woman she loved, who was the man she loved. And yet she had loved (did love?) that green-eyed man in the hut, too. But that person might not be the man who was Dr Greenman now. 'Possibly John ... I mean Dr Greenman ... is simply seeking his brother and an answer to a mystery. He told me he was dead.'

'Yes. That too. But it cannot be easy to mourn a beloved brother, then travel across the world to see if he might still be alive, only to face that your brother has been alone, neglected, living on charity and turnip stew for twelve years.'

'The food will be better now. I've arranged for money to be sent regularly, with the first draft telegraphed to Mother Antill today.'

'Of course you have,' said Miss Lily gently, in the tone that meant that while the young Sophie Higgs had believed money and determination could achieve whatever she wanted it to, Sophronia Vaile, Countess of Shillings, knew better. 'Dr Greenman has a look of Rose,' Miss Lily added quietly. 'The same green eyes.'

'But Danny looks just like the portrait of you — of Nigel — as a child on the staircase,' said Sophie quickly.

'Sophie, my love, there is no way to ever truly tell who is the father of our children. But you do know this: they are loved by you, by me, by Green and Jones, and always will be. Perhaps you must give Dr Greenman the chance to love them too.'

'Perhaps?' asked Sophie.

'You are right. There is no perhaps. If he asks —'

'He may not ask,' said Sophie desperately.

'I think he will. I saw his eyes. His hands shook, which is why he held them behind his back. He will ask.'

Sophie nodded dumbly.

'I would like us to travel to the hospital early tomorrow morning,' Miss Lily changed the subject deftly. 'You and me, rather than you and Nigel. Is that ... acceptable ... to you?'

'Yes. I've missed you. Missed you desperately.' Who was Miss Lily? Friend, mentor, mother substitute? No, none of these, or all of them, and more. She was herself, and there was no one like her.

'I have missed myself too,' said Miss Lily lightly. 'Would you mind leaving at six o'clock?'

'Why then?'

'I would like us to talk to Matthew before his wife and brother arrive. Just you and me.'

Sophie knew once again that Miss Lily did not mean Nigel. 'You think Matthew really is Major McDonald?'

'I think he might be. And I think he may talk to the two of us, when he will not to Mother Antill, or his wife or brother.'

Sophie did not ask why. The girls Miss Lily trained were very good at questions — gentle, charming questions. One could not charm without compassion. One could not be compassionate without understanding. She accepted another crumpet, nibbled, tried to understand.

A man with neither voice nor hands, hideously scarred, who screamed at night remembering sights no one apart from him could understand. What had he felt, twelve years ago, when he had understood what he had become? What was he feeling now?

Chapter 12

Never weep for what you cannot do, or even what you fail to do.
Keep your tears for others, to give you strength to try again.

Miss Lily, 1913

Sophie drove. She was, in fact, a more experienced driver than Nigel, having found her way across war-splattered Belgium and France while the Earl of Shillings was being chauffeured both to and from the battlefront and at home. But no woman of sensitivity would suggest she should drive when a man could take the wheel.

But Miss Lily, of course, was different. Sophie even found herself wondering if Miss Lily were able to drive, before smiling at the thought. Nigel and Miss Lily shared the same body, and the same skills. But if they had been the same persona there would be no need for Miss Lily to be with her that morning.

Nor would Sophie have been so grateful that she was.

The sun had more warmth there than at Shillings, but the wind slithering along the fields was colder, although Green had still laid out silk for her to wear: a dull gold dress, its colour accentuating her hair, high necked and low waisted, with a coat of the same silk that had a caped lambs-wool collar in thin stripes, like a most elegant tiger, felt-lined and warm.

Miss Lily wore silk too, in silver grey. Sophie remembered the afternoon Miss Lily had explained to the girls sitting on the hearth by the fire that the sound of silk, the scent of it, whispered 'woman' in a way no fabric also worn by men could do.

The Ritz had provided another hamper. Sophie suspected the hotel would have found them a performing elephant and a troupe of jugglers if they had needed them. Though, now she thought of it, Rose and Danny would appreciate the jugglers.

The hamper contained more coffee in a Thermos, held in place inside the lid by a strap. Straps also secured the coffee cups, the saucers, the plates, cutlery and damask napkins to lay under the brioche, for surely no client of the Ritz would risk crumb marks on her frock.

Sophie spread the napkin on her silken lap and nibbled as she drove, as Miss Lily broke the brioche into manageable pieces and spread them with jam and butter for her. They paused just before the turn-off to the hospital to drink the coffee. Sophie was glad of the flood of energy.

If this did not work two lives might stay shattered, and maybe other lives, as well.

This time the door was opened by a taller nun. She led them through the courtyard, then apologised, in French, for leaving them. 'It is time for the men's breakfast. This takes a while, you understand. Some can feed themselves, at least the easier foods, but others cannot.'

Sophie opened the stable door. This time the room smelled of real coffee and fresh bread, and the rich, buttery scent of croissants. She smiled. Mother Antill had lost no time using the new funds for her charges.

The man in the first bed eyed them: two women, with shining hair not covered by a wimple, clothes that subtly showed the shapes beneath, smiles that acknowledged him as a man. The other men in this ward could only listen to the click of women's heels on the cobbled floor. The man in the last bed listened too, his hand stumps carefully wielding a long piece of French loaf spread with jam.

'Excuse us interrupting your breakfast, Matthew,' said Sophie quietly. 'It's Lady Shillings again. Sophie. This is Miss Lily; she is a relative of my husband.'

No answer. But he had heard her. He bent his head to push the last of the narrow loaf into his mouth, then rested his stumps in his blanket-covered lap and chewed. The two chairs still stood by the bed. Sophie moved them so the partition gave them privacy. They sat.

He waited.

Sophie waited too, expecting Miss Lily to speak. Instead she glanced at Sophie.

What was she supposed to say? She had assumed Miss Lily had a plan for this particular conversation. But it seemed Miss Lily was leaving this to her.

I am no longer the student, Sophie realised. Miss Lily was leaving this task to the one who — perhaps — had been the most successful of her 'lovely ladies'.

Sophie placed her fingers gently on what had been a man's hand, moving her fingers slightly in what might have been a caress. Or not. The man looked sharply in her direction, as if trying to force his ears to see where his eyes could only dimly make out a shape.

'I knew a man in 1915,' said Sophie softly. 'He had no eyes. His whole head was covered in scar tissue, red ridges instead of hair. He married his assistant accountant after the war. They manage the accounts of a factory together. I am godmother to their daughter.'

The man was silent, but he listened.

'I flew from Australia three years ago. The woman pilot who flew me to Europe had been a nurse. She lost most of her face rescuing the pilot of a burning plane. He lost his sight. They are married now, running an aeroplane route through northern Australia. It was a shock to see her face,' she added, 'but only the first time. The second time I looked in recognition. The third time I looked at her I saw her beauty. They are happy, the two of them.'

The man twisted his head in an impatient gesture.

'No,' said Sophie, 'I am not pretending that the world would see her beauty, nor even understand their happiness. But their friends see *them*, and not their scars. Or rather they accept those scars as evidence of their determination, their love as well as their pain.'

Once more the man was still.

Miss Lily leaned forward. 'There is a woman who loves John McDonald,' she said, her voice a soft caress. 'She intends to devote her life to him. If he will not return to Australia with her, she intends to return here, to help tend him.'

The man in the bed gave a brief jerk of shock.

'The question you can't stop asking yourself, of course,' continued Miss Lily, 'is what John McDonald has to give to her.'

'Nothing.' The word was no more than a breath, a croak. The sound seemed to surprise the man on the bed as much as Sophie.

'Are you sure?' asked Miss Lily, and surely the man could sense the smile, that deep and perfect smile, the one that had charmed for decades now. We are partners now, thought Sophie with relief. Miss Lily and I can work together ... 'Mrs McDonald loves, and asks for love. Can John McDonald give her love?'

The man sat still.

'Love is love, no matter what has happened to the body from which it comes. Can John McDonald give the woman who loves him companionship, listening as she talks about her day? Caring about her day? Caring for her? Can John McDonald give her that?' Miss Lily's smile grew deeper. She leaned forward again, touched his ankle, then ran her hand slowly, so very slowly, up his pyjama-clad leg. 'Children?' whispered Miss Lily. 'Can John McDonald give her children? A baby to hold in her empty arms, arms that will remain empty unless he fills them. Mrs McDonald knows her husband lives. Somehow she has always known, in her heart, that he is living. She will not marry again.'

'Unless her first is dead.' The words were only just intelligible, the bitterness profound.

'I think she would not believe in his death, especially now she has found him after he was supposed to have been dead for so long, unless she saw the body. And if she did see that body, after looking for him for so long and then succeeding, only to find tragedy again, I think the heartbreak would be so great she would not risk loving, or trusting, in marriage again.'

The man on the bed was still, except for the blinking of his lashless eyes.

'Can John McDonald give her a child's laughter?' whispered Miss Lily, her hand still resting gently on his thigh. 'Can he give her grandchildren to cherish when she is old?'

The stumps of the hands moved to mound the blanket less revealingly about his loins.

How had Miss Lily known, thought Sophie wonderingly, that John McDonald could still father children? For if he had not been able to, this conversation would only have made him more determined than ever to spare his wife.

Miss Lily sat back, her hands now in her lap. 'Your wife loves you very much,' she said quietly. 'But it is not just that. She knows you, John, even after everything. She told Sophie yesterday that she recognised the scent of you, after fourteen years. She did not even know it was possible, until she did. You are the man she loves, the man she knows. Not the man you were fourteen years ago, but the man you are now. She has spent weeks with you, and she is not a fool. You are who she wants.'

He lay back against the pillows. It took a minute for Sophie to realise he was crying, for the gas had burned his tear ducts along with his eyes.

'John?' Sophie turned. Mrs McDonald stared at her, fury gathering in her small form. 'What have you been saying to him, the two of you?' she demanded, bending over the man in the bed like a small tiger in blue wool. 'How dare you upset him like this?'

'Harriet ...' Once again the word was more breath than voice and yet intelligible. Mrs McDonald gave a cry.

'Love you,' said the voice. 'Have always loved you. Did not want to be a burden ...'

'A burden? John!' Mrs McDonald flung herself against him, sobbing. The scarred stumps of arms closed about her, protective, as if they would never let her go.

Miss Lily stood. Sophie followed her. It was only then that she saw Dr Greenman standing watching her, his brother, his sister-in-law and Miss Lily.

Chapter 13

True empathy means feeling another's pain, but also their joy. It takes time to learn, my dears, but empathy is possibly the most selfish talent you can have. Once you have true empathy, the more you lose, the happier you can be that someone else has gained.

Miss Lily, 1913

The three of them stood in the cobbled courtyard. It had rained in the night. Mud oozed between the stones. The men from the stable ward were limping out into the feeble sunlight, helping one another. Perhaps they too wanted to give the couple in the last cubicle privacy. Sophie hoped they would be happy in their fellow patient's joy.

Miss Lily pressed her hand. 'I will tell Mother Antill the good news. You will take your brother with you today?' she asked Dr Greenman.

Dr Greenman nodded, his face closed to all emotion. Perhaps he, too, did not yet know what to feel, though he did not look as strained out there as he had in the stable ward.

Sophie thought again of the man by the gate, his hut, the song and silence of the bush around him, the wide sky above and the far blue horizon. Even the smells of the ward, the sight of rows of beds, must bring back memories hard to bear. He looked at Miss Lily, not her, as he answered, 'Yes. Harriet and I are staying at the Ritz. I am sure they can make arrangements for John too. There is a lift.'

We might have seen them there, thought Sophie. He might have already seen Danny and Rose. And then: the Ritz. Money. The man who had lived in the hut by the gate at Thuringa had been penniless, except for threepences given to him for opening the gate. Burrawinga was evidently a prosperous property, and such families usually had other investments too. And had he returned to his profession?

'I will be inside when you need me,' said Miss Lily. She smiled at a pair of men limping past, then made her way into the main building.

'Who is she?' asked Dr Greenman. He did not look at Sophie directly.

'A close relative by marriage. My teacher. My best friend.' All true, thought Sophie. Almost, indeed, the whole truth, though this man would not know it.

'How did you manage that, you and ...?'

'Miss Lily.' Sophie shrugged. She could not say, 'Miss Lily knows exactly how to arouse a man.' Nor was she able to casually remind Dr Greenman that his brother would by circumstance have been denied — release — for many years.

She had once thought she knew this man, his simple goodness, the way he could see to the heart of love. She could have spoken of what had happened in the old stable to John. But to Dr Greenman? 'There's a seat over by the fence,' she said. 'We can talk privately there.'

He tucked his scarf into his coat. A well-cut coat, even fashionable. But then all his clothes must be relatively new. 'Do we need to talk?'

'You know we do. And I think your brother and his wife need more time alone.'

He nodded at that. They crossed the courtyard. The breeze hit as they left the shelter of the buildings, the scent of ice and pig and omnipresent turnip. Sophie sat on the rough wooden seat. Dr Greenman hesitated, then sat as far away as the seat would allow.

'You recognised your brother?'

'What?' He had expected her to talk of them. 'Yes. Almost at once. The set of the shoulders, the shape of the feet. Even the same stubborn set to his chin when he wouldn't acknowledge our voices. But I didn't want to force him into a life he didn't want.'

'He longed for it,' said Sophie. 'He simply didn't want to be a burden to those he loves.'

'I see that now. Thank you,' he said grudgingly.

A breath. A moment only, but such a long one. 'You said he was your twin.'

'We always thought of ourselves as twins. We were born on the same day, to different parents. His father died, and my mother. My father and his mother married when we were two years old, though he kept his father's surname. We even looked so much alike we were taken for twins, especially in school uniform.' He shrugged. 'In times of stress we tend to go back to the beliefs of our childhood.'

'I searched for you when I woke up that morning,' she said quietly. 'I thought you had fled from me. I left, thinking I had hurt you, forcing you back to a life you didn't want. The telegram about Nigel had arrived at Thuringa by the time I arrived home ...'

'And a month later you had married him. Countess of Shillings. You must be proud.'

She couldn't see whether he meant to sting her with that. 'I am proud of my husband. He is not his title and nor am I mine. Except, perhaps, in our sense of duty to the people of the Shillings estate. Nigel needed me. He was ill, probably dying. I owed him more than I can say.'

'And loved him?'

'Yes,' said Sophie. 'Though it's not as ... simple ... as that. Nigel had asked me to marry him before I went home to Australia. I loved him then too, but knew my life was elsewhere.'

'And then it wasn't.'

'In the years since then I'd learned how to be myself. I no longer risked losing that by staying in England with Nigel.' Except I have, she thought, a little bit. But perhaps that always comes with marriage and parenthood. She took a deep breath. 'I loved you too. If you had asked me to marry you, I would have accepted.'

'Marry a swaggie who lived in a hut?' She noticed he did not say he had loved her back. Had she loved an illusion?

'Yes,' she said quietly. 'I would have married you, if you had asked. Though I would have gone home to bathe if you'd insisted on continuing to live in the hut by the gate.' Her tone was not quite facetious.

'You had children the year after you left Australia,' he said flatly. 'I read about the birth. Your marriage was quite a sensation in Australia. But the newspapers were tactful. No one mentioned that their birth date was just a little too close to your marriage.'

She did not tell him that she and Nigel had only those few days of physical love, before the surgery necessary to save his life made it impossible. 'Midge keeps me up to date on the Australian news. So does Maria, my old governess, who's returned there. There is no need to be tactful. Yes, Rose and Daniel may be your children. They may also be Nigel's. Nigel knows this, by the way; and had I been able to find you I would have talked to you about the ... situation ... as well. At least,' she added honestly, 'I think I would have. John, look at me.'

'That man no longer exists.'

A man she had loved; still loved in memory and dreams. A man who'd seen beauty all around him, and touched strangers with his compassion.

'Dr Greenman, then,' she said, glad her voice stayed steady. 'Would you have asked me to marry you if I had told you I was pregnant? Or even if I'd stayed and waited for you to return that morning?'

He looked at the turnip fields, not at her. 'I dreamed of asking you to marry me all through that night we had together, and no, I didn't expect we would stay living in the hut. I dreamed of marrying you until the moment I found you'd flown away. Quite literally.'

But who would I have married? she thought. John or Dr Greeman? Who is Dr Greenman?

'You must have some idea which of us is the children's father.' She could feel the effort he was making to keep emotion from his voice, but his fists were clenched in his lap.

She shook her head. 'Truly, I don't. My journey to Australia was ... irregular. My body was irregular too. I hardly knew night from day. Rose and Danny were born slightly late for you to be their father, and slightly early if they are Nigel's.'

'Twins are more likely premature than overdue. Which conveniently makes them your husband's.'

'There speaks a doctor. But firstborn children are more likely to be slightly overdue too.'

'Psychiatrist,' he corrected.

'Ah. I should have guessed. But doesn't that mean you've qualified as a doctor as well?'

'Yes. And served as such in the war. Sadly, the armed forces in their wisdom had little use for doctors of the mind.' He hesitated. 'How did you know my name was Daniel?'

'What? I didn't know.'

'But you called your son ...'

'I called him after the song you sang. "Danny Boy". *Oh Danny Boy, the pipes, the pipes are calling* ...'

'My mother used to sing it to me. My stepmother, but I always thought of her as Mother.'

'I sing it every night to Rose and Danny. It's their lullaby.'

'Ah,' he said. Nothing more, but his hands relaxed. His body moved infinitesimally towards her.

They sat in silence, each at their end of the seat. At last she said, 'Do I call you Dr Greenman or Daniel?'

'Do I call you your ladyship or Sophie?'

'Sophie.'

'Then I am Daniel.'

Was that the beginning of a smile?

'May I write to Midge, to tell her you are safe? She cared about you. So did many people.'

'Yes. I must write to her too.' Daniel gazed at the men, limping around the yard or being pushed in wheelchairs, drinking in the thin French sun. 'I wasn't quite sane, back then. I knew it. Being someone else helped me keep all that Daniel Greenman couldn't cope with locked away. Not just John's death, but all the others.'

Sophie thought of those thousands of crosses he had carved. She had presumed they were for each man he had ordered to his death. But he had been a doctor — were they for the ones he had not been able to save?

'Then you appeared,' Daniel said simply. 'And I found I wanted to live, not as a swaggie by a gate, but as myself.'

'And then I left you. I'm sorry. I'll always be sorry. I didn't understand.'

'How could you? What I was, who I was, wasn't entirely rational.'

'And now you are rational?'

He looked at her with honesty. 'Most of the time. There are still difficult nights. Times when I am — discombobulated. I … I'm still not quite able to reconcile my life as "John" with my life as Dr Greenman, though I know I owe Midge and others both apologies and gratitude. Sometimes I need to spend a day or more just walking through the bush. That seems to bring me back to who I am and when I am, not back in 1918.'

'You can't walk in the bush in France. Is it worse being back here?'

'Yes.'

She wished she could help him, hold him through the nights. Why couldn't a woman have two husbands, if she loved them both? Or even just be there, to hold him as a friend? Suddenly, with anguish, she wished he'd find a woman who could help keep him in the present, safe, happy, not back in all the tumult of the war.

But he had found one, a woman who had been trained by Miss Lily to understand, to have compassion, grace and charm. And that woman had abandoned him, might even have stolen his children, the ones he had longed for. She imagined walking along the riverbank at Thuringa, each of them holding a child's hand. Daniel, who looked like a baby Nigel, Rose, who had Daniel's eyes, green as his name …

But come ye back when summer's in the meadow
Or when the valley's hushed and white with snow
It's I'll be here in sunshine or in shadow —
Oh Danny Boy, oh Danny Boy, I love you so!

'Thank you for not asking me to leave Nigel so you can claim the children.'

He looked startled. 'It never occurred to me that you might agree. You're a countess, after all.'

'I can dispense with the countess bit,' she said drily. 'It is the least important part of my life. But Nigel *is* important,' and Miss Lily, she thought, who I love as much. And Jones and Green, who are family too. Their lives would be ripped as far apart as Nigel's if I left him. 'I married Nigel because he needed me more,' she said. 'Or I thought so then. And, looking at you now, I think I was right. You've survived. Nigel ... I don't think he would have.'

'I heard about his surgery.'

Ah, she thought, Midge told him that too, probably when he heard of my marriage, before he so suddenly left Thuringa. And possibly, as a doctor, Daniel might also guess that Nigel and I no longer have a physical marriage. But love and a life together? We have that. The ways we are bound may not be entirely conventional but they will hold.

'I'm not saying I have no regrets,' she said slowly. 'I ... dream of you sometimes.' He was watching her now, his hands trembling again, but not reaching for her. 'I dream of Thuringa too, and sunshine and proper dusty sheep, not ones that look like they've been washed in Sunlight soap. We'll go back to Thuringa, probably next autumn — English autumn, in time for the spring wattle bloom at home.' She met his eyes. 'But I have never once felt that marrying Nigel was the wrong choice to make, for him or for me. Or for the baby I knew I was carrying. I did try to find you, you know. But you didn't make it easy.'

An uncomfortable silence for a second or two too long. And then, 'I miss the gate, sometimes,' he said. It sounded like forgiveness, and an apology. And suddenly it was as if winter had lifted, and she smelled the crackling bark beneath their feet at Thuringa again. For this was John, and Daniel too.

She tried to keep her voice light. 'You are welcome to go back there, at any time.'

'I might, you know. A kind of camping holiday. But I've returned to real life now.'

'That was real,' she said.

'It was, wasn't it?' He seemed to be only just realising it himself. 'And wonderful.' He was silent for a while, then added, 'I will never regret those years.'

'A beautiful time,' she agreed.

They sat in silence, still as far apart physically, but strangely together now. Something that had niggled at her for months clarified. She took a breath.

'Daniel, as a doctor ... I haven't even asked Nigel this. I haven't suggested it to anyone, in case it is insane. But the twins ... they look so different from each other. I know fraternal twins are no more similar than any other brother and sister. But is it medically possible for twins to have different fathers?'

He looked startled, then thoughtful. For the first time she saw him assess the question as a professional, and that expression was familiar too. I should have guessed he was a doctor back then, she thought, thinking of all who'd come to his hut for help, how he had managed each man with such expertise.

'I've never heard of such a case,' he said at last. 'But then for a case to be known, a woman would have to admit that she'd had ... relations ... with two men within a single month. Medically ... yes, it is indeed possible that you produced two eggs — you must have anyway, to have had non-identical twins. It might be possible that each was fertilised by a different man at different times. But I doubt a court would accept it.'

'Why should it go to court —?' she began, then realised. 'You'd sue for custody?'

'No. But your husband might decide to repudiate an heir he felt was not his own, especially if you have another son.'

85

'Danny looks exactly like Nigel did at his age.' She would not say that Nigel needed an heir to ensure his cousin never took the property. But the question would not arise anyway, she thought. Nigel could never repudiate a child, even one who was not his own. Nor could he not love either baby he had held so often in his arms.

'And Rose?'

'She looks a little like you, especially her eyes. A lot like me.'

'Lucky girl.'

She flushed, hoping it was a compliment. 'Do you want to meet them?'

'Of course.' For the first time his eyes met hers, and his face was gentle despite the certainty, even urgency, in his voice. 'Would that be possible?'

'Of course,' she repeated.

'What will your husband say?'

'We have already discussed it.' She smiled. 'He said of course too. Nigel is a good man, Daniel. A wonderful man.'

A lark sang, somewhere behind them, the first she had heard in all her years in France. Daniel reached across the seat, took her hand and kissed it.

'I'm glad,' he said.

Chapter 14

When you are a child, you wait for the world to become simple when you are an adult and can do whatever you want. A young woman waits for life to be simpler when she is married, in charge of her own house. A mother waits for the simplicity that will follow when her children manage their own lives. But life continues to become more complex. How can it not, unless we stay walled up, with no connections growing between each other or the world?

Miss Lily, 1913

SHILLINGS

HEREWARD

Hereward the butler might have only one hand, and he'd had only two years' experience as a footman at Shillings before he enlisted in the Great War. But he had lived at Shillings all his life, as had uncounted generations of his forebears before him.

Hereward had heard whispers, which he knew how to ignore.

He also knew his duty when a young woman appeared — of uncertain class, even uncertain nationality — in a much-mended white dress, with shoes and stockings that appeared new and a coat that would be suitable for a much older woman of the lower middle classes.

'I am sorry, miss, but his lordship is not at home, nor is her ladyship.'

'I do not want to speak to lords or ladyships,' said the girl impatiently. 'I am here to see Miss Lily Shillings.'

This was interesting. It was also interesting that Hereward had never heard Miss Lily give her surname — nor anyone else use it. But it would be too much coincidence to have two 'Miss Lilys' — unless this girl had assumed a woman surnamed 'Shillings' must come from here. All intriguing, but his duty was clear. Hereward carefully let no sign of his eagerness show. 'I am afraid Miss Lily has not visited Shillings since before the war, miss.'

'Ah, so you do know her! Where is she then?'

'I couldn't say, miss.' Hereward regretted giving more information than necessary. But the girl could have heard that a Miss Lily visited here from many people in the area. 'Perhaps if you would like to leave a note for his lordship, he might know where it might be sent on to.'

'And you do not?' The words were imperious. Spoiled brat, thought Hereward. He'd put her over his knee if she were his daughter. Who did she think she was, appearing at the front door of Shillings?

'I am afraid not, miss.'

'When will this lord and ladyship return?'

'I cannot say, miss.'

The imperiousness vanished. Suddenly he saw the child, limp with weariness after a long train journey and an even longer walk, the touch of desperation in her eyes, the chill as she dragged her coat closed over her dress.

'If you would care to go to the back door,' he said more gently, 'I am sure Mrs Goodenough would give you a mug of hot cocoa and a slice of cherry cake. I will ask one of the men to give you a lift back to the station. There's the 4.10 to London, stopping at all stations.'

'Thank you, monsieur.' The girl had lost all signs of arrogance now. 'You are so kind. I would like some cocoa please, and the cherry cake. His lordship ... do you think he will be gone days or months, monsieur?' The blue eyes looked up at him imploringly.

She had no right to ask; nor was it his job to answer. But he found himself giving her the information anyway. 'Days, I think, miss. Now you go and get the cherry cake.'

She dropped a curtsey to him and his heart melted. A sweet little thing, and probably it was all a mistake, and the Lily Shillings she searched for had no connection with the Vaile family's Miss Lily. He must make sure she had enough money for the train journey, second class. It was too cold in third. And a brown paper bag of mutton and pickle sandwiches perhaps, from the leftover roast, and more of the cherry cake …

Chapter 15

Love comes in many ways, my dears. Never restrict yourselves to what society tells you love must be. If it is truly love, a love that gives and does not hurt, then it is good.

Miss Lily, 1913

Mother Antill wept a little as John McDonald, her Matthew, walked unsteadily to the car, arm in arm with his wife, but they were tears of joy. The other sisters and the ambulatory patients waved farewell.

And now there are only seventeen, thought Sophie, as she and Miss Lily watched John ... *Daniel* ... drive the car down the track between the turnips. She lingered to make further financial arrangements with Mother Antill, then joined Miss Lily in the car. She drove slowly down the lanes, describing her conversation with Daniel, though not the gentle kiss with which it had ended.

'A good man,' Miss Lily said at last.

'That is what I said of Nigel.'

Lily nodded. 'Yes, Nigel is a good man too. I wish, though, I could be with you for the meeting, not him. But your Daniel will expect your husband to be there, to assure him he does in truth know all the details and is comfortable with whatever role Daniel may wish to play.'

'Except their acknowledged father.'

'Except, of course, that.' Lily looked at a cluster of goats, driven along the road by a boy with rags wrapped around the rudimentary clogs that kept his feet from the cold mud. 'Society accepts rolled-down stocking tops and rouged knees, the loss of twenty thousand men in a day's battle and most of a generation of young men, but not children having two fathers.'

Lily is so beautiful, thought Sophie, a beauty age only deepened, not just the elegance of her bone structure but the kindness shining through.

'I so very much wish Nigel could offer him joint fatherhood,' Lily said at last. 'But to do so would confuse the children, even if it were socially possible, and if my cousin even heard the whisper of a rumour he would be quite capable of launching a court case. We can't risk Daniel's succession to the title and the estate. The children must never have doubts about who they are,' Miss Lily concluded.

Sophie glanced at her, this woman who had lived all her life — and Nigel's life — doubting, changing from one and then to the other. How much anguish did that small phrase hold?

Nanny and Amy were delighted to be given a whole day free to explore Paris. Sophie debated between Rose and Danny meeting Daniel at the hotel, or in a park. But the children must be rugged up for a park and their time there would be limited by the cold. And neither the Countess of Shillings nor Sophie Higgs wished to cry in public ...

She realised she was preparing for this meeting with as much thought to strategy as she had once spent on founding a new hospital or factory, or that new line of canned tomato juice that had done so well in the United States, for its health-giving properties and to replace red wine in temperance households — and even to disguise hooch for those who had found a source of bathtub gin.

Tea would arrive five minutes before John ... *Daniel* ... arrived. Cucumber sandwiches, watercress and cream cheese, crab and ginger on brown bread because the Ritz did them so perfectly, with madeleines, perhaps, and small cherry and custard tarts. There must be nothing that said ostentation, but nothing reminiscent of Midge's apple pie or fruit cake by the campfire either. Bread and honey, because Danny loved it, cheese and lettuce for Rose ...

And her dress ... Green had put out a new one, magically arrived only twenty-four hours after the visit to the couturier, hazel velvet, the same colour as her eyes, with gold and green embroidered dragons at the hem and collar and a low-slung thin gold belt ... too like a chastity belt?

Come off it, duckie, she told herself. Breathe. You are a swan.

'If you don't sit still,' said Green, wielding a comb, 'your hair is going to look like a birch broom in a fit.'

'I shouldn't have washed it.'

'Of course not. Nothing wrong with the scent of turnip. All of fashionable Paris is wearing eau de turnip this year.'

Sophie grinned reluctantly. 'I am behaving like an idiot.'

'Yes,' said Green.

'I was perfectly calm before my debut. My heart hardly raced when I first met Queen Mary.'

'But then you didn't care particularly what Queen Mary thought, did you?'

'No,' said Sophie. 'It was just an adventure. Such a wonderful adventure. Do you think the world will ever be as innocent again?'

'It never has been innocent. But you were.'

'Were you?'

Green considered. 'Yes. The maid who travelled to meet the new Miss Lily was innocent.'

'But you didn't marry Jones?'

'I was in his bed within three weeks, so perhaps not quite so innocent as all that. But by then I had met Misako.' Misako was the elderly courtesan who had taught Miss Lily so much. 'I wanted to be like Misako. Not a courtesan, but myself. Lily taught you all to be successful wives. I don't think it ever occurred to her she wouldn't have enjoyed being one herself.'

'She did teach us that marriage was inevitable. Well, for most of us, if we wanted to have influence in the world. Few of us had a choice.'

'I did,' said Green.

'And I suppose I did too. And now I am sedate and married.'

'And if you don't sit still your face will look like a clown's. Part your lips. Just this shade of lipstick, I think ... do sit still ... and only a touch of powder. You'll do,' said Green.

Nigel looked up from the desk, where he had been reading a telegram. 'You are the most beautiful woman I have ever met and would look glorious in a hessian sack. But today you also look completely appropriate.'

Miss Lily could not have said it better. Sophie relaxed. Had he heard Green's comment about Miss Lily? Or had he been too absorbed in his telegram? It was an unusually long telegram, Sophie realised. She had assumed it was from one of the few House of Lords committees to which Nigel still lent his name and, occasionally, his time. He held it out to her. 'I think you should read this.'

Green tactfully slipped out. She and Jones would read the telegram, of course. Nigel would leave it on the desk for them. If it was important all of them would discuss its contents that night. Sophie was not sure how she felt about that. She had always assumed that marriage was a nation of two, but aristocrats were used to having attendants for everything from putting on their boots to supporting their personal crises. Nigel was different only in that his attendants were also friends.

'Sophie?' Nigel looked puzzled at her hesitation.

Sophie took the telegram.

Daniel Theophilus Greenman MD Sydney Dip Psych Edinburgh stop Colonel stop Born 8 August 1890 Father Theophilus Greenman grazier Burrawinga Western Victoria deceased 1916 motor accident stop mother Virginia Anne Greenman née Hillier 1868 D 1890 stop stepmother Elaine McDonald née Fusilier died 1916 stop brother John Gilbert McDonald Major grazier married Harriet Windermere 1913 stop missing in action Somme 1917 stop D Greenman service record significantly insignificant stop demobbed August 1921 delay due influenza epidemic stop whereabouts unknown December 1922 to December 1928 stop attended Burrawinga church Christmas 1928 with sister-in-law

stop gossip only follows stop studied psychoanalysis in New York
stop intends setting up Macquarie Street practice query marry
sister-in-law query politics unknown mental stability minor query
probably trustworthy on all counts fuller report follows yours
Lorrimer

She put the paper down. 'James has been busy,' she said evenly.

'James's secretary and assistants have been busy. James has been attending a Friday to Monday in Northumberland. Do you mind?'

'Asking about Dr Greenman? No. Or rather, yes, I mind very much, but admit the necessity, if Dr Greenman is to play a role in the children's lives.'

Nigel smiled. 'I meant asking James about Dr Greenman without your knowledge.'

To Sophie's surprise she did feel a slight niggle of resentment — James was *her* friend, but of course Nigel — and Miss Lily — had known him and worked for him far longer. But she also felt gratitude that Nigel had not bothered asking her when she was ... discombobulated ... not just at meeting Daniel, but at seeing the change in him.

The greatest shock, perhaps, was that maybe he had not changed so much at all.

Four years earlier she'd thought she'd seen a saint living in a hut by the Thuringa gate and giving out simple wisdom. Instead that man had been an experienced professional, war damaged, but able to assess his own mental state and respond to it and to that of others. But he was still 'John', too. Did that make a difference to how she felt about him? Perhaps it was wise not even to probe how she felt about him ...

Nigel held out his hand. 'Come on. It's time to go.'

Nanny left to investigate the delights of Paris in a haze of lavender water; Amy in a fog of Eau Des Nuits de Paris. Sophie made a note to ask Green to advise the girl. Amy could be pretty with a better haircut ... 'Rose darling, no, we do not hit our brother on the head with a wooden horse.'

'Gogunk!'

'Yes, very probably, but kiss him sorry. That's a good girl.'

'Orse?' demanded Rose.

'Orse orse?' asked her brother hopefully.

'All right, Danny darling, I'll be your horse, but just for a minute. Daddy, will you be Rose's horse? Oh, thank you, don't mind us,' as a small team of waiters (three) brought in a tea tray, cutlery, sandwiches, followed by Daniel, his face cracking to a grin at the sight of the earl and countess galloping about the floor, each with a toddler on their back, and three Ritz staff attempting to look as if this was something they encountered every day.

Nigel stood, deftly placing Rose on the ground and holding her hand. 'Greenman, old chap, good to see you again. How is the patient?'

'Startled to find himself impatient with being a patient.' Daniel looked down at the small boy, who had discovered his mother's belt made excellent reins, and at the boy's mother, slightly flushed with exertion. 'He has begun to speak more frequently and easily, he demands news of home and has eaten an extraordinarily large serving of devilled kidneys and bacon. Harriet has promised there will never be a turnip again in the kitchens of Burrawinga. He even laughed at that.' He glanced down again, amusement overtaking self-consciousness, which was exactly what Sophie had intended. 'Good morning, Sophie.'

Sophie clambered to her feet. 'Please excuse us. Danny, this is your Uncle Daniel. That is all right, isn't it?'

'I believe so.' Dr Greenman's tone was cautious again.

'And this is Rose. Say good morning, Rose.'

'Hello.' Rose beamed as Daniel bent to shake her hand. 'Hello, hello, hello ...'

'Sorry,' said Nigel. 'She's only just learned the word. Can you say hello too, Danny?'

'Good morning,' said Danny, bouncing slightly with superiority.

His sister glared at him. 'Hello!'

'I've brought you something,' said Daniel hurriedly. Sophie noted that somewhere, sometime, not noted in James's summary, Daniel Greenman had spent time with toddlers. He held up a drawstring bag with a picture of a giraffe on it, then squatted and tumbled out a mound of wooden blocks, in squares and rectangles, brightly coloured and each with its own animal.

'No, Rose darling, we don't hit your brother with blocks.' Sophie sat. 'You build them up. One block and then another block. See?'

'Block,' said Danny, with proud clarity.

'Tea or coffee?' asked Nigel, handing sandwiches down to them on the floor.

And suddenly it was easy, the twins absorbing the technique of building towers and, even more fun, knocking them down, smearing crab and watercress into hair, tablecloth and Daniel's trousers, but nothing a wet cloth could not wash off, and finally giggles edging into yawns. Both children were surprisingly compliant as Sophie put them down for their afternoon sleep in the bedroom next to the suite's living room.

'All they need is three adults' complete attention for an entire morning and luncheon,' said Sophie quietly, as they looked down at the sleeping children, the room suddenly extremely quiet.

'Perhaps every family needs three parents,' said Daniel, then seemed to realise what he'd said. 'Speaking professionally,' he added.

'You're not a Freudian?' asked Nigel, moving into the living room again and sitting on one end of the sofa. Sophie sat next to him, Daniel in an armchair.

Daniel shook his head. 'Freud is a master, of course. His concept of the subconscious is revolutionary, but I've been more concerned with the differences between neurasthenia, battle fatigue, soldier's heart and hysteria.'

'And your conclusions?' asked Nigel.

'That those labels may be useful for War Office clerks, but not for a doctor. The kind of warfare we have seen is one of the greatest traumas possible, but ten men can have exactly the same experience, with ten quite different reactions. In some men it may trigger problems they could otherwise have coped with. Others have the enviable ability to look forward, not back, though even there, problems may arise suddenly and unexpectedly — at a birthday party, perhaps, or hearing fireworks in the distance. No, my motto is, understand your patient then find out what works for them. Which is possibly older than Hippocrates.' He took another sandwich.

'Will I ring for more tea?' asked Sophie.

'Not for me, thank you.' He glanced at his pocket watch. 'I need to get back to John and Harriet. John still needs help physically, and prefers not to ask Harriet.'

'What will they do now?' Sophie asked quietly.

'Speaking as John's brother ... John and Harriet will go back to Burrawinga. He has agreed to a male nurse-companion. We've got a good manager there. Hopefully John can be part of it all again, and it's a small enough society for people to get used to his appearance. Speaking as a doctor, I know a Melbourne therapist who should be able to make walking easier for him, and I think more exercise will help too. Mentally it's going to be far harder than they both think now.'

He shook his head. 'They are both in the "it's a miracle" phase and not thinking about future problems — and there'll be a lot of those — but I think they'll make it. Possibly those years in hospital might actually help — John learned to accept being nursed there. There was a lot of love too, even if an excess of turnip.'

'And you?' asked Sophie quietly.

'I'll stay at Burrawinga for a while, but they need me out of the way.'

Ah, thought Sophie, so possibly there was truth in the rumour about Daniel and his sister-in-law, at least potentially. Or maybe he was just concerned that his brother might think so.

'I plan to set up practice in Sydney. And you intend coming back to Australia?' The question was slightly more intense than a social pleasantry would have been.

'Next spring — the Australian spring.' The question was meant for Nigel — Sophie had told Daniel this yesterday. But she had answered instead. 'Nigel has promised I needn't experience the next English winter.' She met his eyes. 'Will you want to see the children?'

'Yes. As often as I may.'

Once again she was filled with longing for the twisting river, the scent of hot sand. Danny and Rose needed to play barefoot in the shallows, watch cockatoos swinging from the trees outside the homestead. She glanced at Nigel. 'Then perhaps we should sail to Australia sooner.'

Nigel smiled at her. 'Yes. And stay longer.' He turned to Daniel. 'May we dine with you and your brother and sister-in-law before you leave? A couple of times, if it's not too much for Mr McDonald.'

Daniel looked startled. 'Of course. But we may not be good company just now.'

'The best of company,' said Nigel lightly. 'But it would be good to forge a strong link between our families, if you are to be Uncle Daniel.'

'Ah, I see. Thank you. A good idea.' Daniel hesitated. 'I'd like John to meet Rose and Danny, but his appearance might scare them.'

'We have scarred men on the estate.' Sophie did not add that Nigel had deliberately created work on new tree plantations for those whose appearance made it difficult to find other jobs. 'The children will be fine. Exhausting, sticky and rambunctious, but fine.'

'Tonight, then? I'll check with Harriet, but I'm sure she'll agree. She's more grateful than she can say. As am I. Will you bring your sister too? Harriet said she was the one who convinced John to ... to come back to us.'

'I'm afraid Lily had to go back to England early this morning.' Nigel leaned back in the sofa. 'By the way, I am considering a change to my will, something you would need to agree to, though, Greenman. You too, Sophie. No need to answer now, but would you think about sharing the children's guardianship with my secretary, Jones, should anything happen to Sophie and to me?'

Dr Greenman stared at him. 'I ... I am not sure what to say.'

'We are not planning on immediate decease,' said Sophie. She glanced at Nigel, slightly overwhelmed at how quickly this new relationship was being woven. 'But it is a good idea.'

'As their Uncle Daniel?'

Just like it is 'Aunt Lily', she thought. 'Yes, as Uncle Daniel, and only ever that. It's important neither child is ever confused about who they are, and that there is no question about Danny's inheritance. Legal fees alone would be crippling, not to mention the blight on his life.'

'I agree,' he said quietly.

'You are always welcome at Shillings. And that hut on Thuringa is yours forever — or whatever building you might like in the future in its place. I'd like you in our lives too.' Suddenly she realised that she meant it. For months John had been a friend, before that one night when he had been a lover. Now, miraculously, perhaps the friend was back.

She had always liked him. Even more miraculously, Nigel not only liked him too, but accepted that her feelings for Daniel did not affect her love for him. Nigel, of all people, could understand that a person might have more than one face to show to the world — or even to themselves.

And one day, just possibly, if Daniel came to Shillings, she might be able to explain that their children had not three parents but four — and Daniel could meet Miss Lily too.

Chapter 16

A child usually knows exactly who they are. But it may take years
for them to accept that knowledge in adulthood. Many never will.

Miss Lily, 1913

'You don't like *Alice in Wonderland*?' Mrs Maillot put the book down. She had taken to reading to Violette each afternoon as they sat beside one another on the sofa in the living room.

Violette looked for a tactful refusal. 'It is ... not real.' She no longer called the older woman madame, nor Mrs Maillot. The day would come, she thought, when Mrs Maillot would ask her to use 'Mama', though not till Mrs Maillot was sure the position of Violette's mother would not be claimed by another.

Mrs Maillot smiled. 'That is supposed to be its charm.'

Violette shrugged. Fantasy led to stupidity, and stupidity could end in death, like the pretence of certain villagers that the Boche could be their friends, and the refusal of so many to accept that the hungrier people grew, the more savage they became. This 'Alice' would not have survived long in wartime, or in the ... readjustments ... afterwards if she had confused her fantasies with the reality around her.

Grandmère had taught her adopted granddaughter what a girl in the post-war world must know: that the best way to kill a collaborator was with a knife struck just there, into the kidney, so they died almost immediately and quietly, with little blood; how hemlock could be disguised in a liqueur; how felt could be soaked in evaporated urine for an improvised explosive; and how the tears of an old woman or a girl would mean no one guessed that you had set that explosive under the railway bridge.

For only a fool believed war would not come again. Grandmère had not been a fool. And she had learned all too well only to trust the smallest possible number of comrades.

Violette only dimly remembered the war years. The 20s had been more vivid: the return of men who had lived with violence and who saw no reason why it should be entirely put away, men who believed that all women should be owned by a man, be it a father or husband, and any who were not so owned were fair prey.

Grandmère had shown her how to deal with men like that too.

She missed Grandmère. Grandmère could turn stale bread, two onions and a hard heel of cheese into a soup for an emperor. Mrs Maillot, on the other hand, turned a very good piece of beef into grey leather, with grey gravy and grey potatoes too. And she approved of books like this *Alice in Wonderland*.

But that would change when they reached the south of France.

For Violette had a plan. If — when — she killed Lily Shillings, she would need a new life. Mrs Maillot needed a fresh start too. Down in the south of France they would be free of the London fog blanketing the crouching bungalows, the yellow grey sky, the smell of coal in that small house where only small lives could be lived.

All they needed was money. As soon as Violette had seen Shillings she had known money could easily be obtained. A woman who lived in magnificence like that would wear jewels, almost certainly pearls, and rings, and perhaps a brooch. That woman would not interview the most embarrassing girl claiming to be her daughter in the hall, where servants might overhear. She would take her to a drawing room, which would undoubtedly be rich in small valuable items that could be secreted under her clothes.

Miss Lily Shillings might even offer to pay an allowance. That would be tempting — years of money, and no worry about interfering police. But it would not be justice; nor would it be revenge.

A few weeks earlier justice and revenge had been all she sought. Now she was going to take whatever she could manage from Shillings to support herself and Mrs Maillot in a land with warm, clean air, and where they spoke a civilised language. Mrs Maillot might find it strange at first, but the fresh air and warmth would be good for her, Violette thought firmly. She was also sure the older woman would do anything, including follow her to a foreign land, rather than lose a daughter a second time.

Violette touched Mrs Maillot gently on the hand. 'Will you be all right when I go to Shillings tomorrow?'

Mrs Maillot did not buy newspapers, but she and Violette did visit the library, and there Mrs Maillot had seen the photo in the *Daily Mail* — 'The Earl and Countess of Shillings Return from the Continent'.

It was time. Time for one life to end, and hers and Mrs Maillot's to truly begin.

'Of course I will, my darling girl. You must wrap up warmly. I will wait at the station again for you to return on the evening train. But if ... if you do decide to stay I will phone Shillings,' said Mrs Maillot with uncertain determination. 'I must hear from your own lips that you have found your mother, that her family will accept you. I must know that you are safe.'

Violette smiled. 'I do not think an earl will murder me.' He would not have a chance to.

'But nonetheless, if you are not on the train I will go to the call box at eight o'clock tomorrow evening. I will write down its number for you too. If you are in trouble someone may answer it and fetch me.'

Who? wondered Violette. They had yet to meet any neighbours. Even at church Mrs Maillot had not greeted anyone. Her life seemed to have been sliced away by the death of her husband and daughter.

But she smiled and nodded anyway. 'I will be back before eight or expect your call,' she lied. Instead, if this time she did find her mother and exact the retribution she deserved, she would send Mrs Maillot a telegram from the train station telling her not to worry, and that she would contact her soon. It might not be possible to discreetly kill the woman who had abandoned her.

She would need to vanish. That would not be hard. She had already chosen the clothes from the wardrobe of the dead Monsieur Maillot — trousers that could be worn under the coat. Mrs Maillot had loaned her a coat, and her dress would do as a shirt. She would hide her hair under a hat, and pull a too-tight chemise over her bosom. A boy, not a girl or man. Enough of a disguise to reach the Channel ...

And that might be all that would be needed. For she did not think that the family of Lily Shillings, those aristocrats, would admit who had killed their relative. They might tell the police about a mad girl, perhaps, who had attacked poor Miss Shillings for some unknown reason. But they would not want it known she was Lily Shillings's bastard daughter. Nor, perhaps, would they even want her caught, to tell her story.

They might not even mention the thefts, in case the jewellery and whatever other items she might take led to her capture, and headlines in the *News of the World*.

A little disguise only, and for a short time, then Violette would become Daisy, springing up anew.

Chapter 17

There are two ways to achieve power over another: slavery and domination, or service, understanding what the other person needs and wants, and providing it. The latter sounds like sainthood. It isn't. It will be you, of course, who will decide what the other needs, though hopefully with empathy and compassion.

Miss Lily, 1913

SOPHIE

It was good to be home.

They had spent another month in Paris, while the McDonalds waited for passage home on a ship that could accommodate a wheelchair.

Sophie and Harriet McDonald had walked in the sunlight each day, Mrs McDonald pushing her husband in his wheelchair, a hat and scarf concealing his face from those who might stare.

They talked of Burrawinga, of Thuringa, of horses, dogs and children.

It was a hesitant friendship at first. Sophie Vaile, née Higgs, was not of the squattocracy. Indeed, she had first come to England to be remade into a level of respectability sufficient to become a squatter's son's fiancée. Now, as a countess and mother of the heir to an ancient title, she was socially well above Mrs McDonald, while simultaneously several rungs below her.

Within two days none of that mattered.

John McDonald did not try to talk during these outings, partly because he was only beginning to articulate through his scarred lips, but also because the world bewildered him, even as he enjoyed it. He was in shock as well as joy, as was his wife. Luckily both realised it. They treated themselves gently: walking, talking, eating and watching, his brother and the Vailes their only companions.

Sometimes Daniel accompanied them, and Nigel on rare occasions too. But Nigel understood that social ties are essentially wrought by women, even if they do so on behalf of their men. If the McDonald–Vaile connection was to be easy, Sophie and Harriet must like each other.

Luckily they did.

Now and then the children also went on these walks. As Sophie expected, neither showed anything but transient interest in John McDonald's scars. Rose had traced his face gently, as if waiting to see if her touch hurt, then, reassured, gave him a slobbery kiss and toddled off after pigeons. Danny had shaken his hand, a skill he had only just acquired, looking only curious when the 'hand' presented turned out to be a stump.

Both then happily departed in search of ice cream or pomme frites with Uncle Daniel, ostensibly to leave Sophie and Harriet to talk. If Harriet noticed that Rose shared the intense green eyes of her brother-in-law, she did not mention it.

Sophie also spent part of those weeks in Paris conferring with her agent, who almost successfully hid his knowledge from her that this close attention by his employer was not needed except, perhaps, by her.

In between she was … coaxed … by Green to the new fashion house of Schiaparelli, who had not yet proper headquarters, and believed that the ancient Greeks had given to their goddesses the serenity of perfection and the fabulous appearance of freedom.

Elsa Schiaparelli had discarded the chemise, believing that clothes should not only give freedom, but celebrate the body beneath them. Sophie wished Miss Lily could have attended these visits too, but an experienced fitter might be too perspicacious; nor could Miss Lily abandon undergarments as Sophie might. Sophie found that she could not ask if Green had already given the fashion house Miss Lily's measurements — if that had been done, had Miss Lily asked for it, it could be a sign that she intended to return sometimes once more.

The new fashions were adorable. Pleated overdresses in lace and chiffon, shorter knee-length silk sheaths below: the natural female shape had returned after nearly a decade of flat chests. Sophie, whose chest was decidedly not flat, rejoiced.

Divine suede culottes, much like men's Oxford bags, but shorter; evening dresses that clung to the shoulders and bust but then hung in tiers of pleats, allowing one to run from a charging polar bear, if by any chance the fireside rug should come to life; even man-style suits cut to show the female figure, though with larger buttons and embroidered collars, topped by fur-trimmed coats or velvet cloaks, diamonds daringly hung on ribbons, instead of gold chains, or crafted into ivory or ebony and ringed with topaz.

Only once, at a private showing, the models parading in creations madame was sure la Comtesse would adore, did Sophie see a small woman with slightly too blonde hair being shepherded into another room, an older man in smiling attendance.

Sophie had carefully forgotten the woman who was her mother, or had at least placed her in a locked room in her memory. On her father's death she had reduced the monthly payment to her. It was enough to live on, but not to afford 'Schiap's' clothes. But the deeply self-centred woman who had borne her had, unsurprisingly, found another protector.

She almost didn't care.

'Almost', however, was enough to reduce her pleasure in houses of fashion. It was time to head home.

It was strangely sad to wave to the McDonalds and Dr Greenwood as their car left to take them to the ship. Sophie had expected to miss Daniel, but in the past month Harriet, and to a lesser extent John, had become friends whom she missed almost as much. Those who were not just marked by war, but who had refused to bow down to its ravages, would always have a bond.

The first small breaths of spring gusted warmth and blossom as they drove down the lanes. The snow had melted. Even the rain showers seemed made of brighter drops than in winter. Each tree's leaves were at a different stage of opening, from bud curl to pale green. Cuckoos called, and woodpeckers tapped.

At last they drove through the Shillings gates. The lawn was spring green, and snowdrops clustered by the lichened walls. Shillings had always wrapped itself around her, even when she was Miss Lily's student before the war, though Thuringa was more deeply in her heart.

Now, with the mellow stone and mossy tree trunks, the hedges that had grown small communities of flowers and ferns over centuries, and Hereward and the staff lined up to welcome them, this was home.

And it was a lovely home, she admitted next afternoon as she blotted a letter to Cousin Oswald, so perfectly managing her businesses in Australia. Waking to the sounds of the children down the corridor had been a delight, as was being served at breakfast by Hereward, and deciding the day's menus with Mrs Goodenough.

Nigel was out on the estate to admire six new breeding sows and the growth in the new plantations. She had a letter from Emily, inviting her to an 'African Safari' at their London house to raise funds for a regimental widows and orphans fund; a more welcome letter from Giggs, now living happily with her mother-in-law on the estate her son would inherit; cards from seven women she had met once and only vaguely remembered, offering social delights that varied from a Tahitian Breakfast to a supper 'with artistic dancing', which probably meant half-nude and untrained. A hilarious note from Ethel also awaited her, about the responses of East End mothers seeking family planning, or, as Ethel put it, 'Not-Family Planning'.

David had even invited them to Balmoral with Queen Mary's blessing though, unusually tactfully for David, it had been an unofficial invitation — one did not turn down formal ones.

Sophie did not want to go — court protocol bored her, and court conversation bored her even more. Poor David, who had to endure so much of it. They would use Nigel's health as an excuse.

She had a library full of books, some of which she might even wish to read, a divine new wardrobe she might try on, a pony to choose as a birthday present for her goddaughter, darling Mouse's child, and a whole estate's worth of households to visit and benevolently interfere with. She might even plan another glasshouse in which to grow flowers for the London market and provide at least three jobs for ex-servicemen or widows.

And yet ...

Her youth had been full of the excitement of being in England, a colonial challenging society and winning, then the war and its aftermath. She had restructured her business and stood for parliament — and then the flight across the world to Nigel. Life could not always be as *urgent* as all that when one had children.

She looked at the garden beyond the window, spring-wet grass rather than snow-melt sludge, yellow daffodils shoving their heads into the light. Daniel, Harriet and John would be on their way back to Australia now, while she just sat there ...

What did women in her position fill their lives with? Supporting their husband's political career? Nigel no longer seemed to want one. Nor had he the stamina perhaps, even if he managed to be successful. Costume balls and luncheons? Playing roulette on the Riviera? She smiled at the thought. The only people she wanted to ask for luncheon were busy — Midge and Maria in Australia, Ethel running her clinics (her mind still boggled at the concept of Ethel instructing the fecund women of the East End of London in the use of Dutch caps), Anne, who she had liked enormously the year before, back on an archaeological dig in Mesopotamia, the Dowager Duchess of Wooten too frail in mind and body ...

For a moment she thought enviously of Hannelore and her Herr Hitler. At least she was working to change the world as Miss Lily's protégées had been trained to do. I need a cause, she thought, or at least a project. But what could she do here, isolated at Shillings, intending to leave for Australia before next winter?

The library door opened. 'Yes, Hereward?'

'Excuse me, your ladyship, there is a young person at the door. She wishes to see Miss Lily, your ladyship.'

Not a 'young lady', but not someone to send around to the back either. 'What does she want?' Collecting for charity, perhaps, though Hereward would have asked one of the members of the Ladies' Guild to wait in the hall, or in the drawing room if she were an acquaintance.

Hereward experienced just-visible pain in not being able to answer this question to his mistress's satisfaction.

Sophie put down her pen. 'You explained that Miss Lily is no longer in residence?'

'Yes, your ladyship. The young person has called before, while you were in France. She is more — insistent this time, your ladyship.' Hereward's face became even more impassive. 'She has just claimed that Miss Lily is her mother, your ladyship.'

Sophie's first reaction was to laugh. Then caution returned. If a deluded young woman thought Miss Lily was her mother, then denying it was even possible would not stop her claim, not without proof of why it was so — a proof she certainly would not receive. And if this 'young person' had been simply clearly mad, Hereward would have called the police.

'What is her name?'

'She calls herself Violette Shillings, my lady.'

'I need to ask his lordship about this. Show her into the small drawing room when I ring,' Sophie said at last. The small drawing room had been Miss Lily's sanctum. It was also in the wing of the house below their bedroom and could be reached by the side stairs, where the servants or other guests would not see Nigel ascend, and Miss Lily descend. 'We don't wish to be interrupted.'

She slipped the letter into its envelope, then went to tell her husband that his alternative persona seemed to have produced a child.

She found him not at the piggery, but in the field below the orchard, inspecting a bull. A very fine bull, who would service many cows. Human society would be so much more convenient, Sophie thought, if the best male specimens could be put to stud, leaving all other arrangements to love. 'A visitor,' she said quietly.

'Excellent choice,' Nigel said to the farmer — Roger Rothomley, Greenie's second cousin ... or was he twice removed? They were confusingly inter-related here. 'If you'll excuse me old chap, I'd better attend to this.'

She and Nigel walked to the house arm and arm, while Sophie explained. 'What on earth are we to do with her?' she finished. 'The girl must be deluded, of course.'

'Possibly not,' said Nigel.

Sophie stared at him. 'You can't be serious. Whatever do you mean?'

Nigel shrugged. 'Maybe nothing.'

'Or something. What?'

'I'll explain if it's necessary. Sophie, I'm sorry, I don't really have the right to explain unless I have to. But if this "young person" wants to see Miss Lily, then she should see her.'

'Don't you think it would be safer to say we don't know where she is?'

'But we do know,' said Nigel quietly.

'Nigel, you aren't her father, are you?'

He smiled. 'Not unless she is in her thirties and half Japanese.'

'I think Hereward would have mentioned if she had been Japanese. Besides, he described her as young.'

'And she is looking for a mother, not a father ... Come on. It will take time to change. I don't want to keep her waiting too long.'

Chapter 18

Some lives flow like quiet rivers. Others have waterfalls and rapids disrupting them. I have found that when an early life is full of waterfalls, your acceptance of their existence means waterfalls tend to keep appearing.

Miss Lily, 1913

Transforming Nigel into Miss Lily was not going to be as swift as Nigel had hoped. He had forgotten Green was staying up in London for a few days and was not expected back until the afternoon. Sophie suspected a dalliance, or even no dalliance but the pretence of one, to make it clear to Jones that love and friendship did not mean marriage, or not for Green.

Nigel needed to shave and his wig needed restyling from the evening elegance in which Lily had last appeared to something more suitable for the afternoon. Nor, as ever, would he let Sophie help with the transformation in the small dressing room adjoining their bedchamber.

Finally, intensely curious, she went downstairs to the small drawing room and rang for Hereward. 'Tea,' she instructed when he appeared. 'Crumpets as well as cake and sandwiches.' Toasting crumpets was a useful activity when conversation flagged. The best friendships, Miss Lily had said, were made while toasting crumpets. 'Please show Miss, er, Shillings in.'

'If you would like me to remain, my lady?' enquired Hereward.

She smiled at him. 'I am sure I can manage. Thank you.'

'I could ask Mr Jones ...'

Jones would be assisting Nigel. 'Mr Jones has already been informed. Thank you, Hereward.'

Hereward backed out, his posture expressing reluctance, deference, impassiveness and a willingness to protect her ladyship against tigers or young persons. Impressive, thought Sophie. She sat, waiting for the click of Miss Lily's heels. But Hereward ushered the interloper in first, with Ackland, the first footman, behind him, carrying the tea tray and Dorothy following with the cake stand.

'Miss, er, Shillings, my lady,' announced Hereward.

'Thank you, Hereward. Please leave the tea things. I will pour. Miss Shillings, it is good to meet you. Do sit down.'

Hereward and his minions vanished behind gently closing doors.

The girl — for she was only a girl — did not sit. She stared at Sophie suspiciously. 'Why is it good to meet me?'

Belgian accent, thought Sophie, not French. Interesting. Her white dress was too young for her — she was probably thirteen or fourteen. New shoes, machine-made but of reasonable quality.

And the girl was beautiful. Blonde hair, curling naturally in a simple bob under her chin; perfect skin, blue eyes, a fine-boned face that was instantly familiar ...

And a coincidence, she told herself, nothing more.

'I am glad you are here because I was bored,' Sophie admitted frankly. 'Hereward said that you believe my husband's relative, Miss Lily, is your mother. That is impossible, but not boring.'

The girl glared at her. 'She is my mother! How can it be impossible? Why should my grandmother lie to me?'

'I can think of many reasons for the impossibility, including the fact that while I have a relative by marriage called Lily, our family name is Vaile. Shillings is our title. It is also unlikely that our Lily was anywhere near Belgium when you were born, or even conceived.' She smiled frankly at the girl. 'I assume you were born in Belgium, and in wartime?'

'Yes.'

'Lily was elsewhere during the war, nor was it a time for a casual visit to Belgium. And I can think of many reasons why someone might lie, including an attempt to get money.'

Sophie held up her hand as the girl stepped forward in anger. 'I am not accusing you or your grandmother of lying. I am merely saying I can think of good reasons — even kind reasons — why it would be better for a motherless child in a poor and war-wracked country to be told she has an absent and well-connected Englishwoman as her mother.'

'It is true!'

'Then tell me the circumstances. Please do sit down. Tea or coffee? Though I can call for cocoa if you wish.'

The girl grimaced. 'Not cocoa again. And I do not like tea.'

'Coffee then. Please, have a sandwich. I recommend the cherry cake. May I call you Violette?'

The girl shrugged, a graceful shrug. 'It is my name. What do I call you?'

'Your ladyship,' said Sophie wryly. 'Now, tell me why you think we are related. Ah, Lily!' She stood as the door opened, then moved to kiss Miss Lily's cheek. She smelled once more of roses with subtle undercurrents. 'This is Miss Violette Shillings.'

Blue eyes under blonde hair stared at the same colour eyes, under hair that was almost the same shade, except for Miss Lily's carefully placed streaks of grey. The resemblance was unmistakeable. No wonder Hereward had not called the police.

But Sophie believed Nigel completely when he said he could not have fathered this girl. His brother and father too had died long before this girl could have been conceived. His second cousin did not resemble him and, anyway, had spent the war safely as a clerk in a Birmingham office. There were surely no other close relatives who might be this girl's parent — she and Miss Lily's other 'lovely ladies' had carefully hunted through Debrett's in that winter before the war trying to find any.

Miss Lily sat, her back as always to the light, clad in a fashionable low-waisted grey silk, pleated for the last four inches above the hem and unmistakeably Schiap's work, surely purchased by Green in Paris, and a silver chiffon scarf at her throat. She smiled, that perfect, inclusive Miss Lily smile. 'My dear, before you call me Mother, I have to tell you frankly — I have never had a child.'

Violette shrugged again. 'You would say that.'

'This is true.' Miss Lily smiled at her again, warm, accepting. No one but Miss Lily ever smiled like that, thought Sophie. That small taste of Miss Lily again in France had only reminded her how much she missed her.

'An unmarried woman of good family cannot openly acknowledge she has had a child,' Miss Lily continued. 'But of course unmarried women do have children, and there are accepted ways to cope with this. If I'd ever had a child, it would have been adopted by a tenant on this estate. The child would become my protégée, educated, cared for and very much loved. If his lordship had not wanted that — and some men would not — there is money enough for a child to be adopted overseas. But I would have visited often —'

'But you did not!' said the girl fiercely. She spat, neatly, on the carpet. 'I have not come here for money. Or for a mother. You do not deserve a daughter.'

Miss Lily looked at her seriously. 'Then why have you come?'

'To kill you,' said Violette.

Chapter 19

The problem with 'duty' is that once you have accepted it applies to you, its demands never end. Each of you, my dears, need to decide: do you want a normal life, or duty?

Miss Lily, 1913

Sophie reached for the bell pull. Violette moved faster, a knife at Miss Lily's throat. 'Move back, onto that chair,' she directed Sophie, nodding to one far from the bell pull.

'Why?' asked Sophie. 'If you are going to kill Lily anyway — who is not your mother, by the way — why should I not call for help before you stab me too?'

'Because you want to hear why I am going to kill her. And because she needs to hear what she has done before she dies.'

'That sounds almost reasonable.' Sophie moved away from the bell pull, her heart pounding. She felt an unruly desire to laugh. This was melodrama — *East Lynne* with Sarah Bernhardt in the lead: 'Dead! Dead! And never called me mother!'

And yet the knife was real, as real as the girl's anguish.

Miss Lily moved, slowly, pushing the knife a little way from her neck. 'Then tell us,' she said quietly.

'You wish to hear? You wish this ladyship to hear as well?'

'Yes,' said Miss Lily.

'Very well.' Violette put her hands — the right one still holding the knife — into her lap. 'I heard this from my grandmother, you understand? A good woman. A trustworthy woman.'

'I accept that,' said Miss Lily.

'In 1914 the Boche had invaded our country. The things they did, the things they had been trained to do to make us fear them, my grandmère told me of these things.

'Many left, became refugees. Others stayed. Some, like Grandmère, stayed to fight. They became La Dame Blanche, The White Lady. Thousands of them, but secret, most known only to their best friends, and the best friends only known to their sisters ...'

'I know of La Dame Blanche,' said Sophie quietly. 'They collected intelligence in plain sight, and passed it to Britain ...'

'Yes. That is why Miss Lily came under another name, for secrecy, but Grandmère knew her real one. Why you came.' Violette nodded to the woman next to her. 'You came to live among us, to pass information back to England. But also, Grandmère said, you came to have a child. By 1915 there were many unmarried women who had children, raped by the Boche. Women like Grandmère pretended they were the orphaned children of a daughter, killed in the bombing, or made up another tale, so the children did not live in shame.

'When I was born, Grandmère said I was her granddaughter. The villagers, of course, knew this was not true. But the Boche were fooled.' Violette's blue eyes met Miss Lily's. 'But you know this.'

'I don't,' said Sophie. She had lost all desire to laugh now. If they kept the girl talking perhaps Jones or Hereward would come, or Miss Lily would be able to grab the knife ... 'Did she pretend your mother was her daughter too?'

'My mother — her,' Violette gestured slightly at Miss Lily with the knife, 'was not there, not since I was a few weeks old. There had been a railway bridge. The English sent explosives to blow up bridges. A man is too noticeable in wartime, but a woman? You blow up a bridge, sit and cry, Grandmère told me, and the Boche, he comforts you instead of dragging you away. "Monsieur, I am so scared," you cry. He may even buy you coffee ...

'Grandmère had two daughters, Charlotte and Suzanne. Suzanne and you, Miss Lily, you go to destroy the railway bridge.

And, poof, it is blown up. But Suzanne does not come back. You do not come back. Instead the Boche come. They make Charlotte stand against a wall and her friend Colette too. The Boche say they planned the bridge attack. They make Grandmère watch as they bayonet them, many, many times, before they die. They bayonet Grandmère too, in the left hand, so that she remembers. And then they go.'

'My dear,' murmured Miss Lily. 'I am so sorry. To have lived with this anguish, and now to tell it to strangers. This must be heart-wrenching for you.'

Violette stared at her. 'A good word — heart-wrenched. I will remember that one.' She gathered herself and returned to her story. 'There is only one way the Boche could have known about Charlotte and Colette. Someone must have told them. And who could it have been, for only five women knew of the plot?

'But Grandmère would not believe Suzanne would have told the Boche. She could not believe her Miss Lily would tell them either. Others said she was a fool to trust a stranger. It was a mystery, one with no answer, even once the war was finished and the Boche were gone.

'Grandmère had money, money you had left with her. That money kept us, all through the war and after. Not well, you understand, but enough, an old woman and a child. We moved to the next village, where there was a cottage enough undamaged, we grew our vegetables, we kept some geese. Grandmère did sewing, turning old clothes into new. There was enough money for me to go to school, to take singing lessons when Soeur Marie said my voice was good. Grandmère was ... heart-wrenched ... but we had each other. There was no grave for you or for Suzanne, but every Sunday we left flowers on Charlotte's at least. We prayed for all of you, for my aunts, for my heroic mother, who had died facing the Boche.

'I was four years old when you came back to Belgium. Were you looking for us?' Violette looked at Miss Lily contemptuously. 'You did not find us. Because the moment you walked into our village everyone knew that if you were still alive, then it had been you who had betrayed my aunts. The only way you could have walked free from the Boche was by selling my aunts, betraying them, allowing them to be killed while you waited out the war in prison, perhaps, escaping from revenge back to England once the war had ended. You did not care about the women you left to die. You did not care about your baby daughter, who must now live with the shame of what her mother had done. You saved yourself.

'Perhaps you returned to Belgium because you thought no one would know what you had done. Perhaps you thought that all who suspected your crimes would be dead, or that once the war was over no one would care. But La Dame Blanche, it still exists. Collaborators must be killed, or cast out, that was what Grandmère said. The others agreed. The Boche are gone but they will come again. No one ever betrayed La Dame Blanche, except for you.'

Dazed, Sophie thought, was this 'return' when I was in Belgium with Green and Jones? But Nigel did not come with us, Miss Lily did not come with us ...

... unless Lily followed us. Was that why Green vanished, to 'visit friends', while I worked out the business contracts in Brussels? Was she meeting Lily, once again helping Nigel to be Lily?

'Only you were not killed,' said Violette, savagery behind her eyes. 'Many want to kill you. But you are English, and one day the organisation you worked for might be needed again. But after that, no friend would speak to me again.'

'Grandmère told me your real name then, how you lived in an earl's great house in England. Then five years ago Grandmère died,' said Violette flatly. 'No one would take me in by then, not the daughter of a traitoress. I go to an orphanage, then the sisters send me to a kind lady who offers me a home.' She spat again. 'A home where kind gentlemen come who like the pretty girls. I had the knife I used to kill the geese. This knife I used on one of them. I left. I used the voice, the pretty singing voice, that Soeur Marie had trained. I eat from rubbish bins and sleep in doorways so I save my pennies to get to England. Sometimes I think I should go to Soeur Marie, but I do not want to be a nun.' She shrugged. 'And in Belgium perhaps the police look for a girl who used a knife on a man, too. Perhaps even Soeur Marie, she would feel she must give me to the police.'

Did Violette kill her abuser? Sophie wondered. Somehow she did not think so, despite the lessons in killing collaborators, perhaps even seeing them executed. But she did believe this girl was capable of murder.

'And all the time I know this happened because of you. My aunts dead, because of you. Grandmère's hand injured, because of you. I must fight my way out of that room with the old man and all because of you. And then I think,' said Violette calmly, 'that I will kill you.'

'And that will make it right?' asked Miss Lily gently. 'Killing me will make the women of La Dame Blanche accept you? You will have a life again?' She shook her head. 'It won't work like that, my dear.'

Sophie stared at her. Lily couldn't be admitting that this story was true. It was impossible that she could be a mother. Nor could Lily have worked with La Dame Blanche while Nigel was with his regiment in France.

'If you kill me,' said Miss Lily quietly. 'You will be taken by the English police, and hanged. I do not want this to happen. Truly, my dear, after all you have been through you deserve a life, and happiness ...'

'I will escape from your police ...'

'And be found.'

'I am very good at not being found,' said Violette.

'Perhaps. Yes, I think probably you are. But wouldn't you rather have a mother? One who did not mean to abandon you? One who will love you, look after you?'

Violette laughed sharply. 'You pretend that you love me?'

'No,' said Miss Lily.

'Then what do you —?' Violette stopped, as the door opened. Once more the knife was at Miss Lily's throat.

'Lily!' said Green, Jones standing behind her. 'Hereward said —' She stopped as she saw the girl, the knife. Jones reached down as if tying his shoelace.

'Green, darling, I am glad you are here,' said Miss Lily calmly. 'This is Violette, your daughter, the one you thought was lost.'

Green fainted, just as Jones's blade pinned Violette's sleeve to her chair. Miss Lily pulled out Jones's knife. She kneeled by Green, supporting her. Violette stood, dazed, her own knife still in her hand. 'Green, my dear, it is all right now … Sophie, ring the bell for more tea, please? Jones, could you help me?'

Sophie rang the bell, staring at the scene. She had never realised how alike Green and Miss Lily were. Green was generously endowed bosom-wise, but the very shape of their faces, their blue eyes.

Jones stayed in the doorway, staring at the girl, then at Green, now blinking in Miss Lily's arms. 'If she is your daughter, then who is her father?'

'You, of course,' said Miss Lily. 'Your Christmas leave in 1914, I expect. Green?'

'Yes,' whispered Green.

'You didn't tell me?' Impossible to tell the emotion in Jones's voice. Possibly he himself did not yet know either.

'I didn't want to worry you,' stammered Green, still gazing unbelieving at Violette. As Sophie watched, the girl lifted her skirt slightly, and secured her knife under her garter.

Green's voice still shook. 'And then I thought that she was dead.'

'Not worry me!' Jones stared at her, then back at Violette. 'I had a daughter and you didn't want to worry me?' He turned and left the room.

'I think I hate you all,' said Violette.

Chapter 20

*Life is constantly unexpected. That is its charm. Most of the time,
at least.*

Miss Lily, 1913

SOPHIE

Green sat, sipping sweet tea, on the sofa. Violette sat as far from
her as possible. But at least, thought Sophie, she wasn't trying to
kill anyone. Jones had not returned.

'I was injured,' said Green finally. 'That was why I didn't come
back. The explosion — well, let's just say that we weren't trained
sappers or engineers. I knew nothing of the plot until that night.
Suzanne was killed. I'd been trying to stop her, but I reached her
too late. I ... I ran. I don't know how far I ran ... I woke days
later, in hospital ...'

Violette snorted. 'Easy to say. Convenient, n'est-ce pas?'

Green impassively lifted her skirt, her petticoat. The scars
stood out, red even after all these years.

Violette stared. 'You may have been hurt another time.'

'I might have,' said Green wearily. 'But I was not. I was
wounded in October 1915. The people who sent me to the
village tried to find you or, rather, your aunts and grandmother.
At last they told me your Aunt Suzanne had died, that your
Aunt Charlotte, her friend Colette and your grandmother were
killed by the Germans in retaliation for the destruction of the
bridge and train, and that they had killed you as well. Probably
the villagers told any questioner that to keep you and your

grandmother safe, especially if she was still working for the Dame Blanche.

'I ... I believed you were dead. Of course I believed it. No one betrayed you, not me, not Suzanne. Probably the Germans found out who Suzanne was after they found her body next to the detonator. That may be why they killed Charlotte and Colette — neither of them would give the Germans information. That would be why your grandmother moved, in case the Germans decided to question her again or kept watch on her associates in the village, and so she could continue her resistance work. And you have explained why, when I went back to Belgium, I couldn't find your grandmother or anyone who would admit they had even known Madame Larresse.'

'Our name is Dumarche,' said Violette.

'Your grandmother must have changed her name, too, when she moved villages. It would be safer. I did leave flowers on the graves of Charlotte and Colette,' Green added quietly.

Violette frowned. 'But if your name is Green, why did you pretend to be Miss Lily Shillings? That was not even the name you used in Belgium. And Mrs Maillot, my friend now, says that a relative of the earl should be called Vaile, not Shillings.'

'I was doing other war work,' said Miss Lily quietly. 'But my name was known in intelligence circles, and the powers that be decided it would be useful if there were two of us for a while.' Sophie noticed she had neither confirmed nor denied that she was Nigel's half-sister. She had once assumed Lily was Nigel's cousin. Possibly their ostensible relationship was fluid. 'Miss Green here took my name, as no one she was likely to meet would know me.' It was even pretty much true, thought Sophie. 'As for my name, my mother was not married to my father. I'm the earl's half-sister, and an illegitimate one. They gave me the name Shillings as I was not entitled to Vaile.'

And that was a fairly good cover story, thought Sophie, close to what Grandmère had been told. And a safe one to give to a volatile young girl, as there were no records of either a Lily Shillings or a Lily Vaile if anyone tried to investigate the truth.

'I'm sorry,' said Green simply, still gazing at Violette. 'I … I could say I didn't abandon you, but I did. Even being with La Dame Blanche when I was pregnant was abandoning you too, knowing I might be killed, which would have meant your death too. I could say that it was war, that I was trying to liberate your country, but that does not excuse me. A mother's greatest duty is to her child. I failed you. Time and again, I failed you. And nothing can put it right.'

'Rubbish,' said Sophie.

They all stared at her. She shrugged, hoping hers was as graceful as Violette's earlier one. There were gaps in Green's story, and Violette's, and Lily's, too, large ones, but this was not the time to explore them.

'There is a lot you can do to put it right. You can begin to be a mother. Violette, you do not have an aristocrat in your family tree, I'm afraid. Green is my maid. An extremely good one, and my friend as well. She is also extremely well paid. We think of her as one of our family. Whatever you need or want — within reason — you can have. Education —'

Violette snorted.

'Don't rule it out. Have you ever even thought what you could have if money were no object? You can travel with your mother, dress most beautifully, learn to fly a plane or explore the Amazon, if that is what you crave. Greenie, do you want to be her mother?'

'Of course,' whispered Green.

'Well?' Sophie asked Violette.

'Fly an aeroplane?' asked Violette thoughtfully. 'Ladies fly aeroplanes?'

'Two I have known.'

'You will do no such thing!' said Green. 'Aircraft are far too dangerous —'

'Perhaps a mother who left her baby to blow up a railway bridge might allow her daughter some latitude,' said Miss Lily quietly.

Violette looked at each woman thoughtfully. 'I like your dress,' she said to Miss Lily. She turned to Sophie. 'Your house is most pleasant. I may live here?'

'As long as you promise not to kill anyone. Or use a knife for anything except cutting up your food. I am serious,' Sophie added. 'All of us in this room have known what it is to fight for our lives. All of us know that once you have had to kill or even accepted you will do it if necessary, then you are profoundly changed. So I do want your promise. As you said, this is my house. If you and your mother are to stay in it — as I very much hope you will — then you must give me your word.'

'I promise,' said Violette. 'I will not stab anyone.' She paused, then added, 'Or, if I must, I will tell you first.'

'Good enough for now,' said Sophie. 'I am glad you like good clothes. Greenie, darling, I think you have your first task as a mother. Clothes, whatever of mine might fit, and the Blue Bedroom, I think. That was the one I used when I first came here.' She smiled at Violette. 'I was almost as prickly as you are back then, though I didn't try to stab anyone. But we ... all of us ... have a lot to teach you, if you would like to learn.'

'Perhaps,' said Violette.

'That is a beginning. Greenie, would you like me to come with you?'

'No. Thank you,' said Green. 'I think ...' She stopped, as if trying to straighten out all that had happened in the past thirteen years, as well as what must be done now. 'Would you mind if Violette used one of your nightdresses for her first night here? I will make other arrangements tomorrow.'

'You have complete charge of my wardrobe, as always,' said Sophie. 'Have a good day, Violette. We will meet again at dinner. All of us.' She stood. 'Welcome to Shillings, my dear,' she said.

And suddenly she was back nearly sixteen years earlier and Miss Lily was welcoming her.

Chapter 21

There are times when even the most finely tuned charm fails.
I recommend a slightly longer than usual hat-pin, topped with a
pearl and kept extremely sharp, or a letter opener, of better quality
metal with a keener point than is usual.

Miss Lily, 1913

SOPHIE

Miss Lily took a slice of cherry cake. Her hand trembled slightly as she held her cake fork. 'Do you think that was wise, Sophie?'

'Having Violette stay here? Probably not. But we can't send her and Green to a hotel. Green is family, and Violette has been abandoned once. We can't abandon her again.'

'And Jones?'

'He and Green will have to sort it out. Or he and Violette. It's interesting she doesn't seem to have wondered who her father was. But then she has lived in a world of women most of her life. Or perhaps she was afraid that her mother was raped, and did not want to know she had a father capable of that.'

'Jones is my best friend.'

'I thought I was your best friend.'

'You are my wife.' Miss Lily looked at her dress, her ringed hands, then shook her head, suddenly helpless. 'He is my oldest friend, then. This will tear him apart.'

'Then maybe when he has put himself back together again he will be even better than before. Lily, you know what I am going to ask, don't you?'

'Yes. Why was Green using my name?'

'Not just that. You and Nigel and Green and Jones. You've had a life together I've never shared. Decades of it. You've given me hints, over the years. I haven't pried.' Sophie stopped, then admitted, 'Perhaps I didn't want to know. But now I do. I want to know about the relationship between you and James too. I know there is one, has been one for a very long time. I guessed that when you arranged for me to meet him as a suitable husband. And, yes, I did realise it was an arranged meeting. Of course I did.'

'Ah,' said Miss Lily.

Sophie looked at her steadily. 'You will tell me. Nigel wouldn't.'

'You could try asking him,' said Miss Lily.

'Nigel is my husband. He wants to keep me as his wife, I think, so he can continue to be a husband. Nigel's wife does not need to know about Lily's past.'

'You are … perceptive,' said Miss Lily. 'You always were. I love you, you know. Whoever I am.'

Sophie smiled. 'I've always known that.'

'Very well.' Miss Lily took a deep breath. 'I've always told you the truth, just not the entire truth. The rape when I was a young soldier on the North West Frontier, the years in Japan when Misako taught me to be a woman of grace and charm. Jones was there for all of that, of course. Then Green arrived from Shillings, trained by my mother to be the perfect lady's maid, and she taught me to be an Englishwoman. All that is true.'

'And leaves most of your life unaccounted for,' said Sophie. 'Yours and Green's and Jones's.'

'Exactly,' said Miss Lily.

'So where does James fit into it?'

Miss Lily looked at her hands. She still wore a wedding ring, the only external link between her and the Earl of Shillings — an oddity for a single woman, but Sophie felt deep happiness it was still there.

'We were staying in the south of France. I couldn't face England yet. Nowhere fashionable, just a fishing village, with a small but good hotel. And I met a friend from school, perhaps the only close friend I ever had back then. He was ... different ... too, though neither of us admitted it even to ourselves back then. No, he did not feel he was a woman. He liked men. He was on holiday, with his lover, being discreet, like me. He had begun to make a name for himself in the Foreign Office. I stared at him across the hotel dining room. He noticed the stare, noticed me ...'

'And recognised you?'

'No. But knew he had been recognised, and that his relationship with his lover was fairly obvious. He looked so terribly afraid. And so I told him who I was, and how I came to be there, and he understood, or at least he understood my feelings about as much as I could understand his.'

James, thought Sophie and then, no, James is too young to have been at school with Nigel. And she was reasonably sure James was not a homosexualist. 'What is his name?'

'Morton Langton-Montgomery. Monty. He died in 1919, one of the first influenza victims. He was in disgrace by then, cast into some Foreign Office backwater, as were all of those who had too openly pursued peace with Germany, trying to keep power balanced between us. It is so easy to believe in hindsight that there was never any chance of peace.

'Monty and I talked a lot, in those first weeks in France. He envied me the ability to be myself, for most of the year at least — Nigel Vaile must put in an appearance now and then, but mostly I was free. I told him I envied him having a purpose in his life. I did not want to drift, and yet Miss Lily was doing just that ...

'And that was where we ended it. But six months later a letter was forwarded to Cairo — Jones and Green and I moved every few months back then, so that no one would get to know us too well, or begin to question my background too closely. Yes, a drifting life.

'Monty offered me another kind of life. Miss Lily, travelling with her maid, and her butler, could find information that a member of the Foreign Office could not.' She smiled at Sophie.

'Everything I told you girls about wishing to teach women to use the only power they had was true. But my growing involvement in Monty's world meant that others selected the girls who stayed here, coaxed their families to let them come to an isolated manor house in England ...'

'You were a spy,' said Sophie bluntly. 'Recruiting other spies, even if they did not know their friendship might be used to gather intelligence.'

'At times. Mostly I was what you might call an agent of influence. Sometimes an extremely persuasive influence. Egypt, Japan again — it was so good to be back there — ensuring the continued alliance with England. Thanks to Misako I understood the culture far better than any Englishman. Australia — you would have been just a child then, four or five. James wanted to know if your federation might diminish the former colonies' loyalty to the Empire. I was able to tell him that possibly the contrary was occurring, that the new nationalism meant you all wanted to show England what Australia was capable of.'

'And so England killed more than sixty thousand of our men,' said Sophie. 'Cannon fodder to spare the English.'

Miss Lily looked at her, startled. 'I didn't know the numbers ... I didn't think ...'

Sophie rescued her. 'Did you like Australia?'

'Very much. Little culture, but one can create culture.'

Sophie raised one eyebrow, very much as Miss Lily had taught her, and her friend laughed ruefully.

'I am sorry, my dear. That was discourteous.'

'Perhaps a little,' said Sophie. 'And when did James come into all of this?'

Lily reflected. 'Monty introduced me to James in 1912 or so. James is the only one now in the intelligence community who knows that Nigel Vaile and his occasional half-sister Lily are the same person. It was ... necessary ...'

'Because he fell in love with you after his wife died?'

'Perceptive woman. Not quite but, yes, there was ... an attraction. James accepted who I am, even if he didn't understand. I was useful and he liked me. You can rely on James Lorrimer for two things: loyalty to his country and loyalty to his friends. And then the war.' Miss Lily steepled her hands. 'I could have been valuable, despite my association with the peace with Germany movement. I could have redeemed myself. But the Earl of Shillings had an inescapable role to play to lead his men to war, the men from his estate. Miss Lily was forced to vanish for the duration. Which of course left those who knew of her with the impression she had washed her hands of England altogether.'

'And so Green became Miss Lily, a loyal patriot for the war effort, and anyone who matters knew she was working for our government,' said Sophie slowly.

'Yes. Green was given the birth certificate of a Lillian Shillings, showing her to be the illegitimate child of a woman who died young on the estate, as well as letters of introduction ...'

'I hadn't realised how alike you and Green are physically.'

Now Miss Lily raised an eyebrow. 'Not a coincidence, my dear. My grandfather regarded the women of Shillings as his property. My father did too, to some extent. In return the families were given money, or better acreage, or their children positions here in the house. Green is probably Nigel's cousin, or even the half-sister we pretend I am.'

'Does she know?'

'Of course.'

'And she isn't bitter?'

'This is England, my dear. We all know our stations. But Green truly is my friend. She had no financial need to work after the war. I thought she stayed away from Shillings because of Jones. That relationship has never been easy. Possibly being with you allowed her to continue the styling she enjoys and could no longer do with me.' Miss Lily shrugged. 'And the life she led with you in Australia was certainly more interesting once Jones and I were no longer working in intelligence. I had no idea about Violette.'

Sophie thought of the young woman now, hopefully upstairs and being introduced to the world of luxurious clothes and elegant hairdressing. 'I'm just a little ... concerned ... about Violette being in the same house as Rose and Danny. She kept her knife,' she added.

'I know. But it would have been easy for her to find another, in this house. My father left a whole wall of swords, muskets and throwing knives in the billiard room', said Miss Lily with a touch of exasperation. 'But as you say, we have little choice. But I think Rose and Danny are safe. Violette's anger will be aimed at Green now. Green is fond of the children but not doting, so Violette is unlikely to seek revenge by hurting them.'

But there was doubt in Miss Lily's voice.

'We do have a choice, you know,' said Sophie. 'We could leave for Australia tomorrow, just you and me and the children. Let Green and Jones and Violette work out if they can be a family.'

'And risk her stabbing Hereward?' murmured Miss Lily.

'Hereward didn't win those medals and lose a hand serving cocktails. I suspect he would be a match for Violette.'

'And you would see Daniel Greenman again.'

Sophie was silent.

'Do you wish to?'

Sophie met her eyes. 'I love Nigel. I love you.'

'That wasn't what I asked.'

'Then the answer is that I love my husband. I know my duty to my family. I don't want to see Daniel again until he has found a woman to share his life with, till we can be friends and nothing more.' And till my own physical passion ebbs a little, she thought. Till my body no longer aches sometimes in the night ... 'Do you miss the world of espionage?'

'Very much to the contrary. I am like a swallow who has at last come home. I've served my country. Nigel has as well. We have given all that could be expected of us. I want to live his life here, watching the children grow and the crops being harvested, pondering nothing more taxing than the choice of clover or mangelwurzels for a forage crop, and should the lower paddock be drained for potatoes.'

And you are twenty-five years older than me, thought Sophie, and have survived a major illness. You have entered the quietening of life, just as I feel it surge within me.

The age gap had never mattered before or, rather, her fire had been matched by his experience. But if Nigel Vaile — with visits from Miss Lily — was to have a quiet life on his estates, broken only by similarly peaceful interludes in Australia, Sophie's life would be circumscribed in exactly the same way.

And Nigel did not know it for, after all, it was she who had quite literally flown to him. He must believe she was content with children, a business she would oversee, an estate, a title, a husband. And why shouldn't she be content?

Because I would like to have convinced the Emperor of Japan to maintain an alliance with England, she thought. I'd have loved to entertain the Fathers of Federation at tea, and gauge their opinions on the Empire. I would like to ... to ride a camel and do whatever Lily, Jones and Green did in Egypt. I want to change the world, and not just by selling it canned comestibles ...

Instead it was time to dress for dinner.

Chapter 22

A good dinner can tell you a great deal about a hostess. A poor dinner can tell you even more.

Miss Lily, 1913

For the first time tonight Shillings protocol was abandoned: a lady's maid sat at the dining table, Sophie at one end, Jones at her right hand, Nigel at the head of the table, Green at his right hand and Violette next, her chair moved as far as possible from her mother's. A formal meal would hopefully impress Violette. It would also be a way to evaluate her ability to cope in polite society.

Miss Lily was indisposed. Sophie wondered how long Miss Lily must remain indisposed, or whether she would have decided to leave by the morning. If Violette was to become part of their household, she was sharp-eyed enough to soon suspect something wasn't quite as it seemed — and with her they could not rely on the loyalty and discretion they enjoyed with the tenants and servants of the estate.

Violette would be another anchor keeping Nigel Vaile permanently as the Earl of Shillings.

Violette sipped turtle soup, small sips, the spoon proceeding away from her as she scooped up the liquid. Her manners, Sophie noted, were excellent. She had assumed Grandmère had been a villager, but despite their cottage Madame Larresse and her daughters must have been educated bourgeoisie.

Violette wore one of Sophie's evening dresses from the year before, a soft blue silk with white fox-fur trim swiftly shortened to the fashionable length with a deeper blue silk scarf as a belt around her hips, the dress ballooning softly over it, and a lace fichu to turn the low-necked gown into one suitable for a thirteen-year-old.

'You look lovely,' said Sophie.

Violette smiled at her with what Sophie recognised as at least two-thirds calculating charm. 'Thank you, my lady.' She turned the smile to Jones. 'It seems I am Mademoiselle Jones now, and not Shillings. A fine name, Jones. I like it better than Green.'

The wrong kind of smile, thought Sophie, and Jones knew it. This girl had never known fatherly love.

Hereward cleared the bowls, the angle of his nose in no way indicating that this young woman, the protégée of the earl and countess, had ever been nor could ever be 'a young person'. Undoubtedly the servants' hall already had almost every detail.

Oysters Rockefeller were served. Violette carefully waited until Sophie lifted her small fork, then copied her. Not Green, Sophie noted. Violette had scarcely glanced at Green.

Violette took another oyster as Hereward offered them again. Evidently she approved of them. 'Where is Miss Lily?'

'She is not feeling well.'

'She is interesting,' said Violette.

She is indeed, thought Sophie.

'I wish she had been my mother.'

Green seemed to shrink. Jones remained impassive.

'Have you thought what you might like to do?' asked Sophie hurriedly.

'I have decided I would like to learn to fly,' said Violette. She let her smile linger on Nigel. 'Your sister said that I might learn.'

'Did she now? Shall we talk of the possibility of flying lessons in a few months?'

Violette's lip trembled slightly. 'You will not let me?'

'Your parents probably will, but I think you need time to get to know them first.'

Violette gave Jones a long look and Green a shorter one. 'I believe my ... mother ... when she says she did not betray us to the Boche. I believe my papa,' again the flash of smile for Jones, 'when he says he did not know of me. They will give me a home

133

and I will not kill them. But do you think I will love them, or they me?' She shrugged, and ate another oyster. 'I do not think so.'

Green closed her eyes, then put down her oyster fork. Jones glanced at Green half in anger, half with irritated love, then helplessly at this daughter, as untouchable physically and emotionally as if she were in Antarctica.

'You are very frank,' said Nigel mildly.

'This is a house of frankness, is it not?'

'Usually,' said Sophie.

'Will Miss Lily be at breakfast tomorrow? She would agree I should learn to fly, I think.'

'Lily will be leaving early tomorrow morning, if she is feeling up to it of course. She spends most of her time on the Continent these days. You were lucky to find her here at all.'

'Where on the Continent?'

'She travels.'

'That sounds most interesting, just to travel as one wishes. There will be a telephone call for me soon. A woman who has been most kind to me.' Violette ate her last oyster. 'Are there more oysters?'

'Probably,' said Sophie. 'But it is not good manners to ask. Sometimes the butler offers more, but not tonight. Other courses will be served.'

'What?' asked Violette with deep interest.

'That again is something a guest does not ask, at least not at table. Who is this woman?'

'A good woman, a truly kind one. Her daughter died. I think she would have liked me to stay to be her daughter. I must tell her now that I have found my mother, and another home.'

A flash of anguish crossed Green's face. 'You would have liked to be her daughter?'

Violette shrugged. 'I am your daughter, am I not? But I must tell her I am safe, and happy.'

'I'm glad you are happy,' said Nigel.

The smile again, a quite enchanting smile. 'The bedroom is beautiful. Shall I have jewels, do you think?'

'No,' said Green.

Violette ignored her.

'A strand of pearls when you are twenty-one,' said Sophie. 'Perhaps.'

'You are the daughter of his lordship's secretary,' said Jones quietly. 'Not his lordship. We do not dine with him when there is company, nor even every night, and usually informally in the library.'

'And my mother is a servant and you are not married,' observed Violette. 'But may I still learn how to fly?'

'Why are you so interested in flying?' Sophie tried to change the subject.

For the first time Violette's face was open, her gaze unguarded. 'Because when things are bad I have looked at birds and thought how lucky that you can fly away. And now perhaps I can fly too.'

Hereward brought in the saddle of lamb, followed by the footmen with the roast potatoes, parsnips, Brussels sprouts, glazed carrots and Cumberland sauce. 'There is a phone call for the … er … Miss Jones, my lady,' he said to Sophie.

'You may take it in the library,' said Sophie to Violette. 'Hereward will show you the way.'

Chapter 23

When you rise from a chair remember, knees together always, back
straight, a deep breath and inhale as you rise. That way as you
grow older and your bones stiffen you will not instinctively groan
as you get to your feet. Softly tweak your skirt before you rise, no
matter how old you are. It is always good to remind a man what
lies underneath.

Miss Lily, 1913

VIOLETTE

'Violette, are you safe? Did you find her?'

'I am safe and, yes, I found her,' said Violette flatly.

'Miss Lily Shillings?'

'Yes.'

'Your mother?'

Violette hesitated. But the woman who had given birth to her
had not been Lily Shillings; nor was Violette quite prepared to
admit, even to Mrs Maillot, that her mother was a mere lady's
maid. 'No, but she is a friend of my mother, and I have met my
mother now.'

'So Miss Lily is at Shillings now? You actually met her?'
Mrs Maillot sounded strangely insistent.

'Yes, I met her this afternoon.'

'And your mother was there too?'

'Yes.'

'What is her name? Does she want you to live with her? Will
she care for you?'

'I ... I am not sure yet.' Violette was in fact extremely sure that Miss Green wished to be her mother. But she was not prepared to give her name. Did she want a mother who was a maid? A father who might decide he knew what was best for her? A home, however grand, where she ranked with the servants and hangers-on, no matter what the earl's wife said about friendship. Violette had already heard the servants whispering about Miss Green eating in the dining room, certainly a first and for her benefit, and so unlikely to be repeated.

'Did your mother say why she called herself Lily Shillings?'

Ah, that was complicated, and something Violette did not want to explain on the telephone, with many people at all the exchanges between here and London listening in. She could not mention La Dame Blanche.

'She was not married, and so did not want to give her own name,' she temporised. 'But Miss Lily was kind when she found out.'

'You have met the earl? How did he take your arrival?'

Of course, thought Violette indulgently, Mrs Maillot would be impressed by members of the aristocracy. 'Yes. And I met his wife. I am dining with them now.'

'Oh, my. Violette ...' There was a strange note in Mrs Maillot's voice. 'Is Miss Lily dining with you too?'

Violette considered her answer. Her mother was dining with them, but not Miss Lily Shillings. 'No,' she said at last. 'She is not feeling well, and she leaves for the Continent tomorrow.'

'Are they close? Miss Lily Vaile and the earl?'

'I do not understand.'

'I ... I am just interested. I just wondered how they get on together.'

'I do not know,' said Violette. 'I have not seen them together yet.'

'But surely when you arrived and saw Miss Lily, the earl would have been there too. It is his household.'

Violette shrugged. 'Well, he was not. I did not meet him till dinner time. But they are both kind and Miss Lily's clothes and her ladyship's, are most beautiful. The earl says Miss Lily does not live here.'

'Where is her home?'

'I do not know that she has one. He says she travels. She will be leaving again if she feels well enough tomorrow.'

'Where will she go?'

'I did not ask,' said Violette slowly. Why was Mrs Maillot so curious?

'I'm sorry for so many questions. I ... I just want to know how much you are truly accepted by the members of the household, that is all. Aristocrats can ... can have their fancies, be kind and then forget those they think are their inferiors.'

Inferiors. I am their inferior, thought Violette. It hurt. She had known she was a bastard, but had taken comfort from the knowledge she was a well-connected one. But to be the child of the maid Green, and the man Jones! Green did not even wear evening dress.

'My dear, I ... I want you to know you are always welcome here. Always. My heart is with you. You must know how much ... how very much the last weeks have meant to me.'

'To me also,' said Violette. For it was true. Mrs Maillot was the first person who had accepted her, loved her, with no duty to do so. Miss Green might want a daughter, but she did not know her. Mrs Maillot had picked her up from the street ...

'My dear ...' A hesitation on the phone line. 'Please, will you do something for me?'

'But of course.'

'Could you slip away now, and ask Miss Lily where she will be next? I will stay on the phone.'

'But that will cost you many threepences. And Miss Lily is not my mother, as I have said ...'

'Please, my dear. Don't let anyone see you.'

This was ... strange. But Mrs Maillot would have a reason, and this was obviously not the time to explain it, with others listening.

Violette put the receiver down gently, slipped out the door, then along to the small drawing room and the stairs at the end of its corridor. She had seen the room Miss Lily went to when they had all gone to change for dinner.

She knocked quietly. No answer. She opened the door.

A lovely room, papered in cream silk with a faint pattern of leaves. A cream coverlet, and hanging in the dressing room the gown Miss Lily had worn this afternoon.

Such lovely clothes. Violette could not resist opening the cupboard door.

Evening dresses, silks and such soft satins. And carved wood boxes. Violette stilled. Jewellery?

She lifted the lid of the largest.

No jewels. A wig, blonde, with faint grey streaks.

Was Miss Lily bald? Or had her hair thinned, like Grandmère's? But why was she not wearing it then, if she was not here in her room? Impulsively Violette returned to the bedroom. She lifted the coverlet to see if the sheets were still warm. That would tell her how recently Miss Lily had lain here.

The bed was not made up.

This was peculiar.

Quickly she hunted for papers, letters, in the drawers, even under the bed, in case there might be a case. But there was none. No papers, not even a writing desk, nothing but underwear, and that not the thin silk she had expected, but slightly padded.

Was that the fashion now that flat chests were no longer admired?

But she could not linger here. A servant might arrive to make up the bed, or Miss Lily might return from ... Violette tried to think of a reason why a woman who needed a wig might leave her room without it, where servants could bring a bath, or remove her chamber pot.

And Mrs Maillot was waiting on the phone. Violette slipped the door open, and checked the passageway was empty. But the servants, too, would be down in their hall tonight. No one saw her as she made her way back to the telephone.

'Hello?' She was proud she knew the correct way to speak on a phone. 'Mrs Maillot? Miss Lily is not in her room. There are no letters there, no papers at all. Just her clothes. Perhaps she has left already,' she offered. She knew that wealthy women had clothes 'sent on'.

'Why do you think that?'

'There were no sheets on her bed. But no, she cannot have left. Her wig was still in her dressing room.'

'A wig?' asked Mrs Maillot carefully.

Violette laughed. 'I think Miss Lily perhaps is vain. Her chemise is padded even, to increase her bosom! But maybe it's several wigs. She is so rich, after all. I will ask his lordship if Miss Lily is still here, and where she will be next.'

'No!' said Mrs Maillot sharply. 'There is no need. It was just curiosity,' she added, her voice back to its quiet, motherly tones. 'You know how I love the society pages. It is so wonderful you have met an earl and a countess! But you must go back to dinner. It would be impolite to stay away too long. I will telephone again tomorrow night,' said Mrs Maillot. 'And always, always you are welcome here. Sleep well, my dear.'

'And you.'

Violette replaced the phone in its receiver. She gazed around the library quietly, deep in thought, till Hereward coughed at the doorway. 'I will show you to the dining room, Miss, er, Jones.'

She smiled at him. 'Thank you.'

Chapter 24

It is a human instinct to try to take away pain. You will learn that usually this is not possible. It is better to acknowledge that it is there, to comfort but not try to deny the anguish.

Miss Lily, 1913

SOPHIE

'Talk,' said Sophie. She and Green were in her bedroom. Green shook her head as she hung up Sophie's dress, then reached for the nightdress on the warming rack by the fire. Sophie lifted her arms to be fitted. She could dress herself perfectly well — a talent many of her wealth never acquired — but this was what Green expected to do, had done for her since she became her maid after the war.

But did Green still wish to do it?

Green pulled the warming pan out of the bed and set it on the hearth. 'Everything has been said.'

'I really meant to ask how are you feeling, but that is stupid. I can't possibly understand what you are feeling, even if you describe it at length. But if you'd like to cry, I'm here.'

Green sat suddenly on the edge of the bed. She began to shake as Sophie held her. At last she sobbed.

Sophie let her cry. Nigel must have heard or else he would be there by now. Hopefully he was having a quiet talk with Jones.

'He blames me,' said Green at last.

'Jones?'

'Yes. Huw bloody Jones. I would have told him! I was ready to take her to England.' I was just waiting until the arrangements were made. One more day and we'd have been gone.' Green scrubbed at her eyes with her handkerchief. She had worn a Sunday dress at table — not an evening dress, but not her uniform either. Now, characteristically, she was dressed as a maid again. 'There would be a fishing boat, probably, and then a larger boat a little way out at sea. Huw was due leave, though we didn't know exactly when. I would have been waiting for him, and Angélique would have been too.'

'Not Violette?'

'No. I hadn't had her baptised — I wanted Huw — Jones — to be there, perhaps even see if we could be married first, so she would seem legitimate. James Lorrimer might have arranged that. But I can't take her name away now. It's been changed too many times already,' said Green bitterly. 'How does the stupid man think I could have told him I was pregnant? In a letter, to be read by the censor and his Commanding Officer? For all I knew they'd have him up on a charge, at the very least report him and make him sign away part of his wages, as they did with married men. I had to wait till I could see him.'

'You didn't think to tell him after the war?'

'That he'd had a child and lost her before he even met her? After he had lost a wife and child before? It would have been cruel.'

And honest, thought Sophie. And a permanent link to Jones that Green obviously had not wanted.

Green stood and grabbed a hairbrush angrily. 'I suppose we should get married. But, knowing Huw Jones, now that there is actually a reason to get married he probably won't want to.'

Jones was one of the least temperamental people Sophie had ever met. He would be reasonable about this too, once the shock subsided. But this was not the time to say that to Green.

'If you keep brushing like that I will end up bald.' Sophie took the hairbrush from her and began the required hundred strokes each side. 'I don't see why you need to marry.'

'Everyone else will see the need.'

'For a while, perhaps. It would be different if Violette were younger, or if you couldn't give her a secure home without marriage. But, after all, you both live in the same house anyway. Greenie, darling,' she tried to find the words, 'I know it is unfair when you have only just found your daughter. But she is what, nearly fourteen? In a few years she will have her own life — one that hopefully has you in it, but not necessarily with you. Dad used to say, "Children are only borrowed."'

Sophie felt a sudden longing for him, the man she had loved and admired completely. 'He was middle-aged when I was born, his only child, yet he arranged for me to come to England, leaving him behind. I only had a few months with him after I came back from the war. Even if you and Jones were married, Violette would be learning to be independent, at school, perhaps, then married.'

'I can't see her going to school.'

'I can,' said Sophie with feeling. 'Though I would pity the school. But Greenie, darling, speaking as the fairly respectable Countess of Shillings, I don't think you need to be bound to Jones for the sake of the few years left that your daughter will be with you. You and she and Jones will still be together whether you marry or not.'

'Yes,' said Green with feeling, not quite slamming the dressing table drawer.

'What do you want?' asked Sophie gently.

'I want my baby back,' Green wailed. 'I want Angélique! I want to feel her in my arms, to hold her, hug her. My arms are so empty. I want to teach her to sew and take her to the circus ...' The tears began to fall again. 'And I can't have any of it. None!'

'The sewing is possible,' said Sophie, incurably pragmatic. 'And you might take her to the circus. Though she might then demand an elephant to ride.'

'She is going to be trouble.' It was almost an apology.

'Yes, thank goodness. I was becoming quite bored.'

'I know,' said Green.

'Were you bored?'

Green considered, wiping away the last of the tears. 'Only a very little. I think I have been happy, the last two years, being here, being with Huw. His lover, but not having to cook his breakfast and darn his socks. Knowing I did not have to be his lover tomorrow, if I didn't want to, but knowing too that I probably would want to be and keep wanting to ...'

'Nigel says he has earned a peaceful life at home.'

'I think perhaps I have too,' said Green. 'Perhaps I even want one now.'

Sophie grinned. 'I doubt your motherhood is ever going to be peaceful.' She did not add that she had asked Hereward to set a footman to watch the door of the Blue Bedroom, just in case its inmate decided to steal the Botticelli in the hall or the Constable in the library or a silver coffee pot or two. Or burn down the house.

She had no doubt Violette was who she claimed to be: the girl's fury hid too much anguish. But she also knew that past horror led to instability. A girl who was used to a life that was dangerous, hidden and at times bizarre would expect her future life to be like that too. Her expectations might even create it.

Shillings contained Sophie's children, husband, friends. Her people.

She would make sure they were safe.

Chapter 25

Some men think size matters most to their lovers, or their wealth or the ability to do clever things with their fingers. On the contrary, I have always found sexual success depends mostly on one's partner's empathy, imagination, and a sense of fun.

Miss Lily, 1913

VIOLETTE

There was a footman in the corridor outside the bedroom, seated behind a ... a thing ... tall, with a pot on it. His legs were stretched out, so presumably he was going to sit there all night.

Violette was not experienced in the homes of noblemen, but she assumed that footmen were not usually perched about the house each evening. This one was watching her.

A nuisance.

She shut the inch of door she had unobtrusively opened, sat on the bed — the luxurious bed, with a satin cover and linen that smelled of lavender, just like the far thinner sheets had with Grandmère — and considered.

She could stay here. It would be sensible: security and comfort.

Sensible however had never been a major feature of her behaviour, nor Grandmère's.

If she stayed here she would be the daughter of servants. The woman called Green clearly did regret losing her child, but she did not know Violette and, quite possibly, would not like her when she did.

Men, in Violette's experience, were more easily manipulated than women. She was reasonably certain she could manage Jones. But did she want to? She had slightly more experience of fathers than of noble houses — there had been fathers in the village where they lived, all of whom expected their daughters to do as they were told. It could be wearying, having to manipulate a father all the time.

Her ladyship had said that Violette could do whatever she wished. But evidently did not include learning to fly, which she had suggested to see what their reactions might be. 'Whatever she wished' might only be chosen from those activities selected from a narrow menu of school and helping in the house, which here might mean helping to tend her ladyship.

The clothes of her ladyship and Miss Lily — who had not appeared again — were the greatest inducement to stay. Violette's greatest pleasure, after manipulating fools, was gazing at beautiful garments, their flow, their cut, their fabric and ornamentation. But clothes were not enough. For now, for the first time since Grandmère's death, there was someone who *did* love her, someone whose life she could change with warmth and comfort. And the south of France!

Violette had seen the south of France often in the illustrated papers. Aristocrats and film stars sunning on the Riviera, beaches and bathing suits and handsome men who might be useful, plus many, many gorgeous outfits that with good fabric she might even imitate with her needle. All she needed was money.

She used her knife to unpick the stitching that had sewn Mr Maillot's trousers, shirt and jacket onto the lining of her coat — the disguise she had expected to need once she had killed Lily Shillings. She quickly slipped them on, shrugged the coat over it all, and then slid the men's shoes and hat into the pockets.

She inspected herself in the mirror. With her hair loose she still looked like a girl, if a trifle bulky. If a servant saw her now they would only wonder why she wore a coat indoors.

She opened the window, then tested the wide window ledge. Solid. Excellent. A well-maintained window was a rarity, in her experience. She crept out, sat, twisted, bent till her fingers held the edge of the ledge, then grasped the bare ivy stems and dropped.

Ivy was not enough to take the weight of a girl, even one as slim as Violette. But it was enough to guide her fall so that she didn't land too heavily on the ground. She peered in the nearest window. A curtain and darkness. She had not seen what this room was, but it seemed likely to be unused at this time of night, when the servants would be asleep. She lifted the window.

It didn't move. She hadn't thought it would. She wrapped her sleeve about her knife and hit the glass sharply, only once. It cracked, but did not shatter, and the noise was not loud. Nonetheless, she waited.

Ten quiet minutes later she quickly pushed at the glass again, removing shards piece by piece until the way was clear, then slid inside past the curtains. She lit a stub of candle retrieved from her pocket and looked around.

A wooden table, with silver serving dishes on it, and cleaning cloths. Tempting, but a silver tureen would be noticeable, unless she pretended to be *enceinte*. She grinned at the idea but quickly rejected it. Silver teaspoons: yes.

She opened the door quietly, waited, then slipped down the hall towards the library. She had noticed some most useful items there. The most useful of all, of course, were the pearls in her pocket that she had palmed when ... such a good child ... she had gone to say another good night to the woman who had borne her. Three very long strands of such large pearls should keep her and Mrs Maillot nicely for many years. Violette opened the library door and reached for the small painting above the desk.

Chapter 26

Love, friendship, justice: each has been constructed by people, for people, so we can co-exist. Do not expect fate to deal with you with justice. It does not know the word.

Miss Lily, 1913

SOPHIE

'She's gone,' said Green grimly.

Sophie woke, sat, looked hopefully for the cup of tea and Bath biscuits, and saw none. The bed beside her was empty. Nigel had slept in his own room that night, as he did sometimes when he was in pain, and his restlessness might disturb her.

'Violette?' and then more urgently, 'Rose and Danny?'

'In their nursery, still asleep.' Green glared at her. 'You didn't think my daughter would harm your children, did you?'

No more than you did, if you have already checked on them before coming here, thought Sophie. 'Are you sure Violette hasn't just gone for a walk?'

'Hereward fetched Jones. The window in the butler's pantry has been broken, and the Blue Bedroom's window is open. Samuel was in the hall all night and didn't see her leave.'

'Which means she didn't want to be seen,' said Sophie slowly. She pulled the bell, as Green evidently was not going to bring tea and she needed it. 'But she broke in again. Why?'

Green looked at her mutely.

'What has she taken?' asked Sophie.

'We don't know yet. Your pearls to begin with. Do you want my resignation?'

'Oh, don't be silly.'

Green frowned at her.

'I'm sorry, I'm sorry, I'm sorry. Can you forget I employ you for a few minutes? And that Nigel's bloody ancestors employed yours and impregnated half of them for the last thousand generations? Of course I don't want you to resign. I thought ...'

... that we were a family, thought Sophie, if an unconventional one. But she supposed that even in families one person might decide to remove themselves ...

'Your *pearls*,' repeated Green.

'I heard you. Giggs gave them to me and I loved them, but they're just jewellery. And, yes, I know,' she said wearily, 'that it is easy for the owner of Higgs's Corned Beef to dismiss the loss of tens of thousands of pounds' worth of pearls. Ah, Amy, tea please, two cups, no, three, extremely strong, and with a vast amount of toast and honey, not just biscuits. Quickly, if you'd be so good.' She waited till Amy had left. 'Has Jones gone to find her?'

'He rang from the station. No one boarded the milk train except a young man.'

'Ah. I hope he has followed the young man.'

'He should catch up with the train before London. He'll be able to check anyone who gets off at most of the stops after that. Sophie, are you going to call the police?'

'Of course not.' The door opened again, revealing an earl, not tea, but just as welcome. 'Nigel, darling.' She lifted her cheek for a kiss. 'I've called for tea and toast.'

'Good. The Rembrandt from the library has gone.'

'Clever girl, to recognise a Rembrandt.'

'And cut it from its frame,' said Nigel grimly.

'Someone has trained her well. Or badly. You know what I mean.'

Green sat numbly on the dressing stool. 'I'm sorry. I ...'

Sophie swung herself out of bed and took her hand. 'You don't know what to feel.'

'I know exactly what I feel. Angry. Manipulated. I ... I know what I *don't* feel.'

'Love?' asked Nigel quietly.

Green nodded. 'I don't love her. I loved Angélique. I loved her desperately, but I don't even know her now, this Violette. Do you think she guessed? That she knew I didn't love her as I should, and that's why she left?'

'Possibly,' said Sophie. 'I ... I don't think motherhood is quite that instinctive, not if you haven't seen her for most of her life.'

'It should be,' said Green miserably.

'Greenie, darling, it may still work out.'

'How?'

'I don't know,' said Sophie honestly. 'What was this grandmère of hers like?'

Green smiled. 'Formidable. She was the driving force behind what would become La Dame Blanche in the whole region, though most of us only knew a very few other members. Safer that way — each group would have contact with a single member of one other group. The old lady once slit the throat of a soldier trying to rape the fishmonger's wife, then strangled the companion who came looking for him with her stocking. A useful technique for any woman — you slip off a stocking, tie a slip knot, loop it around their neck as they come towards you then fall back, letting your weight do the strangling. Then you put the stocking back on — it only takes seconds, completely quiet, and the stocking shouldn't even be laddered.'

'Thank you. I will remember that technique the next time I am bored at a dinner,' said Sophie drily. 'What happened to the men's bodies?'

'Madame had them arranged carefully in the forest, trousers at their ankles, so that it looked as if they had been ... interested ... in each other, and one of their comrades had killed them in revulsion or jealousy. No reprisals on the village for those two, at least.' Green seemed calmer relating her wartime stories.

'Where had the grandmother learned all this?'

'I taught her,' said Green. She glanced at Nigel. 'Some of it I knew already. Mr Lorrimer also arranged for a few weeks' training for those of us heading into Belgium.'

'You didn't think to come home when you found out you were pregnant?' asked Nigel.

'My pregnancy was partially why I was in Belgium. What home? You and Jones were in France. I was unmarried! How could I come back here? The scandal would have been all over the estate. And at my age too. A sixteen-year-old unwed mother may be forgiven. A forty-year-old one? And besides, my pregnancy was a useful disguise. No one suspects a pregnant woman of violent sabotage.'

'At least Violette didn't blow up the glasshouses,' said Sophie. 'Oh, Greenie, I'm sorry, I didn't mean it like that.'

'Yes, you did.'

'All right, yes, I did, but tragedy is easier if you can find something to smile about. Oh tea, wonderful!' as the bedroom door opened. 'Amy, thank you. On the dressing table, please.'

Tea might not solve a problem, but drinking it was a comfort and a pause.

Chapter 27

Men too often ignore women. Many a wife has had an interesting life as a mathematician or botanist and her husband hasn't noticed, especially if their work is published only under their initials. No, I am not suggesting a discreet academic career for you, my dears. I am instead strongly advocating that before you marry, you find out what fulfils you, fascinates you, and then forge a life that will allow you to achieve it.

Miss Lily, 1913

VIOLETTE

A man's hat, clothes and a carpetbag found in the housekeeper's room fooled a half-asleep station guard in the pre-dawn light. Violette alighted at the first junction, changed her clothes swiftly in the toilet block, thankfully deserted at this hour of the morning, then bought a ticket to Edinburgh, just in case anyone enquired who had bought a ticket that morning, and where they might be travelling to. The journey to Edinburgh would mean changing at London, and the railway station nearest Mrs Maillot's home was on the London line.

The tickets took all the money she had, apart from a few pennies; nor, she knew, would the pearls, the silver spoons or the painting be easily converted into cash. Pearls could be rethreaded into smaller necklaces and go to a pawnbroker, but finding a buyer for the painting was beyond the skills she had learned from the girls at the orphanage.

The Riviera, however, would have wealthy people, and where

there were wealthy people there would be others who supplied whatever they might want. In a year or two Violette was sure she could dispose of the Rembrandt — one of the few artists whose name she knew. They would not get its true value, of course, but enough to buy a cottage.

No one seemed to have noticed her, not muffled now in Mrs Maillot's coat with a cloche hat pulled down over her ears. She felt secure enough to alight at the right station, well before the 'change all' at Waterloo. Of course Mrs Maillot was not there to meet her — they had spoken only the night before and naturally she would expect her to stay with her new mother. Perhaps she should have divulged to her her intentions. But no, not with all the operators listening in, including the Shillings operator who would have certainly warned his lordship ...

Fog curled around the doorsteps, wisps as thick as scarves but nothing like the choking coal smog that could spread across the city. A baker's cart rattled down the street, the horse plodding in the mud, the baker's boy darting back and forth as he placed the loaves in bread bins left by the back doors. Violette expected Mrs Maillot would have cut back her bread order already to save money. Or perhaps she would be living only on tea and toast to save money after the extravagant beef roasts.

Violette let her fingers linger on the pearls in her pocket. Soon Mrs Maillot would have caviar and champagne. Violette had never consumed either, but they were obviously something she and Mrs Maillot deserved.

Violette opened the front gate, hesitated, then walked around the back. The baker had been. Two loaves, she saw in surprise, a brown cob and a high white. She knocked, the smile ready on her lips.

'Yes?' A man stood there, unshaven, in a red dressing gown. She blinked at the unfamiliarity and then again because he *was* familiar. His was the face in the photo on the dresser. The red dressing gown had been one of the sad souvenirs in the wardrobe.

'Mrs Maillot?' asked Violette.

'Sorry, miss, don't know her.' The man began to close the door.

For a second Violette wondered if Mrs Maillot could have taken a lover, one who very closely resembled her dead husband. 'But I am Violette. I live here with her. She will want to see me.'

The door swung open again. 'You what? Hey, Joanie!' His body still blocked the door.

A woman appeared, also in a dressing gown, one of Mrs Maillot's. A girl peered from behind them. A most familiar girl.

'This lass says she lives here. Says a Mrs Maillot does too.' He turned back to Violette, 'You stay right there, missy. Georgette, run down to the telephone box and call the cops. I reckon this Maillot woman is the one who's been living here while we've been up with Auntie Flo.'

'That's my coat!' said the woman indignantly. 'You take it off this minute.'

The coat held the pearls and the painting. Besides, the day was cold.

Violette ran.

The man would pursue her. The police too, undoubtedly, notified by Shillings and by the people in Mrs Maillot's home ... the house she had taken for Mrs Maillot's. But before then someone from the house must get dressed, run to a phone box, and then the police must be called, and a policeman would have to bicycle through the mud and listen to the story ...

When did that family arrive? Last night? But Mrs Maillot called me last night ...

She had to think. This was impossible, but impossible things happened, Grandmère dying or the son of the family next door returning to a welcome home feast then hanged from the oak tree the next morning as a collaborator. Nothing in life was as it seemed.

The fog was rising. Good. It made it easier to hide. She turned a corner and began to walk swiftly to the station beyond the one where she had alighted.

She was hungry, she was cold, and she was scared. The last two she could ignore, as she had so often, but she must find food today. Without food you could not think clearly. She had to think well.

So. If the house was not Mrs Maillot's ... she turned another corner ... Mrs Maillot must have known the family would not be there, somehow got the key, coaxed Violette into staying only until the family were due back. And, yes, for the past week she had been saying, oh so regretfully, that she would miss her so much now the earl and his family had returned.

Manipulated. But why? She was not important.

The earl was. And possibly his half-sister. Yes, the questions last night had certainly focused on the sister, the 'Miss Lily' Violette had thought was her mother.

Blackmail? A member of the aristocracy's illegitimate child was possibly blackmail-worthy. She would kill Mrs Maillot if she tried to blackmail Miss Lily, who was not her mother anyway ...

Her face was cold. Violette realised it was wet too. Tears. Of anger, of betrayal, of disgust at herself and her foolishness, taken in by so little kindness, tears because she would almost certainly never see Mrs Maillot again, because she had nowhere in the world that would give her shelter, unless she went back to Shillings, where they would not want her now, even if they did not call the police, and she didn't even have the train fare to go back there anyway.

The most important matter then was to get as far away as possible, in case the man back at the house really had called the police. And then food. But there had been no café at the railway station, nor any that she knew of nearby where she might forage in a rubbish bin, though most café owners had an arrangement with a pig man, so you might need to search several bins before you found stale bread or half-eaten cakes a careless waitress had thrown out.

It was too early to enter a café and sit at a table not yet cleared, where the previous customer had left crusts, or even a remnant of pie. So she must walk, and keep walking, despite the cold, despite the trembling, which was just cold for she was used to fear, would *not* be trembling because of that, would not waste her energy thinking of betrayal, of the woman who had pretended to love her, of how everyone had betrayed her all her life, even Grandmère with her death ...

She would *not* think of that. She must calmly keep walking like a ... what did they call those people who had that new fad of walking for pleasure? Hikers, that was it. She would walk like a hiker at least until mid-afternoon, till she found city streets, and a café to sing outside where there were lanes behind that she could vanish into.

Because if the police nabbed her for the theft of the coat they would find the pearls and the painting and she had nowhere she could leave them and no one to help and nothing had ever been quite as desperate before ...

The car came slowly around the corner, shining grey in the yellow fog.

The car stopped. A man got out and turned to look at her, not unkindly, over the silver roof.

'Get in,' said Jones.

Violette obeyed.

Chapter 28

Always breakfast well. Your day's decisions will be far more rational.

Miss Lily, 1913

The café was at least ten miles away, and filled with men in overalls. The tea tasted of stewed dishcloths; the plates were piled with fried eggs, fried sausages, fried potato, bacon, canned beans in tomato sauce, with slabs of bread and margarine.

Violette ate. So did Jones. Neither had spoken since she had slid into the car, just as a policeman bicycled around the corner. Jones had tipped his hat to him as they drove on, stopping here where Jones evidently knew the menu, at least well enough to say, 'The lot for both of us.'

At last he cleaned the egg yolk off his plate with the last of his bread, a gesture she did not expect he used at Shillings. He smiled as he saw her watch him munch the yolk-soaked bread. 'Old habits die hard. Nothing better than fresh bread soaked in the last of a fry-up.'

'Miss Green said you had been a butler.'

'And Nigel's batman in the last war, and long ago on the North West Frontier too.'

'Are you taking me to the police?' It would take more senior ones than a fat man on a bicycle to take charge of the thief of a countess's pearls and a Rembrandt.

'No. Why were you running?'

Violette considered. But there was nothing to be lost in telling him. He might even have an explanation. So she told him everything, from the meeting with Mrs Maillot outside the Lyon's Corner House to her hopes of creating a sanctuary for the woman she thought had loved her.

Jones listened, then nodded at her suggestion that Mrs Maillot had intended to blackmail Lily Shillings about her abandoned illegitimate child. 'Possibly. Or maybe she hoped you'd open the door for a gang of thieves one night, for a bigger haul than you've made off with by yourself. But the questions about Lily are ... interesting.'

'But as Miss Lily is not my mother there can be no reason to blackmail her.' She shrugged. 'A maid is not useful to blackmail. No money.'

'Green's done all right but, no, I can't see anyone blackmailing her. They'd be lucky to escape with all their limbs.'

Violette stared. 'Miss Green would fight people?'

Jones grinned. 'You think you inherited your sweet temperament from me? You're your mother's daughter. I saw her slice a man's thumb off once in a bazaar in Morocco.'

'Why?'

'His hand was holding a rope, with a child at the other end. Don't know what happened to the man — we didn't stay to find out — but the child was adopted by a baker and his wife, a hundred miles away.' Another grin. 'And you stole Sophie's pearls from her. Brave girl.'

'I ... I did not know Miss Green was like that.'

'Lucky you're her daughter, then. She won't slice your thumb off.'

'What will she do?'

'Cry. She's crying now, I reckon. Your fault, and mine too. I haven't ... behaved well over this.'

'You are a nice man.'

'Thank you. I am also a surprised man. But talking it over with Nigel ... there was no way Greenie could have let me know about you at the time. And afterwards ... well, my war was bad. I have just discovered that hers was worse.'

'She truly wants me as her daughter?' asked Violette slowly.

'Let's just say she wants her daughter and you're it. You'll get used to each other.'

'And you? Do you want a daughter too?' She did not use guile in her tone. She wanted the true answer.

'I had a daughter,' he said slowly. 'She died. Honestly? No, I don't want another child. I didn't do a good job of looking after the one I had, off with Nigel most of the time. But that's irrelevant. I have a daughter. You could be worse.'

'I am a thief,' said Violette indignantly. 'I have stabbed a man, and maybe killed him, and attacked other men too, when they deserved it. I wanted to kill my mother!'

'Like I said, you could be worse. You could be a boring little sweetheart. If I'd wanted one of those I'd never have fallen for Green. Or Lily.'

'You loved Miss Lily too?'

'Not like that,' said Jones quietly. 'Never like that. But, yes, I love Lily. Part as her friend, part as her father, or uncle maybe, as I'm only a decade or so older than her.'

Violette pushed away her empty teacup. Men were obviously waiting for their table, and their own fatty portions of fried pig adorned with bloody-looking baked beans. 'What do we do now?'

'We go home.'

'Home is Shillings?'

'Unless you have another one.'

'No. I ... I have nowhere else. What ... what will the earl do with me?'

'I have no idea,' said Jones cheerfully. 'Send you to bed with no supper? He won't call the police at any rate. Or set the dogs on you.'

'I did not see dogs.'

'Which is why he won't set them on you. Sophie's more volatile, but you're probably pretty safe from her too.'

'Probably?'

'Probably,' agreed Jones, standing up from the table.

'And Miss Lily?'

'She is no longer there.'

'That is a pity. She is … interesting.'

'Yes,' said Jones. 'Lily is interesting.'

'You know she wears a wig? She is vain, n'est-ce pas?'

'I've learned it's best to take Lily as she is, and not make judgements,' said Jones, leaving the change on the counter as a tip.

Violette waited till they were in the car again, such a comfortable car with leather as soft as a caress, the polished wooden dashboard, even a small rose in a flower holder near the steering wheel. Who put a fresh rose in a car each day, and in late winter?

'If they let me stay,' she asked carefully, 'what will happen then? After they have forgiven me, perhaps?'

'What do you want to do? Were you serious about wanting to learn to fly?'

'No. Though one day, perhaps.'

'Somehow I can't see you as a lady's maid, nor a housekeeper. Or cook.'

'I am a very good cook.'

'Till the day you put arsenic in the hollandaise. Just joking. Tell you what, how about I start off teaching you jiu-jitsu?'

'Jube eat you?'

'No, jiu-jitsu. It's something you learn in the east — how to kick two men in one leap while you strike another in the neck. Deadly, but a matter of balance and strength, not size and weight.'

'Does Miss Green know jiu-jitsu? And Miss Lily and the countess?'

'Greenie does, and Lily. I don't think Nigel has taught Sophie.' Jones considered. 'He hasn't really had a chance since they married. He had a major operation, and still needs to take care. She'd probably like to learn.'

'I think that I would too.'

They drove in silence for a while. The fog thinned and so did the houses on either side. A wet cow stared at them mournfully.

'I'd better ring them to let them know to expect us,' said Jones, stopping outside a telephone box. 'Should have done it before. They'll be worrying.'

'About the pearls and painting?'

'About you.'

Violette absorbed that. 'Oh.'

'Violette, do I have your word that you will not injure any of my family, friends or household?'

'Yes.'

'And you won't run away again?'

She considered his question. 'I cannot promise that.'

'Good.'

'Why good?'

'It means you were telling the truth when you made the first promise. Probably.'

'I always tell the truth, except when I am lying.'

'Good enough,' said Jones.

Chapter 29

*You will notice I do not urge you to any particular political path,
my dears. Each of you, I hope, will follow your own. But do be
prepared to turn right at the next star on the right if it seems brighter.
And always have a contingency plan in case your star should fade.*

Miss Lily, 1913

HANNELORE

Miss Washford sat on the silk-covered sofa and sipped her coffee.
Her high-heeled shoes matched the dark green of her silk Chanel
dress, though her now-dark hair had been recently cropped
slightly too short for the current fashion. No one would ever
recognise this woman as the lower-middle-class Mrs Maillot.

'A wig,' said the prinzessin thoughtfully. 'She said she saw a
wig?'

'Yes, Your Highness, and a padded camisole, nor even a sign
her room had been recently occupied.'

'That is most interesting,' said the prinzessin slowly. 'A grey
and blonde wig. Why not stay blonde, for vanity? To be there, so
suddenly, just when she is needed, and then to be not there, even
more suddenly. You are quite sure that Violette never saw Lily
Shillings and the earl together?'

'I asked her directly, Your Highness.'

'And there was no clue at all where Miss Vaile might be
travelling to now?'

Miss Washford sipped her coffee again. 'None, nor any
mention of where she had been, either.'

Miss Washford's father's surname, Hannelore had been informed, had not been Washford but von Grüner. Miss Washford's mother had changed her daughter's name when she married her second husband, the English stepfather. Miss Washford had kept her stepfather's name but also retained her loyalty to Germany.

In the weeks when it seemed war with Germany was inevitable, Miss Washford had offered her services to the German embassy. The embassy officials had been inclined to dismiss her: what help could a woman be? Luckily the interview had been interrupted by a young count, the uncle of the Prinzessin von Arnenberg. That meeting had led to Miss Washford being most useful to the fatherland in the war. As indeed she hoped she was useful now. Being useful was also — usefully — lucrative in these hard times.

'I believe the earl was deliberately vague about where his sister had been, as well as where she might be going,' she answered.

'Just as his wife is,' murmured Hannelore. 'Interesting. A mother finds her daughter, but the woman who saw this most touching reunion does not join them for a family dinner that very night. She is not well enough to dine, but well enough to travel. The brother who trusts her enough to have left her so often in charge of his estate does not even care where she might be going, or keeps it secret. Thank you, Miss Washford. You have been invaluable.'

'I am glad you think so. I don't believe I could have found out more even had it been possible to stay at that house any longer.'

'The earl's absence for so long was inconvenient,' agreed Hannelore. 'Especially as Miss Lily was not there, even though he was absent so long.' She stood. Miss Washford stood politely also. 'I believe my uncle has arranged payment?'

'He has, Your Highness. He has been most generous. Please do call on me if you have any further work I might help you with.'

'Of course.' Though she would not. Hannelore could not risk being seen with a woman familiar to a girl who might well become part of the Shillings household.

She rang the bell. The butler showed Miss Washford from the room.

Hannelore sat in silence.

She had thought, at first, that she had an answer to Miss Lily's continued disappearance. A child — a very late-in-life child, but still possible — might mean drastic changes to her life, for she could not imagine Miss Lily farming her own child out to strangers, nor bringing scandal to her friends and family by letting it be known the child existed.

Introducing Violette into Miss Lily's household, with continued contact with 'Mrs Maillot', would have meant a way to find out where Miss Lily might live, or travel to, as well as a way of persuading her to further the Nazi cause.

But now it seemed Miss Lily did not have a child. But she did have a wig, mysterious appearances and disappearances, and both Nigel and Sophie were quite unnecessarily reticent about anything involving her.

Twenty years ago, even ten, the Prinzessin von Arnenberg would not have considered the possibility that the Earl of Shillings might lead a double life. But erotic games and gender shifts were not just commonplace but fashionable in the Weimar Republic's Berlin. The more she thought about it, the more 'possible' became 'probable'.

So, she had ... probable information. She had the means to use it, too. Hannelore continued to sit, thinking about the repercussions of what she planned to do.

For there was now a problem. A major problem. If, as now seemed possible, Miss Lily and the Earl of Shillings were the one person, they would find Hitler's views on such matters abhorrent.

Hannelore herself did not share the Führer's views on this particular matter. But that was such a small part of his political agenda. If — when — he achieved power, what could he do about it, except make such activities illegal? There were already laws against homosexualists in England. It simply meant one must be discreet, unlike poor Oscar Wilde who wished to shout his desires in every newspaper across Europe.

If she approached this carefully, discreetly, with compassion, as Miss Lily herself had taught them to use, surely no one would be hurt by this, she told herself, certainly not Sophie — who she loved, even as she envied her.

Hannelore smiled. Who would have thought, all those years ago, that the Prinzessin von Arnenberg would ever envy Miss Sophie Higgs, corned-beef heiress from Australia?

Sophie would not like the trickery, of course. But Hannelore had also recognised her friend's restlessness. It was familiar because she too had felt that way until Herr Hitler showed her a new future for Germany, and Europe.

Like all of Miss Lily's 'lovely ladies', Sophie needed a cause. Hannelore knew she had attended Bolshevik meetings with Lady Mary, and then to Hannelore's relief abruptly attended no more. But National Socialism would fill that void, even if Sophie could not accept that yet.

Hannelore glanced at the clock on the mantelpiece. She must dress for Mrs Donald C. Ottaway's Venetian luncheon: 'Such larks, Prinzessin. Gondolas on the Thames. And Venetian costumes, of course.'

'Don't Venetians wear much the same as we do?' Hannelore had met several Italians the last time she had been in Paris.

Mrs Ottaway stared at her. 'Not present-day Italians, darling. The real ones.'

'Real' meaning five hundred years earlier, perhaps. Hannelore wondered if she would be more of a real princess if she wore a glass slipper and arrived in a coach shaped like a pumpkin? Mrs Donald C. Ottaway would probably adore it.

But one must be seen and one must be seen to smile; and possibly among those on the chilly gondolas there would be some already sickening of this febrile gaiety: men and women she might invite to dine, or even to tea. Such a productive meal, tea, Miss Lily had always said ...

The door opened again. 'His Royal Highness, the Prince of Wales.'

Hannelore rose. 'David, how delightful!' More delightful than he knew, she thought, as the next stage of the plan could not be put into place without him. And such a plan — a plan that might change the history of Europe.

All her life the Prinzessin von Arnenberg had been taught she could play a part in history. Now, at last, she would.

'You are glowing, Cousin Hanne!' said David lightly. 'I am not interrupting anything, am I?'

Hannelore metaphorically cast Mrs Donald C. Ottaway and her gondolas out the window. 'Nothing serious, my darling David. A hundred lovers are waiting for me on the tiger skin rug upstairs. But they can wait ...'

'You did say come to tea.' He smiled. 'But a tiger skin sounds far more interesting. Especially with you.'

'But my tiger skin is already occupied by my hundred lovers.' She sighed melodramatically. 'Tragic, to have one's tiger skin occupied by boring lovers when the Prince of Wales finally comes to tea. But it is only mid-morning, and I am sure you don't really want tea. Is it too early for a cocktail?'

'Not today,' he said, a trifle grimly.

She rang the bell. The butler appeared — he would have known she would ring almost at once and had waited outside the door. 'Cocktails. A Prince of Wales — brandy, champagne and a touch of Cointreau. Am I correct, David?'

He bowed over her hand. 'Sadly, you are always correct.' He kissed the hand. 'Far too correct.'

The butler backed from the room.

'David, darling, do sit.'

'I would rather make love to you, even if we cannot use the tiger skin.' He was not serious. They both knew it.

'I don't dare face Freda's wrath.' Though the current royal mistress was not the jealous type; far from it — Freda was known to even encourage her friends to 'care for David' when, as a married woman, family affairs meant she was temporarily unavailable.

But David was always careful not to have affairs with any eligible women. Marriage with a German cousin would not be wise, politically, but Hannelore was still — just — eligible as a wife. Which meant ineligible as a mistress. Though not, luckily, as a friend.

She observed him and the smile that did not change his eyes. 'David, what's wrong?'

'I have decided I am a poodle.'

She waited for him to explain.

'I am primped by my valet, just like a poodle. All I need is a bow in my hair. And then I am shown off to the world, as if I were the star of Crufts. I make a speech about nothing. A photograph. A poodle would do as much good and probably play the role better than I.'

'I understand,' she said quietly.

'I am supposed to open a garden show this morning. A garden show! Two hours of looking at flower displays and saying, "Jolly good" and "I say, well done, old chap". Do you know there is even talk of having parliament pass a law to forbid me from flying?'

Hannelore waited till he had sat down on the sofa, then took the chair opposite him. One waited for permission to sit in royalty's presence, but after all, Hannelore was a prinzessin, even if there was no longer a German throne.

'I truly do understand, David. You were born to be a king. It is in our blood, our bones, and it has been taken from us as surely as if we had faced a firing squad. Once I, too, thought I would make a difference to the world. And after the war?' Hannelore shrugged. 'I was nothing.' She reached over and took his hand. 'But I am nothing no longer, David.'

'Thanks to this politician of yours?'

'Some are calling him a saviour.'

'Hanne, my sweet, I cannot invite a German politician to England. My father would not allow it. The press would have a field day. I must be Prince Perfect —'

'Then send an emissary to talk to him, assess his views. Someone you trust. Let him meet Adolf Hitler in your place. David, this is a chance for true peace, and not just between our nations. You know the danger of bolshevism as well as I do. No royal house is secure while bolshevism spreads across Europe. Everyone like us is at risk, even if they do not see it, refuse to see it. They drink and dance and laugh as if there is no danger lurking from slums to drawing rooms.'

David looked at her, half serious, half flirting, wholly intrigued. 'Whom should I send?'

'Ah,' she said. 'I know the perfect pair. And so do you.' She moved next to him on the sofa.

Chapter 30

*Life is rarely as expected. This is diverting when you are young. It
is not quite as diverting as you get older.*

Miss Lily, 1913

The library door opened. 'The post has arrived, my lady. Will
you read it here?' Hereward had carefully failed to look curious
when his mistress had arrived an hour earlier than usual for
breakfast, turning the kitchen into a small, speedy circus with
Mrs Goodenough as its ringmaster, conjuring the usual array
of scrambled eggs, coddled eggs on buttered asparagus toast, as
well as thinly sliced liver and bacon and an offer of a ham, or
cheese or fines herbes omelette to replace the kedgeree that took
too long to create in ten minutes. Better no kedgeree at all than a
second-rate one from Mrs Goodenough's kitchen.

'Thank you, Hereward.' She put down her coffee cup. Green
was upstairs, ostensibly cleaning a spot from Sophie's newest
dinner dress and probably sobbing. Nigel, who'd had a bad night,
was breakfasting in bed on toast and tea. Jones was hunting a
girl who was at best a thief and at worst ...

... she would think what the worst might be later. For there,
on the silver salver, were two letters postmarked Madeira.
She recognised the handwriting on neither envelope but knew
instantly who they were from.

She picked up the one in the most delicate hand first.

The SS Lady Grey
Cape Town
My dear Sophie,

   *Once again I must thank you and your sister-in-law for giving
me and John back the lives we thought we had lost forever.*

Sophie skimmed the next page — an easy voyage so far, the
two male nurses hired to care for John were proving excellent,
and the stewards so kind too. She had bought small gifts for
the children — possibly too many, but how could one resist? —
which would arrive separately, and she was always hers, with
love and gratitude, Harriet.

She put the letter on the table for Nigel to read, then, slowly,
carefully, picked up the other, deeply glad Nigel was not here to
watch her as she read it, nor Jones nor Greenie.

My dear Sophie,

   *This is the letter that says what I could not say in France, for to
do so would have implied that I expected you to act upon it. So this
will be posted from Madeira and you will not be able to respond till
we reach Melbourne.*

   *Quite simply, it is this: I love you. I loved you long before
the night of the election. It was you, I think, who brought me
back to who I am, who healed the damaged soul that left the war,
who could not bear four walls enclosing him, much less the scent
of hospitals or antiseptic, who was fit only for the company of
kookaburras.*

   *I had excused myself from the world beyond the gate, you see.
I had seen so much anguish, so much death. Surely I was owed a
life of leaves and birdsong. I expected Harriet to marry again, once
a year or two of grief had passed, and she was well provided for.
I left the world and found a gate to open and close as others directed
me, the simplest of lives a man could have.*

   *The peace healed me, slowly. I might even have returned. But
why should I? I had done my duty, had seen too much. Then you
entered my world. Sophie Higgs, who had seen as much as I had*

170

and yet kept going, fighting not just for the wounded in the war, but for decent lives and decent jobs for them in peace. Sophie Higgs who was beautiful and far more vulnerable than she would ever admit. Sophie, who was both of the world I'd left behind and in my new world too, of gum trees and the glinting river.

I had so many plans that morning. No, I would never have expected you to live in a hut. John would have become Dr Greenman again, a brief source of gossip for a while, but I didn't think you would mind that. Sophie Higgs had not given herself to a man until that night. Why should I doubt you would give yourself to me forever?

Sometimes I wonder what would have happened if I had waited to leave until you woke. Even if that telegram had arrived just two days later. Would you have agreed to marry me? Having agreed to marry me, would you have jilted me for your earl? Or would you have flown to save him, as a friend, but then come back to me? Would you have been happier if you had?

That too is what I couldn't say in France. I do not believe Sophie Higgs married to become a countess. Nor, though I like your Nigel very much indeed, am I confident you would have married him if you had not felt it was necessary to help to save his life and the people of the estate he cares about so deeply.

He told me, you see, while you and Harriet walked ahead with the children, how you had flown to him, cast out his vampire cousin, arranged his surgery and his recovery. He also told me you had refused to marry him seven years before and had insisted that your true home was Australia.

He is a good man, Sophie. But he knows that at some deep level you are not content.

Hence this letter. It is not the missive of a would-be lover. I am not urging you to leave your husband and I never would. Like John and Harriet, I believe marriage is a merging of two lives and not something that can be cast away and another taken up.

I am however, urging you to talk to Nigel: to return to Australia not just for a short visit, but to see if you are happier here, where you are not subordinated to an English estate and title.

I am also trying not to let my longing to see you, and the children, influence me in this, but of course it does. Take that into account too as you consider my advice.

This is a strange love letter, isn't it? I have never written one before. I am not sure I ever will again. There is unlikely to ever be another Sophie Higgs in my life, a woman I not only love but trust and deeply admire, but who could also understand so completely what will probably continue to be brief lapses, when I am in 1917 once more and find it difficult to fight my way back to the present.

Don't worry: I will not pester you by repeating what I have said here. My other letters to you — and there will be more — will be from Uncle Daniel, giving you news of Harriet and John, of Midge McPherson, whom I will visit as soon as John is settled, of Thuringa and the river, and of the life and medical practice I will slowly establish in Sydney.

My darling Sophie: let me indulge myself by saying those words for the last time. I love you and wish you happiness always.

Yours, forever more,
Daniel and John

Two men, she thought. Am I forever doomed to love men cleft in two? Daniel and John, Nigel and Lily. But Daniel had found himself again. And Nigel?

Nigel was happiest as Lily. She knew it. He knew it. In saving Nigel's life and his estate — and by giving him a wife and two children he adored — Sophie had also separated him from who he truly was. And neither of them could admit it to the other.

A door slammed. No one who lived in this house would slam a door. The breakfast-room door opened.

'I've found her,' said Jones.

Chapter 31

*This is the truth no girl ever dreams of: she too will grow a
moustache as she gets older. I recommend a dextrous maid and
cooling toffee spread across your upper lip, which will take the hairs
with it when it is removed. The method is also useful to remove the
hair on your legs. You may think stockings and a skirt will hide leg
hair. They do not.*

Miss Lily, 1913

SOPHIE

Sophie slid Daniel's letter into the desk drawer, then looked at
the girl in the doorway. She raised an eyebrow.

'I am sorry,' said the girl at last. 'I have brought your pearls
back, and the painting.' She pulled the ropes of pearls and then
a roughly folded square of canvas from her coat pocket. 'I hope
you can glue it back in its frame.'

Sophie winced. She knew little about art. She did, however,
know that one did not glue a canvas to its backing or frame and
that a Rembrandt with creases cutting through the oil paint was
worth considerably less than one intact. 'Are you apologising for
robbing me or for hurting your parents who have done nothing
to deserve the pain that you inflicted? Or are you sorry for
worrying us? Or are you sorry only for yourself?'

The girl considered. 'All of those,' she admitted.

Sophie glanced at Jones. 'Did Violette want to come back, or
did you make her come?'

'No one makes me go anywhere!'

'That answers that then,' said Sophie. 'Perhaps you will tell me why you have decided to return.'

'I had nowhere else to go.'

'Ah. Jones, I think Greenie should be here to hear this, don't you?'

'I do,' said Jones grimly. 'And Nigel.' He left the room.

'Tea or coffee?' asked Sophie.

'You haven't called the police?'

'No.'

'And you are offering me coffee?'

'And cherry cake. It is extremely good cherry cake.'

'I know. But I do not know why you do this.'

'I could say because your parents are my friends as well as our loyal employees, and both my husband and I care for them deeply and owe them a lot,' said Sophie slowly. 'But that would not be the whole truth.'

She smiled at Violette, flirtatious, pretty Violette who had not yet learned how one could beguile other women as well as men. Nor had she learned that the most effective charm depended on understanding the person you wished to please or manipulate.

And once you understood, you felt a little of their joy and pain.

'You are a casualty of the war just as much as Hereward, or any other man injured in the trenches. You were born in war and brought up in its aftermath.'

'So you feel sorry for me?' demanded Violette.

Sophie nodded.

'I do not want your pity!'

'Too late. You have it. But pity would not lead me to offer you a home with us, in my home or homes. I like you,' said Sophie simply. 'You remind me a little of myself.'

Violette frowned. 'We are nothing alike. You are rich, and small, and I am tall and —'

'And ruthless, loyal and extremely interesting.'

'Ah,' said Violette. 'Are you ruthless, loyal and extremely interesting?'

174

'I hope so,' said Sophie evenly.

'My father, Mr Jones, says he will teach me jiu-jitsu,' offered Violette.

'Excellent. I will ask him to teach me too.'

'You really intend to study this jiu-jitsu?'

'Of course. Violette, if you choose to give us the loyalty you gave your grandmother and that she gave her comrades, then we will be loyal to you too.' Sophie heard Green's and Nigel's voices in the hall. 'Can you promise us loyalty?' she asked quickly.

'Yes,' said Violette. 'I kept my other promise to you,' she added hurriedly. 'I did not stab anyone at all.'

'Excellent. Now, let us find out why you left and took my pearls — and why you have agreed to return.'

They sat. Violette talked. They questioned. She answered. She had lost her belligerence, Sophie noted, and her bewilderment was real. She had even let Green tentatively kiss her cheek, though she had not returned the embrace.

Which reassured Sophie. This girl, it seemed, did not lie. Trick, steal, mislead and kill, perhaps. But she seemed to have a genuine distaste for dishonesty, instilled, perhaps, by this Grandmère who had made it the work of her last years to kill traitors.

Why had Mrs Maillot — or the woman who had assumed that identity — gone to so much trouble to fool a beggar girl? And why had she been so interested in Miss Lily Shillings?

The question remained as puzzling for Violette as for them all.

'At first I think she might be a thief and wish me to open the door for her here. But then why would she vanish, just when I might do that? The owners of the house were returning, but she could have said that a water pipe burst, and that she must stay at a boarding house till it was fixed. But there is a thing that is stranger. She was ... believable,' said Violette, wonder in her voice. 'Me? I do not believe people so easily. But I believed her.'

'She had found out all she wished to know,' said Green flatly.

'She didn't have to trick Violette to that extent to discover that a woman named Lily Shillings had given birth,' pointed out Jones. 'She seems to have mostly wanted to know where to find Miss Lily once she left here. You're sure you did tell her that Miss Lily is not, in fact, your mother?'

'Very sure. But she kept asking if I had seen Miss Lily and his lordship together. That I do not understand. Are they not friends?'

The other three in the room were careful not to catch each other's eyes.

'I have only one conclusion,' said Violette. She looked at Green. 'You were a spy in Belgium, were you not?'

'Among other things,' said Green.

'This Miss Lily, has she spied too? Is she away, spying now? That, perhaps, is what Mrs Maillot wished to know.'

Nigel regarded Violette thoughtfully. 'Yes,' he said at last. 'Miss Lily, shall we say, "collected intelligence" in the past. Some may believe she still does that.'

Violette clasped her hands in excitement. 'She is still a spy? Are you all, perhaps, spies?'

'You seem to like that idea,' said Jones.

Violette looked at him in surprise. 'Of course. It would be most interesting.'

Nigel smothered a laugh. Violette looked at him in annoyance. 'It is not amusing.'

'My dear girl, do you really think that if we were spies, now or in the past, we would confirm it to a girl we only met yesterday, who intended to kill one of us and who left abruptly in the night stealing the most valuable items she could lay her hands on?'

Violette looked thoughtful. 'No.'

'Then ask that question again in a year, or two years, or however long it takes for us to trust you. The answer will not be quite what you expect,' Nigel added.

'That is reasonable,' said Violette.

'I am so glad you think so,' said Sophie with a slight smile. She looked at her small jewelled watch on its gold chain. 'Luncheon will be served in two hours. You need a bath, and you need to rest. Sleep, then dress for lunch. Your mother has placed some clothes you might like to try on in your room. She did this, I may point out, when she did not know if you would return or not. Luncheon will be served in the dining room, twenty minutes after you hear the gong.'

Violette stood. 'I like clothes. And now you may all discuss me while I am gone.'

'Exactly,' said Sophie. The four of them watched the girl go out, their faces carefully pleasant till she shut the door behind her.

'Bloody hell,' said Green.

Chapter 32

When you say 'I will do what is right' you still have choices. You can refrain from doing wrong: usually a safe choice. Or you can actively do good. The latter invariably involves sacrifice, small or large, and will annoy — sometimes fatally — those who do not care who they harm.

Miss Lily, 1913

'Someone suspects that Nigel and Miss Lily are the same person,' stated Sophie.

Jones cast a worried glance at his friend and employer, sitting impassively on the sofa next to Sophie. 'And Violette's information doesn't help dispel that suspicion.'

'No,' said Nigel quietly. 'But there is no proof. There never can be any proof. Nor will there ever be, as long as Miss Lily never appears again.'

'There might be gossip ...' began Green.

Nigel shrugged. Such a different shrug from Miss Lily's, thought Sophie. 'Only a small amount. What does a little gossip matter? Especially as neither Sophie nor I are social lions, and we don't matter politically. Nor has Miss Lily been seen except by a very few people for fifteen years. But I don't think there will be gossip.'

'Why not?' demanded Green.

'This woman — let's call her Maillot for convenience — went to an enormous amount of trouble to try to find out about Lily. Cultivating a street child who was singing for her supper, finding a house she could take over, ensuring the owners did not return unexpectedly, which would have needed surveillance. I doubt she did that on her own. It is too large an undertaking just to collect gossip.'

'Blackmail?' suggested Jones. 'A woman connected to a great estate had an illegitimate child?'

'Possibly. I almost hope there is a demand, as that would give us answers. I won't pay, of course. Again, if Lily never returns, then there is no one to blackmail.'

'There is the claim that you have an illegitimate sister,' Jones considered. 'These days that wouldn't even make page two of *News of the World*, especially without a photograph of Miss Lily.'

'And where will Miss Lily be?' asked Sophie carefully.

'Where she has been most of the time since 1914. Travelling — we don't know where. I am sure if it's necessary James Lorrimer will provide a false and ultimately frustrating trail for the curious to follow. But you are forgetting something Violette told us yesterday.'

Has it only been one day since the girl set fire to our lives? thought Sophie.

'There are still witnesses in Belgium who will swear they knew Lillian Shillings and worked with her, while the Earl of Shillings was with his regiment in France. They do not like Lillian Shillings, nor trust her, but that very hatred will make them all the more likely to tell a stranger all about her. They have no need to be loyal to her now. But their testimony would be useful if anyone needed to prove that the Earl of Shillings could not be the same person as his half-sister.'

'Nigel ...' Sophie tried to find the right words. She glanced at Jones and Green, and saw her feelings mirrored on their faces. They too loved Miss Lily. And in condemning her to vanish permanently, denying himself even the momentary reclaiming of self he experienced in Paris, Nigel was slicing away who he truly was.

And that was it, thought Sophie in wonder. Why had she never realised? Nigel was the disguise Miss Lily assumed, not the other way around.

'I am so sorry —' began Green.

'Don't be,' said Nigel flatly. 'This isn't Violette's fault. And if you had never taken my identity in Belgium we might be in far worse trouble.'

He stood like a man about to face a firing squad. No, thought Sophie with a stab of sorrow, like a man who had already been shot and all that was left was shadow.

She had to do something. Someone must do something. They could not let Nigel ... Lily ... face this. Surely something could be done ...

The phone rang in the library and, more dimly, out in the hall. Sophie moved automatically to answer it before Hereward did.

'Shillings,' she said.

'My lady?' It was the operator at the exchange. 'I have a Mr Lorrimer on the line. Will you take the call?'

'Yes please. Put him through. James,' she mouthed at the others. Nigel sat again, looking more exhausted than she could remember seeing him since he had recovered from his surgery.

'Sophie?'

'Yes, James. Is something the matter?'

A pause. James Lorrimer remembered, even if she had forgotten, that there might be several operators listening in, and almost certainly were, to hear any gossip about the Countess of Shillings, though of course they would never mention it, except to their six closest friends ...

'Are you free this afternoon? I was thinking of motoring down.'

'Yes, of course. Nigel and I would love to see you. And the twins will be delighted to see their Uncle James,' she added, to make sure the visit sounded totally innocuous to those who listened in.

'Good.' A hesitation, as if James were choosing his words carefully, but needed to warn her just the same. 'A friend of ours is going to ask Nigel and his sister to go to Germany.'

Hannelore? she thought. But James knew Hannelore had already asked many times and, as many times, been refused.

'This will be a request that will be impossible to refuse,' he added. 'You might even call it a ... decree. I thought you should know as soon as possible.'

'I ... see,' said Sophie carefully. 'We'll look forward to seeing you, James. You'll stay to dine, I presume?'

And probably the night as well, she thought, as it would be too late to drive back to London after dinner. Car batteries were unreliable beasts, all too liable to give out on a dark road miles from the nearest farm house and, she glanced out the window, yes, it was snowing again, soft flat flakes of spring snow that would melt almost as soon as they touched the ground. 'It will be good to see you,' she repeated, then put the receiver down.

And to think that only forty-eight hours earlier she had been bored.

Chapter 33

The art of a well-dressed woman is to make her clothes appear the
perfect choice for the occasion, even a nightdress in a ballroom.

Miss Lily, 1913

What did one do with a thirteen-year-old and far too self-possessed young woman while one held urgent talks with Britain's most senior spy master? Neither of her parents could be spared from the discussion.

A journey to the next town, with Samuel at the wheel of the Silver Ghost, so she might buy necessities such as undergarments, shoes and nightdresses, until appropriate ones could be made for her? No. Samuel would probably decide he adored her, which might be somewhere between a nuisance and a potential disaster, and Violette would wonder why her mother did not accompany her.

A riding lesson? But Sophie's riding clothes would be far too small and could not be altered as easily as a loose-fitting evening gown.

Eventually she decided to tell Violette the truth: this was a private meeting and, if appropriate, one day she would be told what they discussed. In the meantime she was to stay in her room and read fashion magazines, marking the styles and colours that she liked, so that when they went to London she might have a clear idea of the style of clothes she wished to have made. To her relief Violette accepted this as an interesting occupation. She even promised to stay in her room until called. 'Or until twenty minutes after the dinner gong. I will wear the mauve silk in my dressing room. It is too small, but I can alter it.'

'You are too young for mauve. A white dress, or lavender perhaps, or even pale blue would be more appropriate. But not tonight. Our guest will stay for dinner but you will dine on a tray in your room.'

Violette considered her. 'My parents are servants. Perhaps I should eat in the servants' hall.'

Sophie doubted Violette truly wished to eat with servants. This was a taunt. 'Your father is his lordship's secretary. It is not appropriate for you to eat in the servants' hall.' Thank goodness, she thought. 'But you will have an excellent dinner, even if it's served on a tray. If you wish for anything else — coffee, cake — pull the bell and a servant will bring it.'

'Anything?'

Sophie sighed. 'I spoke incorrectly. If you wish for tea, coffee, cocoa, bouillon, hot or cold milk, a glass of water, cake, biscuits, crumpets, toast, sandwiches, a bath, towels, a book, magazines or writing or sewing materials, or any similar items, you may ring the bell and ask for them. But please do not do so more than once. It is not fair to the servants to make them run up and down stairs too often.'

Violette nodded. 'I am sorry I ran away last night. This is extremely pleasant.' She looked at Sophie shrewdly. 'Life here may also be most interesting.'

'I profoundly hope it won't be. Excuse me; I must dress for our visitor.'

'May I watch?'

Sophie blinked. But the girl seemed genuinely interested in clothes. Green could give a commentary on exactly what dress was suitable for this afternoon and why; show her how to dress a lady's hair, select a riband, jewels appropriate for this particular visitor, and possibly a dozen other arts Sophie rarely paid attention to.

'If you like.'

'Quite interesting,' said Violette.

James arrived with snowflakes on his overcoat, which he insisted on removing before kissing Sophie on the cheek. 'Will this wretched weather ever end? You look beautiful, Sophie.'

'I feel haggard and harried, and your compliment may have saved my life.' Sophie felt in fact deliciously lovely after the ministrations of Green, and Violette's evident fervent approval, but men enjoyed being told that their mere presence made one feel glamorous. 'We're in the small drawing room. I've asked for soup and sandwiches to be served. I expect you are ravenous?'

'Yes. You are a marvel, Sophie.'

She smiled. 'You almost make me feel that I am.'

Watercress soup, served in a china cup so James did not feel he was eating while others watched him dine alone. Sandwiches of roast beef and horseradish, cheese with lettuce from the greenhouse, and the first of the forced asparagus rolled in well-buttered, thinly sliced brown bread. Sophie nibbled to keep James company; Green and Jones sat and Nigel paced, restless, staring out the window, which was disconcerting. Sophie had known Nigel in many moods, but never restless.

At last he turned, as James put down his cup. 'Well?'

'You are about to receive a royal visit, or possibly an invitation. The first, I expect, as it will be more discreet. His Royal Highness is going to request that you and the woman he now believes is your possibly illegitimate half-sister be his informal emissaries to Adolf Hitler, to assess his abilities and intentions and help ascertain whether His Royal Highness might be advised to offer him support.'

'A Prince of England supporting a German politician?'

'As much as he is able. Influence, rather than financial support. If His Highness sets his mind to it, the influence could be considerable.'

'Nigel *and* Lily,' said Jones carefully. 'The prinzessin has been urging Sophie to convince Lily to see Herr Hitler. Why does His Royal Highness now want them both?'

James sipped tea before he answered. 'I am afraid I can't answer that.'

'You have a watcher in the home of the instigator of this ... mission?' asked Nigel, still over by the window. 'The Prinzessin von Arnenberg, I presume.'

'Yes.'

Sophie stared. 'You are spying on her?'

'Of course.' James looked at Sophie, then at Nigel, with deep sympathy. 'Old chap, it's been a good run — longer than anyone expected — but I think our luck may have run out. The prinzessin suspects that you and Lily are one person. As blackmail devices go, it is about as good as one can get.'

'I see,' said Nigel slowly. 'If I — or we — refuse to go, she holds the threat of exposure. But if Lily goes — and supports Herr Hitler — presumably she will keep quiet.'

'That is what I believe, too,' said James.

'How do you know all this?' asked Sophie quietly. 'I don't imagine His Highness or Hannelore confided in you.' She remembered the prince's tone of voice, describing James's first wife: 'Rich of course, like all that type of person.'

James helped himself to an asparagus roll. 'These are excellent. Our asparagus still has weeks to go.'

'Sophie has our asparagus beds heated with manure pits underneath them,' said Nigel. 'The Prinzessin von Arnenberg was learning how to influence royal Europe while Sophie was redesigning our glasshouse management.'

'And now you are spying on her,' said Sophie bluntly.

'You disapprove?'

'It depends on what you are doing. And how and why.'

'To protect our country, and, for that matter, Nigel too. To give just one example: it seems that the prinzessin arranged to have a woman of some experience persuade a girl, almost a child, to infiltrate your household. The original aim seems to be to find out whether Miss Lily Shillings had a child, as well as her address, her exact relationship to Nigel, or any other material that might be useful for blackmail. I don't know if Violette said something that made the prinzessin suspect you and Lily as one, or she noticed a too-close resemblance before. In these

... modern ... times, an imposture that would seem impossible twenty years ago would be possible, if improbable, now.

The girl did not know what intelligence she was being used for,' James added. 'She was a temporary dupe, nothing more.'

'Have your intelligence networks found out where this young person is now?' asked Jones evenly.

'Here, I presume, as you were seen picking her up and driving her away in your car.'

'No one followed us back here,' said Jones, his tone still mild.

'No. It was assumed there was no need. The watcher was hidden by the fog. I hope this does explain why it seems advisable to keep watch on the prinzessin's plans.'

James took another asparagus roll. 'There is also a butler who reports to me, and a spy hole — which must be used discreetly — in a shadow below a gas lamp in her drawing room, through which conversations can be observed and overheard.'

'And another spy hole in her bedroom?' Sophie was not sure why she was angry on Hannelore's behalf. Hannelore was betraying her, and Nigel too.

'The prinzessin has given no reason for us to think that any supervision of her bedroom might be useful,' said James calmly.

Sophie was silent. Did James know Hannelore had been raped with bayonets? Had nearly died? That she would not only never take a lover, but never bear a child?

Probably, she thought. The essentials, at least, if not the details.

'You know about Violette?' asked Green flatly. Sophie noticed that she did not call him sir, as a servant would do. 'You know who she is?'

'Yes.'

'Then why didn't you tell me my daughter was still alive?' Green was not quite able to keep the anguish from her voice.

'I'm sorry,' said James quietly. 'We only discovered her existence when the prinzessin located her. As she was bound for Shillings, it seemed best to let things unfold naturally, so the girl did not become suspicious, and pass those suspicions on to the woman who called herself Maillot.'

'She intended to kill me,' said Green.

'You are undoubtedly a match for a thirteen-year-old girl. The fact that you are still alive, and unwounded, would seem to support that.'

Green made a small noise, impossible to interpret.

'Miss Green, forgive me. I know this isn't a matter for levity. It is in fact so momentous that I am not sure how to speak of it. Like you, we assumed the child had died. Madame Larresse, the woman who became her grandmother, was a formidable woman. I only wish we had realised what the prinzessin intended to do with the information before this girl came here.'

'It would probably have made no difference,' said Nigel, still impassive.

'But Hannelore can't ever know for sure about you and Miss Lily!' protested Sophie.

'She probably can,' said James. 'Fingerprints.'

'We're not in a Conan Doyle story!'

'Actually the police now use them regularly,' said James mildly.

'Hannelore can't be sure she has Miss Lily's fingerprints, if they were retrieved from any item in a house where Nigel lives too,' insisted Sophie. 'Do you know if she even has samples of Lily's fingerprints? How could she? She hasn't seen her since the war.'

'As far as I know, fingerprints have not been mentioned,' said James. He hesitated. 'Possibly she would not need proof. Gossip does not need any. Any gossip that damages Lily's reputation, that makes her an object of scandal and curiosity, would destroy the entire network we've spent decades creating.'

'The immediate question really,' said Jones, 'is what are we to do about the request to go to Germany?'

Nigel shrugged. 'When one's prince orders you to be his emissary, one obeys.'

'But Nigel, you *and* Lily —'

'It is the only way to make Hannelore doubt what she thinks she has found out. It's possible. You know it's possible. We will meet Lily there. I can meet this firebrand German, and Lily can meet him on another occasion. Glimpses in the distance can even be arranged, with Greenie in play.'

Sophie shook her head. 'Too risky. Tell His Royal Highness that Lily is still travelling, that you do not know how to contact her, that she is, as always, erratic.'

'Not this time. If *both* Vailes do not obey a royal request, Hannelore will know her suspicions are correct. After all, Miss Lily was in England only last night. She cannot have gone far enough today for a message not to reach her.'

Sophie had never seen Nigel like this, not even during the depression before his surgery. It is because Hannelore was one of Miss Lily's lovely ladies, thought Sophie, and has turned on her; because Hannelore is my friend; because Hannelore is sure of this in her own mind, even if she does not have the proof that would convince a court. She can now use this conviction to compel Miss Lily to appear.

Gossip from a Mrs Maillot could be ignored. But gossip from the Prinzessin von Arnenberg, a close friend of both the earl and his wife, a long-time visitor at Shillings? Hannelore would be listened to. Others across Europe, some of them the 'lovely ladies' Miss Lily had instructed in the years before the war, must have also wondered how Lily was actually connected to the Vaile family. They would be fascinated. All of society would be intrigued.

The gossip would spread like jelly on a hot plate. The Earl of Shillings? Is he, or isn't he ...?

Surely Hannelore would not do that to us, thought Sophie desperately. Maybe I can explain, can make her understand ... 'I'll speak to her —' she began.

Nigel shook his head. 'This is Hannelore's life, Sophie. Don't you understand? It is all she has left. She knows that Miss Lily has influence across Europe and she will not give in until her protégé has been given access to it.'

He crossed the room and kissed her head. 'No escape, my dear. It's over the top with this one. But you need not come with us. Stay here with the children, and —'

'No. If you go, I go.'

'We all go,' said Jones. Green nodded. She, at least, had to go, Sophie realised, to help the complete transformation of Nigel to Lily as needed, to even give glimpses of 'Lily' so that others would assume they had seen Miss Lily and the Earl at the same function, a dance, perhaps, or a crowded café. And why would a lady's maid go with an earl if his wife did not travel with him? 'But what about Violette?'

'She will come with us,' said Jones quietly.

'And what do we tell her?'

'The truth, or part of it. That His Royal Highness wishes Nigel to sound out this German miracle man.'

'Ah, that reminds me.' James reached down into his satchel and brought out two documents. He held them out to Jones.

Jones looked at one and then the other, then back at James, his face impossible to read.

'What are they?' demanded Sophie.

'Two birth certificates,' said Jones expressionlessly. 'One for a Violet Jones, born in Shillings in 1915, one for a Violet Green.'

'It is simpler if she legally becomes a British citizen,' said James. 'She is already a British citizen by parentage of course. But this is ... easier. Whichever one of them you wish to use.'

'I don't suppose you brought a 1914 wedding certificate too?' asked Green bitterly.

'No. But one can be procured, if you would like one.'

'Thank you, but that will not be necessary,' said Green.

'As you wish,' said James.

Chapter 34

Remember this my dears: shock passes so does despair. All lives, if they are long enough, contain anguish and tragedy. The scars will remain. But the feeling of utter helplessness will not.

Miss Lily, 1913

Violette did not wear mauve to dinner, nor did she flirt with James. Sophie had decided that she should dine with them, and not on a tray. She needed to see how the girl behaved in public.

Violette sat, quiet and well mannered, in a white, high-necked dress suitable for a girl who had not yet 'come out'. The dress looked as if it might be a pre-war style, hastily refigured for modern fashion. Sophie presumed Green was already planning her daughter's wardrobe.

Just then she didn't care.

Nigel presided at the head of the table, his face pale, his smile in place. Sophie's heart bled for him. Miss Lily had trained her lovely ladies for almost two decades, instilling in them the need for loyalty to each other, as well as giving them the skills of charm and insight that had then been the only tools a woman might wield in the world of men — and the fortitude to use those skills. Now she had been betrayed by one of them.

But it was more than that, Sophie realised. She had never truly understood why Miss Lily had not returned post-war. Yes, she had tried to strengthen the ties between England and Germany, which made her suspect once the war began. But so had many others, including James. The Great War had not been inevitable. Many, or even most, in Germany had no wish for war, and without the German High Command's successful plan for a coordinated and brutal attack on Belgian civilians, the British people might not have been sufficiently moved to support the declaration. Only once they had chosen — or been manipulated — to aid 'plucky little Belgium' could Germany aim for its true target — not France, but England.

Those who had worked for peace had, for the most part, been redeemed politically, as long as they had not declared themselves pacifists during the war, like Ethel's Quaker brother, and even he had been forgiven for the sterling work Carryman's Cocoa had done in feeding the troops.

Had Miss Lily not returned because women like Sophie Higgs, or Ethel Carryman, now had rights that had seemed almost impossible when Miss Lily began her work? They had the vote, the right to earn degrees, to own their own property, and even the ability to enter professions like medicine. Perhaps they would become legislators themselves.

Most women still did not have the ability to use these freedoms: they remained mothers, daughters, servants, wives. But the upper-crust girls Miss Lily had sought out could forge their own lives, if they wished to; if other, older kinds of duty didn't bind them. Perhaps Miss Lily had decided she was no longer relevant to the flappers of today. And, of course, the Shillings estate and its families had needed their earl to help them recover from all they had lost in the war, from their sons to their horses, their sanity or their limbs.

Hereward brought in the roast duck, redolent with sage and onion stuffing, and spring peas, new potatoes. A good meal, that pompous old writer, Samuel Johnson, would have said, but not a meal to invite a man to. (Horrid human being. Why had any hostess ever invited Samuel Johnson to dine again?) But a meal like this also said, 'James Lorrimer is our friend.'

And James is a friend, thought Sophie, watching him engage Violette in the potential delights of the English seaside. Because James too must have wished to use Miss Lily's influence and ability to move relatively unobtrusively in society over the past decade. She might not still wish to hold her court of lovely ladies, but she had two generations of contacts of which he could have made good use since the war.

And James had either not asked or he had accepted a refusal. And James had what Hannelore did not have: proof.

Hereward removed the duck; he brought in chocolate mousse, managing impeccably with his single hand. Samuel followed with the cream.

Only a few months earlier Sophie had sat here with Hannelore. How could you, Hannelore? she thought. Have you any idea what you have done? What damage you can still cause?

Green was just removing the last of the cold cream from Sophie's face when Nigel appeared in his dressing gown. He sat on the corner of the bed till her preparations for the night were complete.

'Greenie dear ...' Nigel touched Green's hand as she passed, then stood up and kissed her cheek. 'It will work out, you know,' he said.

'We've seen out worse,' said Green. She did not sound convinced.

Sophie had never seen Nigel touch Green in all the years she had known them. The master of the house did not touch a lady's maid, except with ill intentions. Green and Miss Lily must have touched, but not Green and Nigel ...

He is already beginning to say Miss Lily's final goodbyes to her, thought Sophie. And as for her ...

She acknowledged now that in marrying Nigel she had thought she would have Miss Lily too. Sophie was not sure how she loved her — not as a mother, and certainly with no schwarmerei or sapphic desire. There are not enough words for love between women, she thought. Sisterhood, comradeship ... none of them was enough.

She sat beside Nigel on the bed and held him. He rested his head on her shoulder, his eyes closed as if he was trying to see the past or even, perhaps, another future.

At last Sophie said, 'We can leave for Australia tomorrow. Have you thought of that? Drive to Southampton, take the first ship on which we can get passage and then travel on to Australia from whatever port we end up in.'

Nigel leaned back against the bedpost. He smiled at her gently. 'I think one of the things I love most about you is your ferocity. Cyclone Sophie.'

'But it's true. We don't have to stay here. We can be gone long before David asks or orders you and Lily to do anything.'

'He is Prince of Australia too.'

'But it would take us weeks to get there. Weeks too before we could get back to England. I suspect David would want to speak to you in private about this, anyway. He wouldn't risk a telegram, or even a letter. The whole point is that no one must know the heir to the English throne is interested in a German politician.'

'We would need to come back to England some time, Sophie. Shillings may run beautifully, but it needs a master. Or mistress. Someone who loves it. This will be Danny's one day too. He needs to know his land. All we'd be doing by leaving now is delaying the inevitable. Even if this Hitler fellow vanishes, as he probably will, Hannelore will find another cause to support. Nor can we risk antagonising her by disappearing before she can put her plans into action.'

He glanced at himself in the mirror, something else Sophie had never seen him do, then looked away. 'We need to do this, Sophie,' he said at last.

'To obey a prince? He's just a man! You are worth a hundred of him. Or to give in to Hannelore's blackmail?'

'No,' said Nigel softly. He took her hand. 'To convince Hannelore she is mistaken. To make Miss Lily safe forever.'

Chapter 35

The test of true beauty comes at fifty. It is then that half a century of expressions have been etched upon the face, be they joy or discontent.

Miss Lily 1913

VIOLETTE

She was not going to meet the prince! This, in Violette's opinion, was unfair. Had not the king himself declared that his son should marry an Englishwoman? Which she was now, according to the piece of paper that officially made Mr Jones her papa.

Violette had even behaved herself most beautifully at dinner, and coffee afterwards, and even at breakfast the next morning. She had not flirted with Mr Lorrimer, though as an expert in susceptible men, Violette was not entirely sure she *could* have enchanted him. But nonetheless, her manners had been most excellent, and where she had not been sure what to do, she had watched her ladyship for guidance. She was entirely respectable enough to meet a prince!

Being Miss Green's daughter might have been an embarrassment, however, had not that most interesting Mr Lorrimer sent within the week yet another two pieces of paper, these ones asserting that her parents had been married and had then divorced.

It was slightly bewildering, suddenly having two parents, neither of whom she wished to kill. Violette even quite liked the man she now called Papa — and being legitimate, as well as having a house which was not quite a palace to live in and being — officially it seemed — the protégée of the Countess of Shillings.

But only slightly. Violette's life had been event-filled from her birth. And now the Prince of Wales would visit! His equerry had called that morning to say His Royal Highness would call in on his way back to Sandringham. An unofficial visit, which meant the staff would not be lined up outside to bow or curtsey to him as he entered the house, so that he could not even catch the eye of the beautiful and now entirely English, almost, young lady, who would be attired most perfectly in white.

She could catch a glimpse of the prince from upstairs, her ladyship had suggested, as long as she was not too visible. She might even help in the nursery, as the prince would quite possibly ask to see the children.

But if he met her there Violette would seem to be a nursery maid. A prince would never marry a nursery maid, nor even make her his mistress. Being a royal mistress was respectable, it seemed from all she had read, even if being the mistress of any other man was not.

Besides, Violette was not a nursery maid, though she quite enjoyed playing with Rose and Daniel, as long as it was always quite clear she would never be a servant, like her mama.

It was impossible not to feel a little contempt for the woman she still thought of as Green, content to serve another woman instead of having a life of her own, as Violette would have, especially as there seemed to be an unlimited amount of Vaile — or Higgs — money that might be spent on finding out what that life could be.

Exactly what her life would entail she had not yet decided. Possibly she might become a couturier, designing garments even more beautiful than those in Paris, or an aviatrix. Or, of course, she could become the Princess of Wales.

This required a plan. The earl, it appeared, was to have a private talk with the prince in the library. The library doors opened onto the terrace. What could be more natural than the protégée of the countess wandering in the orchard and gardens, picking flowers, thus getting prickles in her most flattering white dress, and so needing to enter discreetly through the library door, flowers in her arms and, perhaps, a few tucked in her flowing blonde curls? She would then find in complete surprise that the library was occupied by a young, handsome prince. She would blush, laugh, apologise, offer him a flower …

What prince could resist?

She waited till the car drove up, till the prince had entered. Violette glimpsed him from above the stairs, as her ladyship had suggested. Smaller than he seemed in the photographs and thinner too; nor was he smiling — until her ladyship greeted him.

Men did smile when her ladyship spoke to them, and women too. Even her mother was able to make people smile, though she did not use the art as often as the countess. That deserved further study. But not today.

Violette waited until her ladyship emerged from the library, then slipped down the servants' stair and out into the kitchen courtyard. From there it was an easy stroll to the orchard, full of lichened trees bearing hard green cherries and still miniature apples, pears, quinces and medlars, then through the orchard to the carefully cultivated 'wilderness' with its cornflowers, in full bloom now, and far more suitable for a beautiful maiden's careless gathering than the formal roses from the beds nearer the house.

Violette glanced at her wristwatch, a gift from her parents for all the birthdays she had not celebrated with them — a birthday was something she had not celebrated before, but sounded most pleasant, certainly. She would give the men an hour to talk …

She drifted back towards the house, cornflowers in her arms, matching the blue of her eyes exactly.

The day was warm and, yes, the library's French doors were open. Most perfect. Violette halted at the sound of voices unmistakeably 'discussing'. She would wait for the discussion to be over, for the lull when a prince would welcome the sight of a beautiful maiden emerging like a summer day in winter …

'I say, old chap, you are taking this awfully well.' The prince's voice, high and light.

'I must confess to being mildly curious about this Hitler fellow myself, and a summer journey through Europe, with a few days staying with one of Sophie's oldest friends, sounds delightful. I haven't seen Berlin since before the war.' That was the earl's voice. 'But Sophie simply doesn't understand how close our ties with Germany have always been. Her only experience was during the war and just after it. Besides, she misses home.'

'Australia!' The prince laughed. 'Terrible place. I was black and blue at the end of it. Everywhere I went people swamped me, touching me — or rather swallowing me in a football scrum. Whenever I entered a crowd, it closed around me like an octopus. I can still hear them: "I touched him!" And if I were out of reach, then a blow to my head with a folded newspaper appeared to satisfy the impulse.'

'Hopefully an earl will not elicit the same impulse. But we won't stay in Sydney long in any case. Sophie wants to see her estate again, Thuringa. She calls it the "true Australia".'

'Ah, yes, I am familiar with the true Australia too. Mayor's wives in flowered hats and a million flies ... and the native stockmen! They are the most revolting living creatures I've ever seen, and I have been to Africa and America, and you do see some specimens there, old man. But the Australian darkies are the lowest known form of human beings, quite the nearest thing to monkeys.' The prince seemed to think he had made a joke.

A pause. Violette thought the earl's voice was not quite as relaxed as he wished it to seem as he replied, 'I think Sophie is very attached to some of the native stockmen. Her farm manager is Aboriginal.'

'Not really? Well, Sophie is Australian after all, old chap. No offence meant. You know I adore her.'

'Of course. None taken.'

'At least Australians are good British stock. Some races are simply superior to others, and of course some people too. Even if my own family ... You know about my brother, the one with epilepsy.'

'I was sorry to hear about his death.'

'My dear chap, no need. That is exactly what I meant. The poor boy was close to being an animal towards the end. Degenerates and the unfit should not be allowed to breed, or even live if they are a burden to themselves and society. That is part of the creed of the Hitler chap that interests me. Have you read that book of his?'

'*Mein Kampf*? Yes. The prinzessin sent a copy to Sophie. Sophie doesn't read German but I suppose the prinzessin thought she could have it translated. Or that I'd read it to her.'

'One of my cousins gave it to me. It's the most fascinating work ever written, don't you think?'

'Interesting, certainly.' Violette wondered if the prince could hear the less obvious emotions in the earl's voice. She thought perhaps he did not. Even a prince, it seemed, might not be very bright. 'My German probably isn't as fluent as yours, sir,' added the earl. 'I may have missed the full force of his arguments.'

'Herr Hitler says that if we'd had the courage to kill twenty-three thousand Jews at the start of the war it would have been over in a year. It was the Jewish bankers and war profiteers who kept it going. It's a jolly good point.'

'I'm afraid I don't agree, sir.'

'Even poor bally old Wilhelm suggested that the Jews be gassed. He was right on that point, at least.'

'If I might say, sir —' began his lordship.

It was as if the prince did not even hear him, or had heard agreement, not dissent. 'Degenerates are taking over the world, according to this man Hitler. Sexual depravity of the worst kind. He's correct about that too. Makes one wonder what else he has a nose for, what?'

It was surely time to enter the library. The discussion was over. The earl was increasingly uncomfortable with the conversation, although he hid it well. Violette was sure now that the prince was not the kind to pick up on the feelings behind the polite words.

Possibly, as a prince, he had always assumed that everyone about him agreed with him, and so had never thought that true feelings might be unexpressed.

And suddenly she had no wish to waft in. Life had given her little respect for men who could be manipulated. And it was obvious that this man so easily could be, even if he were a prince, or perhaps because he was.

And he was not kind. It would be interesting to be a princess, certainly. But Violette believed she had at last met two men who were truly kind: her father and his lordship. Even to be a princess she did not want to be bound to a man who was not kind, who could make light of the death of a brother who had epilepsy, like poor Mademoiselle Lamonte in the village. Mademoiselle Lamonte was often dazed and shaky, but Violette had liked her, and Grandmère explained the condition that she suffered from.

Mademoiselle Lamonte had not been an animal. Violette had a sudden image of the prince behind bars in a zoo, an animal himself, and all the people he so unthinkingly classed as animals gazing at him, and throwing him bananas.

She turned and walked quietly back towards the kitchen. She would use the servants' stairs again and present these flowers to her mother, who would be pleased, even though she would also look at her sharply and wonder why she had been given them, for her mother was not someone as easily manipulated as that imbecile prince. But she would, perhaps, accept they had been gathered on impulse.

She might even guess what Violette had intended. But Violette was sure of one thing. The family — including her parents — was about to travel across Europe, to stay in the palace of a princess in Germany. And there was no way Violette was going to permit them to leave her behind.

Chapter 36

It is necessary to tell a child 'no' so they understand what is acceptable and what is not. A man in power, unfortunately, is rarely told, 'No, that is wrong.' He may be chastised when he is a child, but as an adult believes himself wise simply because there is no one to teach him that he is not.

Miss Lily, 1913

SOPHIE

'Well?' asked Sophie, as they waved at the royal car proceeding up the driveway, followed by the two other cars carrying the prince's long-suffering guards. At least she had made sure they'd had a good lunch. David too often simply forgot his attendants, leaving them hungry and thirsty in the car or anteroom.

'We are going to tour Europe towards the end of summer,' Nigel informed her. 'Not the south of France or Paris ...'

'That's rather good — France would be far too hot. Even the fashion houses would be closed.'

'We are to stay at His Highness's request at a hunting lodge by a lake in Germany. It seems Hannelore has arranged it with the owner, for our pleasure.'

'What! Not Dolphie's lodge in Bavaria?' Sophie had a too vivid memory of her 'rescue' of Hannelore after the war, the night she danced with Dolphie, almost agreed to marry Dolphie, before she realised where his loyalties truly were.

'Not Bavaria.' Sophie had never told Nigel about that episode, but she was fairly sure Jones and Green had. His sympathetic tone now confirmed it.

'Why can't we just go to Berlin or wherever this politician is, and get it over with?'

'David says that would be too conspicuous. We need to look as if we are having a simple family holiday. The children will be with us too.' Don't worry. The lodge will be vacated for our use.

'I don't want Rose and Danny in Germany.' Sophie considered. 'Nor do I want to leave them here. Not if we will be away for weeks.'

'It will be more like months. Darling, Nanny is extremely competent.'

'Of course she is competent. But I am not leaving my children.'

Nigel looked at her, amused, as they entered the hallway. 'What about when Danny goes to boarding school?'

'Why should he? I never went to school. And you hated yours. You said it was sheer torture.'

'Darling, that is simply what is done —'

'It is what your family has always done. Mine hasn't. We will argue about it in six years' time,' said Sophie, with the calmness of someone who intended to have her own way. 'And continue to argue about it every time you suggest boarding school. Very well, Danny and Rose will come with us. Herr Hitler will meet us at the lodge?'

'No. Once again that would be too obvious. We will continue on to Berlin then stay with Hannelore for a few days, in her aunt's house. We will meet her politician then.'

'Which aunt? Hannelore has about five hundred aunts scattered through the royal houses of Europe. Doesn't royalty do anything other than breed and marry?'

'Quite a lot, but breeding and marrying are their main occupations. I don't know which aunt yet. David said Hannelore would arrange it all.'

'She has managed him well, hasn't she?'

'Yes.'

Sophie glanced at him as they climbed the stairs to change before dinner. 'What's wrong?'

'If you'd asked me this morning I'd have said David was a friend,' said Nigel slowly. 'A good chap, chafing at not being able to do more for the people he will rule one day. But now ...'

'What did he say that upset you?'

'Nothing much more than things I have heard him say before, though even "not much more" was fairly bad. But it was also the way he said them, as if he didn't even hear when I disagreed. He is too easily influenced, and by the wrong people. And I am not the kind of person he listens to.' Nigel gave her a wry look. 'He is also not desperately bright.'

'You've only just noticed that? I have a feeling you may be exactly the right person to assess Hitler for him. You will at least tell him the truth, and perhaps even get him to accept it.'

'Am I? I don't know. I think David has already made his mind up, after reading that wretched book — or at least believing what Hannelore and others have told him is in it. He won't think differently, no matter what I say.' Nigel attempted a smile. 'He might, however, listen to you.'

'Nigel.' Sophie paused on the step. 'David said something that really did worry you, didn't he?'

'Yes. He spoke of ... degenerates. People like his brother, like your native stockmen ...'

'What! How dare he?' Aboriginal stockmen who refused to work — usually under slave conditions — were no longer chained at any of the properties near Bald Hill. Children with dark skin were even permitted to go to school — if they could live with the prejudice shown there. But it had taken Sophie years of persuasion, and finally, tactful financial bribery, to achieve it.

'Degenerates such as me, if David knew the truth.'

'You are not degenerate,' said Sophie fiercely.

He smiled gently. 'No, my dear, I know I'm not. I have spent my life doing whatever good I can. I am not a saint, far from it, but I've done my duty, no matter what it has cost me.' Nigel met Sophie's gaze. 'I don't think David will.'

Sophie thought of all the engagements David had failed to attend, the cavalier manner in which he left the ceremonies bereft of their centrepiece. So easy to sympathise with him, of course. But duty was duty and it was inseparable from privilege. How could his family trust him with important matters when he conspicuously failed to meet simpler responsibilities?

'When do we leave for Germany?'

'In a couple of months. There should seem to be no connection with our summer in Germany and David's visit.'

'Are we taking Violette?'

Nigel smiled. 'I think so. Best to keep her under our eyes.'

Sophie considered. 'That is probably the safest approach.'

Nigel grinned. 'I noticed her lurking outside the library with an armful of cornflowers. I think she intended to accidentally wander into the library and enchant David.'

'She saw you'd seen her and didn't risk it?'

'No, I am quite sure she had no idea that I'd seen her — there's that small window in the corner that most people miss, but it gives an excellent view of the gardens. It was Violette's own decision not to join us.'

'Why? She's not exactly a shrinking violet. Oh dear, a terrible play on words …'

'She isn't, is she? But I think Violette might be a good judge of character, despite being taken in by the Maillot woman. After all, she has not killed her mother. She even seems to be growing fond of Jones.'

'I'm glad. But you think she didn't like what she heard of David this afternoon?'

'I didn't either,' said Nigel.

Chapter 37

Marriage of course is inevitable — I of all people know how few opportunities an unmarried woman has. But we spinsters do have one advantage. It is much easier to travel with just one's maid and groom, instead of transporting a household.

Miss Lily, 1913

There was much to get done if they were to be away from Shillings for a part of summer as well as winter.

One of the tenant farmers had died, leaving no sons to take on the tenancy. Luckily, despite the war, there were enough younger sons of other Shillings tenants wishing to run a property of their own, but the choice of which was a delicate business for Nigel to negotiate.

Sophie had also decided that their extended time away was a perfect opportunity to electrify the house, with a new battery shed off the back courtyard, as well as to install bathrooms. No more exhausted maids lugging water up one or two flights of stairs.

Each two bedrooms would share a bathroom, except for her own and Nigel's, using space taken from the present dressing rooms, far too large these days now there was no need for crinolines or even the bulk of several court dresses. Her own bathroom would contain that glorious luxury, a shower. Showers were common in Australia, even in quite poor homes, but Sophie had yet to find one in England.

There'd also be a bathroom for the nursery, two small bathrooms made from a disused stillroom for Mrs Goodenough and Hereward, as well as an extra lavatory that all staff might use, and two large bathrooms on the floor that held the staff's bedrooms, one for men and one for women, though with three bath stalls and 'conveniences' in each one.

The staff would no longer have to tread out to the 'bath house' in the courtyard on their designated day once a week, returning shivering with wet hair in mid-winter, nor use the pungent privy behind the courtyard walls. They might not be pleased, however, when Sophie made it clear that they were to bathe each day, not just 'top and tail' in the mornings.

They can fill in the old privy and plant honeysuckle over it, thought Sophie, to remove the memory of its stench.

All this meant long discussions with an architect, carpenters and plumbers — none of whom seemed to agree — as well as an extremely young man who assured her that he and his brother were experienced electricians and showed her recommendations from various great houses to prove it.

She relished the hard work. It would transform Shillings, and lighten the staff's workload enormously — she had ordered electric vacuum cleaners and irons too, and electric heaters throughout the house. Even better, the planning kept her from brooding about the journey to come, and its implications for Nigel and Lily.

In the meantime there were the everyday house and village duties, as well as letters. Wonderful, blessed letters.

Sydney, Australia
Dear Sophie,

Thank you for the photographs of Danny and Rose. Please thank Miss Green for me and congratulate her on her skill with the camera. The photographs of my adopted niece and nephew now sit on my desk.

Yes, I do have a desk now, of reassuringly professional mahogany, and chairs and sofa in brown leather, in very satisfactory rooms in Macquarie Street, with a view of the harbour if one leans out the window. I even have patients, thanks to the good offices of Mrs Midge Harrison, who has testified to her contacts within the Country Women's Association that I am 'just the ticket' for men suffering what the British government forbade us to call 'shell shock'.

It is not the practice I planned to have here, but Midge is correct. It is the one I am perhaps best suited for. It requires no Freudian nor Jungian analysis, but an understanding and even experience of causes and effects. It also helps when I confess that I too suffered from the malady, and still do at times, and how I learned that living in the present is the best antidote to the anguish of the past.

Anecdotes like the tale of Rose and the toy elephant you sent me in your last letter help greatly in making one feel it is 1929, not 1917 — thank you, I treasure both the story and the letter. Please tell my niece I have every sympathy — if someone had promised me an elephant and then given me nothing but a knitted toy I might well have tried to drown it in my custard too. Like Rose, I also detest custard.

I have promised Midge to spend a Friday to Monday with them. She seems to have coped with my transition from John to Daniel Greenman surprisingly well, as have all my other friends there. It is extremely moving how easily they have accepted me.

My brother is progressing excellently, though I am sure Harriet has already told you all the news. The setback on the voyage here seems to have settled now that he is back in familiar surroundings. He has forged a friendship with one of the cattle dogs. It sleeps at his feet during the day and is even allowed inside! But I think Harriet is glad of anything that gives him happiness, even a cattle dog in the parlour.

Several of the stockmen also bear major legacies of the war. I think that has helped the local people accept what John looks like now; nor is he left alone among people who cannot conceive of the years he lived through.

Thank you once again for the photographs and the stories of your children. Give them their adopted uncle's love and do enjoy your summer in Europe. I am just one of many, however, who look forward to your family's visit home this winter.

Midge is already planning the welcome home and 'meet the earl' lunches — plural, of course, though it will be some weeks before she is prepared to share you with the neighbourhood, no matter how excited they are over the visit from aristocracy. I have even managed to bathe in some of Nigel's reflected glory. One small girl asked me if you have golden chamber pots. I told her your golden pots are kept for extremely special occasions. Please do not disillusion her!

I am so very much looking forward to your homecoming.

Yours truly,

Daniel Greenman

Sophie read the letter for the fourth time since it had arrived two days earlier. She was more concerned by what it did not say than the words on the page. Daniel had not mentioned where he lived, nor that he had been making new friends, only visiting the old ones he had known as John. Maybe he thought she wouldn't be interested. More likely there was little to say. This new life must be almost as difficult for him as for his brother. His brother had Harriet's help. Daniel had no one closer than Bald Hill.

She put the letter back in the drawer and picked up her pen from the stand again. There was much to sort out before they left, including instructions to Cousin Oswald at Higgs Industries in Australia, and to Mr Slithersole in the London office.

The new line in baby food was proving popular, and she wished to move from simple stewed fruits to 'Baby's Chicken Dinner' and 'Beef and Vegetables', both of which could be produced using the same factory equipment as the corned beef that had been the foundation of the Higgs empire.

Which reminded her: she must have all business mail directed to Mr Slithersole while they were away. She also needed a competent secretary — one who could take dictation and type — waiting for her in Sydney. So much to organise ...

Sophie Higgs had set out for Europe nearly four years earlier with a small satchel, though she had accumulated more luggage on the way. The Countess of Shillings and her family, it appeared, must travel not just with trunks of clothes, her maid and her husband's secretary, but her own butler, a chauffeur, Nanny, and Amy as a combination nursery and lady's maid in training.

The library door opened. 'Are you free to see Mrs Goodenough, your ladyship?'

'Thank you, Hereward. I am always free for Mrs Goodenough.' Sophie turned and smiled at the cook–housekeeper.

Mrs Goodenough had kept her supplied with cherry cake and much else during the war years and through 1919, that even harder period before the Armistice finally ended the war with the Treaty of Versailles, her hospitals full of influenza victims, as well as those still recovering from war injuries. But Sophie had already visited the kitchen that morning to meet the new kitchen maid — Green's second cousin twice removed, and Hereward's niece — and to approve the day's menus (family meals as, hopefully, no visitors would suddenly decide to arrive in their wretched motorcars). What could Mrs Goodenough want now?

'I'm sorry to disturb you, your ladyship,' Mrs Goodenough gave the short bob that always embarrassed Sophie, though she supposed those born aristocratic hardly noticed it. 'But it's about this new electric stove that's coming while you are away.'

'Yes, Mrs Goodenough?'

'It's just at my age, your ladyship — well, I'm not getting any younger and learning how to cook all over again at my age …'

'Truly, there is nothing to worry about. I'm assured that the electric stoves work exactly the same as the wood- or coal-fired ones. You just set the temperature you wish. So much cleaner and less work. You'll fall in love with it by the end of the day.'

'Yes, your ladyship.' Mrs Goodenough did not sound convinced.

'And the electric lights will make life so much easier. No more changing the gas lanterns every few days, or trimming wicks …'

'But what if the house blows up, your ladyship?'

'Why should it?'

Mrs Goodenough shook her head. 'I've seen pictures from that power company, your ladyship. It's got a bolt of lightning on it. It was lightning that burned down old Trueman's cottage twenty years ago.'

'This is ... harnessed lightning, Mrs Goodenough. Perfectly safe.'

'At least there will be no danger to the family with you all away, your ladyship.'

Was that a thinly veiled, 'It's all right for you — we are the ones who will get burned in our beds'? But, no, Mrs Goodenough seemed truly glad the family would be safely far from Shillings if there were an explosion.

Sophie gave a reassuring smile. 'You will love the Frigidaire too, and the bathrooms. No more carting water to the bedrooms. I'm sorry that the construction will make a mess.'

A slight bristle at that. 'Nothing we can't handle, your ladyship. I promise all will be immaculate when you return.'

'I know it will be. You are a treasure, Mrs Goodenough, and one for whom his lordship and I are grateful every day.'

Sophie turned back to her correspondence as Mrs Goodenough left, pride, at least temporarily, overcoming trepidation. And surely she *would* find life far easier after the electrification of the house?

Sophie only felt slightly guilty that she would miss all the noise and dust. While she suspected the bathrooms would take at least twice as long to construct as the builders promised — no builder she had ever met managed to keep to schedule — surely all would be done by the time they returned from Australia.

Nigel had promised her a whole six months in Sydney and at Thuringa. She longed to see Maria again and Midge, to introduce her children to Thuringa. To see Daniel, said a whisper ...

She picked up her pen once more.

Darling Ethel,

    That visit by the police sounds truly terrifying, though luckily for them, not you. The officer has obviously not met anyone like Miss Ethel Carryman before.

    Don't you dare get arrested for peddling contraceptives but, if you do, please get a message to me so I can bail you out. If we have left for the Continent, I am enclosing the card of Mr James

Lorrimer, who I am sure can arrange for your release. I will even
have a quiet word with him, saying you will contact him in an
emergency and explaining all the sterling work you have done, and
still do.

I am quite serious, my dear — your work is too valuable to
have you wasting away in prison and, if you do wish to stand for
parliament again, a criminal conviction may stand in your way.

I must say though, I did smile at the vision of the embarrassed
police constable asking you in strictest confidence about —

'Your ladyship, I'm sorry to interrupt but ...'

'Yes, Nanny?'

'Mr Hereward says there is no need to take the children's
quilts to Germany, your ladyship.'

'I am sure Mr Hereward is correct, Nanny. The lodge and
house where we will be staying are sure to have whatever bedding
we require.'

'Fleas, your ladyship,' said Nanny darkly. 'And bed bugs and
worse. You should have seen what the men brought back after
the war.'

'That was ten years ago, Nanny. I am sure they have ...
cleaned things up by now. But the children will need travelling
rugs in the car. They can be used on beds as well if necessary.'

Nanny looked reassured. 'An excellent suggestion, my lady.
Thank you, my lady. But I will stock up on flea powder, just in
case.'

Sophie finished her letter to Ethel, then dipped the pen in the
inkwell once more.

Dear Midge,

*Congratulations on your record price for a ram! I am glad Harry
is so chuffed. Please tell him how pleased I am about the new fire-
tanker too. It was indeed a sterling effort ...*

'Your ladyship!' The voice seethed with justified indignation.

'Yes, Violette?' Sophie placed the pen in its holder once more.

The girl radiated innocence and anguish. 'I promised I would tell you if I planned to leave again, your ladyship.'

'Do you plan to leave?'

'I must! I do not wish to, but she is impossible! To live like this — I cannot do it!'

'Your mother is the impossible one, I presume?'

'Who else? Just because I went to the fair in the village with a boy — a most respectable boy, the son of the grocer who delivers to us here — she tells me it was not a proper thing to do, that I ought to have asked her permission and your permission. I cannot live like this, like I am a child ...'

'Your mother might have been worried the young man might ...' Sophie hunted for innocuous words.

'Have tried to kiss me? Molest me? He is a nice boy! And, besides, I have my knife.'

And Violette knifing a young man who tried to put his hand under her skirt would have meant ... Sophie was glad she didn't have to pursue exactly how much trouble that would have meant. But there was another matter as well.

'I think your mother might hope for a more ... suitable alliance for you than with a grocer's son.'

'Ah.' Violette was arrested by this suggestion. After some thought: 'I did not think of that. It is difficult, your ladyship. I thought because my mother is a servant I am lowly born, but she is a superior servant?'

'A most superior one, and your father is a gentleman.' Or is now, thought Sophie, despite his humble antecedents. Jones had spent enough time as both butler and batman to assume both the accents and demeanour of a gentleman, as Green could those of a lady. But it was difficult to work out exactly where a child of theirs stood in Britain's decreasingly rigid class system. Anywhere she wished to stand, quite probably.

On the other hand, she could not imagine Violette contentedly married to a village grocer, though she could quite see how the grocer might have hopes of an alliance with the 'big house' for his son.

'You can marry anyone you please I think, Violette. But if you wish to do so you must guard your reputation.' Yes, that was a tactful way to put it. 'If you associate with a grocer's son, people will think you should marry a grocer's son. But in the next year you will meet businessmen, politicians, aristocrats and after that property owners in Australia. They would not be impressed if they heard you had walked out with a grocer's son.'

Violette sat, her anger forgotten. She had also apparently forgotten one did not sit unless one's countess had given permission. 'I am going to like Australia, I think. May I learn how to use a boomerang?'

'I ... I don't think anyone at Thuringa has any. They are used further north, I believe.'

'That is a pity. They look a most useful weapon. I have been practising riding, your ladyship, so I can ride with the cowboys.'

'Excellent. But we call them stockmen.'

'I have read every book in the library about Australia too. I promise I will take care of Rose and Daniel if we are held up by bushrangers.'

'I am sure you will. Violette, I suspect if you apologise to your mother she will apologise to you. Then you can tell her that I think that you and she should go to London to fit you for evening dresses.'

'Ones with no bosom, like you wear?'

'I think you mean low cut. No, low-cut evening dresses will not be suitable until after your debutante year and after you are presented to the queen —' Sophie stopped at the expression on Violette's face.

'I will be presented to the queen? Like the girls in the illustrated papers?'

Sophie had not really considered the matter. But there was no reason why Violette should not be presented at court. Ironically Sophie herself had been presented informally, as her family was in trade. Violette, as the daughter of a secretary, was — theoretically — more acceptable. And surely David would arrange it for them — anyway it was at least four years away and by then Violette might have decided to lead an expedition up the Amazon ...

'Yes,' she said recklessly.

Violette bounced three times, kissed Sophie's cheek and ran out. She must really find the time to teach the girl how to walk or, rather, float like a swan. Swans could float extremely quickly if necessary ...

'Your ladyship, the vicar wishes to know if you might be free to discuss using the grounds for the summer fête in your absence ...'

Sophie closed her eyes briefly. All this just to meet a minor German politician, leader of a party that had one seat in the German parliament, who, in ten years, everyone would probably have forgotten.

She forced the perfect, vicar-meeting smile to play on her face. 'Of course. I am always free for the dear vicar. Thank you, Hereward. Please show him in. Would you mind ringing for tea too? I'm sure Mrs Goodenough will have some of the meringues he likes ...'

Hereward coughed neatly. 'There is also the matter of awarding the prizes at the Ladies' Guild Sale of Work, your ladyship. As you won't be in residence my aunt wishes me to ask if you could present the prizes earlier.'

'When would that be, Hereward?'

'Next Tuesday, your ladyship. I apologise for presuming, your ladyship.'

'Not at all, Hereward.' Sophie discovered yet another smile, though if this kept on her supply might dwindle. 'I'm always delighted to support our wonderful Ladies' Guild ...'

Chapter 38

Who am I? My dear, ask me that again when you know who you truly are.

Miss Lily, 1913

Violette stepped into the library as if she had every right to be there, which indeed she did, though not, perhaps, to sit at the desk and open the as yet unsealed envelopes of her ladyship's correspondence.

Violette liked the library. The smell of leather-bound books and the neatsfoot oil with which their covers were rubbed each spring by an elderly expert gentleman who came from Oxford especially for the task; the lavender furniture polish; and the early roses that now stood in vases around the room. Mostly she enjoyed the scent of leisure. A room like this was maintained because those in this house had time to use it.

Violette liked Shillings. She admired her ladyship; she respected her father; she liked his lordship; and she accepted her mother. She took deep delight in the dresses and accoutrements suitable for a young lady, and even more in those that were not suitable now but that one day she would wear. The meals were superior even to Grandmère's, which was an accomplishment she had not thought England capable of (neither had Grandmère).

But Grandmère had deserted her, just as her mother had done. True, neither was at fault. But Violette knew that security lay in relying only on oneself. Which was why she had taken to slipping into the library before Hereward collected the mail to learn a little more each day about this new and complex world in which she had found herself.

She opened the first letter.

My dear Emily,

Thank you so much for your invitation to the Elizabethan Ball in aid of the orphans of British Officers. I am sure it will be a credit not just to your organisational genius but to your compassion in aid of such a worthy cause. Sadly Nigel and I will be travelling on the Continent, but please accept this as a token amount towards the cause ...

Not interesting at all, except for the size of the bank draft enclosed. Violette's life had been bounded in francs and pennies. Now, it seemed, hundreds of pounds were no more than threepences. She picked up the next envelope. Ah, a fat one and going to Australia too.

Dearest Midge,

Another English spring has been and gone! Every year I forget how extraordinary it is — the thousand shades of green, the bees drunk on blossom, the air like wine, bare fields suddenly sprouting grass and sheep and cows back from their sheds and enclosures. But of course you would know this as you have experienced several English springs. You seem so much part of the land I love that it seems impossible you grew up in New Zealand and went to school here in England for a while.

Spring is finally summer and, even more finally, we are almost ready to leave for our German summer holiday. I thought for a while we might have to hire a dozen charabancs to fit us all in but that, it seems, would be déclassé for the household of an earl. Our trunks and footmen will be sent ahead, with only the bare essentials in two cars to care for us — like a butler, maid, nanny, nursery maid ...

It should be exciting but I am not excited, just mildly harassed. I think the time has come to engage a housekeeper. Mrs Goodenough served her dual role while Nigel did not entertain and there was no family here, but I have always had the luxury of others to look to household duties and am extremely bored with those I am having to direct.

I know this is not a tactful complaint to make to a farmer's wife (will we ever have a time when a woman who farms and has a husband will be known as a farmer too — which you most certainly are!). But truly, your cook, kitchen maid, gardener and Mrs Siggs who comes in to 'do the rough' are really all that a good household needs. It is just that our household is so much larger.

It was lovely to hear about your 'brats'. Please tell Lachlan he has my full permission to pot rabbits on Thuringa. My own brats are thriving, despite Rose's recent adventure. Nanny said she looked away for only two seconds and Rose was gone. Violette discovered her in one of the dog kennels, sharing the inhabitant's bone. Or, rather, not sharing it. The poor animal looked quite put out.

I do love having children. It's strange — I never thought I would. Or, rather, I never thought I wouldn't, but didn't see them as a major factor in my future happiness — and yet they are.

Violette is becoming one of the family, though I am concerned about her. She should be at school, but has stated she does not want to go, and what Violette doesn't want, she doesn't do. Nor can I see her as a teacher, nurse, lady's companion or typist, which usually only leaves marriage. But she is still young and Nigel says she is quite capable of choosing her own future, if we let her see enough of the world to choose what it will be.

I have married a wise man, Midge, just as you have. We are both blessed with our husbands.

Only three months now and I will see you again, and Nigel, Rose and Danny will be with me and you can meet them too. We will return briefly to London to do some business there before we board the ship and sail from Southampton, but won't come down to Shillings, which may still be in the hopefully not too appalling chaos of electrification and installing bathrooms.

Home! I cannot tell you how much I'm longing to hear cicadas again, or show Danny and Rose emus and kangaroos.

Please give my love to Harry, and to your 'brats', and to you always,

Sophie

PS Giggs and Timothy visited us for a few days last week — both thriving. Giggs sends her best wishes.

PPS Would you like a cuckoo clock? I gather they are rather the thing where we will be staying.

Violette put the letter back thoughtfully, then crossed to one of the leather armchairs so anyone who came in would never suspect she had been at the desk.

Interesting. Violette had not realised her ladyship was still so Australian. She had thought it was something that her patroness had cast off, like a moth-eaten cardigan, when she married. Why would a countess want to return to a land at the bottom of the world? Soeur Marie had shown them Australia on a map. It was far away from everywhere. It had much desert, and animals that jumped, and the most poisonous snakes in the world, which sounded most interesting, and must make the inhabitants either brave or extremely careful and possibly both. Admirable, but not a land you would long for.

And yet her ladyship did.

The words her ladyship had written about Violette herself were interesting too. Violette approved of the sentiments. She would indeed find her own way, but she was not sure that it would include marriage.

The most interesting part of that letter had been what was not in it. Her ladyship had made no secret that she did not wish for this 'holiday'. But she had not told the woman who seemed to be one of her closest friends that the true purpose of going to Germany was so that his lordship could assess a German politician for the prince.

Violette had been told this was confidential, a matter only for the earl, his wife, her parents. But something else was planned too for this venture. She did not know what. She even felt that perhaps her ladyship did not know what it might be, either. But she had come across earnest discussions between his lordship and her parents, who broke off when they realised she was near.

She must find out. The betrayal by Mrs Maillot still hurt — not just that she had given affection to one who did not exist, but that she had been fooled. Violette had never been fooled before. She did not intend to let it happen again. Ignorance too often led to death.

The sound of the luncheon gong echoed in the hallway. Violette smiled. She had visited the kitchens that morning. Luncheon would be trout au bleu, from the stream in the Shillings park, dill sauce and new potatoes, with asparagus and strawberries from the gardens and cream from the home farm dairy. This was most superior to toasted cheese at the Worthy's Teahouse.

This afternoon she would ride with her ladyship and her father about the estate, then play with the children for a pleasant hour. Her mother, inevitably, would then find a useful task for her to learn, like removing a soup stain from silk.

And through all of these activities she would listen. Violette was good at listening. For the time might come when she would have to decide whether to disappear once more — for a time, or permanently perhaps — or play a part in whatever his lordship intended.

This house was most pleasant, and the family too. But she had no solid role there. Being called a 'protégée' meant nothing. Parents who had done without a daughter for nearly fourteen years might well decide they had no need of one again, especially as they now had the legal power to compel her to go to school (as if a school could keep her!), or to apprentice her (the same) or simply leave her at Shillings while they adventured across the world.

Ignorance had cost Violette's adopted aunts their lives; nor had Violette been able to save Grandmère. Grandmère had been good to her, and Violette had loved her, but Grandmère also had made no provision for what might happen to Violette after her death.

Violette had no intention of ever trusting anyone else to decide her fate again.

Chapter 39

Summer strawberries, the wild ones gathered in the forest, not the cultivated ones ... every life should have just a little gluttony, my dears. How can you understand the desires of others if you do not indulge just a few yourselves?

Miss Lily, 1913

SOPHIE

The German fir trees made a dark tunnel above the road as the two Shillings vehicles bowled along it, stopping only twice for flat tyres and then a boiling radiator, competently attended to by Lloyd, Hereward's youngest brother, only twenty and therefore unscathed by nightmares of war, and still with limbs and lungs intact. He glowed with an innocent joy each time he tended to a motorcar.

This road had, of course, not been built for motorcars. It was even more unsuitable than most, with many stretches almost too steep for the cars to manage at all. The third time the Silver Ghost faltered the adult passengers got out; the drivers, Jones and Hereward, unloaded the luggage and carried it to the top of the hill, while the family and the females walked.

The trees thinned as the walkers reached the crest, revealing a small alpine meadow open to the sun and occupied by four giant pale-brown cows, each wearing a bell that jangled like a more emphatic version of the Thuringa bell birds back home.

The grass there was too green. The German hills were green too, dappled occasionally with deer that looked like they had been crafted as 'Souvenirs of Germany', and the snow-capped mountains in the distance were far too regular and foreign.

The longing for home overtook her again. Sophie hungered for the stocky dark brown and white Australian Herefords; she craved trees whose branches did not form an almost impenetrable canopy, but instead angled their leaves to present as small a face to the moisture-sapping sun as they could. She also needed friends, she realised, and not just via letters.

The last four years had given her a husband, and children, and she still had the companionship of Greenie. She loved all of them, and Jones, and her Shillings family. But Greenie was decades older than her. These last four years had been spent almost entirely without the company of friends of her own age. Those she had in England were too far away, and too occupied with their own projects, to share tea and much needed conversation.

At least there would be Midge back in Australia. But when they returned to Shillings she needed to reassess her life. Retirement from the society of the world might suit Nigel. It did not suit her. Though there were no other 'great houses' near Shillings, that did not mean she might not find female companionship among the professional or business classes from which she'd come. If that lowered her social rank within fashionable England, they could lump it. Perhaps she needed a flat in London, or a club. Opening Shillings House was far too extravagant an ordeal, but staying at a Women's Club for a few days each month, to attend to business directly at the Higgs office, and to catch up with Sloggers, Ethel, and yes, even Lady Mary, would be good ...

The unburdened cars crept, complaining, up the road till they reached the crest too. A cow made a sound that was somehow not the decorous 'moo' of English cattle, nor the longer, stroppier sound of Australian livestock. Sophie looked around the meadow. The cows were moving to the other side, their bells clanking, and there was a convenient absence of cow droppings there by the road. 'Luncheon!' she called.

Four picnic baskets, five picnic rugs, a scatter of cushions, one teddy bear and one stuffed zebra, both with chewed ears, and two small children in knitted reins to stop them investigating the cows too closely, were relocated to the meadow. Violette and Green unpacked the baskets while Jones and Lloyd decided the cars should make several journeys to the hunting lodge carrying a small part of the luggage each time, returning finally for the passengers.

'It can't be far as the crow flies,' said Jones, map in hand.

'Pity we're not crows,' said Green, as Violette fluttered her eyelashes at Lloyd, who was, fortunately, very focused on the Silver Ghost and not on an attractive young lady clad in a dust-coat and veiled hat. 'Here, you'd better take this to the others.' Green pointed to the fifth basket, intended for the servants' luncheon. Apart from her, and Nanny and Amy still holding the children's reins, the servants would tactfully eat on the other side of the line of cars. Jones would sit with the servants so that he and Lloyd could discuss the cosseting of cars.

'What is it today?' asked Jones resignedly. Sophie had given up scandalising European hotel kitchen staff by trying to persuade them that their Shillings employees should eat the same food as the family. Indeed, their own luncheons took so long to unpack, eat and pack again compared to the fresh rolls regarded as appropriate chauffeur food that if the staff ate as their employers were supposed to, they'd have only travelled half the distance each day that had been planned.

'Fresh rolls — brown of course — cold sausages and cheese again, and I slipped in a few bars of chocolate. I might even save you an apple.'

'You are a wonder of a woman.'

'And don't you forget it,' said Green.

Sophie removed her dust-coat and veiled hat — thank goodness the fashion for pale limbs had vanished with the war — and lay back on the grass. A dandelion brushed her cheek, blown out to grey fuzz.

'Mama?'

'Ooph.' Sophie tried to sit up again — but Rose sat on her stomach, Danny on her feet ...

'Mama play ball?'

'After lunch, darling.'

'Play ball now.'

'Lunch first, Miss Rose,' said Nanny firmly.

Sophie lifted her daughter off and sat up to gaze at the last hotel's concept of a luncheon for aristocratic travellers — cold chicken; quails roasted in grape leaves; a galantine of duck already beginning to melt in its jar — all of which showed more experience with picnics on castle lawns than ones held fifty jolting miles away. There were also bread rolls — white, for People Who Matter, salade russe, a hunk of Roquefort and another of brie, late-season asparagus and early-season apples, a mess that was for one disconcerting second remnants in a surgeon's bucket and then resolved into what had been sponge cake with raspberries and cream. It would probably still be delicious spooned up with the cutlery they had brought from home, for Heaven forfend that an earl should dine by the roadside with a fork that did not bear his crest, just as the (crestless) Shillings china occupied the third basket.

Champagne, wrapped in damp napkins, and barley water for the children; and stone jars of ginger beer, still cold …

Sophie accepted ginger beer and gazed at her family — Nigel, shadowed eyes, but smiling as if concerned about nothing except helping Violette to asparagus; Violette, sitting between Nigel and Sophie, which coincidentally put her as far away as possible from Green; Nanny feeding Danny mashed carrots and potato and Amy dabbing at Rose with a napkin as she gnawed at the leg of chicken she insisted on holding herself.

She wished she could tell Nanny that self-reliance was more important than neatness; but Nanny would not believe her, especially not when it concerned a girl.

The sun in the midsummer sky was still deceptively high when lunch and the ball game were over, and they descended in the motorcars again. This time only one flat tyre marred their progress.

Alpine meadows gave way to fir trees again, then fir trees to beeches, all lime-green dapples, all shadows and sunlight, and then at last two gateposts topped by lions. They had arrived.

The driveway curved among trees that were more regular now, with glimpses of a lake that also seemed too impossibly beautiful to be natural, with a small island just off centre, topped by what looked like ruined Roman columns. Swans swam by, looking as perfect as if they had been painted. The drive curved again ...

'Oh, my,' said Sophie.

They had been promised a hunting lodge. This was a castle, the kind made from icing sugar for an indulged child's birthday party (her own at eight years old, for example). Four turrets, long winding steps leading to a perfect door, yet all in miniature, no larger than Shillings. And yet something was missing ...

Sophie glanced at Nigel. He grinned. 'What is the one thing a real castle always has?'

She shook her head.

'Defence walls. Turrets were first designed as lookouts for pouring boiling oil on your enemies. Narrow windows were created so archers could fire out and not be hit. Low doorways mean you can easily top off the head of an intruder. This imitation was built about forty years ago, I'd say.'

'Why forty?'

'That was when Ruffi's father married his mother. American. Her people made their money in margarine and custard powder, I believe.'

'Is that more or less respectable than marrying an Australian corned-beef heiress?'

'Corned beef is far superior to margarine and powdered custard, my darling, as are you. Ruffi's parents died when the Russians took their estates in 1916. They were Hannelore's neighbours. Drat,' he added. He nodded towards the front door.

'Hello, hello,' said Sophie. 'What have we here?'

The staff were lining up, the butler and housekeeper at the head of a line stretching down to the tweeny, or whatever the German equivalent was. And the man in a red velvet waistcoat and green cravat must be their host — a host they had been assured they were not going to have.

'I thought we were supposed to have this to ourselves for the month.'

'Either Hannelore lied, or our host has changed his mind. Meanwhile, we pretend we expected this all along,' said Nigel quietly.

Jones braked, but let the castle servants open the doors for Sophie and Nigel.

'Ruffi, old chap.' Nigel shook hands with the man in the red waistcoat. 'Absolutely top hole to see you again. We met at the Embassy in 1912, wasn't it? May I present my wife, Sophie?'

'Charmed, my dear.' The heels clicked. The mouth pressed to her hand was wetter than the occasion demanded. Ruffi was forty, perhaps, and just beginning to be rotund. His eyes sagged sleepily in wrinkles that Sophie suspected came from nightclubbing, not the open air. 'You have captured a beauty, Vaile. But then your family always has.'

'Thank you so much for your hospitality, Count von Hegenhof,' said Sophie.

'Call me Ruffi, my dear. Everybody does. Especially as our wretched government has banned all titles. Not that anyone pays attention ...' Ruffi ushered them through the lines of curtseying and bowing servants. Sophie cast a glance back at the children and Green and Jones. Even the twins were being bowed and curtseyed at. But there was nothing she could do politely except be ushered inside.

A hall, with a giant fireplace either side, large enough to roast the many oxen that had undoubtedly met just such a fate; a long staircase at the far end with too much gilt on the banisters; carved doorways leading left and right; and all about them trophy heads, taxidermied on the walls: deer, with antlers and without, two bears, a surprised-looking elephant, a lion, despondent, three tigers ... and yet Nigel had said the castle was only forty years old.

'You hunt?' she asked Ruffi. He bent close to her, just slightly too close. 'Confidentially, my dear, my father bought them all from a Jewish importer before the war. The old man couldn't hit a wall at ten paces and nor can I. But what is a hunting lodge without trophies?' Ruffi smiled. 'My interests are different.' The eyes were half closed in a look that was not ambiguous at all.

An hour later Green had dressed Sophie for dinner. Her clothes had been carried up in the trunks, supervised by Hereward, and they had already been pressed and hung by the castle staff. That night's garment was one of her more formal gowns — one she had expected to keep for Berlin, with silver lace over burgundy velvet, shoes in matching fabric — and she wore her diamonds: necklace, bracelet and a brooch pinned to a feathered toque for her hair, suitable for a formal dinner with one's new host, for she would not otherwise have worn diamonds in the country.

It could be worse, she thought. Her room adjoined Nigel's. Hereward had obviously insisted that Green, Jones and Violette be installed nearby, not in the servants' quarters two floors up, and Nanny and the twins were down the hall. They seemed, in fact, to have all this floor in this wing of the house to themselves, ensuring at least a degree of privacy — there was even a small private sitting room across the hall from Sophie's bedroom.

We can tolerate this, she thought, as the gong boomed for dinner. Not that they had any choice. But if this were a prison, it was a delightful one. The 'castle' even had central heating and bathrooms with mahogany, porcelain and gold fittings, presumably demanded by the American margarine heiress and, possibly, thought Sophie, considered suitable for an Australian purveyor of corned beef.

Hannelore would have suggested a 'holiday' in this place for a reason, before their meeting with Herr Hitler. But, on reflection, she doubted Ruffi's castle was meant to remind her of her place as a member of the nouveau riche. For all Hannelore's machinations, she still believed the prinzessin liked her, that she was even, in some deep way, loyal to her and to Miss Lily too.

Perhaps this was merely to be the holiday it appeared, a way of separating their lives in England from their experience to come in Germany, so that they could look more impartially at the issues the miraculous Herr Hitler put forward. But why was there now a host — one she suspected that Hannelore felt as little liking for as she did? Surely Hannelore would not think that a holiday with Ruffi would make them more sympathetic to Herr Hitler, or even feel more kindly towards herself.

So why were they here?

She took Ruffi's arm as they entered the dining room. He wore white tie — no newfangled dinner jacket. At least no animal heads adorned the walls there: only ancestors' faces, all long nosed and none bearing any resemblance to Ruffi. Sophie wondered mischievously if they had been purchased at the same time as the animal heads, and the portraits of the true ancestors had been lost along with the estates up north. Nigel sat opposite her, for there was no other company. Ruffi, it seemed, had not married, though he did not explain the absence of a wife or hostess.

Carp in wine sauce was served by Ruffi's butler, not by Hereward, who must be seriously annoyed that his right to serve his master was usurped. But a butler in residence outranked the one who was visiting. Sophie stared at the fish head on the plate. The head was recognised as the most choice part of a carp, but she didn't like the way its dead eyes stared at her.

'I never serve soup,' said Ruffi. 'So wishy-washy. You will like the carp. I have the fish live in a pond of fresh water for a month to remove the taste of mud. Of course we never have eaten carp's head at court. Nor even pork knuckle.' He laughed, dabbing sauce from his chin. Sophie looked at him enquiringly.

'The Kaiser's withered arm,' Ruffi explained. 'He could not use a knife to cut his food and so, of course, none of us was permitted to use a knife and fork either. Currywurst, day after day, and Königsberger Klopse, with Spätzle. His favourite meal was Kartoffelsalat, potato salad. Even a one-handed man can manage that. I have never eaten Kartoffelsalat again.' Ruffi shuddered. 'For a time I wondered if the whole court would turn into a potato.'

'You spent much time at court?' Sophie managed a smile that Miss Lily would have been proud of. Nigel looked amused.

'Of course. I was His Royal Highness's right-hand man. Or perhaps his left.' Ruffi smiled at his little joke. 'One needed … tact … in dealing with His Highness. I remember one morning he came down with a freshly slaughtered hare strapped to his left arm. He was sure the strength of the hare would transfer itself to the limb. But of course it did not.'

The plates — and most of the carp's head on Sophie's plate — were removed. A boar's head was borne in next. It had bright blue eyes, presumably glass, and sat on frills of endive so it looked as if the creature had been given an Elizabethan ruff.

'I was one of the White Stag Dining Club,' Ruffi stated. 'Created by His Majesty, and supposed to be a secret, but now,' he shrugged, 'the secrets have gone the same way as royalty. At every meeting each member had to tell a joke.' Ruffi raised an eyebrow at Sophie. 'The kind I could not tell in your company, of course.'

At least not with my husband here, thought Sophie a little grimly, as Ruffi patted her hand.

'On entering the dining room we all had our backsides slapped by the flat of His Majesty's sword too. One slap for each member, but for a young man he liked,' Ruffi raised his eyebrows suggestively, 'he might have three slaps, or even five. We would count them, to see who was the current favourite. The Kaiser was always in uniform of course — he had hundreds of uniforms for different occasions, all different. By preference, he ate sitting on a saddle at the dining table. Luckily he did not demand that of us all.'

Was he joking? But Nigel was calmly eating his boar with sauerkraut and potato dumplings as if he had heard all this before.

'We had such fun!' Ruffi patted her hand again.

Try that once more and I'll bite it, thought Sophie. But of course she would not. She was the Countess of Shillings now, and even if she were not, she could not risk what was in effect a royal commission.

'One of the Kaiser's favourite games was doughnuts,' continued Ruffi. 'Perhaps we should try it after dinner. An officer places his helmet by the fire and guests must try to throw a doughnut so its hole lands over the spike. The ladies would sometimes climb up onto the sofa, or the men on chairs. All was permitted as long as one did not step upon the hearth rug. His Majesty would run around the room, suggesting vantage points.'

And that man engineered a war in which millions died and many millions more were injured, or damaged for life, thought Sophie.

But tonight, across Britain, other leaders who had so ineptly played their strategic war games with the Empire's troops might be at a costume ball or playing mah jong, or anything else just as trivial. For surely only those capable of filling in their time with inanity would have the capacity to ignore the tragedy of the war they commanded.

'I remember one dinner,' Ruffi continued dreamily, 'at the hunting lodge of Prince Fürstenberg. The chief of the army danced in a pink ballet skirt! "His legs are so fine," the Kaiser said, just as the poor man dropped down dead. A heart attack. The dinners were not quite the same after that. But of course the Kaiser's greatest love was for women's hands.'

And yours is gossip, thought Sophie. Was this why they had been sent here, to see how gossip about Nigel might be spread across the Continent?

Ruffi swallowed another forkful of meat, leaving the vegetables untouched. 'He had perfected the art of removing a woman's glove. Every woman at court had to wear one long white glove, leaving the other hand bare. But it was the gloved hand he would kiss. It took quite ten minutes to remove the glove, and another five for the kiss itself, pressing his lips to the very centre of her hand. Plump hands, by preference, and the softer the better, but never scented. It would make him quite cross, to miss what he said was the essential scent of a woman's hand.'

'How fascinating,' said Sophie, trying not to look at the boar's bright eyes. The meat had been carefully carved from the underside, so the head with its tusks seemed undamaged. She wondered, slightly hysterically, if each boar's head was given fresh eyes, or if cook kept a small carton of them to reuse. If we have caviar next, I will scream, she thought.

'But you, Ruffi.' She forced her eyes to look artlessly up at his. 'What are your interests now?'

'Why, pleasure, my dear. What else is left to us?'

'Indeed,' she murmured. She took a small bite of the dumpling served with the boar — she had been unable to eat its flesh — and it turned to glue in her mouth.

What am I doing here? she thought. I have extended a business empire across the world, founded hospitals, relief systems, stood for parliament and almost won ... Yet I sit here powerless while this useless man gloats about scandals of the past and do nothing, can do nothing, because I am a wife now and must protect the reputation of my husband.

Sophie glanced up to find Nigel looking at her. He understood. And because he understood she remembered that she was a mother too, and his reputation as well as hers would determine those of their children and, after all, this was not for long. A few months at most, and they would be gone, back to the clean air of Australia where she would resume her life again ...

Frozen meat, she thought, as an antidote to all this indulgence. Higgs needed to move into refrigeration, not just canning. If frozen beef and lamb were already being shipped to England by others, what else might be frozen and exported? As soon as they arrived back she would arrange for Johnny Slithersole to instigate the necessary research ...

'And of course I have my collection,' said Ruffi, still smiling. He pressed her hand, then lifted it to his lips, almost but not quite touching it. 'One day perhaps, before you leave, I must show it to you.'

'It sounds delightful,' said Sophie, carefully not asking exactly what he collected — the second-hand knickers of royalty, perhaps, or ancient Roman erotica.

The footmen removed the boar, its eyes still sightlessly staring. Caviar was brought in (of course, thought Sophie, mildly hysterically), a thousand dead fish eggs, like tiny glossy black eyes, with the smallest of new potatoes and tiny forks made of some pink shell for them to eat with.

Chapter 40

*The world runs on secrets, of course. Few people acknowledge
their secrets even to themselves, much less to others. Governments
keep their own counsel, especially those that have been elected.
Knowing secrets brings you power, but once you enter that world of
'intelligence' it is impossible to step out of it again.*

Miss Lily, 1913

VIOLETTE

Violette hesitated in the narrow hall that led to the servants'
stairs on one side, and the baize door that led to the rooms her
ladyship, the earl, and her family occupied.

She was not a servant, and she and her parents slept on the
same side of the baize door as her ladyship. But even so, each
meal, they must dine in the room set aside for visiting senior
servants, on the same floor as the servants' hall.

She wore linen, not a servant's serge, but she must still use this
servants' back staircase. If she wished to leave or enter the house
she must use the back door only.

She did not wear a servant's apron, but today the family —
her ladyship, the earl, the children — had ridden in a horse-
drawn carriage around the district, while her day had been spent
darning her ladyship's clothes, removing stains from fabric,
creating the exquisite being that was her ladyship, instead of
herself, a glorious Violette.

Violette snarled internally. (Externally she kept her face
delightful always, or nearly always, in case someone might be

watching.) She had been promised a family holiday where she could walk through any door she wished. This had not happened.

On the other hand, it was only the woman who happened to be her mother who had informed her that she must spend today invisibly darning a ripped hem. Her ladyship had given no such order. Was Violette bound to obey the whims of her ladyship's maid, simply because that woman had borne her nearly fourteen years beforehand? No.

Violette glanced out the window, where the midsummer sun hung indestructibly in the sky, as if it could not conceive of winter, and made up her mind. Head high she crossed to the baize door, and opened it, then walked down the small hall that led to the main staircase down to the Great Hall.

Which was where she met Count von Hegenhof, walking up the stairs as she walked down.

Violette hesitated. She would not curtsey to him, she decided. Her ladyship had not curtseyed, and anyway had not titles been made illegal by the German government? Besides she did not feel like curtseying, she who had been ignored by Heinrich, a servant, with not even a response to her 'Guten Morgen' after breakfast.

'Ah, Miss Jones, is it not?' Count von Hegenhof did not sound annoyed. He even seemed pleased.

So the count knew who she was and that she should be addressed as 'Miss', not simply Jones. This was good, even if he was a Boche.

'The little … protégée of her ladyship …' the count continued, the smile spreading as if he were genuinely amused, not just by her presumption in trespassing beyond the servants' stairs and failing to curtsey, but by something else. Or perhaps Count von Hegenhof assumed that those who climbed the front stairs had a right to climb them, and she had risen in his estimation.

He did not click his heels though or kiss her hand. She was glad he did not try the latter. There was something frog-like about Count von Hegenhof, not his appearance but coldness under the warmth. Nor, of course, would she ever permit herself to be kissed by a Boche.

'I am sorry you missed the expedition this morning,' he said smoothly, the smile still in place. 'I did not expect a Miss Jones, you see, so made no provision for a place for you in the carriage.'

Ah, an acceptable excuse, though Violette could easily have been found a place — but it was good that he thought an excuse necessary. 'I hope at least you enjoyed your lunch?'

Violette regarded him haughtily. Her ladyship did not use hauteur nor condescension when she looked at people, yet managed to look indeed a ladyship. But that was a skill Violette had yet to master. 'I did not enjoy luncheon,' she informed him. 'It was mostly cabbage, and sour, and the pork, it was tough.'

'But cabbage is so good for you, my dear. We have a saying here: A cabbage has a hard heart but it nourishes a man.'

Violette decided one of her less charming smiles might work better. 'A pineapple has a hard heart too and nourishes, but it is delicious. I prefer pineapple to cabbage.'

He laughed. 'May I make amends?'

'How, your lordship?' That might not be the correct way to address a German count — she was more familiar with how people killed Germans than how their titles should be used. But it seemed to do.

'I have a little collection upstairs. It may amuse you. Come. I will show it to you, to make up for the expedition you did not have. Perhaps we might both even have fun with it.'

He preceded her up the stairs. Violette hesitated on the landing, then followed him up, past the third floor, with the servants' bedrooms, then to a small doorway. He took a key from a chain around his neck, unlocked the door, then gestured her through it. She peered up at the narrow winding staircase. It smelled faintly of mouse overlaid with furniture polish, and must go up to one of the towers.

It would be stupid to go up those stairs, leaving a door that could be locked behind her, when no one knew she was there. On the other hand, she was curious and had her knife with her and, besides, it would be far easier to push a man behind her downstairs than for him to grab her.

She walked up the stairs. She had expected them to be worn and slightly slippery stone, but they were well designed, with a solid handrail to one side.

Four bends and another door, unlocked this time. She opened it herself, and looked around inside.

The tower room was round, with long narrow windows evenly spaced around it and a vaulted wooden ceiling. At first glance the contents were incomprehensible: a machine that looked like a see-saw, but that had handcuffs at both ends. She walked over and pushed it. Yes, it was a see-saw. She glanced back and saw Count von Hegenhof smiling at her. He looked even more like a creature that belonged at the bottom of a well, as if in this room he was entirely free to be himself.

She moved to the next machine. It was a curious kind of gate that looked like the base of a guillotine, with two armholes and a cushion on which to rest the neck, but no guillotine above it. Once again there were manacles, though these looked as if they were for ankles, not wrists. A portion of wall padded by a vast velvet cushion, with straps and manacles, confirmed exactly what this room was used for. There was no need to examine the rest of the implements. The house to which she had been sold in Brussels had clients with … less usual tastes.

Violette smiled. She knew exactly how to manage men like Count von Hegenhof. She saw him note the smile, and misunderstand it entirely.

'You'd like to play? Shall we start with this, my dear? It was the first of my collection.' The count stroked the see-saw lovingly. 'It is a spanking machine. The naughty little girl stands here … come, you must try it. I promise I will stop when you say enough. Or would you prefer this one …?' He moved to what might be a swing. Or might not.

He was between her and the door. He was older and stronger and had possibly even learned to box, which was something she had learned that 'gentlemen' did. She, however, had her knife, and many years of most useful knowledge.

Violette sighed mentally. She had promised her ladyship not to kill anyone. Her ladyship probably would not like her to wound her host, either. Which meant she must not use her knife at all. And once she threatened the count with it, he would know she had it. He might try to get her up here again. And next time, he might arrange for Violette to be fetched.

It was better, always, to be underestimated.

Violette gave a small cry, then buried her face in her hands to cover her lack of tears. Two sobs, then a stumble towards the staircase. She heard rather than saw him step back to let her pass.

She fumbled down the stairs till she was out of sight, then proceeded fairly calmly to the doorway. The door was not locked. She used the back stairs this time to go down to the room they had given her as a bedroom. An adequate room, with rich mats upon the floor, brocade curtains and a fire and dressing table, even if it had a wardrobe in it, not a dressing room attached.

'Where have you been?' Her mother looked suspiciously at her from the dressing table, a froth of white in her lap, a needle and thread in her hand.

'Why are you in my bedroom?' demanded Violette.

'I have been removing the lace from the top of your dress for this evening. The lace is not suitable now we are not here alone.'

'You mean I must look more like a servant?'

'I mean exactly what I said. You must look appropriate. Where have you been?'

There was no reason not to tell her mother. Every reason, in fact, why she should be told, so that her parents and her ladyship and his lordship would know about the man in whose castle they were staying. It was only the anger, anger she had been unaware of but that still slept within her that made her say, 'It is not your business.'

'Of course it is my business!'

'Why?'

'I am your mother.'

'You gave birth to me. You fed me perhaps for a very little time. Since then her ladyship has done more for me than you.'

234

'That is irrelevant.'

Violette shrugged. 'You are the one who is irrelevant. Do you love me? Do I love you? I do not even respect you.'

Silence from the woman at the dressing table, then, 'Why don't you respect me?'

'You are a servant. Just that. You serve. You serve good people but, still, you do no more than serve. You have had chances to be more than a servant. And yet, when the war was over you went back to serving. What should I respect about that?'

Green put the white dress carefully on the bed. It was impossible to see where the lace had been. 'It is more complicated than you think.'

'Is it? When I find out the *complications* will I respect you?' Green had not protested, thought Violette, wondering why she felt so empty. Green had not said, 'Of course I love you. I think that you are wonderful, to have survived all these years. I think that you are beautiful, a treasure, my life is full at last ...'

Instead Green said, 'We don't know each other. Not yet.'

Violette shrugged again, without speaking.

The woman who was her mother took a breath, as if calming herself. 'Very well, I will ask you again, not as your mother, but as a member of a party of English people in a strange land and a stranger's castle: where have you been?'

Eh bien. 'The count invited me to see his collection. It is of things that men use to hurt women and ... pleasure themselves. I pretended to cry and then I left. He did not touch me.'

'I see,' said Green slowly. 'Thank you for telling me.'

'I do not think he will ask me again. I do not think he will ask Amy, nor her ladyship. I think he hoped I might agree to be used by him, for money or because he is a count, but when he saw I would not he enjoyed watching me be scared, no more. I was not scared, of course,' she added. 'But I pretended most convincingly.'

Green nodded. 'He will have no shortage of women to play games with, if he pays. The aristocracy is looked up to around here. But try not to be alone with him again.'

'That is good advice. I do not enjoy pretending to be scared.'

'I do respect you,' said Green.

'Good. Tell me, did you ever want a child?'

'No. But once I was pregnant, I did want you. I loved you more than my life, or any cause for which I worked. You *were* my life. And then they told me you were dead and I could not even see your grave. I mourned for you — silently, secretly, but every single day.'

Not — 'I love you now.' Violette wondered vaguely if she had inherited her mother's habit of honesty, though in her case, it was combined with a useful ability to deceive, even if she did not like to lie directly. 'You mourned a baby. It is a long time since I was she.'

Green nodded at the truth of that. Once again Violette wished she hadn't. But it was best to know the truth. Fooling yourself could lead to danger, even death, when there was no one to protect you.

'We do not know each other yet,' repeated Green with a touch of almost desperation.

'I would like you to leave my bedroom now,' said Violette. She had a strange feeling that she was going to cry. She wished to be alone to do it.

Chapter 41

*There have been times when I longed for ignorance, so I would not
know how ignorant I was. But that is cowardice, perhaps the most
common kind there is.*

Miss Lily, 1913

SOPHIE

Sophie woke early the day they were to leave for Berlin. Nigel
lay next to her, still deep in sleep. He had shared her room ever
since they left England. She welcomed him, but did not feel she
could ask him why he had changed the habit of the years since
his surgery.

It was not to protect her. Green had told her of Violette's
experience, but nothing untoward had happened since. After
that first evening Ruffi had been an almost absent host, meeting
them only at dinner. He breakfasted in his room and filled his
days with, 'Meetings with neighbours, my dear, so boring. But I
have prepared some little activities that may amuse you.'

Were the meetings with neighbours political, urging them to
National Socialism? Possible, though Sophie doubted it. Ruffi
had not mentioned politics at all to them. Nor, indeed, had
he seen any military service beyond wearing a uniform while
accompanying the Kaiser.

And the activities he had arranged had been genuinely
amusing, unlike the forced and febrile gaiety she had seen in
Sydney and England. They went rowing on the lake with the
children and Green, Jones and Violette now that Ruffi seemed to

have recognised they preferred to be a party of seven, not four. A small bevy of footmen accompanied them, just in case anyone fell in or dropped their asparagus fork, on a picnic to the small island in the lake with its Roman ruins (commissioned by Ruffi twenty years earlier).

There had been a midnight feast in a firefly-lit forest glade that almost made up for Ruffi's detailed descriptions of every royal scandal for the past fifty years as they ate. There had even been a birthday party picnic for Rose and Danny, with a ludicrously elaborate birthday cake, an exact replica of the castle, but with candles, and a quartet of jugglers who sang 'Happy Birthday' in strongly accented English. The twins had ignored the jugglers, but demolished the cake with joy, while Sophie caught Nigel's eye. Was this, too, a demonstration of Hannelore's affection, or her knowledge of their family affairs?

They had toured the district, in Ruffi's old-fashioned horse-drawn coach, in a hay wagon and in their own cars. The area seemed prosperous — plump children, with shoes on their feet and well-combed or plaited hair, fat cattle and mended fences. Germany — or this part of the country at least — had not known invasion for over a century. Despite the reparations Germany seemed a wealthy land again, trading on investments and loans from the United States. Certainly the income from Sophie's Bavarian contracts had been steadily increasing through the decade. The Weimar Republic seemed successful and, possibly, a most welcome change from the rule of the king Ruffi had described.

Sophie had known the Kaiser was unstable, eccentric and hated England. She had not realised how much even those in the court, like Ruffi — and probably Dolphie and Hannelore — had despised him, even while they accepted his royal authority.

Prosperous countries did not easily change governments. Hannelore had claimed Germany desperately needed her favoured politician and his National Socialist Party to restore its pride and prosperity. Sophie had seen no sign that it did.

And now, thank goodness, they would soon be gone, not just from there but from Germany, the Prince of Wales's demands and Hannelore's political machinations. Tomorrow they would leave for Berlin. Three days there, or a week at most, and they could leave for England, report to David then sail for Australia.

She glanced again at Nigel, still gently snoring. Suddenly she needed time to herself. She slipped into the dressing room, removed her nightdress and slid the first dress to hand over her body, and then stepped into some shoes, not bothering with stockings or even underwear, then walked silently out into the corridor and down the stairs.

Voices came from the kitchens, louder than they would be later in the day. No one expected anyone to be in these rooms now. The front door was still locked, but it was simple to unbolt the drawing room's French doors and escape out onto the terrace.

I am floating across dew-diamonded grass as the morning sunlight ripples upon the lake, she thought, crossing the carpet of green lawns. It was a phrase worthy of any romance novelist, but what else could do justice to the small, white, turreted icing-sugar castle in this morning light, to the swans that seemed to have been recently washed with Pears soap and to a summer-green silk dress that by pure accident perfectly matched the German forest around them, bright with new leaves? Though perhaps that was not accidental — presumably Green had chosen to leave the dress out for the morning for just that reason. Undoubtedly a matching hat or bandeaux waited for her back in the dressing room.

She breathed in the scent of lake, swan dung and lush grass, with the slight musk of forest below it. A pair of deer glanced at her from the edge of the lake opposite, then cantered surprisingly calmly back into the wall of leaves.

Dolphie had once promised she could grow to love Germany. She had not doubted him, even as she tried to explain that her loyalty would always remain with a far harsher land. But she had not guessed at the beauty of a German summer.

'Sophie, darling, slow down ...'

Sophie turned and smiled as Nigel came towards her. 'I was just thinking this was perfect, and now it is even more perfect.'

'You don't mind my joining you?'

'Of course not. I just didn't want to wake you.'

He kissed her cheek, then took her arm. 'Shall we take a sedate pre-breakfast promenade? Do you remember your pre-breakfast walk on your first morning at Shillings?'

She laughed. 'Then Miss Lily explained to me exactly why a guest does not take pre-breakfast promenades, including the chance one may embarrass the master of the house returning from an illicit night with his lover. But I doubt Ruffi would be embarrassed in the slightest.'

'On the contrary, I should think,' said Nigel. 'After you left the dining room last night he told me how Catherine the Great had pulleys installed so she could copulate with a stallion, having decided that only a horse had the equipment to satisfy her. He said he had considered having a set made for his castle.'

'Were you duly shocked?'

'Only at his lack of originality. I first heard that story on the North West Frontier in my first year in the army. I think I heard it for the fiftieth time in 1918, just before the Armistice.' His expression grew more sombre. 'He also told me in considerable detail about his liaison with Hannelore's grandmother twenty years ago.'

'I wonder if Hannelore knows?'

'Almost certainly. It was Hannelore's grandmother who advised Hannelore to come to Shillings. I doubt she desired Ruffi, or even liked him — she was a woman of considerable taste — so there would have been other reasons for the affair.' He shrugged. His face had lost all its earlier joy now. 'Perhaps it was just to bring the families closer. Hannelore must have considerable influence with Ruffi to have persuaded him to accommodate us this summer, especially as she cannot have expected you to ... entertain ... him in return.'

Sophie was silent. Nigel looked at her with sympathy. 'Losing friendship can be even more painful than the loss of a lover.'

Sophie shook her head. 'The problem is that in a strange way the friendship is still there. I ... I think Hannelore would still risk her life for me. I probably would for her, if it weren't that my life is no longer mine to risk, but belongs to you and the children. She has brought us to Germany because she believes it to be right, thinks that I will even eventually agree with her. But ...'

'But it is the way that she has gone about it,' finished Nigel.

'Blackmail is not comfortable,' said Sophie, trying to keep her tone light.

'Blackmail doesn't end,' said Nigel. They had reached the lawns mown about the lake. The swans paddled towards them, hopeful. 'We've partially confirmed Hannelore's suspicions simply by agreeing to come to Germany. It just increases her power over us.'

'But no matter what your ... the ... circumstances, you'd have agreed to see this Herr Hitler once David asked you to.'

'Possibly. Even probably. But I would also have explained that it was impossible for me to arrange for Miss Lily to meet him. It is Miss Lily's influence she really wants, remember, not mine.'

Sophie nodded. She had tried to think of a way Green could convincingly take Miss Lily's place in Berlin where Hannelore would notice her. But while the women of La Dame Blanche had never met Miss Lily, Hannelore knew her well. Hannelore had also met Green, though possibly not noticed her particularly, or even recognised her and Jones on the night they had helped Sophie escape from Dolphie's hunting lodge. But Hannelore would immediately notice any deception. She might even expect them to try to deceive her, even if she did not know how.

The best they could do was Nigel's stipulation that Miss Lily was now retired and unwell and so would appear for only one day, to speak with Hannelore and then be introduced to Herr Hitler. Miss Lily would wear gloves — perfectly acceptable, and no chance of leaving incriminating fingerprints. But no excuse for Nigel's absence on that same day would be sufficient to erode Hannelore's belief that Lily and Nigel were one.

And if Miss Lily did not volunteer her support for Herr Hitler? Would Hannelore demand that, too?

'It's my fault,' said Nigel slowly. 'I was overconfident, sure that no one would recognise me. And if they did ...'

'We were only women and therefore powerless, apart from our charm as "Miss Lily's lovely ladies"? And so we were, before the war. Any scandal we spread would have rebounded on us, to be associated with such a decadent setting as Shillings would suddenly have become. That shame would also hurt Miss Lily's friends in so many countries, too.'

Sophie smiled at the memory of their last day there, so unlike the quiet, dignified Shillings she had first known, with Rose and Daniel going bump, bump, bump down the staircase on their bottoms, and Nanny scandalised, but unable to intervene while the children's mother chose to bump down stair by stair beside them.

No more 'lovely ladies' for Shillings, though the children would have friends to stay, and she and Nigel would have visitors over as a sedate married couple, even if Ethel did arrive on a motorbike.

'I should have cut the connection with Hannelore when I returned to England,' she said slowly. And yet she had risked her own life to save Hannelore, had loved her like a sister.

That was the worst of it, she thought. For Hannelore was no villain, demanding money. Possibly, even probably, she would never act on the unexpressed threat, never do anything that might hurt her friend.

But even probably was too great a risk.

Sophie gazed at the swans, now paddling back to an interesting clump of reeds. 'Do you think I am sufficiently swan-like in my movements after all these years?'

Nigel lifted her hand and kissed it. 'I think you are perfect.' He met her eyes. 'And, if I do not say it often enough, every day I give thanks for the miracle that you married me and gave me two children and the happiest two years that I have ever known.'

'That ... that sounds ominous, as if you were heading off to war and might not return. Darling, what is the worst that Hannelore can do? Yes, I know what she can *try* to do — have us support this wretched man financially, even join his political party, support an alliance with Germany in the House of Lords, have Lily at least write to her friends, urging support. But if you refuse? We could simply sail for Australia till the gossip blows over.'

'But it never would,' said Nigel. 'Think of Ruffi last night, with scandals that are decades old. The Australian papers, too, would love the gossip. What of Danny and Rose, growing up with that?'

'But if Miss Lily never appears again ...' Sophie took a deep breath of air. 'That is it, isn't it? That's what you plan after Berlin? The scandal might be survivable — but only if Miss Lily vanishes forever after Berlin. Hannelore can never prove what she suspects. If Miss Lily disappears for good, 'somewhere in the East' perhaps, there can never be photos of her, nor fingerprints. Few if any who have know her will tell any journalist that they ever knew her, except possibly as a Vaile relative who spent quiet months at Shillings.'

'Pretty much,' said Nigel, though something in his tone made Sophie uneasy. He looked out at the island. 'Do you think we need Roman ruins at Shillings?'

It was an obvious attempt to change the subject, but Sophie accepted it. 'No more than we needed the Egyptian columns your horrible cousin tried to install when he thought you were going to die. I am very glad you didn't die, Nigel.' Miss Lily gone, she thought. Why didn't I realise before this was what Nigel — and probably James too — had planned? Miss Lily's network must not be tainted by scandal.

'I am glad I didn't die too,' said Nigely lightly. 'And as my cousin has no sons his line will never inherit, even if Danny has no children.'

Sophie didn't ask who would inherit then. Impossible to think of Danny ever dying. But she had lived through the Great War, when almost every family in Britain and the colonies had lost a son. There must not be another!

And yet in her heart she knew Hannelore was correct. The Great War had never entirely ended. The tensions that drove it were still there: White Russians still fought the Red; France believed so deeply in the inevitability of another German invasion that it was still insisting on those crippling reparation payments.

She almost wished the next war would come soon, while Danny was still too young to fight in it, and Nigel and Daniel and Jones now too old.

Perhaps this politician really was the answer: an alliance between Germany and England, and France too, against their common enemy. The Bolsheviks might, just conceivably, keep the peace — for Britain and her Empire, at least. German territorial ambitions would be directed northwards and east, to reclaim the German lands Russia had taken. Perhaps Herr Hitler really would make Europe safe ...

She shivered. 'No talk of dying. You are going to live to be a hundred and four and Danny will have six sons by the time he inherits the title, and his oldest son will be eighty before he becomes earl.'

'Very well, I promise — no more talk of dying. Time we turned back for breakfast,' said Nigel.

Sophie nodded. 'I'd like to write a letter before we leave. Jones can post it on the way to Berlin. I don't like the idea of Ruffi reading my correspondence.'

'I feel the same way. I have some letters to send too.' He leaned over and gently kissed her on the lips. 'In thee I've had mine earthly joy,' he quoted.

She stroked his hair. 'And you will always be my Lancelot.' They walked back to the margarine heiress's perfect German castle together.

Chapter 42

Knowing you have found beauty that will always stay with you in memory and with joy is the most profound triumph of any journey, literal or otherwise.

Miss Lily, 1913

Sophie sat at the far too ornate, too small and entirely too inconvenient desk in her sitting room. The margarine heiress had evidently not expected her guests to write more than a few words on a visiting card. But the paper was good, the nibs sharp, the ink fresh and the pen wipers embroidered with Ruffi's crest.

Darling Midge,

Your letter finally reached us! How lovely that Dr Greenman has been visiting you. I am so glad he looks well, and seems to be settled in Sydney. I am even happier that he intends to visit often, and has no need to hide away as in those years at Bald Hill. Sometimes there are 'happy endings' to stories, aren't there? I hope there is much more happiness to come for the man we knew as 'John'.

I am writing this hastily before breakfast from a far too pretty German castle where we have been holidaying for the past month to soak up the European summer. I apologise for its brevity, but I may not get time to write again as we leave here today after breakfast. By the week after next we should be back in England and embarking on the Margaret Marshall for Australia, so any letters I write after this may arrive after we do! I keep thinking that I cannot wait to be home again, and then reminding myself I must.

The children have grown so much this summer! Rose is now speaking in full sentences. Of course they are almost entirely

incomprehensible but I am still most proud. Danny's articulation,
on the other hand, is perfect, though he wisely keeps to one- or
two-word utterances. At the moment he is saying 'good morning',
'good afternoon' and even a 'good evening'! He greeted Nanny,
me, his father, his breakfast and his toy zebra yesterday morning,
but refused his sister a simple 'hello'.

It is delightful that they are so different, and not at all like
bookends. I wonder if I will ever stop marvelling over them. I am
relying on your 'brats' to show them all the joys of a country
childhood — including the ones it is best parents do not know
about. I never had older children to show me illicit activities and
things, only 'suitable friends'. I don't want my children to ever be
restricted to the 'suitable'.

There is not much more to write or, rather, our time is mostly
composed of walks by the lake or hay rides and meals that go on
forever — I am sure that the castle consumes at least three pigs a
day. None of it is at all as interesting as … we are coming home!

Give my love to Harry and the 'brats' and to Thuringa and of
course to you, always,
Sophie.

Sophie put down the pen and wiped the nib on Ruffi's family
crest, the heads (what else?) of boar and deer on a gilded shield.

What would Midge say if she knew of Lily? Her pragmatic
Australian friend might simply hug her and say, 'Darling, we are
all made as we are.'

Midge might also hug her and say, 'Darling, I understand. But
others mightn't. For the sake of the children, perhaps it would
be best if they don't meet Nigel or … Lily. But you and I can still
meet. At church, and the CWA perhaps …' And soon Miss Lily
would be gone forever, except brief moments of privacy with her
and Green and Jones. Even Rose and Daniel would never know
'Aunt Lily'. She could not bear this charade. But she must. Nigel
was right. There was no other choice now.

And they would succeed — must succeed — in disarming
all of Hannelore's suspicion, while leaving her to exist, even if

only barely seen. Even now Green and Violette were packing her clothes, and Nanny was preparing the children. One final meal and the waiting would be over and they could begin the real purpose of the journey ...

And soon Miss Lily would be gone forever, except brief moments of privacy with her and Green and Jones. Even Rose and Daniel would never know 'Aunt Lily'. She could not bear it. But she must. Nigel was right. There was no other choice now.

Breakfast was always served cold: a dark-fleshed, double-smoked ham on the sideboard, game pie, a platter of pale, cold sausages and a selection of cheeses with small triangles of black bread, pickled walnuts and pickled onions. Only the rolls that were served instead of toast were hot, in damask-lined baskets: round white rolls with onion seed tops, and flaky croissants rich with yellow summer butter, which Ruffi insisted were Austrian, not French at all — 'Stolen from us, like so much that is German that the traitorous French purloin' — and coffee or chocolate, either thick with cream.

To Sophie's surprise Ruffi was already in the breakfast room that morning as she and Nigel entered.

'Ah, the Wandervogel are about to depart!' Ruffi stood, bowed to Sophie and then pulled the bell. 'Fresh coffee, Heinrich.' He held out Sophie's chair for her. 'I was wondering if you were still communing with the swans.'

She smiled at him. 'You see everything, Ruffi! The swans and I had a most enlightening conversation. Do they stay here all winter?'

Ruffi shrugged. 'Yes, I believe so. I spend my winters in the south of France, or sometimes Morocco. So amusing, Morocco.' He grinned at her. 'You should have advised the swans to do the same.'

'I think your swans are as happy here as we have been, Ruffi.' Nigel helped himself to the rolls Heinrich the footman had brought in, while Hereward carried the coffee. His bearing seemed to say: coffee outranks hot rolls in the servants' hall, but these barbarians do not know it.

'We have encroached on your hospitality long enough.' Sophie spread cherry jam on her croissant. The pale sausages looked extraordinarily like a platter of deformed penises. She'd had to fight an urge to giggle at them each breakfast time.

'Nonsense. But as you insist.' Ruffi shrugged. 'I have told Heinrich to have my things packed also.'

'You are leaving too?'

'Of course! Do you think I would not escort you to Berlin? And once you are there,' he raised his eyebrows, 'there are most interesting places I can show you, ones that my dear cousin Hannelore certainly would not.'

'Then perhaps I should not see them either,' said Sophie.

Ruffi patted her hand. Sophie wondered if she might have a pair of gloves made, with spikes to keep off hand patters, and especially hand kissers. 'What is the point of being in a city where no one knows you if you do not take advantage of it? And what else is there for you to do in Berlin? Its fashions are Parisian second hand. But the night life ... or even sometimes in the mornings; you will find it deliciously decadent.' Ruffi raised his eyebrows again at Sophie. 'And most educational. Ah!' His tone changed. 'Here is a parting gift to you — kedgeree for breakfast! Hannelore said it was your favourite but it has taken the kitchen a while to find the recipe.'

'How delicious,' said Sophie, thinking of the long and bumpy journey ahead of them. She helped herself to what she hoped was an enthusiastic-looking portion.

Nigel stood. 'If you'll excuse me, I have some final arrangements to make.'

'Of course, dear chap.' Ruffi patted Sophie's hand yet again. 'This may be my last chance to be alone with your so lovely wife. You are such a lucky man, Vaile.'

'I know,' said Nigel. He smiled at Sophie, then left the room.

Deserter, thought Sophie. 'You will be staying with us in Berlin?' She tried to make her voice sound eager as she forked up

248

kedgeree. It was far too buttery, ridiculously rich in smoked fish and curry powder. Kedgeree's charm was its hints, not a slap in the mouth.

'Sadly not. Hannelore's aunt has quite a small establishment. But I will make sure you see everything.'

'You are so kind,' said Sophie. What else was there to say?

Chapter 43

Beware of following your dreams, my dears. Dreams change as you learn more of the world. How many girls who dreamed of being princesses found that the role of minor royalty is opening flower shows and bearing heirs, with no time to even assess the broader issues of the day. A mistress, on the other hand, has both power and freedom, especially with a husband who approves of her role.

Miss Lily, 1913

VIOLETTE

Violette spread tissue paper between the layers of fabric in her ladyship's trunk; Green glanced up from her folding to check the work, and nodded approvingly.

The holiday had improved since the first day at the castle.

True, she now used the servants' stair to get to the rooms she and the family occupied, but by choice, she told herself, so as not to meet the count again. She and her parents still dined downstairs, an upper servants' meal, invariably of roast pork, potatoes and cabbage, when those upstairs dined on venison, turkey, salmon and varied other delights, including a dessert of thin layers of pastry, cream and wild strawberries. She'd even had to make do with black bread instead of white rolls or croissants for breakfast.

When we are in Australia I will eat croissants for breakfast every day, she thought, with much cherry jam.

At least Violette had accompanied the family on their expeditions in the countryside, like the previous week's journey up a snow-topped mountain to a meadow where the flowers still bloomed, even now in August. They travelled in small carts filled with hay and topped with soft blankets because motorcars could not reach so high.

Today, however, she must travel with Nanny and the children, and eat brown bread sandwiches cut in the shape of circus animals to amuse the children, who had not even *seen* a circus yet. She must help her mother pack her ladyship's clothes, just as if she too were a lady's maid, while her father checked his lordship's trunks had been attended to correctly.

She hesitated, listening. That was his lordship's voice, and her father's. The door opened. His lordship said, 'Green, I think we need to discuss …' he stopped when he saw Violette.

Green (Violette still refused to think of her as 'mother') smiled at her. 'Go and stretch your legs. It'll be a long journey.'

Five minutes before she had wanted to do just that. Now she said, 'But you need help packing.'

'It's nearly done. Go.'

'Of course. Thank you,' said Violette. She presented his lordship with one of her best smiles, then slipped out, then up the servants' stairs (no carpet … pah!) and slipped into the servant's bedroom above her ladyship's. Kept empty, naturally, for a maid slipping back for a handkerchief might interrupt the entertainment of the count gazing through the spy hole to the room below.

Violette had discovered the small spy holes in her bedroom and her ladyship's on her second day at the castle. She had pointed them out to her mother, who had merely shrugged and said, 'Of course.'

Her mother was entirely too reticent about matters Violette needed to properly understand.

This spy hole seemed to be used solely by the count, who was breakfasting with her ladyship below. Interesting that his lordship wished to talk to her parents when both her ladyship and the count were safely out of hearing.

Violette pushed at a slightly discoloured section at the base of the wall. It opened to reveal a small passage in the wall between the rooms. The three were still talking, his lordship sitting on a dressing chair, her father pacing, Green standing immobile, as if considering.

'I don't like it,' her father was saying. 'It's too dangerous, Nigel. Far too dangerous.'

His lordship leaned back on the chair, 'I can see no other way out. Neither can James.'

'You should at least tell Sophie.'

'No,' said Green. 'Sophie has to remain out of this. The prinzessin knows her too well. The wrong words at the wrong time, an expression that is not quite right ... the prinzessin has been born and bred playing politics. Sophie is a brilliant organiser, but she has little experience of intrigue.'

His lordship shut his eyes. 'I wish I could tell her. I think she could carry it off. But Greenie is correct, Jones. Cyclone Sophie must be ... unabated ... if this is to succeed.' His lordship opened his eyes and stared out the window at the mountains where his family had so recently been picnicking. 'I only hope she will forgive me.'

'She loves you,' said Green softly.

His lordship smiled. 'I know. That has always been both the joy and the dilemma.'

'I still don't like it,' repeated Jones.

'We've been in worse situations.'

'Yes. And each time we had a plan. This is too ...'

'Dramatic? Theatrical? Final?' suggested his lordship.

Jones gazed at him, his expression impossible to read. 'You are my oldest friend. It ... it is not easy to face losing you.'

'It may not come to that. I hope it doesn't come to that.'

'We need more contingency plans,' said Green, almost desperately. 'We have always had back-up plans before.'

'We can't know what we are going to face this time,' said his lordship quietly. 'Nothing can be counted on. Even here we expected to have the lodge to ourselves ...'

'There'd still have been local servants, potential spies,' said Green.

Like me, thought Violette.

'The main thing is to keep Sophie and the children away from risk. And Violette.'

His lordship smiled again, a strange smile, taking in both of her parents. 'We always knew it might come to this,' he said quietly. 'Remember that last day in Japan, when you prepared to board an English ship for the first time with Lily? If just one person guessed, we agreed we'd give it up.'

'But no one did guess! Not in all these years,' said her father.

'Because until my marriage Lily and Nigel did not move in the same social circles. But once I was married to Sophie, who had friends like Hannelore who knew Lily, that separation became impossible. And it will become increasingly impossible as the children grow older. It can't go on like this. I should have realised nearly four years ago that this was inevitable, whether it was initiated by Hannelore or someone else. But back then I expected to die. I have had nearly four more years than I expected. Four wonderful years.'

He looked from Jones to Green. 'We have had our times, haven't we?' he said. 'So much friendship. So much adventure. None of us guessed we'd have so long, so much.'

Green sat on the other dressing-room stool, the mending forgotten. Jones sat on the window ledge. 'What would we have done,' he wondered, 'if someone on that ship from Japan had guessed?'

His lordship shrugged. 'Bought a small Scottish island, for select friends only. Or a Moroccan fort, no Europeans allowed. Or gone back to Japan.'

'And gone mad with boredom within six months,' said Green.

'There is that,' his lordship admitted. He raised an eyebrow at Green. It was a gesture that reminded Violette of someone. 'Have you been bored these last four years?' he asked.

'I wouldn't call it bored exactly.' Green glanced at Jones. 'I have been happy.'

'Not the same thing.'

'No, it isn't. Well, at any rate, I'm not bored now.' Green stood and reached for the sheets of tissue paper. 'I'd better get on with this before the little miss returns.' Violette realised with a shock that Green was speaking of her. 'She hasn't enjoyed the way she has had to live here. That girl needs to learn a bit of gratitude. She could be starving in the gutter.'

'Not her,' said his lordship, and suddenly he looked weary, more tired than Violette had thought possible. 'But I have enjoyed it. The last months, probably, of the only marriage I will ever have. An island of calm before we strike out for the shores of war. I ... There is so much I am going to miss.'

Green crossed over to him. To Violette's shock she kissed the earl on the forehead. 'There's a lot we're all going to miss. But we're with you, Nigel. Always and in every way, just as we promised all those years ago. The three of us, together.'

'Always,' echoed Jones, as Green picked up the tissue paper again.

Chapter 44

Friendship matters. Every woman needs five friends to whom she can confide everything, though it may not be the same five with whom you share each tragedy, joy or problem.

But when those friends are far away, and letters take far too long for guidance, remember the advice of friends who are always with you: those of memory, and those you will find between the leather bindings in the library. An author may be two thousand years departed from life, or far older even than that, but they may still become your friend.

Miss Lily, 1913

James Lorrimer, His Majesty's faithful servant — and the more-faithful-still servant of his nation — stood to greet the woman on the other side of his desk. She was not a 'lovely lady'. He doubted she had even made her debut, much less been presented at court. His butler, in fact, had even hesitated before announcing 'A ... lady to see you, sir.'

Six feet tall if she was an inch, with shoulders like a navvy's, hands that looked capable of handling vats of her family's cocoa — or empires, for that matter — and the face of a friendly horse. No one like her had ever stood in that study before. But just now James Lorrimer needed someone with broad shoulders — physically and metaphorically. And he had always been fond of horses.

'Ah, Miss Carryman. Thank you so much for coming.'

Ethel Carryman grabbed his hand, which he had not expected — one did not shake hands with ladies — and pumped it up and down enthusiastically. 'Wouldn't have missed it for the world.'

James withdrew his fingers, hoping they were not irrevocably bruised. 'Miss Carryman, you realise this mission is going to be dangerous.'

She grinned at him. 'Mr Lorrimer, I've been teaching family planning in East End slums to women who've had ten kiddies, and whose husbands expect them to lie back, open their legs and be given yet another one, or get a black eye instead. The coppers try to arrest me for talking about contraception at least twice a week. They haven't managed it yet. And I did have my moments in the war. Don't talk to me about dangerous.'

'You like danger,' he observed.

The grin grew wider. 'Aye. Noticed that, did you? Sophie always said you were a noticing kind of chap.'

'Did she now?' James murmured.

The grin faded. Ethel Carryman met his eyes squarely. 'Sophie trusts you. She trusts me too. And I'll tell you this for nothing: I'll do anything for Sophie.'

'Even if it involves hurting her — hurting her badly — to avoid a worse tragedy?'

She looked at him shrewdly. 'Are we talking a tragedy for Sophie here, or just for your political schemes?'

'My schemes are for my country, Miss Carryman, not for my own advancement.' Which he did not need. Independently wealthy, of a family who had been refusing titles since the fifteenth century, James Lorrimer was esteemed by whichever party was in power. 'But yes, the Empire's safety *would* be compromised by what we are trying to avoid. Sophie too would be badly harmed, and so would her children, and the title, for what that's worth.'

'It's not worth a lot to me, but the Shillings people are. I'll do what's needed.'

Not 'try to do', James noticed with amusement. This extraordinary woman was confident she would achieve whatever she set out to do. 'I gather your nephew runs an airline.'

Ethel nodded. 'Five planes now, seven pilots.'

'Would you trust him, both to be discreet and to fly to Germany and back?'

'Yes.'

The one word was enough. James had arranged the rest, but this final step was the most important.

Nigel Vaile was his friend. Sophie Vaile, nee Higgs, was the woman James Lorrimer had loved for fourteen years, and had hoped might be his wife. But his personal feelings must remain irrelevant. What mattered was that the extraordinary network of contacts across the world, from Japan to the Middle East, created by 'Miss Lily', must not be compromised. Miss Lily herself might vanish, or even die, with no repercussions. But having her demolished by scandal would be disaster.

'Thank you, Miss Carryman. The ... arrangements should be finalised tomorrow. If you and your nephew could be ready to fly to Berlin by then, I will explain exactly what will be involved.'

'Just say the word, and Bob's your uncle,' said Ethel cheerfully.

James Lorrimer smiled. He had once met the politician for whom that phrase had been coined, a man who had his position because 'Bob' had been his uncle.

'Excellent.' He looked at his watch. 'I wonder, Miss Carryman, are you free for dinner tonight?' He surprised himself with the invitation, and he saw she was startled too. He didn't think that happened any more frequently to her than it did to him.

'I usually just have cocoa and bread and cheese for supper. That "dining" malarkey takes too much time.' But he could see longing in her eyes.

'There's an R in the month, Miss Carryman. They have oysters at the Ritz again now summer's ended. Do you like oysters? Their soufflé potatoes are also superb. As a change from bread and cheese?'

The grin came again. Not a charming grin at all, but one he found he was enjoying. 'You're on,' said Ethel Carryman.

Chapter 45

Some finishing schools attempt to teach their students to walk
elegantly by balancing a book on their heads. This only trains them
to walk with a faintly terrified stare, eternally waiting for the book
to fall off. Instead imagine a friendly puppeteer holds your head and
shoulders erect and still with his strings, and your spine extends
deep into the soil, balancing you between soil and sky. Yes, Sophie,
I accept that a kangaroo balances on its tail, but hopping around
the ballroom — or when being presented to Her Majesty — is not
the image one wants to give.

Miss Lily, 1913

'Unter den Linden,' breathed Ruffi. 'The heart of Berlin.'

Sophie looked. Four rows of trees, presumably lindens, with bright green leaves and a slight scent of honey above the smells of horse and car exhaust and pigeons, pretty shops and the solidity of what could only be embassies and banks.

'And that is the Adlon Hotel — it is where the Palais Redern used to be. Magnificent!'

Sophie was not sure if Ruffi was referring to the hotel or the palace.

He gestured out the window again, his gloves as immaculate as they had been this morning. 'And that is the Ministry of Culture.'

Another stately building. Culture, it seemed, was most serious in Berlin. 'And that is the famous Brandenburg Gate,' which Sophie had never heard of. Miss Thwaites's education had focused on the kings and queens of England, with a short detour into the 'gardens of Italy'.

They passed the Ministry of Finance, 'With cellars full of gold,' said Ruffi. It was the first time Sophie had heard a note of bitterness in the light voice. But then all of Europe knew that any gold the ministry might glean must go not just to reparations for war damage to France, but to repay loans from the American bankers who had helped finance both sides of the war until the United States of America had thrown its hat in with Britain.

And yet the city looked prosperous, more so than London, despite the thin-faced newspaper sellers, many in tattered uniforms, one armed or one legged or scarred by gas, propped up on shooting sticks along the footpath, despite the match girls whose desperate smiles at potential customers hinted that they would sell far more than their boxes of matches.

Double-decker trolley buses proceeded along the broad, well-maintained roadway, accompanied by more motorcars than horse-drawn vehicles. Even the horses seemed well fed and many of the signs in the shop windows were in English and French as well as German, as if to announce, 'We live in a cosmopolitan city, the largest in Europe, the industrial centre of the world.' American loans and investment during the past five years had made the German middle and upper classes the wealthiest in Europe, even if the poor, or those crippled in the aftermath of war, still struggled or died, for the most part forgotten by those who would rather look at a prosperous present, not the tragedy of the past.

Hannelore's aunt, it appeared, lived at Grunewald.

'It used to be such a hike to come out here,' said Ruffi. 'That is the correct word, is it not? Hike? But now even ordinary people can ride out here on the tram.' He gestured at a conveyance rattling by on the rails. Apart from the tram's clatter the street was quiet; it was tree lined, with mansions behind well-tended gardens of more trees and shaped hedges and neat beds of perennials.

The Silver Ghost stopped. Jones opened the door for Ruffi. He bowed to Sophie, clicked his heels and kissed her hand, damply but thankfully without the relish or flourishes of the ex-Kaiser. 'Vaile, old chap, I will see you tonight, eh? A little fun.'

'You are too kind,' murmured Nigel. 'But I retire early these days, as you know.'

Ruffi's smile did not waver. 'Then I will show you Berlin tomorrow. Both of you.'

'Hannelore may have other plans, or our hostess —' began Sophie.

'I will send a message.' He shrugged. 'Your hostess does not like the "vibrations" of the telephone.' Another heel click and Ruffi was gone, back to where the chauffeur waited in his own car, behind those ferried across the Channel from Shillings.

Vibrations? thought Sophie. She had only heard the term from those who believed in séances — and from mechanics, referring to vehicles. But at least they were temporarily free of Ruffi.

The Silver Ghost drove through the gates — quite discreet gates — and up a gravel drive to a stuccoed house, comfortable but not lavish, a pale pink façade above cream marble stairs leading to a modest portico, and no serried ranks of servants bowing or curtseying.

The door opened. A manservant, not quite haughty enough for a butler, bowed, as the other cars drove around to the servants' entrance. 'Your ladyship, your lordship. The Prinzessin Elizabat and the Prinzessin Hannelore are in the sun room. Please follow me.'

They followed as a maid appeared to direct Nanny, Amy, Rose and Danny upstairs.

The hall floor was marble, the walls adorned with an astonishing number of niches and plinths holding nude figures, all extremely athletic rather than erotic, with bunches of flowers, a spray of leaves, or even what looked like a large bundle of asparagus, hiding the most erogenous zones. Pilasters were painted, with stucco trim, all in a symphony of creams and pinks.

It also smelled delicious, a perfume Sophie recognised as almost, but not quite, that of the pot pourri that scented Shillings. She peered into what was evidently a drawing room as they passed. The room seemed strangely empty, with delicate chairs situated where surely no one would ever sit on them, and a pink-tiled stove at one end giving out a small amount of heat that, despite the summer warmth, was welcome, for the marble seemed to breathe out cold.

The manservant turned into yet another hall, slightly smaller, leading to two oak doors carved with leaves and flowers. He opened them and announced quietly, 'Her ladyship and his lordship, the Earl and Countess of Shillings, Your Highnesses.'

At first all Sophie could see was greenery: ferns twice as tall as herself; full-grown trees, peach trees, lemon trees and, yes, that was a lime. And pineapples and half a million orchids ...

The second impression was glass — three sides of glass walls, a domed glass ceiling, slightly fogged with moisture, and sunlight, so much summer sunlight, golden beams magnified ten times, so bright she had to blink to clear her sight.

'Sophie! Oh, Sophie, it is so good to see you.'

Sophie blinked again. Hannelore stood before her, blonde hair in perfect coils about her head, colour in her cheeks and what was surely genuine joy in her voice.

She was also entirely nude.

Chapter 46

*All wise people will tell you that age has beauty. But one must ask
why that must so often be so emphatically said ...*

Miss Lily, 1913

The once cruel scar on Hannelore's hip was now a faint pink
line. Her breasts were high and had no stretch marks, thought
Sophie enviously. She looked beautiful, happy, and entirely
unselfconscious. 'We did not expect you for an hour at least.
Sophie, must I put on a robe? Truly, we would not have taken
you by surprise like this. You are not offended?'

To Sophie's surprise she felt like laughing. She did so, with
true delight. 'On no account. It is beautiful to see you, and I
mean no double entendres, or perhaps I do. Nigel darling, you
agree, don't you?'

'Always,' he said, though Sophie noticed he tactfully looked at
Hannelore's face, and not below.

'Aunt Elizabat, may I present Sophie, my dearest friend, the
Countess of Shillings, and her husband, Nigel, Earl of Shillings.
Sophie, Nigel, this is my aunt, the Prinzessin Elizabat.'

Sophie glanced at Nigel again. He too looked amused.

'Call me Elizabat, do.' Another woman walked from behind a
tree bearing small red apples, older, also nude and beautiful. She
might have been Eve in the Garden of Eden, if it hadn't been for
her hairstyle, softly and far too evenly grey to be natural, and
arranged in neat marcel waves around an almost unlined face. 'I
too must apologise for meeting you like this. We expected Ruffi
to insist on taking you on a tour of what he believes is the "true
Berlin". All my friends are naturists, of course, and it did not

occur to me to tell the servants to ask you to wait in the drawing room rather than bring you straight here. It is such a depressing drawing room, too. No earth, no sky above, no leaves or running water. But Hannelore said that you both have such a love of all things natural. I have heard so much about you, Sophie, not just from Hannelore but from her uncle on her father's side too.'

'How is Dolphie?' asked Sophie, keeping her voice even and her smile, she hoped, perfect.

'Hard at work,' said Hannelore. 'He is at the Paris embassy now. But you must be tired and need refreshment. A bath upstairs, or perhaps ...' Hannelore gestured behind the apple trees. Sophie saw a small round marble pool, gently steaming, while what seemed to be a natural waterfall wriggled its way down a scatter of rocks for a final sparkle into the water.

She could feel Nigel's unspoken laughter, even though she refused to catch his eye. Was this a trick by Hannelore to make sure that Nigel was, indeed, male? But surely she could not think a woman had been allowed somehow to assume the title. 'Indeed, we are both rather tired ...'

'But would love to bathe with you here,' said Nigel. 'It is a custom I grew used to in Japan. Mixed bathing is natural there.'

'It is natural everywhere,' said Elizabat eagerly. 'What is more lovely than the human body? It is our clothes that keep us apart, that tell our social rank, that keep our feet from the energy of Mother Earth, keep the caress of wind and water from our skins.'

Another maid — clothed — appeared behind them, evidently to take their clothes. Sophie fixed her smile more firmly, and slipped off her shoes and then her stockings. The maid undid the buttons of her dress. Beside her Nigel too was disrobing. She tried to think of possible punishments for him later, for she was *not* used to mixed bathing ...

'There is no need to disrobe completely if you feel uncomfortable,' said Hannelore pleasantly.

'Of course I'm not.' Sophie made her own smile more brilliant. 'People bathe naked in the river all the time at Thuringa. The stockmen go for a splash after work most days ...' Not that she had ever joined them, nor the school children either who, lacking swimming costumes, always swam nude, the girls at one river bend, the boys at another.

But I've been bathed by hired hands ever since I was a baby, she reminded herself. So many maids had washed her, clothed her. Greenie saw her nude every day, and while only two men had ever seen her naked body — she had made sure she stayed well out of sight of the peephole at Ruffi's castle — one of them was Nigel, who was there and already down to his underpants. He pulled them off, showing the scars, long, purple red and ridged from his groin almost to his waist, even the stitch marks still vivid. He stepped over to the pool, then sank into the water. 'Wonderful,' he murmured. 'There is nothing like warm moving water on the skin.'

Sophie removed her own chemise, her stockings and garters, then her camiknickers, trying not to compare her body to Hannelore's. Her breasts were definitely lower than they had been three years ago, her nipples a mother's, not a maiden's. She reminded herself yet again of aspiring to swan-likeness, and stepped into the water.

It was less confronting once she was sitting down. The water was almost opaque, turning their bodies into flesh-coloured squiggles, and covered her breasts. Elizabat sat on one side of her, Hannelore on the other.

'How long have you been a naturist, Prinzessin?' asked Nigel pleasantly.

The prinzessin beamed at him. 'Elizabat, please. Since 1919. My Jakob died of influenza. I was so cast down, cast out, perhaps, of all that I had known. Our estates lost, so many of our family lost, Hannelore I knew not where. The whole world seemed insane.

'A friend took me to a lecture. That was all we had, back then, parties and lectures.' She smiled and added, 'And if we were lucky, a potato. The lecture was by Dr Hirschfeld. The dear doctor! He explained that war is an illness, an illness of society. Until we embrace our bodies, our sexuality, society will always sicken, and look for war or other vices to distract us from what we have avoided for so long. Ah, Gerda, thank you.'

The maid who had taken Sophie's clothes now proffered a tray: tall glasses of what looked like orange juice, slices of very brown bread spread with a substance that was definitely not butter, and slices of an orange-coloured melon arranged with raspberries, strawberries and dates.

Sophie took the juice, sipped and smiled. 'Passionfruit as well as orange?' she asked.

'How clever of you!' said Elizabat.

'We have passionfruit growing at my home in Australia.'

'Wild? They must have a greenhouse here. Such a healthy country to grow up in Australia must be. Do try the bread. It is home-made, as is the nut butter. What kind of nut today, Helga?'

'It is Brazil nut and walnut today, Prinzessin.'

'It sounds delicious.' Sophie took a slice. Actually it wasn't bad, especially after the pig-based cuisine of Castle Ruffi. She took a strawberry and then a slice of melon. To her surprise the water was soothing her, relaxing her. She leaned back and felt her body lift slightly, almost floating. She shut her eyes, then opened them to find Hannelore smiling at her. 'I knew you would like it after the first shock.'

'All right, it was a bit of a shock. But all this,' she gestured at the trees, the flowers, the fruit, the arch of glass glowing in the afternoon sunlight above them, 'it's truly wonderful.'

'My thoughts exactly,' said Nigel. He too looked peaceful. This will be good for his scars, thought Sophie, and Hannelore too leaned back, as if all good things had come to pass now her friends had joined her at last.

The peace vanished. Sophie suddenly realised that this must be the most cunning part of Hannelore's plan. A man might seem to be a woman, carefully dressed, but not nude in a marble pool, and not when his hostess had seen a scar that could not be faked or disguised. Now Nigel had bathed, it would seem odd if the broad-minded Miss Lily did not.

As if to echo her thoughts the prinzessin asked, 'Your sister arrives late tomorrow night, I believe? Hannelore says you are all meeting this Herr Hitler she is so interested in.' The tone could refer to a stamp collection or a passion for mah jong. Prinzessin Elizabat was not a National Socialist, it seemed. It also appeared that Miss Lily was assumed to be Nigel's sister, or half-sister. It would be useful to know which, thought Sophie, trying not to giggle at the thought of asking these people exactly who her husband's presumed relation might be.

'The Führer is looking forward to seeing the two of you and Miss Lily at five o'clock tomorrow.' Hannelore smiled too innocently at Sophie and Nigel. 'He has also kept the entire afternoon free for you the day after. It will be so good to have two whole days with Miss Lily again. Just like the old days, but now with Nigel too. And the children. I cannot wait to see the children. Will you have them brought down before dinner, or should I go up to them? They must have grown so much over summer.'

Sophie tried to find a crevice in the conversation, to say that … that they had just had a telegram from Lily, that she could not arrive until the day after tomorrow, and so would not be staying there. Impossible that she could stay there now.

No, that wouldn't work. How could they have picked up a telegram on the journey without Ruffi noticing? But maybe they could pretend to call her … yes, that would work, if they could find a telephone nearby. She would be in Berlin as expected but would be staying with old friends …

'That sounds delightful,' Nigel was already saying. 'But I am afraid Lily will not be here until tomorrow night. She hasn't been well, but when asked to do this …' He glanced at Prinzessin Elizabat.

'You may speak freely in front of my aunt,' said Hannelore, her eyes watchful.

'You understand that I am here semi-officially, to report back to His Royal Highness? David knows Sophie. He trusts her. He is also anxious to have my sister meet Herr Hitler so she can add her assessment to mine. But David has never met Lily. He would like Sophie to be able to make her own opinion without my sometimes ... extremely persuasive ... sister. So there must be two separate meetings, one with Sophie and myself, and another with myself and Sophie and Lily, the next day. The afternoon I think you said? That would fit in well, as Lily will arrive here tomorrow night.' He smiled at Elizabat. 'We did not expect your hospitality to extend to her too. It is so kind of you. She will love your conservatory.'

Sophie tried to keep all expression from her face. How did Nigel think he was going to manage this?

'Miss Lily too knows the beauty of the human body?' asked Elizabat.

'Most decidedly,' said Nigel.

Chapter 47

*Do I remember being young? I am not sure. But the only thing
children truly have in common is their youth. One does not assume
that all middle-aged men are similar, so why should children be?*

Miss Lily, 1913

VIOLETTE

Her bedroom was a good room, if odd — a plain wooden floor,
well-polished, the wooden walls painted with trees and flowers,
and even the ceiling too. Shutters, not curtains, a very hard bed,
a pink porcelain stove surrounded by pink tiles that gave off
sufficient warmth for the season.

The room was even on the same floor as her ladyship and his
lordship. But it still was, decidedly, a servant's room. Worse,
from the bottom of one of the trunks Green had produced a
black serge dress, white apron and white cap for her to wear.

Violette glared at her. 'I will not!'

'You will,' said Green grimly.

'I do not have to stay with you!'

'Don't be silly. What would you do in the middle of a strange
city?'

Violette met her eyes. 'You forget, I have managed quite well
in strange cities. I will sing and men will give me money. And I
speak German too.'

'Last time you went off by yourself you ended up betrayed and
penniless.'

'That was because I was searching for my mother. It distracted me. I do not make that mistake again.' Blue eyes met blue eyes.

Green sat on the bed's white coverlet. 'Violette, please. This is important. I can't explain to you what is happening now.'

'Why not?'

'Because I do not know you well enough yet to trust you fully.'

Violette considered. Any other answer would have met with refusal. But this was the truth. And reasonable. 'How long must I be a lady's maid?' she asked at last.

Green's body lost its tenseness. 'Until we leave this house. Possibly a little longer. I cannot say. But you are booked on the ship to Australia as Miss Violette Jones, daughter of Mr and Mrs Jones, in a first-class suite next to her ladyship's. You will dine with the family at the captain's table.'

'In evening dress?'

'In evening dress suitable for a thirteen-year-old.'

'I will be fourteen on the voyage.'

'I know,' said Green softly.

Suddenly Violette needed to know. 'Will I have a birthday party?'

Green nodded, so quickly Violette knew this too was the truth. Her mother had already planned this. She suspected that the evening dresses would be the most beautiful ones that 'suitable' clothes could be. 'A cake at dinner,' said Green, her voice not quite steady, 'and the orchestra will play "Happy Birthday", and you will dance a waltz with your father, and perhaps the captain too.' She met Violette's eyes. 'And there will be presents in the morning, suitable for her ladyship's ward, and more presents at Christmas time in Australia, and you will never have to play at being a maid again.'

'Unless I choose to,' said Violette slowly. 'For a maid is invisible at times.'

Green sat quite still. 'That is true,' she said at last.

'Then I will be a maid now. An invisible maid. I will even do what you tell me, and ask when I do not know what to do.'

'Thank you,' said Green quietly.

'And one day you will tell me why?'

'It is not my story to tell.'

'No? Are you, perhaps, a maid to be invisible?' The thought had just occurred to her.

'Not entirely. I was trained as a maid. My ... work has sometimes entailed more than that, but I truly enjoy the profession, at least with those I have the privilege to work with.' She hesitated, then added, 'I think, on the ship to Australia, even before perhaps, you will be told everything. Or at least what we have been doing the last few months, and some of what we have done before.'

'His lordship will tell me?' asked Violette perceptively, then stared. Why should that make her mother cry.

Green wiped her eyes angrily; Violette knew the anger was not for her, as her mother reached for her hand. 'Your father will tell you most likely, or perhaps her ladyship. And by then you will understand far more of why this journey has been necessary.'

And by then, perhaps, you will trust me, thought Violette. And tell me everything, not the small bit you plan to tell me now. For she was just beginning to believe that maybe she could trust this woman who was her mother.

Chapter 48

Dogs eat. A man dines. A woman feeds her family, her friends, the world around her and, hopefully, she does it with love.

Miss Lily, 1913

Dinner was good, and nowhere near as odd as Sophie had expected. They ate, clothed, in a dining room that evidently had one of those convenient tables that might be shortened or extended. It was compressed to an oval now, highly polished, the silver gleaming. Instead of an ornate central floral arrangement that almost hid those on the other side of the table, a single fresh gardenia had been placed at every setting, their soft scent covering the table like a cloth.

'A Japanese tradition,' said Elizabat, sitting at the head of the table; Hannelore was at the other end, and Sophie and Nigel were facing each other. 'It keeps conversation general — so silly, that convention of only speaking to those on either side, changing your speaking partner at each course as if it were a horse race and you were responding to the signal to go. The meal must last only until the flower wilts.'

Elizabat wore a pale kimono-like pink shift, loose about her body, dark pink at the hem, paler as it rose towards her neck. Sophie doubted she wore anything beneath it. They had been offered similar shifts at the end of their afternoon in the conservatory pool, blue and white with cranes for Nigel, a soft gold and white camellia pattern for Sophie, a mauve and white much smaller flower for Hannelore, with silk slippers instead of shoes.

It had felt curiously liberating walking upstairs wearing such informal clothing on such a warm, relaxed body, despite her growing unease about how this situation might unfold. And yet she still could not believe that Hannelore would do anything to deliberately harm them. She must truly think that the meetings with this Führer would so convince them there would never again be a need for blackmail.

But who else might she have told about Miss Lily's secret? Or what might she reveal in times to come? Dolphie? Hannelore trusted Dolphie, loved him as a brother, not an uncle, this man who had saved her life.

Sophie did not trust Dolphie or, rather, trusted him for many things, including kindness, but Dolphie loved his country too fiercely. Such people were dangerous. Sophie knew, for she was one of them.

Perhaps Hannelore might even share her information with this politician or his aides ...

She became aware that the manservant — certainly not a butler, and nor had Hereward been allowed to take up his duties in so informal a house — was offering her soup. She waited for her hostess to sip, then tasted it. Carrot and chervil, a little thin, but good.

'What did you think of Ruffi?' asked Hannelore.

'A rogue. Why on earth did you send us there? I thought we were to have a family holiday.'

Hannelore laughed. 'Dearest Sophie. Still so charmingly ... straightforward.'

'And you still haven't answered me.'

'It is a good thing you two are friends,' murmured Nigel.

'I offered you a lodge for the summer so you would come to Berlin with hearts and minds clear, not clouded by the latest anti-German or Bolshevik propaganda in the English press. Ruffi had told me he would be in the south of France, but either his invitation to stay there fell through or he wished to spend the summer with you.' She spooned up some soup, then added, 'I suspect the latter. I presume he attempted to seduce you?'

'Speaking about sexuality with openness liberates the mind,' Elizabat said in an aside to Nigel.

'Really? I am afraid I have not always found it so.'

'Then you must meet Dr Hirschfeld. I will ask him to luncheon tomorrow.'

'Ruffi propositioned me only once. I assure you it was not a lack of "sexual openness" that led to my refusal.'

'Nor mine when he suggested that both Sophie and I join him,' murmured Nigel.

Sophie put down her soup spoon. 'You didn't tell me that!'

He smiled. 'I was afraid you might slap his face.'

'I still might. Ruffi has said he will show us Berlin tomorrow,' she added to Hannelore.

'Ruffi does not see the beauty of the human body, only pleasure and pain. He will not show you the true beauty of Berlin either. He may have you for two hours tomorrow morning only,' declared Elizabat. 'We lunch at noon, and then we will relax so you will be ready for this so important meeting.' Her smile took the barb from the words. 'I am glad you did not let Ruffi seduce you.'

Sophie picked up her spoon, and sipped the soup again. 'No one has ever seduced me. I have been the one to seduce.'

'True,' said Nigel. 'It is quite delightful to be seduced by Sophie.' He met her eyes and winked.

Elizabat sighed. 'Dr Hirschfeld says that sexuality is fluid like water. It may be hot or cold or in between. A man or woman may love the other sex or their own, or a little or a lot of each. But I am afraid I have never felt any urge for a woman, even one as beautiful as Sophie.'

'Nor I,' said Hannelore. She sounded amused again.

'The doctor will find us all most boring I expect,' said Sophie.

'Perhaps,' said Hannelore. She sipped her carrot soup.

Soup was removed; small fillets of what turned out to be grated raw vegetables in the shape of fish replaced it, with a sauce of mayonnaise and watercress — odd, but delicious. Sophie regretted that it would be bad manners to ask for more.

'Herr Hitler is vegetarian too,' remarked Hannelore.

Elizabat gazed at her not-fish cutlets and did not reply. So you do not share your niece's appreciation of Herr Hitler, thought Sophie. And yet you offer us hospitality so that we can meet him.

'The trees along your streets are beautiful,' she said, to break the silence. 'I wish Sydney had the same.'

'Sydney is your home town?' asked Elizabat.

'Yes, though Thuringa, my country property, feels closer to my heart. I used to wish Hannelore would visit me there.' She realised she had used the past tense and knew Hannelore had noticed it too.

'Perhaps she still may,' said Nigel pleasantly. 'I haven't seen Thuringa either. We're spending this winter there.'

'And you will see kangaroos!' Hannelore's expression was wistful. 'Sophie and kangaroos and sunlight. I used to dream of them, back when ... in harder times. But the world has so much hope now.'

A large roasted field mushroom for each diner took the place of roast meat, with new potatoes flecked with parsley, and a casserole of peas in a sauce that tasted slightly of lemon without impinging on their sweetness.

'I will never eat a pig again,' said Sophie, then realised she had said it aloud. 'We ate a considerable amount of pig at Ruffi's castle,' she added apologetically. 'And this is truly delicious.'

'Ah, I thought you might be referring to the laws of kashrut,' said Elizabat. 'The Jewish dietary laws,' she added when she saw Sophie didn't understand. 'My darling Jakob was of the tribe of Israel and so I also kept to the dietary laws. And now I keep them in his memory, though with no meat or dairy in the house, it is easier.'

'No milk?' Sophie thought of Danny and Rose.

Elizabat smiled. 'Except for the children. They must have milk and cheese for their growing bones, and fish for their growing minds. Tonight they will have poached salmon, and rice pudding cooked with whole milk and a little cinnamon.'

'Thank you,' said Sophie. 'Children can be so fussy about their food, especially when you are moving from place to place.'

'And nannies can be even fussier,' said Nigel.

'I would not know. Jakob and I were never blessed with children. I think my family were a little relieved, despite my grief. No, Hannelore, you need not pretend, for I know how you all feel. But I loved him, and we were a world of two. A most good world.'

Elizabat turned to Nigel. 'It was your sister who gave me the courage to marry him. I met Lily only once, at my older sister's home. I suppose she will not remember me. I was sitting on a balcony and she sat by me, and asked why I was sad. I told her it was because I loved a man my family did not like, would never like.' She blinked, as if to capture the memory.

'What did Miss Lily say?' asked Hannelore softly.

'She asked how long my love would last, with all my family's opposition, with all the tragedies that every life must bring. I said, "Forever," and she smiled. I will never forget that smile. She said, "There is your answer then. Love, and never waste a second on regret." That afternoon I left the castle, and went to Jakob's house. Oh, his mother was shocked, but she forgave me. And we married and were happy and the army would not take him, not fit they said, but I knew it was not that. I was so glad. And then he died of influenza and my life ended, then began again.'

Elizabat looked at Hannelore. 'My family did not cast me out after all, though of course they did not receive us in public, nor come to my house. But now I have my niece again, as close as any daughter.'

Hannelore reached over and took her hand. 'And you will always have me. It is a new life for all of us now.'

Elizabat wiped her eyes. 'That is most true. So much good is happening now. Have you heard of our most modern Garden City?'

'No,' said Sophie.

'You must see it, the Hufeisensiedlung, the Horseshoe Estate, designed by Bruno Taut, before you leave! It is most interesting. The houses are planned to fit into the landscape, rather than the natural world destroyed for the houses. This first stage has more than two thousand houses, of two storeys and three. And colours, my dear — colour is so important. Vibrant colour on the outside, to give life to the spirit, calming colours in the bedrooms, pale mauve in the study — a spiritual but also inspirational colour. And warm-coloured floors, for those who are depressed look down, and cool ceilings for those who need relaxing.'

'It sounds fascinating,' said Sophie.

'You are imagining new estates for your factory workers?' asked Nigel smiling.

'Perhaps. I have already updated or built houses for most of my employees, but I am certainly interested in new ideas.'

Hannelore laughed. 'Somehow I do not think Ruffi will show you new housing estates tomorrow.'

And yet you let him show us around, thought Sophie, instead of someone more sympathetic to our interests.

Peaches poached in cassis with nut cream were served.

Chapter 49

*Each of you thinks of yourself as one person, my dears. But as you
grow older you will learn that we do not just display different faces
to others, but to ourselves. Even the cliché 'mother, daughter, wife'
acknowledges that. And there will almost certainly be aspects of you
known only to yourself, sometimes such large parts of who you feel
you are, that it seems you are an entirely different person from the
one most people recognise.*

*And this is normal — as long as each of those aspects fits into
the current ideals of what normality may be, or you are able to keep
them completely hidden.*

Miss Lily, 1913

Nigel reached for her in the night. Sophie was not yet asleep, had
not been asleep since they'd come to bed two hours or earlier, if
the chiming clock in the hallway was correct, despite the calming
linden tea they'd drunk instead of coffee.

Tomorrow they would meet Herr Adolf Hitler. It should not
feel momentous, even if their meeting had been engineered by a
prinzessin wishing to fill her empty life, and the Crown Prince of
Britain, who felt his life was even emptier than hers.

Herr Hitler was merely the leader of a relatively small political
party. No matter how good his ideals, it was unlikely his party
would gain more than the single parliamentary seat it had already
won. The National Socialists' reputation in Berlin was not
good — there had been more useful letters from James providing
them with background and context. Fighting in the streets with
Bolsheviks, disrupting Communist Party meetings. They were a

political movement mainly made up of the disaffected, many of whom were ex-soldiers.

Yes, money and support from influential people would help. But money could not make Germany vote for the Nazi Party, even if it could buy them brass bands and billboards to electioneer with, nor could even Miss Lily's influence help to any great degree, especially if she could provide no compelling reason to support the party. Hannelore was letting her enthusiasm for the man and his ideals cloud her judgement.

And yet Sophie had the feeling that tonight's darkness hid a cliff and, once she slept, she would slip over the edge and life would never be the same.

'Sophie?' She rolled into his arms. She felt his hands on her breasts, hips, along her thighs, as if memorising every inch of her and, finally, between her legs. When at last she could breathe again she touched him tentatively. He kissed her gently, whispered, 'No,' and moved her hand to his shoulders. 'It hurts you?'

'A little,' he admitted.

She suspected it was more than that. She felt so warm in his arms.

'Do you feel it too?' she asked.

'What?'

'Change.'

'Things always change.'

'You are evading my question.'

'And you know me well.' He kissed her hair. 'Yes, I feel there will be … changes.'

'What kind? Do you think Herr Hitler will really convert us to Nazism?'

'He doesn't need to. He only needs to persuade us to give an attractive account of it to David. Or an account that intrigues him enough to want to know more.' Sophie felt Nigel's shrug in the darkness. 'Besides, I think David had already made up his mind. Herr Hitler advocates all David believes, too. I suspect David, and possibly Herr Hitler, want us — and Lily — as go-betweens, to liaise when he cannot.'

'But even if David were king — when he is king — it will be of Britain, not Germany. David has no influence in Germany.' She reconsidered. 'Well, a very little, perhaps, with his relatives, but not enough to matter much. Certainly not enough to help Herr Hitler gain power. And fascism in England has even less support than bolshevism.'

'I think this is just one small block in a far vaster structure, to be built over years, not days or months.'

'Then why do we both feel things are going to change soon?'

He stroked her hair. 'Herr Hitler is not the centre of the world, darling. Not even important in our world, except as the excuse that brought us to this. Many, many other things might change.'

'In Elizabat's house? In Berlin?'

He kissed her instead of answering. 'Sleep, my darling,' he said. And in his arms Sophie found that she could.

Chapter 50

A girl selling her body is decadence to one onlooker, an opportunity for another, lust for a third. For the woman herself, the act may come of anguish, boredom, acceptance, pleasure, enjoyment of what little power she has, or desperation.

Miss Lily, 1913

Breakfast was served in a breakfast room and in clothes. Even Elizabat was conventionally dressed, presumably to meet Ruffi, though Sophie was sure her body was not confined by a corset below the lilac silk of her simple shift; nor did she wear stockings, though her brown legs — as brown as her sun-soaked arms — disguised the fact.

Sophie helped herself to porridge. Nuts seemed to have been added to the oats, and the 'milk' served with it was a nut cream, with pots of honey or maple syrup instead of sugar. Fresh peaches sat red-cheeked in a china bowl next to jugs of orange juice and something muddy green, like a waterhole in drought.

'Vegetable juice,' said Hannelore, already seated with her own bowl of porridge in front of her. 'Tomato, parsley, celery.'

'Is it good?'

'I think you would like the orange and passionfruit juice better. It has pineapple in it today as well, I think.'

Nigel served both Sophie and himself with juice, and then served his own porridge. The table held neither toast nor tea and coffee, though a pot on a small burner contained something vaguely brown and bland smelling, possibly dandelion 'coffee' or the American Sanka.

'Ruffi telephoned. He will be here in half an hour.' Elizabat grinned. 'You have made quite an impression on him. Usually he does not rise until midday.'

'It is very good of him,' said Nigel noncommittally.

'You will enjoy our luncheon with Dr Hirschfeld more, I am thinking. But it is good you see more of Berlin. It is the greatest city in Europe now.' Elizabat said it matter of factly, as though it was well-known, not boasting. 'I hope you do not mind, but I have arranged the room next to mine for your sister. I am so looking forward to seeing her tonight. Will she be joining us for dinner?'

'Not till afterwards, I think. We should not wait for her, in any case.'

Sophie kept her eyes on her porridge. Nigel had refused to tell her how he planned to deal with this. Perhaps he was still not entirely sure himself. If this Herr Hitler proved to be impossible, maybe he would say he would not let his sister see her. But Hannelore would surely never follow someone so totally unacceptable.

And tonight? It might be just feasible for Nigel to retire early to bed, then for Miss Lily to appear; for her to breakfast, pretending that Nigel had an early appointment, with Ruffi perhaps. It might even be enough to fool Elizabat.

But Hannelore would know exactly why the two were not seen together, and why Miss Lily — the same Miss Lily who had given her students books of Japanese woodcuts to teach them sexual positions — would refuse to bathe naked with other women. And she would leave very sure that Nigel and Sophie knew that she knew.

The doorbell rang. Elizabat rose to greet the caller while Sophie drained the last of her extremely good juice.

The car that awaited them had a female driver. Sophie took her to be an unconventional chauffeur till she alighted, showing jazz garters just above her knees, and ran to kiss Hannelore.

'Cousin Hanne! You are looking beautiful!'

'And you have a nightclub tan and your eyes are far too bright. Cocaine is not good for you.'

'Cocaine is very good for me, as you would find out if you ever tried it. So much energy!' She turned to Sophie. 'I am Elizabat-Marie … our family is most frugal with its names. You are much too young to be shut up here with dowagers!'

'It suits Hannelore.' Sophie smiled at her friend.

'My dear.' Elizabat-Marie waved jewelled fingers. 'Poof! Hannelore is always too serious. You must come and stay with me at Wannsee.'

'Your family lives there?'

Elizabat-Marie's laughter was delicious. 'My family? Of course not. It is my own house. Today, in Germany,' she shrugged, 'and in England too, I am thinking, there are too few men and many of those do not want wives or families. Wannsee is a place where women can live their own lives. There is the Women's Automobile Club. Do you drive?'

'Yes.'

'Excellent! And sail? It is quite the fashion now to have a small yacht on the lake, or even a paddleboat.'

'Bare knees,' said Ruffi dreamily from the back seat of the car. 'So many bare knees. With dimples.'

Elizabat-Marie ignored him. 'And golf of course. You must play golf.'

'Of course,' said Sophie, who never had and profoundly hoped she never would have to. Occupations designed to fill in empty parts of life had never appealed to her.

'The course is perfect. Somebody said the grounds look just like a woodcut from above — the slopes, the grass, the future trees, the colourful trousers of the caddies.' Elizabat-Marie gave Sophie a sidelong glance. 'Quite handsome caddies. But come, I am sure you are longing for a coffee after Aunt Elizabat's most healthy food.'

'And sausage,' said Ruffi. 'We will take you first for coffee, and much sausage.'

It was an old-fashioned beer hall, with a carved, wood-panelled ceiling and painted wooden posts, and shelves high up around a room that displayed every possible container to drink beer from, from pottery steins with lids to porcelain, stoneware and glass from every era. The waitresses wore Bavarian dress, the walls were painted with presumably authentic mountain scenes, and an almost authentic thunderstorm played every half-hour, followed by Rheinish girls doing a jig below the wax grapes hanging from the vine-clad ceiling.

Sophie had refused the wild west bar next door, which came complete with cowboys, on the grounds that she would rather see 'the true Berlin'.

Ruffi smiled around his beer stein. Despite his offer of coffee he did not drink it himself. 'Ah the true Berlin. Drink up and I will show it to you.'

'Try the cheeses,' said Elizabat-Marie, pushing the plate of sausages and cheeses towards her. 'They are most good.'

It was a bit like being fattened for an agricultural show. Sophie nibbled on a slice of cheese, tried to move the cream aside on her coffee, then wiped off the cream moustache. Nigel had not touched his, nor eaten either. He reached for her hand under the table and kept hold of it while Ruffi chattered.

'And this is Friedrichstrasse,' said Ruffi half an hour later, as proudly as if he had cobbled the street himself. 'In the old days, ah, I wish you had seen it then. The centre of all that was fascinating about Berlin. The girls, ah, the pretty girls, each one a different price, according to their speciality! They seemed to walk on silk, with feathers in their hats as opulent as any countess.'

'And now?' Sophie could tell Nigel was feigning interest.

'A few girls. See the Kunstkeller there? The cellar has a nude sculpture gallery, quite a good one, and sometimes the most sophisticated dancers. But no touching, so what is the fun of that? Some of the bars still sell wheat beer with raspberry juice. They are almost the only place you can buy it now.'

'Sounds revolting,' said Sophie frankly, gazing at the Kunstkeller window. Its glass seemed stained with dust no amount of washing could ever remove. 'No wonder nowhere else sells it.'

Ruffi looked pained. 'It is traditional.'

'So are cannibalism, starvation and walking in the snow with no shoes. Thankfully civilisation moves on.' Sophie gazed along the street. The next shop sold ... knick-knacks? Something that looked like a musical toilet roll holder, liqueur glasses in the shape of ivory skulls, but also ordinary milk bottles ... 'What does that sign mean?' she asked Ruffi.

'You must learn German, my dear. It says, *The Association of Former Nurslings*. A joke, you see, for the bottle will be filled with schnapps, but not good schnapps, not here. And that sign says *Useful and hygienic underpants*.'

'Made of rubber, by the look of them,' murmured Sophie, as Elizabat-Marie turned a corner, past a shop selling amber and then another full of anatomically correct glass statues of women with their organs, from heart to spleen to ovaries, floating inside them. Tables and chairs appeared now, a café opening onto the narrow footpath and yet another sign she could not read.

'*Strictly kosher*,' translated Ruffi. 'Everyone, you see, comes here, even the Chosen People. And that is the most convenient portrait gallery in town. Bring your photograph in and by the end of the day our footman can collect your portrait.' He glanced at Sophie, who was looking instead at the next window, where girls, dressed only in stockings, garters and camisoles, busied themselves creating original etchings. 'You are bored.'

'My dear Ruffi, you are so kind, but bored is not quite what I feel ...'

'Where we go next,' said Ruffi, 'you will not be bored.'

It was a cellar, a small door on the street leading to narrow steps down below.

'Three marks.' The man — if he was a man — held out a bored hand.

Sophie stared around inside. It must still be only ten in the morning, and yet here it could be midnight, and perhaps the dancers had been there since then.

The room was large. One wall was made entirely of glass and painted with a scene of alps and flowers, even lit gently from behind with an alpine glow. The other mirrored walls made the room seem even bigger.

A woman dressed only in a man's swimming trunks danced past, her arms around a man-sized teddy bear, correctly dressed in full white tie. On the other side of the room two women in Spanish dress, marred only by the length of their waxed moustaches, gazed into each other's eyes.

The orchestra, mostly wind instruments, were dressed only in underpants and suspenders, which at least made their genders clear, apart from some who might be small-breasted women or bosom-endowed men.

Two bearded nuns in full habits that ended at their gartered thighs danced cheek-to-cheek beside her. Up on stage, bathing-suited young men with oiled muscles hit each other on the head with beer tankards, in a display that presumably meant something.

'Sit,' said Ruffi, ushering them to a table. He picked up a slightly greasy sheet of cardboard. 'This is the menu.'

'I'm not hungry,' said Sophie apologetically.

Ruffi and Elizabat-Marie laughed. 'Not for food! For the companions,' said Ruffi. 'You may have an Amazonian — a big-thighed woman, built for other women, not for men. Or perhaps a minette, a boy who has not yet grown hair, dressed in a ballet skirt perhaps. But if you do not want a change of sex,' he smiled, 'you may have a racehorse — they love to be whipped — or dominas, if you prefer the lash yourself. We are too early for my favourites, I'm afraid.'

'And those are?' asked Sophie evenly, as two men clad in pink silk knickers and extremely small camisoles tangoed past, though the tired-looking orchestra played a waltz.

'I like the demi-castors — girls of good family who work here only after school. And table ladies! From the best families only — I have known some of their brothers at school — and so expensive. But exquisite, I assure you, and quite well trained.'

'How efficient,' said Sophie coldly. Suddenly she was tired of pretence. Was this outing designed by Hannelore too, to show Nigel that transvestism was accepted in Berlin or, if not accepted, so well understood that it would easily be detected? She looked at the small jewelled watch on her wrist. 'I am afraid we are due back for luncheon.'

'But you have seen nothing!' protested Ruffi.

'And it has been enough. Thank you,' said Sophie.

Chapter 51

Shakespeare said imitate the action of the tiger. I find considering strategy as far in advance as possible far more advisable.

Miss Lily, 1913

VIOLETTE

Violette and her parents had breakfasted with the servants, on porridge, brown bread and apples, but the cherry jam was good and she enjoyed the linden tea. Grandmère had made linden tea.

Violette did not admit to anyone how much she missed Grandmère — sometimes not even to herself — but each sip made her long for the old woman, her strength, her courage, her determination that what should be done would be done, despite Germans, the law or others' opinions.

She and Green sewed, and after that they lunched on a thick vegetable stew with barley, which she did not like, and more of the brown bread, then had tea — or rather a mid-afternoon meal with a drink that was not tea — then downstairs again with the servants, who only spoke German but did not realise that she did too.

She hated them, of course. She hated all Germans. But she smiled and ate even more brown bread and cherry jam, and drank her linden tea. As they reached the top of the servants' stairs afterwards, Green hesitated. 'I'll meet you in our room. Your father and I need to discuss something with you.'

'Is it the telegram that came from James Lorrimer to his lordship late last night?'

Green stilled. 'How do you know about that?'

'I saw the boy arrive on his bicycle. I saw my father take it and bring it to his lordship. Then I went to his lordship's room late last night and read it.'

Green stared at her. 'How dare you? You had no right!'

Violette shrugged. 'I know something is happening. And I know that her ladyship does not know.'

'Shh. Very well, come in here.' Green hauled Violette by the arm, unnecessarily and far too hard, as Violette had every intention of joining her.

Her father was dressed as a gentleman, not the valet he had been for the past summer. He looked most handsome.

'She has read the telegram,' said Green shortly. 'Stole into their room to read it.'

Jones regarded Violette. 'Did it tell you anything?'

'It said, *Glad you are enjoying your holiday old chap stop all well here stop business concluded just as you wished stop happy holiday stop.*'

'And his lordship is having a happy holiday.' Jones turned back to the arrangement of his tie.

'And that is not what it was about.' Violette looked at him impatiently. 'I'm not a fool. Grandmère was in La Dame Blanche. I know that telegrams like that mean something different from what they seem to be saying. Why send a telegram so ... so unimportant? Besides, I used the spy hole at the castle.'

Jones turned to her slowly. 'So what do you think is happening?'

'I do not know,' said Violette frankly. 'But I think it will begin tonight. And I wish to be part of it.'

Green began to say something. Jones gestured gently for her to be quiet. He turned to his daughter again. 'Why do you wish to be part of it?'

'Because. Perhaps, I am bored. Perhaps, because I like his lordship and he is worried.' She considered. 'More than worried, despairing even. Her ladyship is worried too but you said back at the castle she does not know, so there is more for her to be worried about. But mostly — you say I am your daughter. If I am truly your daughter then prove it by letting me join you in this, not,' she gestured in disgust at the black serge dress, 'by playing maid and sewing.'

'It is because you are our daughter that we don't want you to be in danger,' said Jones quietly.

Violette snorted. 'Of course it is not that.' She regarded him. 'Well, maybe partly that. But mostly you do not trust me. You do not trust me to keep a secret. You do not trust me to be able to act as it is necessary.'

'To obey orders?' replied Jones.

She met his eyes. 'I obey orders well if I need to. I did with Grandmère.'

'You were younger then. Perhaps less ... angry.'

'And I am older now, and I *use* my anger. And I speak German. I can even look like a German Mädchen. I have my knife and you have been teaching me the jiu-jitsu. And also I am beautiful, and know how to smile so people do not suspect me.'

Jones looked at Green. 'Well?'

'It isn't our decision,' said Green stubbornly. 'Nigel and James didn't include Violette in any of this.'

'Nor has this plan ever been carved in stone. We've always known we'll have to adapt as we go. I trust her,' he added. 'And she will be useful. You must see that. Otherwise it will be just me and Nigel. I will be far less conspicuous if Violette is with me.'

And not her mother? Violette held the question back.

At last Green nodded. 'Very well. I ... I don't like it. If this goes wrong I want my misgivings on the record.'

'If this goes wrong we may be dead,' said Jones frankly. 'And Violette —'

'I am very good at not being dead,' said Violette. 'And I have not let anyone I liked be dead either, except for Grandmère. Knives do not help the pneumonia. So what do we do?'

She felt excitement trickle. This was what she had been born for, lived for. Not for being a dutiful daughter, a ladyship's protégée. Not for wearing lovely gowns, although she liked them, and not for dining at a captain's table.

For this.

'In an hour's time you and I will leave through the library window. You will wear evening dress. Adult,' he added to Green. 'Make her look as sophisticated and wealthy as you can.'

'Pearls and the dress of silver net over deep blue velvet,' said Green. 'Low neck, pearls on a silver riband.'

'That sounds right. No make-up beyond a dab of powder. I don't want her taken for a young prostitute.' He turned to Violette again. 'We are going to a café. A ... strange café ... but you must look as if you feel comfortable there, just a little interested. You are simply a broad-minded girl playing tourist with her father. Can you do that?'

'Of course.'

'If his lordship comes in you will pretend not to recognise him: her ladyship too. And if anything happens you will protect her ladyship. Get her out of there.'

'And his lordship?'

'I will take care of anything else. So will his lordship. But her ladyship will be taken by surprise. She may even feel she has to protect you. Use that instinct, if you can. Promise that whatever happens you will get her out safely, not let her try to help his lordship.'

'Do you really think she can manipulate Sophie?' demanded Green.

'Probably,' said Jones. 'But if not, Sophie will still be safer with Violette than trying to help Nigel and me.'

'I wish I could be there,' said Green wretchedly.

'You know why you can't.'

Green nodded.

'There is more,' said Violette. 'This is just a scrap of a big plan. I want the rest.'

'Very well.'

She stared at him. 'You will really tell me?'

Once more he glanced at Green. 'I think she does need to know. She is intelligent enough to possibly work it out anyway.'

'Of course I will,' said Violette.

'I can't tell you now. No time. Nor here, in case someone overhears. But I will tell you in the car. You must promise me one thing.'

'What?' asked Violette cautiously.

'You do not tell anyone. Do not even hint at the knowledge. Not now, and not ever, unless your mother or I give you permission. Especially do not tell her ladyship. She must not know of this. Can you do that?'

'Yes. And his lordship's sister, when she arrives tonight? Does she know this plan?'

'Oh, yes,' said Green feelingly. 'Miss Lily knows all about it. You can say what you want to Miss Lily, too.'

It was as if soda water had replaced the blood in her veins. She felt alive, and truly happy for the first time since Grandmère became ill. She was trusted, a member of a group again, part of a plan, with a purpose. And tonight she would be doing something ...

'Don't forget your knife,' said Jones.

'I never do,' said Violette, affronted.

Chapter 52

Every one of us thinks we are unique. We are, of course. But as one gains experience and empathy one begins to realise there is no one thing unique about any of us, merely the unique way the very similar lives of the human jigsaw are put together.

Whatever you feel, whoever you are, there will be others who are much the same as you and feel the same, who will reach out to you with understanding.

Miss Lily, 1913

Sophie had expected a young suave exploiter, someone who would be at home in the cellar they had just visited, as well as capable of exploiting a vulnerable and wealthy widow. Dr Hirschfeld looked more like a grandfather, even slightly like her own father: wrinkled, luxuriously moustached, blunt faced and kind eyed. He was even dressed conventionally as he sat at Elizabat's right hand at the table, despite Nigel's title entitling him to that place of honour.

'Always I have been interested in the subject,' he said, accepting another glass of lemon water. His English was excellent, and his accent was American. 'A doctor of the body first, but slowly I found that the body follows the mind. But there was one case ...' He took off his glasses, as if to see the past, not the nut loaf and endive salad on his plate. 'A young army officer. I had been treating him for depression, more than thirty years ago now. But then he killed himself. Selbstmord is the name of it in German, self-murder, for that is what it is. He left a note for me.'

Dr Hirschfeld rubbed his eyes, and Sophie saw all the tears he had once shed for the young man in the action. 'He said that despite his best efforts, he could not control his desires for other men, nor had he the strength to tell his parents about them. The poor boy could not even use the phrase homosexual, so abhorrent was it to him. His body and his mind had become abhorrent to himself. Can there be a fate much worse? But he ended the note by saying that the thought that I, Dr Hirschfeld, could contribute to a future when the German Fatherland would think of people like himself with more justice, sweetened the hour of his death.'

Dr Hirschfeld looked around the table. 'No, he was not my lover, as my detractors say. He was a young man I loved as a patient, nothing more, nor did he feel more for me. But in all my travels across the world, in every culture, it is the same. So many, many young men and women kill themselves, self-murder, because society cannot acknowledge what is true.'

'And what is that?' asked Nigel quietly. Once again he had eaten almost nothing.

'That some women love only women and some men love only men. Others love only the other sex; and others love men and women both. Some may be born with the features of a man or a woman, but the heart and soul that is the other. I have given these people the name "transvestite".'

'What of someone who might feel a wish to be both, at different times?' Nigel's tone was politely conversational.

'Perhaps it is because society will not let them combine the role of male and female at one time? Or perhaps they *are* both. Do we all not become different people in different circumstances? The son is not the same person as the father, or the husband. Why then can a man not be a woman, or a woman a man, at times too? Who can choose who they truly are? Who can choose who to love? Why must they choose? Surely it is the love that matters. If we are all made in the image of God, then each one of us is beautiful.'

Sophie carefully forked up endive.

'True. So very true,' murmured Elizabat.

'And so it is my life's work to free sexuality from its prison, so it can flower and we can bloom with it.' Dr Hirschfeld replaced his glasses, but did not eat, as if he still remained with the tragedy of that long-ago death.

'We have just seen a club,' said Nigel expressionlessly, 'where that kind of thing was celebrated.'

'I doubt it,' said Dr Hirschfeld flatly. 'I imagine you were taken to a club that delights in the shock, the decadence, that perverts the true innocence of loving sexual desire to make money. Do you think that all those whom you saw felt the desires they pretended? There are many like that in Berlin today, some greedy, many desperate to survive. Those are not what I talk about.'

He looked steadily at Nigel. 'There are other clubs, clubs for the sincere, and for those like us, who wish to show that we accept them and do not simply seek amusement. There is one I know well.' He smiled. 'It even has an English name, the Seahorse Club, not far from my clinic. A former patient of mine owns it. It is not a place where the half-naked do the tango. You may drink coffee, or perhaps schnapps. You may eat a quiet meal with good conversation. It is a café like any other good café in the city, but it is also a place where those who feel their bodies do not fit with what society expects may be truly free.'

'Free for an hour, or an evening?' asked Nigel. He sounds as if he is only making polite conversation, thought Sophie. She hoped no one else could see the slight rigidity of his hands as he held his knife and fork.

What would life be like for her, for Nigel, if he were free? If they were both free, with no personal or social repercussions for their children, or political damage to James's intelligence network, if society just acknowledged that life and love could be gloriously diverse as long as that love was good, and she could openly live with, love, be married to the person she loved as both Lily and Nigel, and who loved her?

She looked around the room. How could matters of such importance be confined in this conventional setting, the cutlery just so, the plates the prescribed thumb length from the edge of the table, despite Elizabat's claim of freedom in matters of the body?

294

'People should be free for their whole lives,' said Dr Hirschfeld fiercely, 'and that is what we fight for. And too long humanity has pretended a woman must be only her ovaries, a child bearer, the servant of her husband. For too long we have held that the only true man is the blue-eyed warrior — I mean no offence, sir, to your blue eyes or military background.'

'I do not think of myself as a warrior,' said Nigel quietly.

'That is good. For that is not who we humans are at our heart.'

'Then who are we?' asked Sophie. To her shock she liked this man, trusted him. If Herr Hitler was as surprisingly insightful as Dr Hirschfeld perhaps Hannelore had been right to bring them here. She wondered what Dr Hirschfeld thought of Herr Hitler. Possibly, probably, he disliked him, having been beaten by fascists. But she could not ask. It would antagonise Hannelore, and today was too delicate already. But the followers were not the man. Nothing she had read about Herr Hitler seemed to indicate he would support Dr Hirschfeld's work. Indeed, he seemed against all forms of ... decadence. But then so did every politician. What were Herr Hitler's true beliefs, ones he might not share openly — yet? Herr Hitler himself might be more intelligent and open-minded than his reputation suggested.

'We do not know who we are,' said Dr Hirschfeld. 'Not yet. How can we? Once I thought I knew. But now?' He shrugged. 'When we have lived rightly, openly, with love and compassion and sexual freedom for many years, let us ask the question then and it may be answered.' Once again he looked at Nigel. 'Will you inspect my clinic before you leave?'

Nigel shook his head. 'It sounds fascinating, sir. But I am due back in London in a few days. Another time, perhaps. But we could see the Seahorse Club tonight, after our meeting. A short visit only, before we dine.'

Hannelore made a small sound of protest. 'But Lily is coming tonight,' she said, sounding truly anxious.

Sophie glanced at her quickly, then lowered her eyes to her nut roast. Why did Nigel want to complicate an already difficult evening? Or perhaps this was part of a plan ... Green as Miss Lily might arrive, talk with Elizabat, then leave on some excuse ...

'It will only be a short visit,' Nigel said. 'Lily intends to come back with us to England for a few months, so I'm sure she won't mind missing our company for another half-hour.'

Sophie once again forced herself to focus on her nut roast, to slice a Brussels sprout. That was obviously not the plan, then. Of all places, Shillings was where Greenie couldn't possibly successfully impersonate Miss Lily when Nigel was there too, and where she was accessible to Hannelore or anyone else who came to call.

Anger simmered, mixed with anxiety. Why wasn't Nigel confiding in her? Had he reverted to his old life with Green and Jones, thinking she was too inexperienced in intrigue to be included?

Nigel nodded politely to Dr Hirschfeld, and then to Elizabat. 'Will you excuse me? I must ask Jones to find a telephone to send a telegram for me.' He smiled at Hannelore. 'I'd like to confirm to His Royal Highness that we will still be seeing Herr Hitler this afternoon. I am sure he will want to be free for a briefing as soon as possible.'

David was more likely spending the evening in a nightclub and would remember Herr Hitler only when Nigel returned, or when Hannelore smiled at him again. What was this so urgent telegram?

'Of course,' said Elizabat, as the nut roast was removed — almost as much as had been brought in — and a far more tempting-looking savoury of tiny mushroom dumplings in a tarragon sauce replaced it.

Chapter 53

For years I thought that if enough people of goodwill worked together war might be avoided. But it only takes one spear for a whole flight of arrows to follow. One day, perhaps, the human race might outgrow war, just as we are beginning to put aside cockfights, bear-baiting and prisoners torn apart by lions for our sport. One day. Perhaps.

Miss Lily, 1919

What did one wear to meet a lower-class politician who had the patronage of a prinzessin and other royalty, or former royalty at least. And five o'clock was such a difficult time, unless it were a cocktail party, which this most certainly was not. Hannelore had said Herr Hitler was abstemious, as well as vegetarian, and even abhorred the smoking of cigarettes.

'Greenie, what dress do you think?' Her maid was staring out the window at the trees lining the footpath below. 'Greenie?'

What was wrong with Green today? Green glanced back. 'Any of the dresses on the bed should be suitable.'

Sophie looked at the assembled dresses: no red or claret colours, she noticed, not for a politician so fervently anti-Bolshevik. An off-white shantung silk with draped collar, three-quarter sleeves and brown trim, almost business-like; a plain green, silk, armless sheath with a matching high collared coat, decorated along the edges with small jade beads; or a dark blue linen dress piped in white.

These were quite different looks. She could ask Hannelore what Herr Hitler might prefer ...

She was being stupid. Herr Hitler was supposed to be impressing them, not the other way around. 'The green silk,' she declared. 'Then if we go on to the café afterwards you can remove the coat and give me the green and gold chignon wrap and gold headband. I'll need to change my shoes too.'

'I won't be with you,' said Green. 'I gather that Prinzessin Hannelore has arranged a motorcar for you all. There isn't room for me.'

'We can take both cars then,' said Sophie impatiently.

'I need to be here,' said Green. 'You forget, Miss Lily is supposed to arrive tonight. I need to prepare.'

Sophie looked at her carefully. 'I expect Nigel will say she has been detained. Or flatly tell Hannelore he does not think his sister or His Royal Highness should support their National Socialists, and so Lily must see Herr Hitler alone tomorrow,' she suggested, giving Greenie the opportunity to tell her more.

Green turned, and began to take out the jewels suitable for the green dress.

'Is he really going to attempt a quick change as soon as we get back?' demanded Sophie. 'That won't work — Elizabat will expect to see Lily arrive. Unless Nigel plans to climb out the window ...'

Green was still silent.

'Please tell me you are not going to try to impersonate Lily here. Hannelore knows her too well. You might convince her at a distance, but she'd realise you weren't Lily after a few words.'

'I'm aware of that,' said Green flatly.

'But you do know what Nigel has planned?'

'Yes,' said Green simply.

'And yet you don't tell me? I thought we were friends.' And Nigel was her husband. She was astonished at the degree of pain she felt. Jones, Green and Nigel or Lily had been together for so many years, but she had thought she was one of them by now.

'The plans have to keep changing with circumstance,' said Green, not without sympathy. 'They've had to change again today. Nigel says it's best that you don't know.'

'Why?' Sophie tried to keep the hurt and anger from her voice. 'So you three don't have to bother to keep me informed of the latest changes?'

'Sophie, my dear.' Greenie rarely used 'your ladyship' now, even in public. But neither did she often use Sophie's name. 'Because you need to look surprised.'

'I can look surprised.' Anger was taking over. 'I am extremely good at pretending emotions I do not feel, like charming army officers who want to send soldiers suffering from shell shock back to the front line. If I could manage to look as if I found those officers a delight instead of wanting to bite their ankles I can manage anything.'

'Sophie.' Green spoke softly. Sophie was surprised to see tears in her eyes. 'This is going to be hard. I don't just mean hard to pretend. I … I am not sure I can bear it.'

'Greenie, what on earth —?'

'Don't ask what is happening. Please, just don't ask. Don't ask Nigel or Jones. Just know that we do have a plan, and that Miss Lily will be here tonight and, if all goes well, the Prinzessin Hannelore will swear for the rest of her life that Nigel and Lily are two, not one, and that she should never have suspected otherwise.'

'But that isn't possible!'

Green hesitated. 'There is one possibility. I don't know if this is the plan we will use — as I said, everything may change. Jones is not just sending a telegram to James — he will wait for an answer, and directions, too.'

'You obey James?' It had never occurred to her that James might direct proceedings, rather than simply suggest them.

'Of course.' Green seemed surprised at the question. 'There are several options already, but one is that I become Miss Lily for Elizabat. She has never looked closely at me, a servant, and she has only met Lily once, and briefly. "Miss Lily" will arrive earlier than expected, just after you leave.'

'But Hannelore will know you are not Lily at first glance!'

Green gave a strained smile. 'Not at first glance, and not in candlelight. As soon as I hear the car I will go upstairs. Hannelore will see a glimpse, no more.'

'You will meet Herr Hitler without her?'

'That is still to be decided.'

'Greenie, darling, that is going to make Hannelore even more suspicious. The only thing that will stop her blackmail is if Hannelore sees someone she believes is Lily with Nigel, in the same room.'

Green hesitated. 'Something like that is going to happen.'

'But it can't!'

'There is one way that it might. Only one. One I cannot tell you, one that it is almost too hard to speak of, much less to do. But Lily, Jones and I have spent decades building up a network that cannot be destroyed by rumour. If we do our work well, then after tonight Miss Lily's network of friends — a network Mr Lorrimer regards as perhaps the most vast and important Britain has because few within it even know that they are linked — can never be compromised.'

You speak like a spy, thought Sophie, not like a maid, nor even a friend. She was only now beginning to realise the significance of Green's decades of experience. 'And to do that I must not know what is planned?'

Green nodded mutely.

A deep breath. 'Very well.'

'You're not going to argue?'

'Cyclone Sophie demanding to take charge? Not this time. Greenie, you three have been doing things like this for most of your lives. I'm a beginner — and I never want to be more than a beginner either. But I wish Nigel had told me that ...' She tried to find the words.

'That we have a plan but have to keep you out of it?'

'Yes. Exactly that. And I'll tell him so. Not tonight,' she added, seeing Green's sudden alarm. 'Whatever this is, it's going to be tricky, and you'll all need to concentrate. But when it's all over, Nigel Vaile is in for a lecture on the rights of wives.'

'When it's all over,' said Green, her voice muffled. Was Greenie crying again?

'Greenie, is this dangerous?'

'Of course. We are in a foreign country — one where we are still regarded as the enemy. You are visiting the leader of a party known to have street battles with the communists. Not just roughing up, but real fighting where people are killed.'

'We're not going to a party meeting, and if we see a street battle we will head in the other direction. Is that what you are worried about?'

'No,' said Green.

'Then what ...? No, all right. I'll let you three *professionals* focus and I'll be properly decorative, shocked and whatever else you plan that I should be.'

'Thank you,' said Green. She crossed the room and hugged Sophie briefly. Sophie could feel her trembling.

'Greenie, darling, this isn't putting you in danger, is it?' Not when your daughter has just found you, Sophie thought, not before you have had a chance to be mother and daughter again.

'I'll be fine,' said Green. 'Come on. I need to do your hair.'

Chapter 54

A so-called 'small' life may have a large effect. You never know which lever will move the world.

Miss Lily, 1913

She found Nigel in the nursery, or rather the rooms that Elizabat had set aside for the children for their stay — a playroom, as well as bedrooms, and rooms for Nanny and Amy. Nigel had Danny on one knee, and Rose on the other. Sophie assumed the action pained him, but not enough to impinge on his joy with his children.

'And this is the way the farmer rides,
Clop clop, clop clop,
This is the way the lady rides,
Trit trot, trit trot,
And this is the way the gentleman rides
A-gallop, a-gallop ...'

The children shrieked as his knees moved like a galloping horse.

'This lady also gallops,' said Sophie.

'And this is the way your mother rides,' amended Nigel. 'Which is any way she pleases.' He kissed both small heads, one blonde, one dark, then placed the children carefully on the floor — polished wood, of course, for Nanny would not permit the dust of carpets under her charges.

The twins crawled off. Both walked well now and ran whenever possible, but towards the end of the day they preferred to crawl when they needed to get somewhere swiftly, like to their mother's stockinged legs.

Sophie quickly held them at arm's length before they could wrinkle her stockings, then bent and kissed them. 'We'll go to the park tomorrow,' she promised them.

'Daddy come to park too?' demanded Rose.

Sophie glanced at Nigel. He shook his head slightly. 'Daddy may be busy,' she said, for surely Miss Lily would be in residence then, however that was going to be achieved, or meeting Herr Hitler. 'Now have a delicious dinner and sweet dreams.'

'It was nut roast for luncheon, your ladyship,' said Nanny darkly. 'Who knows what these foreigners will think is suitable for supper? I have asked for bread and milk, just in case it is indigestible. And they have promised me some stewed apple. We can't move our bowels properly on rice puddings, can we?' she asked the children.

'Zebra,' said Danny, heading for his toy.

'Park 'morrow,' said Rose, making sure.

'Nigel, we'd better go if we are not to be late.' He was staring at the twins with an expression she couldn't quite read. He bent to kiss the children again, then swiftly left the room. He did not look back.

Hannelore's motorcar was a large one, the driver separated from the passengers in the back. The young man wore what looked like a brown uniform, and a flat brown cap over shorn hair. He opened the door for Hannelore to enter first, then Sophie, then Nigel. He did not ask for instructions but began to drive along the tree-lined streets then back towards the centre of the city.

'Are we going to the party headquarters?' asked Nigel.

'Herr Hitler will meet you at a friend's house. It is more discreet.'

'A friend of yours or Herr Hitler's or both?' enquired Sophie.

'A friend of the Führer, a friend of mine, and a friend of the party,' said Hannelore. She looked out the window instead of at them as she spoke — the only sign of her discomfort. If indeed she felt any.

'Why the discretion?'

Hannelore didn't look at her now either. 'You may be recognised. Nigel may be recognised. The Führer will certainly be recognised.'

'I thought you wanted us to support Herr Hitler publicly?'

'Yes. But not too publicly. Not in Germany, and not yet. You must know how much ... ill-feeling ... there still is in England towards Germany. Even the queen's own relatives must visit in secret. We need to build up a league of friendship between our countries and those who rule them before anyone thinks to work against that friendship happening.'

'A league of friendship,' murmured Nigel. 'A kind of private league of nations?'

'But between people of goodwill, not nations. People of importance across Europe who wish for peace, who understand the threat of bolshevism, who understand,' Hannelore looked at Sophie, 'that prosperity leads to a contented people, and contented people do not wish for war.'

'Yet Germany already seems to be flourishing.'

'Some of Germany. The middle classes, buoyed by loans from America. But bolshevism would not be so strong here if there was not widespread unemployment or poor wages even when jobs can be found. It is said that Berlin has even more communists than St Petersburg.'

'Leningrad,' corrected Sophie.

Hannelore met her eyes. 'I will not speak that man's name. The Bolsheviks killed my cousins, the tsar, poor Nicholas, and darling Alexandra and their children. They were your prince's cousins too ... Ah, here we are.'

The house was in a mixed area of family homes, but many with what seemed to be offices on the ground floor — lawyers, perhaps, or doctors — or maybe dog groomers, thought Sophie, as a perfectly coiffured poodle stalked past on a lead held by a woman dressed in a maid's black dress.

One house even looked like it might be a small private clinic, the kind that middle-class women might stay in if they did not have room — or money — for an obstetrician and midwife team to stay in their own houses, but did not want to go to larger hospitals, filled with undesirables, whether human or germ.

The driver stood to attention — he had not bothered with this back at Elizabat's house — then opened the door for Hannelore before going around the other side for Sophie and then Nigel.

It was a good house, with no sign in the window advertising professional services. There was a neat hedge on either side of the flagged path, and a carriage house which now seemed to be a garage. The chauffeur presumably lived in the flat above it instead of the groom. The only thing slightly out of the ordinary was a small poster in the window by the front door: a swastika, the insignia of the National Socialist Party.

The door opened at once. Someone had been watching for their arrival.

'Hannelore, Liebling.' The woman wore peach-coloured satin, low waisted and almost certainly Parisian, with a single strand of pearls around her neck, instead of wound around her arms in the present style. Fiftyish, with the slightly stiffer air of command of German aristocrats compared to the relaxed but no less imperious English, thought Sophie, though, admittedly, she had known only four German aristocrats to compare to English ones.

'Liesl, these are my dear friends, the Earl and Countess of Shillings. Sophie, Nigel, this is Liesl von Hargenheim.'

Liesl von Hargenheim inclined her head in a way that clearly meant, 'My title is as honourable as yours, or better, but, as the Weimar Republic has abolished it, and you are only English, I do not need to impress you with it.'

'He is in the library.' The 'he' was almost reverent. 'He is expecting you.' She crossed to a room down the wide hall — good wood panelling, if a trifle over-carved, and two tiled stoves — and knocked on another door, carved wood once more.

'Kommen Sie,' the words from the man inside were perfunctory, the tones middle class and business-like.

Liesl von Hargenheim opened the door. 'Die Prinzessin von Arnenberg, mein Führer, und ihre Freunde, Frau Vaile und Herr

Vaile.' Hannelore had obviously given her friend her family name.

It hadn't occurred to Sophie that the Führer might not speak English. But of course from such a humble background he would not have learned it at school or university. Nor had she realised that Nigel's and her titles, too, might not be used in Germany, especially as Hannelore's still seemed to be recognised. Was the use of titles in Berlin as relaxed as its sexual mores?

She had thought her title meant nothing to her. It seemed that it did. Or, at least, she resented having it removed by an enemy — a former enemy — and one who might, or might not have, played a part in Hannelore's blackmail.

Brown leather furniture. Elizabat had said Herr Hitler was vegetarian, but possibly sitting on dead animal hides did not count. Herr Hitler might simply regard eating animals as unhealthy. A brown wooden desk, highly polished, obsessively neat. Another man, ferret-faced and thin lipped, and obviously not the Führer, sat in one of the room's armchairs. Four younger men, curiously identical as skittles, dressed in the same brown uniform as the driver and with the same straight-ahead gaze of those who saw what they were ordered to see, sat on hard chairs at the back of the room, almost hidden in the shadows. The young men stood as the newcomers entered, not quite at attention, but all facing the desk.

And sitting at that desk: a small man, dark haired, the small moustache, with kind-looking blue eyes that crinkled with pleasure as he saw Hannelore. He stood and made what was not quite a bow, and certainly not one with clicking heels, just a small inclination of the head. But then this man was not a gentleman, had not even been an officer. 'Prinzessin! Es ist so gut ...' The voice was quiet, controlled, almost nondescript.

So this is Herr Hitler, thought Sophie.

Chapter 55

The most powerful people are not strong individuals. They are those who can change their personality to suit their audience. Their souls sway with whatever 'belief' gives them control. How do you recognise them? That is the trouble, my dears. They can make very sure you don't. And too many of their followers do not wish to recognise that they have given their free will away at all.

Miss Lily, 1913

'Mein Führer, meine Freunde, Sophie Vaile, und deine ihr Ehemann, der Graf von Shillings …' Herr Hitler's blue eyes met Sophie's as Hannelore repeated the introductions. He smiled at her, and she felt in that moment that she was the only person in his world, that this man could see into her heart, and truly cared about what he saw there. His eyes held hers, still bathing them in warmth, as he said something too fast for Sophie to follow.

'The Führer says he is so very happy to meet you at last,' translated Hannelore.

Nigel stepped forward and held out his hand. Herr Hitler grasped it, shook it twice. 'Herr Hitler, es ist so gut …' began Nigel.

Sophie had not realised that Nigel's German was so fluent. She had known Lily had many close German friends and had spent time in Germany. Some of Nigel's war (of which he spoke little) had been spent interrogating German prisoners, trying to gain their trust. Yet, strangely, she had never made the connection that of course her husband would have learned German too.

The brown-uniformed young men sat down again on their hard chairs. Herr Hitler gestured to the thin man on the other side of the desk.

Hannelore sat in another of the armchairs then gestured for Sophie to sit in the one next to her. Herr Hitler seemed to be introducing Nigel to the ferret-faced man in the other armchair.

'That is Herr Joseph Goebbels,' said Hannelore quietly. Evidently she was to translate, as well as explain the situation to this ignorant 'Australien'. 'Herr Goebbels is one of the most important men in the party, the Gauleiter of all of Berlin. Three years ago, only a week after he had been placed in charge, he organised a march of our Sturmabteilung, or storm troopers, through one of the areas where the communists hold sway.

'It was dangerous — terribly dangerous. The communists have their own local army, the Roter Frontkämpferbund. Their motto is "Beat the fascists wherever you encounter them!"'

Herr Hitler was conversing with Nigel now. Hannelore continued her explanation, as Sophie tried to pick up some of the few words of German that she understood.

'The communists attacked our march. It became a full-blown battle but we won.' Hannelore's face shone. 'Since then the Sturmabteilung has disrupted every communist meeting they can, a hundred men, two hundred men at a time.' Hannelore met Sophie's eyes. 'The Bolsheviks are our true enemy, Sophie. The ones who kill those who do not agree with them, who steal property and call it liberation.'

Sophie looked at Nigel. Herr Goebbels had joined the conversation with Herr Hitler now. 'What are they saying?'

'Nigel is explaining that David asked him here informally, because of course David cannot come himself, but that David is vitally interested in peace between our countries.' Hannelore paused than added, 'Nigel asks how the Führer became interested in politics.'

The small man at the desk spoke. Sophie did not understand most of the words — Herr Hitler must know she did not understand. And yet it was as if he spoke to her too, spoke to her very heart, spoke to the young men who sat behind them too.

'Now he is telling his story,' said Hannelore. Sophie was shocked by the adoration in her voice. 'It was 9 November 1918, two days before the Armistice. The Führer was in hospital, blind after a mustard gas attack, his eyes burning in his skull, his lungs dissolving, unable to see, to speak, hardly able to breathe. He knew he was going to die.'

Sophie shuddered. She had tried so hard to stop that gas being used. She'd failed. Thousands had died; thousands more had been blinded, horribly burned or lost their voices for life. This man was one of them. And yet his face was unscarred, his voice clear, his eyes tired but bright.

'He heard the whispers down the line of beds, how the communists in our army had betrayed us, were refusing to fight; how they had allied themselves with those who had been our allies but were now our enemies, the Russians.

'We outnumbered your forces. Even with America joining your war effort, we had more men, better equipment and superior training by far. We were winning the war! But when our soldiers were corrupted and would not fight ...' She shrugged. 'The strike spread. And so even though our armies were winning our soldiers began to desert, the Kaiser must resign, and we must agree to a ceasefire.

'The terms Germany agreed to were fair, but as you know, no treaty was signed for almost a year. By then our army had been disbanded but yours had not. And when the French demanded our lands we had no choice but to sign a treaty so different from the one we had agreed to the year before. Betrayed by the rot in the heart of Germany.' Hannelore's voice shook. How much were those Hitler's own words, wondered Sophie, and how much were they Hannelore's?

The small man was still speaking, his eyes bright, his voice calm but passionate. Hannelore translated again. 'I was a man destined for eternal night, enduring hour upon hour on my pitiless Calvary. On that day 9 November, the little sight I had began to vanish and turn black. Stumbling, I groped my way back to my bed. I threw myself down, trembling, anguished and burying my burning head under my pillow and the covers.

'Day after day I lay there, enduring the pain in my eyes, but the pain in my soul was greater. It was in those days, desperate not for myself, but for my country, I resolved to be a politician. I must rise again, and live. I must live for my country!'

It was impossible not to be moved by the sincerity of the quiet voice, the sheer presence of the small man with his odd haircut and tiny moustache, his body so insignificant behind the desk, his passion a flame across the room. Sophie glanced at Nigel. He too seemed moved.

'Und nun?' asked Nigel.

'And now,' translated Hannelore. She listened, then began to give the Führer's words to Sophie. 'Now we in Germany and in England must find our traditional friendship again. Our wars are not with each other, have never been with each other. If twenty-three thousand Jewish bankers and protesters had been killed in 1914, the war would have been over in months. Our leaders have been betrayed by the Jewish bankers and war profiteers, the Jewish film makers who glorify war and try to destroy society from within.'

'Ich verstehe nicht. I don't understand,' said Nigel.

The Führer smiled at him. 'This is why your prince's opinion is so important and that of people like you and your wife, and the Prinzessin von Arnenberg,' translated Hannelore. 'Superior people in mind and body. Humanity deserves a future where the decadent, the unfit, cannot just breed, but are outbred by the superior people. We must improve not just our society, but humanity.'

Adolf Hitler looked about the room, his eyes still fervent, his hands clasped quietly on the desk. 'Go out and look at Berlin tonight.' His voice was still quiet, controlled, Hannelore's even softer, translating. 'See how the soul of Germany is debased. It was the Jews who brought the pornographic art form called movie theatres to Germany, to America and England where they can spread their filthy propaganda on the screen. Look at Jewish so-called scientists, the so-called doctors of the mind, like the man Freud with his psychoanalytic filth, like Bloch and

Hirschfeld, who use science as an excuse for debased ideas of homosexualists and worse, that destroy the sacred institutions of marriage and the family.' Herr Hitler gave a thin, sad smile. 'The only vice Berlin recognises now is chastity.'

Nigel spoke again. This time Hannelore didn't translate. Her hands were in her lap, as if she tried to stop them shaking. She had obviously not expected this part of Hitler's vision to be expounded tonight. Sophie heard the word Hirschfeld again. Hannelore looked as if she were going to interrupt, then sat back again.

What was being said? Surely Herr Hitler could not know that Hannelore's aunt was a supporter of Dr Hirschfeld, that they had lunched with him that very day at her house.

'What are they saying?' whispered Sophie.

'Nigel says he has met Dr Hirschfeld,' said Hannelore, without further comment, or defence of the doctor. Ah, thought Sophie, so someone else in this room speaks English, someone Hannelore does not want knowing quite how close her connection to a 'degenerate' doctor was.

Nigel stood. He reached his hand across the desk. Herr Hitler took it in his, then stepped out from behind the desk again, making his small almost-bow to Hannelore and to Sophie. Once again Sophie felt as if his eyes were searching for the bond that linked them. There was no such bond — the very opposite of a bond — and yet such was the strength of Hitler's gaze she almost felt that somehow it must be there.

Herr Hitler spoke to Nigel again.

'The Führer is thanking Nigel for his visit. He hopes that his report to the Prince of Wales will bring peace and understanding between our nations.' Hannelore paused, as Nigel began to speak.

'Nigel says that he will indeed be reporting to His Royal Highness.' Hannelore stopped translating suddenly.

'What is he saying?' demanded Sophie in a whisper.

Hannelore shook her head. The Führer said something quick and harsh. The man Goebbels replied, barking a command to the young men in uniform. They stood, this time facing Sophie and Nigel.

What was happening?

Nigel turned to Sophie. He took her hand and kissed it, his face clear and determined, a smile of ruefulness and love. 'I have just told Herr Hitler I will indeed make my report to the prince. That I will say that it is strange that a party of peace needs its own army and with it violently attacks its opponents, rather than merely defending itself. I will tell him that my good friends who are Jewish, but not bankers, and those who are bankers, but not Jewish, will be most interested in Herr Hitler's ideas about evil bankers, as would my mother have been, who was the granddaughter of a rabbi.'

Nigel added quietly, 'I also told him I liked and admired Dr Hirschfeld and that we are now going to visit the Seahorse Club that Dr Hirschfield recommended we visit, where we can see homosexualists and others who feel they must hide who they are from society, sit in peace and friendship, the true peace and friendship that he pretends to desire but I do not think he can ever feel.'

Hannelore put her hand beseechingly on Nigel's. 'Please, do not do this.' She turned to Herr Hitler, her words too fast for Sophie to make out even one of them, but evidently an apology, even, perhaps 'He does not mean this' or 'I can convince him. Give me time.' Nigel watched her, smiling calmly.

He turned back to Herr Hitler, but spoke in English, letting Hannelore translate. 'The prinzessin and I will talk to my sister when she arrives later tonight. I am sure the prinzessin will urge Lily to visit you, but I will advise her against it. Lily will make up her own mind, of course, just as the Prince of Wales will.'

Hannelore was translating Nigel's side of the conversation for Herr Hitler. It was impossible to read his reaction. Goebbels looked openly furious, his almost fleshless hands twitching as if the slimmest control was holding him back from physical attack.

'Gute Nacht,' said Nigel pleasantly. 'Hannelore, we will wait for you in your car.'

He took Sophie's hand again. A man and his wife did not hold hands in public, or not in the best social circles. But still he held it as he reached to open the carved wooden doors, as they walked down the hall, through the front doors hurriedly opened by a uniformed manservant and then to the car, where Hannelore's brown-uniformed chauffeur opened the door for them.

Sophie climbed in first, then straightened her skirts. She waited till Nigel had settled next to her and the chauffeur had shut the door. There was still no sign of Hannelore.

'Well,' she said, 'you've done it now.'

'Not quite,' said Nigel quietly. 'But this is the beginning.' He leaned over, careless of who might see them, and kissed her lips. It was a long kiss, almost as urgent as their kisses had been in that brief period of passion before his surgery. Sophie was breathless when they finally parted. She also found that she was crying.

'What you did was right,' she said. 'I ... I am so glad I am married to a man who does right.'

'I am forever blessed to have a wife who thinks so. I hope you think what I do next is right too.'

'What will that be?' She looked at his expression and nodded. 'You're not going to tell me, just like Jones and Green won't tell me either.'

'Best not yet,' said Nigel.

'If you say so, I accept it.' She realised she meant it too.

Nigel bent towards her again. 'I love you so very much,' he said.

Chapter 56

History is rarely simple. If it seems to be, those who have told the story have collaborated so only the 'real' events are remembered.

Miss Lily, 1920

Hannelore came out of the house about twenty minutes later, alone. The chauffeur bowed, opened the motorcar door for her and bowed again after she entered. 'Zuhause, bitte,' she said.

'Nein,' said Nigel.

The chauffeur waited, trying not to show curiosity.

Hannelore turned to Nigel, her face granite. I have never seen her angry before, Sophie realised. Anguished, frightened, anxious, filled with delight and kindness, but not angry. 'Why did you do that? Say that? Do you really intend to go to the Seahorse Club!'

Nigel gestured for the chauffeur to close the door and move to the front seat behind the glass between them. 'Because, with the wrong people supporting him, that man might be dangerous. Now?' Nigel shrugged. 'He may be presenting himself as a saviour, almost a religious one, with that talk of his Calvary. Which I must say, as a practising member of the Church of England, I found … presumptuous. If I had not read his book I might even have believed him sincere, a man like myself who has seen war and knows its horrors and is determined that it will not happen again. But a man who hates war does not have his own private army.'

'You do not understand how things are here,' protested Hannelore desperately. 'The Bolsheviks already have their army. An army in Berlin, and other armies elsewhere, as well as the Soviet forces.'

'Your country has a police force. It is the government that should control unrest, not a civilian who reports to no one but himself.'

Hannelore stared at him, anguished, almost motionless, her gloved hands rested in her lap as if carved by Michelangelo centuries before. 'You do not understand. You cannot understand. All we have lost, all we still have to lose —'

'I think I do,' said Nigel lightly.

Sophie grabbed Hannelore's shoulder, forcing her to turn. 'What that man said about killing Jewish people, about homosexualists. Hannelore, Elizabat's husband was Jewish.'

Hannelore looked puzzled. 'What has that got to do with it? He was not a bad man, as people like that go. I liked him, though of course I did not visit formally while he was alive. But you of all people must know of the Jewish war profiteers —'

'Actually, I don't know any. My father is not Jewish, but he made an extremely large profit from the war, though the money he made from that has gone to creating jobs, to building hospitals and rehabilitation centres. My friend Ethel's family made millions from their cocoa business in the war. They are Quakers, not Jewish, and they too do good with their wealth.' She thought of Daniel Greenman, and his work in psychiatry. 'The Jewish doctors that man spoke of — they work for humanity, not against it.'

Hannelore shrugged, as if the matter was of no importance. 'The "Chosen People" have always been a problem, even if some among them are not so bad. Sophie, you know some races are inferior. You must.'

'Why must I?'

'You are Australien,' Hannelore gave it the German pronunciation. 'You have seen the Aboriginal people of your land. You have told me how they work for you.'

'You ... you think they are *inferior*?' Sophie had never felt a desire to slap anyone before. Yet this was Hannelore, compassionate, intelligent Hannelore. 'Two of the most wonderful people I have ever met were Aboriginal. My present farm manager is Aboriginal and, yes, there is prejudice, but I'd back his intelligence, courage and wisdom against any of the aristocrats in the House of Lords.' She looked at Hannelore steadily. 'I am a successful businesswoman. Very successful. I employ the best. He is the best.'

'I think perhaps sentiment —'

'Sentiment has nothing to do with it. As for homosexuals, four of my nurses were sapphists. More, maybe — their private lives were their own business. I only knew because I had to comfort three of them when their lovers died. Extraordinary, strong women who gave their lives for others, and if the whole world was made up of women like that, it would be much better.'

'Just a trifle short-lived,' murmured Nigel.

Sophie glared at him. 'What do you mean?'

'Darling, a world only of sapphists would mean no babies. Or would you let one of us men live to breed your new race?'

How could he, of all people, trivialise this? thought Sophie. And now, of all times. She was almost in tears, remembering the friends she had lost, their courage, their love for their patients ...

Nigel knocked on the window, and spoke in German to the driver. Sophie recognised the name of the club Dr Hirschfeld had mentioned.

'I am not going there,' said Hannelore stiffly.

'Why not?'

'You know why not!'

'Because you do not like the people we will meet inside?'

Hannelore met his eyes. 'You know that is not the case. I do not agree with Herr Hitler on this, although I cannot say so publicly. Why else would I suggest to Elizabat that you meet Dr Hirschfeld today, but to show you what my real feelings are? But to go into that club! We will be seen. There will almost certainly be gossip.'

'And you arranged our stay with Ruffi to remind us of the power of gossip, didn't you?' asked Nigel gently. 'Well, we will now go to this club to show that we are not intimidated by gossip, nor will we ever be.'

'I will not!'

'Yes, you will,' said Nigel calmly. 'You are going to sit with us and have a calm drink while you watch the people your Führer believes are so decadent. And if you behave with tolerance and impartiality you will have a chance to meet Lily tonight and convince her that her brother is biased and that she must meet Herr Hitler herself. She probably will,' he added. 'After all, she has come all this way to do so. But Lily and I respect each other. If I ask her not to meet him, she won't.'

'You are blackmailing me?'

'Yes, a little pre-dinner blackmail. Do you enjoy it too?'

'I don't know what you mean,' said Hannelore stiffly.

'Of course you do,' said Nigel. 'You have blackmailed me into coming here by persuading the heir to the English throne to have me — and Lily — meet Herr Hitler for him. That it was not a direct command is irrelevant. I am loyal to my country and to its royal family.'

And you are not mentioning the true blackmail, the implicit threat to reveal you and Lily as one, thought Sophie. You are even promising she will meet Lily tonight.

But she still could not see how that would be possible. Perhaps Nigel planned to provoke Hannelore now into saying or doing something that would give an excuse for Lily not to stay at Elizabat's. But how? There would be no way now to even contact a presumed-to-be-travelling sister to tell her of the change of plans.

She felt Nigel's hand in hers again. He smiled at her: a smile of such love, such calm confidence, that she felt her uncertainty ebb. He knew what he was doing and she had accepted that she must not question it.

Hannelore looked out the window. She did not redirect the driver, nor ask him to stop.

Chapter 57

*I have lain, half-dead, wishing myself wholly dead, with friends'
and strangers' bodies all around. I have lived almost three decades
since then and, in each of them, those I have loved have died,
not as dramatically, but at what is so tragically called 'our natural
span'. You would think I would be used to death by now. Yet each
loss is a tragedy.*

Miss Lily, 1918, to the Dowager Duchess of Wooten

The respectable homes with ground-floor offices vanished as the
car turned the corner. No tree-lined streets here, but shopfronts.
The first window advertised painless castration for cats and
dogs; in the next the mannequin of a young dark-skinned woman
wearing only a loincloth lounged next to a long-leafed tree that
bore the sign *Zwei Pfennig Zigaretten*; the next held a family of
mannequins in traditional German 'harvest' dress. To Sophie's
relief the shop seemed to be selling traditional clothing, rather
than offering an entire family to a 'discerning clientele'.

They turned another corner.

This street was more crowded. Cramped, narrow-fronted shops
sold birdcages, carbide lamps, old top hats, shoes 'hardly worn',
bootlaces, portraits in 'gold' frames and ostrich feathers. A liquor-
seller stood by a rickety bench on the footpath, with large glass jars
of clear liquid and rows of glasses and a sign that said, *Eine Mark*.

A woman lay unconscious, blood trickling from her mouth,
outside a more crude tavern, presided over by a man who seemed
a cross between an ape and a mountain. Passers-by carefully
ignored them both, as well as the two rouged children, ten or
twelve perhaps, a boy and a girl dressed identically in short

skirts that showed their stocking tops and garters, rouged knees, their thin singlets, even their lipstick identical as well.

The car pulled to a stop. The driver turned enquiringly to Hannelore, his face as carefully expressionless as a stone. 'Wait here,' said Hannelore stiffly. 'We will not be long.' She spoke in English, which the driver evidently understood. But the message is for me, thought Sophie.

'I think it's that door across the street,' said Nigel. Sophie wondered if he had asked Jones to find the location for him, for there seemed to be no street numbers.

They crossed the road, weaving in and out of the traffic. No trolley buses here, but more motorcars than horse-drawn vehicles. Sophie presumed the customers, if not the vendors, were reasonably well-off.

A woman in chiffon, which showed inadequate lace underpants beneath and nothing more, nudged Nigel suggestively as they reached the footpath. He ignored her. The woman laughed drunkenly, and yelled something that sounded like a threat.

'What did she say?' Sophie asked Hannelore.

Hannelore's face was pale. 'She said he is leftover,' she said tightly. 'That come the revolution our kind will be gone!'

A street merchant held up arms draped with neckties. 'Every one only one mark each! Only a mark! Straight from Hollywood!' Variations on the words had been spoken so often since Sophie came to Germany that she needed no translation.

The door they sought was blue and freshly painted, with a discreet seahorse engraved at its top. There was no name on the door, nor any other sign this was a café. The shop to one side of it sold gilded birdcages, some a mere semi-circle on a chain, others almost as elaborate as Ruffi's castle. On the other side an even smaller shop sold cigars.

The door opened. Sophie had expected stairs leading down to a cellar, like the one Ruffi had taken them to that morning. Was it only that morning? It seemed as if the world had turned a dozen times since then. Maybe time was eating itself and no one had yet noticed.

Instead she saw a conventional anteroom, with hooks on which to hang coats and umbrellas. A woman stood there in the customary black dress and white apron of a maid, red cheeked, plump, the smile motherly. It was only if you were expecting it that you saw the faintest sign of an Adam's apple. 'Kommst du?' she said, using the familiar pronoun. She took their coats, led the way through the anteroom and opened the next door.

It might have been a parlour for extra-large memsahibs. Round tables set with chintz tablecloths, coffee cups and sherry glasses, plates of cakes or small savouries, and men and women at each table. There was no semi-nudity, no rouged knees, no obvious drug-taking. So quiet and so normal ...

And it is normal, thought Sophie, thinking of Dr Hirschfeld's words. Normal not as in 'everyday' or even usual, but normal as in natural, not like the frenzy of that morning, for Herr Hitler was right in at least part of what he said about the decadence of 1920s Berlin. The displays Ruffi had shown them pushed beyond the boundaries of what humanity should be, caring for each other, civilised.

This room was civilised.

The woman showed them to a table. They sat. Hannelore looked tense, but not especially shocked, Sophie thought, at the sight of what were — probably — a clientele as well as staff mostly comprised of men dressed as women, and women as men, or rather, dressed as they knew their true selves to be. Yet despite Hannelore's words, Sophie suspected that even if she did not acknowledge it to herself, Hannelore was indeed prejudiced. Would she have stooped to blackmail if she had found out that Sophie had perhaps had an illegitimate child, or even was not legitimate herself, and so not the Higgs fortune heir? She did not think so.

But Hannelore would keep the secret. If they helped her and her Führer.

Nigel ordered whisky. Sophie longed for a cup of tea. As unobtainable here, probably, as in other Berlin cafés. Even coffee would come with a mountain of whipped cream.

'Pfefferminz Tee, bitte,' said Hannelore. Sophie nodded that she would have the same.

She looked at her friend. 'Herr Hitler would not like this café.'

'No,' said Hannelore stiffly.

'He will not like that you are here with us. He would like the fact that you lunch with Dr Hirschfeld even less. But that gossip does not worry you?'

Hannelore gave a weary smile. 'Herr Hitler does not like my title, the one I officially do not have but everyone still uses. He accepts my rank is — helpful. Herr Hitler does not like my political influence either — a woman should be for Kaiser, Kirche, Küche, her husband, her church, her kitchen. He most certainly knows that Elizabat's husband was Jewish. Adolf ...' it was the first time she had used the man's Christian name to them '... does not demand that those who support him be perfect, only that we agree on what matters most.'

Hannelore's smile grew almost amused as she turned to Nigel. 'The Führer probably even knows that your mother was not Jewish, but he will understand why you lied.'

'You know who my mother was?'

'Of course. Did you ... forget ... that I came to Shillings to study with Miss Lily? Of course I looked up your family in Debrett's, and asked about it too. Your mother's uncle was an Anglican Archbishop.'

'Every family has its skeletons in the cupboard,' murmured Nigel. 'So why did I lie?'

'As defiance. To say, "I will not support you; I will warn His Royal Highness not to support you." But you see, David hates all that is Jewish almost as much as the Führer does.'

'And you?'

Hannelore shrugged. It was still the most graceful of shrugs. 'Very well, as you insist. Yes, I knew my uncle's family. They are not the monstrous creatures the Führer or David and even Dolphie talk about.'

'Dolphie didn't like your uncle?'

'He didn't approve of him.'

'You've given yourself away, you know,' said Sophie.

Hannelore looked at her queryingly.

'You said "I knew his family." You do not see your uncle's family now.'

'No,' said Hannelore slowly. She smiled at the waitress as she placed teapot, china cups and saucers, then Nigel's whisky on the table. Nigel sipped it. He had hardly spoken. Why does he look at me like that, thought Sophie, as if he is drinking me in more deeply than the whisky?

'It is not, ah, tactful to know my late uncle's family now. Elizabat understands that too, though she is not political. Sophie, is there any politician, any king, with whom you agree in every way? Must a politician be a saint of perfect judgement?'

'Wanting to kill twenty-three thousand citizens is not a small misjudgement,' said Nigel quietly. He looked at his watch then took Sophie's hand under the table.

The café was filling up. A small group came in and spread themselves around a table nearer the wall. Sophie glanced at them, then looked again. Jones! And that young woman, looking a decade older than her real age, in lipstick, subtle rouge, a low-cut dress and pearls twisted fashionably around her arm — My pearls! thought Sophie — was Violette.

She glanced at Nigel. He must have seen them and knew that she had seen them, but carefully made no sign. If Hannelore had noticed the group, she had not recognised those who would have been almost invisible to her as servants.

Hannelore leaned forward earnestly. 'Is there no way I can persuade you to change your report to the Prince of Wales?'

'I don't think it matters what Nigel reports,' said Sophie.

Both Nigel and Hannelore looked at her questioningly. Across the room a beautiful woman, or a beautiful man, began to waltz with another, just as lovely, to music only the two of them heard.

'Herr Hitler has great personal magnetism,' said Sophie carefully. 'He promises you what you want, what you have not admitted you want, even to yourself — regaining the estates in the parts of Germany Russia took after the war. He promises to give you back the influence you lost with those estates. But Hannelore, his party may win headlines with their private army, but they do not win votes. Herr Hitler appeals to the lost, the bitter. The more prosperous Germany grows, the less appeal his party will have. He himself ...?' She shrugged. 'I would not be surprised to see him elected. He is persuasive. But to have all of Germany under his sway? It would need a cataclysm almost as great as the war itself.'

Hannelore said nothing.

'How fast is the party growing?' asked Sophie gently.

'Not quickly. That is why we need contacts.'

'You think the patronage of an English Prince of Wales will help?'

'No,' said Hannelore frankly. 'But I needed David to get Miss Lily here. It is *her* contacts — her German and Austrian contacts — who will be far more useful.'

'Less than you think, probably,' said Sophie. 'You and I were once Miss Lily's lovely ladies. Miss Lily taught us charm, political savoir faire. But she also taught us to think for ourselves, instead of letting our fathers, husbands or brothers think for us. Miss Lily might convince her friends to listen to Herr Hitler. But surely most know about him and either support or reject him already.'

She laid her hand on Hannelore's. 'My dear friend. This is 1929, not 1919. It is not the time for a party of loss and bitterness. People want pleasure, not politics and fighting in the streets. Not more fighting, please.'

Nigel sipped his whisky again, still holding Sophie's other hand. 'Hannelore, this may be our last evening together. You and I can meet Lily together tonight, and discuss with her whether she will see Herr Hitler. I'll advise her it is a waste of time but, as I said, she will probably go anyway.' He smiled. 'Lily takes her own advice and does not let her brother construct her politics for her.'

His eyes were bright, his skin slightly flushed. I have seen men look like that before, thought Sophie. Men who had been getting well, but who had smelled the first faint sweet whiff of gangrene and knew that by the morning they would be dead.

Men waiting to 'go over the top' by moonlight, sipping each bright second of life.

Suddenly she was desperately scared. She glanced up at Jones and Violette again. They seemed to be quietly talking to each other, drinking mint tea.

Nigel flicked his eyes down to his wristwatch, then back to Hannelore. 'You wanted a hero for Germany. You found one. But the man we just met will promise everyone what he intuits they want, so he can gain power. Once he has power in Germany he will not stop. Those who love power for its own sake never do. He will want not just Russia, starving and war-torn, but all of Europe, including England and her Empire and the Empire's resources.' He smiled at Hannelore again, that strangely too-bright smile. 'A man who has himself called the Führer? Who compares himself to Saint Paul on the road to Tarsus? No matter what power that man gains, he will be hungry for more.'

'That is not true! You do not know him. You cannot know him after a single meeting.'

Nigel ignored her. 'Sophie, my darling, I have something in my eye. A smut from one of the motorcars, I think. Would you mind going to the ladies' retiring rooms to dip my handkerchief in water?'

'Let me see!'

'No, truly, I just want to wipe it, but I might trip if I try to find my way myself.'

And you want to say something privately to Hannelore, thought Sophie. Something perhaps you do not want her friend to hear, or maybe that you do not want Hannelore to know that I know. A counter-blackmail, perhaps.

She would ask him later. And keep asking until he told her. She had no fear that he would lie to her. Nigel might not always tell the whole truth, even letting a listener assume something quite different from the real story. But if he didn't refuse to tell her, he would not make up something in its place.

She squeezed his hand as a signal to say she understood what he was doing, then stood and made her way over to the discreet sign saying *Damen*, though exactly who might be Damen here she was not sure. Nor did it matter, in the privacy of a cubicle …

The room exploded. The door first: it splintered. She saw the glint of an axe. Men in brown uniforms thrust into the café, boots pounding, hands punching faces, pushing over chairs.

Not the axe, she thought. Please do not let them use the axe again. She tried to make her way back to their table, but customers were standing, running, shouting, screaming …

She could no longer see Nigel, nor Hannelore. Jones was gone from his table too, and Violette …

'Your ladyship, stay here.' Violette's voice was calm, only as loud as it must be to be heard by Sophie. Sophie felt firm hands around her wrist.

'I must get back to Nigel,' said Sophie desperately.

'Stay here.' A command. Violette's knife was in her other hand, but to protect her, not threaten her. A man in brown with a brown cap over short brown hair strode towards them, saw the knife, retreated.

'Nigel!' cried Sophie.

Violette expertly pulled them back towards the shelter of the corridor to the toilets. 'My father is with his lordship. Please, your ladyship. I must keep you here.'

And suddenly large men with large muscles were surging through the room. The men in brown were retreating. A man in a pink chiffon tea dress and a waxed moustache sat up shakily, rubbing what would probably become black eyes. Waiters and waitresses were straightening tables. The splintered door shut.

'Call an ambulance,' said Jones's voice.

'Go to his lordship now,' Violette told Sophie quietly, though she went first, clearing a path for Sophie among the broken chairs, the bruised bodies, none, Sophie registered automatically, having suffered any real damage. The brown-uniformed men had just been making their displeasure at such quiet, well-mannered 'decadence' felt, thought Sophie, as she stepped over a broken platter and saw Nigel —

Nigel. Nigel lying on the floor. Nigel with blood streaming bright red down his face. Nigel with blood seeping from his stomach where Jones pressed hard with a reddening cloth.

'No time for an ambulance.' The speaker wore an immaculate black Chanel suit, red high heels and the hint of a five o'clock shadow. 'There is a clinic around the corner. I am Dr Andreiss.'

The doctor looked around. 'We need a stretcher. There, that tabletop will do. Don't release the pressure,' he added to Jones. 'Careful! There may be head injuries ...' That to Sophie, kneeling, taking Nigel's hand.

'Nigel,' she whispered.

'In thee I've had mine earthly joy.' The words were almost too soft to hear. His eyes closed. His breathing shallowed.

'You are not to die,' said Sophie shakily but fiercely. 'I flew across the world so you would not die. You have to live! For me! For Rose and Daniel. You have to live for Shillings. Please.' She found her sobs impossible to stop. 'Please, just don't die.'

Arms about her — Violette's. Who could have known such a spiky girl had such comfort in her arms.

Four waiters lifted the tabletop, Jones still pressing down on the bloody cloth.

Sophie followed them out, Violette's arm about her waist. Hannelore was ... somewhere. She did not care about Hannelore now.

Nigel. Nigel.

A waiting room. A Berlin private clinic's waiting room should be different from one in London, Sydney or Paris, but this was not. Wooden floor, a carpet not quite Persian, but doing well, chairs of astonishing hardness and discomfort, paintings of hills and trees that were meant to give comfort or, at least, not add to the anguish.

Waiting rooms. Places where one waited. In the hospitals she had founded, in the surgery she had created for Nigel at Shillings, she had had the authority to don a gown and mask, to enter any room she liked, as long as she did not disturb the surgeon or the team, not that men and women who operated under shelling that within seconds might create a cater where they were standing were likely to be put off by a lone woman standing quietly and still. Praying quietly. Waiting quietly. A waiting woman.

I am a waiting woman, she thought. It is a woman's traditional role, but I refused to let it apply to me. All through the war, women waited while I did things. And now I am the one who must wait and there is nothing I can do, no preparations, no organisation, no 'Wouldn't it be better to ...?'

I am a waiting woman in a waiting room.

Jones waited also. Did Elizabat know? Probably not, for she had no telephone, unless Hannelore had sent the driver with a message. Miss Lily was supposed to arrive tonight, Sophie remembered. Perhaps Green was even now pretending to be a travel-weary Miss Lily. But whatever Nigel had planned would not happen now.

And when it did not happen, Hannelore's suspicions would be confirmed. For surely if the sister of an earl, in surgery, situation critical (such a good word — critical ... it is critical that you give my message to ... it is critical to keep stirring to make a good white sauce ...) was in the same city then she would come here to hold his hand as soon as a message could be sent to her, be here as Nigel convalesced, because of course he would convalesce, there was no alternative. *None.* Sophie had flown to England so he would not die and so he *would* not die, would *not* die. It was critical that Nigel wouldn't die ...

'Tea,' said Jones, and suddenly he sounded like the batman he had been when Nigel had first known him, the batman who had decades later accompanied him to the Great War, the only way a commoner could stay with an aristocratic friend. And when Jones said 'tea' in that voice you drank it and found it warm and, even if it tasted bitter, it was a miracle, finding tea here. Miracles happened and so Nigel would not die ...

How long had it been? Sophie glanced at her watch. But she hadn't looked at it when they first came in so she had no concept of how much time had passed.

Green should be here too, she thought. Green loved Nigel too. It was not fair that Green and Jones had lived decades with Nigel, and she'd had less than four years.

'Sophie.' Hannelore tried to hold her hand. Sophie had hardly even registered her presence, nor Violette's, sitting quietly next to her father. Sophie clasped her hands hard in her lap so Hannelore could not touch them.

'You did this,' she said.

Which was both totally unfair and totally incorrect, for surely Hannelore did not support the brown shirts. Nor would she have asked them to raid that café that particular night to eradicate a British envoy who might turn the Prince of Wales against der Führer. Surely she would not have suggested that Nigel be killed before he could report back to England. For Hannelore knew, even if Herr Hitler did not, that Sophie was as capable of reporting to the prince as Nigel, and as close to him.

All this must be the work of others, probably the fox man Goebbels in his armchair, with his young men like brown-clad marionettes.

But Hannelore had brought Nigel to Berlin, blackmailed him to Berlin. Hannelore invited the doctor to lunch who had mentioned the existence of this café, a place where Nigel had been tempted to spend just a short, defiant time in the company of others like him, the man who was a woman, the woman who was a man, people who were both, or neither, and in that small place, for that small time, that did not matter.

Nigel had not even had time to finish his whisky. No time to meet, observe, to feel, perhaps for the first time in his life, that he was surrounded by those who understood the anguish on which his life was based.

I understand, she thought. Then realised: I do not. For she had never wanted to be anyone but Sophie Higgs. Even knowing her father longed for a son to take over his business, had merely made her determined that he accept that a daughter could do as well, or better.

She did not understand. And now, perhaps, she never would.

No! Nigel would live ...

A man in a white gown, white scarf about his head, a mask pulled down, emerged from the door opposite. 'Her ladyship?' he asked in strongly accented English.

She stood. She walked four steps. She said, 'I am her ladyship.'

'Your ladyship, I am so sorry.'

'No,' she said, as if this was a conversation around the tea table. Jones would bring in crumpets to toast. 'I don't understand.'

'Your ladyship, we did our best, but too much was damaged, his heart torn, one lung. There was nothing we could do —'

'Then call another surgeon! One who can do something.'

The gowned man looked helplessly at Jones, at Hannelore, then back at this woman who had always — almost — achieved everything that she desired. 'Your ladyship, it is too late. He has died.'

'People can be resuscitated,' said Sophie stubbornly. She gazed around for Jones. Ah, there he was. She grabbed his arm urgently. 'Jones, we must have another surgeon! Quickly.'

'It is more than ten minutes now, your ladyship. Truly, we kept trying to revive him even after his heart had stopped.'

She stopped then. Life stopped. Colour stopped. Sound stopped all around her. She felt Hannelore's arms and did not have the strength to move away. Felt Violette thrust Hannelore's arms away for her, heard Violette's spit and Hannelore's cry of shock.

'Where is he?' demanded Violette.

'Still in the operating theatre.' The surgeon spoke to Sophie again. 'You may see him in a little while. Truly, your ladyship, we are well equipped for surgery here, and most experienced. We have clients of great importance ...'

Did he think she wanted to invest in the place? 'I will see my husband now.' Sophie was surprised that her own voice sounded so determined and clear.

'We must —' began the surgeon.

'Tidy him? I am used to blood, and body parts. I have seen a hundred piled outside a surgery tent. Nigel is my husband and I will see him now.'

'You will let her see him now,' repeated Violette. Her tone was also calm, and subtly threatening.

The surgeon hesitated. 'It is most irregular.'

Irregular? Nigel was dead. What could be more irregular than that?

Back through the door. A white room, bright lights, a body lying on a scrubbed table, a bloodstained white sheet covering his body to the neck.

Not a body. Nigel. *Not* a body. Nigel. Not a *body*. Nigel. *Nigel* …

She could not think. Why couldn't she think? Her legs were … strange. Not her legs at all. She felt vaguely sick, but that was wrong, for she had seen many surgeries, including Nigel's, and not felt nauseated then …

'Nigel?' She touched his hands. They did not move. She touched his cheek, his cold smooth cheek. She did not draw the bloodstained sheet down. It had been fastened with strings at neck and ankles, perhaps to stop blundering stubborn fools like her from trying to revive the dead.

Dead. He could not be dead. But his skin was white. She felt no breath …

What was wrong with her? The room shuddered when she blinked. She must lie down. She could not lie down.

'I love you,' she said, staring at Nigel, seeing him grow white — no, the world was white, pale white, glowing white. She felt Violette catch her as she fell.

Chapter 58

What should you pay for love? Nothing? No, my dears. The greater the love, the greater the price you pay, whether it be for a husband, wife, a child or your country.

Miss Lily, 1913

Something was wrong. She wanted to be sick but could not open her eyes, much less her mouth. She was in a car and there was a rug over her knees.

At last she managed to speak. 'Stop!'

The car stopped. She fumbled with the door and vomited in the gutter. Not neatly — it splashed everywhere, onto the car, onto a dachshund walking past, its owner yelling something. She vomited again, then retched once more.

Nigel is dead, she thought. He is dead and I am here and all I can think of is throwing up.

Sophie fumbled in her handbag for her handkerchief. It was sodden with Nigel's blood. Sophie stared at it as Violette quickly took it, and handed her a clean one. Violette was still dressed in the unsuitable evening dress. Why had she and Jones been there? To protect Nigel from what had just happened? If so, they had failed. She had failed. All that way and he had died anyway ...

But we had almost four years, she thought. We have two children. We had happiness and I was loved and he was loved and those are the most important things ever in our lives, in his long life past and my long life to come ...

Because she must go on. Rose, Danny. Danny was the Earl of Shillings now, and Shillings must be cared for, for Nigel and for

Danny, for the people there — they were her people now too, just like those of Thuringa and in her factories.

She wiped her mouth, sat back in the car, hands trembling, still not sure she wasn't going to be sick again. 'What is happening?'

'You fainted,' said Jones briefly, as if unable to manage more than two short words.

'I'm sorry,' whispered Sophie. For Jones too had just lost almost as much as she had, more even perhaps, for she had children and a future she must live for, and Jones now had only the past with Nigel. What did he have with Violette and Green? A future, maybe. But no Nigel — no part of Nigel — but she had no Nigel either ... Her thoughts would not stay still.

'We're heading back to the prinzessin's. Hannelore has already taken a taxi cab there. She'll have told her aunt what happened. Don't worry,' Jones added grimly, 'we leave tomorrow morning.'

How? she wondered vaguely. Did Green know yet? But it didn't matter. Nothing mattered now, except to sleep. For some reason she desperately wanted to sleep, and when she woke perhaps it would be real, and even if it did not feel real there would be things to do, travelling away from this place and never coming back.

I should not have come to Germany, she thought. I should have *known* not to come to Germany.

Chapter 59

I became myself, my dears, when I stopped regretting who I truly was.
                                                              Miss Lily, 1913

Jones and Violette helped her from the car. Nausea still buzzed in her stomach and brain. The rose bushes swam like prickly fishes. The door opened. She waited for Jones and Violette to help her up the stairs, but instead Violette vanished as Jones ushered Sophie towards the conservatory.

The stench of conservatory plants nearly made her vomit once again. They were alive. Nigel was dead. She could hear Hannelore in the conservatory, stammering something in German to someone Sophie could not see. Hannelore was perhaps in shock too. Sophie did not care.

She was vaguely aware of Jones behind her. Jones must break the news to Green ...

The conservatory no longer seemed like a haven tonight. Its heat was clammy, the candle shadows ominous, leaves dripping dankly from the steam from the pool. It seemed darker than it had the night before, with fewer candles. Or perhaps some had been extinguished, as Nigel had been ...

'Sophie!' cried a voice. Elizabat's. 'My poor, dear Sophie ...'

Sophie stepped towards her, trying to control her fragmented thoughts. Elizabat stood in the pool, her arms about another woman, blue-eyed, with blonde hair that was liberally streaked with grey, and who sobbed into Elizabat's shoulder without restraint. Both women were naked in the candlelight.

This is how they had planned to trick Hannelore, thought Sophie vaguely, then more urgently. Hannelore must not doubt this is Miss Lily now. If she doubted the gossip might still spread, Nigel's work of a lifetime would be lost ...

But Green's body shook with grief. Impossible to doubt that it was genuine, even if the way she darted into Sophie's arms and hid her face against her shoulder while Hannelore watched, shock warring with shame and sorrow, was not.

Elizabat picked up a robe and slipped it on, then brought one over to Green, sliding it over her shoulders and back like a cloak. 'Sophie, my dear. I have no words. When I lost my Jakob, too, I knew no words could help. Lily, that this should happen ... it is unspeakable that this should happen ...'

Elizabat stopped speaking as Hannelore stepped towards Sophie, still unable to cry, and the sobbing Green. Elizabat's body stilled, as if suddenly turned to ice. 'Stop,' Elizabat said coldly, to Hannelore. 'Do not dare try to offer comfort now. You did this. You brought his lordship to Germany. Now your politician has killed him.'

'Miss Lily,' whispered Hannelore, staring at the grey-streaked blonde hair, the lovely body, the breasts revealed by the unfastened robe sagging a little and skin marked with pale brown liver spots and the softening, crinkling of time, no vast and livid scar tissue across an abdomen that was soft and unmistakeably female. 'Miss Lily, I am so, so sorry ...'

'Nigel would never have supported that man,' said Elizabat bitterly, 'and so your friends killed him before he could report.'

Elizabat tucked the robe more securely around Green's back, then handed her a towel for her hair.

Green turned, her face half-obscured by the towel, her voice trembling with passion. But her posture was Miss Lily perfect, and her accent and even voice Miss Lily's too as she said icily, huskily, to Hannelore, 'He was my only relative! You do not know, cannot know, what he has been to me.'

'Miss Lily,' began Hannelore. She started to move closer again. Elizabat held up her hand to stop her, even as Green herself drew further into the shadows.

'I do not wish to speak to you again,' said Miss Lily's voice.

Sophie shut her eyes at the pain of hearing it again. 'Have the courtesy never to write to me, or mention my name to any person ever again,' said Green, her voice shaking. 'You have taken the father of my niece and nephew, my beloved Sophie's husband. I think you have done enough damage to our family.' She leaned for one last steadying moment on Sophie, kissed her cheek, and then glided from the room, her hands obscuring her face as she wiped her tears.

'I am sorry,' whispered Hannelore again, though it was obvious the departing woman could not hear her. She turned to Sophie. 'Sophie, I believed — I did not mean ... I did not think —'

'It doesn't matter,' said Sophie wearily, carefully blocking the route between the shrubs to the doorway in case Hannelore tried to follow before Green got to her room. Had this been the plan? Nigel would quarrel with Hannelore at the Seahorse Club, taunting her till she lost her temper. She would come back here, glimpse 'Miss Lily', who would use the excuse of the quarrel to vanish. Probably Green had intended to be here, naked, with few candles and many shadows, when Hannelore and Nigel arrived, so that she would be only half-visible in candlelight, then neither she nor Nigel would have agreed to see Hannelore again.

It might have worked, especially as Elizabat, who had never known Miss Lily well, and for such a short time so long ago, had evidently accepted Green's imposture. And why should she not? Or was Elizabat too part of this farrago? Had she agreed to tell Hannelore she had seen both Lily and Nigel together, naked? Surely she must resent her family's treatment of her beloved husband, feel both shock and horror at her niece's support of a fervent racist. But it didn't matter now. Nothing mattered.

'Nothing matters,' Sophie said wearily to Hannelore. 'Nigel is dead and nothing you feel or say will bring him back. I don't care about your politician. I loved you once, you know. You were my dearest friend. I risked my life to save you and you have given me this. My husband gone. My children fatherless —' She choked at the thought of Rose and Danny, asleep upstairs, not knowing they had no father. Danny, Daniel Vaile, Earl of Shillings ...

She almost managed the tears she was so desperate to shed, at the thought of the three-year-old earl, and all that he must bear so young.

'Sleep,' said Elizabat, a little desperately. 'I will bring you a tisane. I know what it is to lose a beloved husband. Sleep now, my dear, and tomorrow ... tomorrow you can think how to go on.'

'Thank you,' whispered Sophie. 'No tisane please. I just need quiet. To lie down.'

Jones put his arms about her waist as she left the conservatory, then supported her up the stairs, looking about him as if to ensure that no young men in brown uniforms might attack them there, then opened her bedroom door. Violette stood there, in maid's uniform again. Jones left, still saying nothing, as Violette took charge.

The fire was lit, her nightdress laid out. Violette began to undo the buttons on Sophie's dress, not quite like a maid, but gently and with care.

'Would you like a bath?'

She smelled of vomit. She smelled of Nigel's blood. She should wash, and go and see her sleeping children.

She could do none of that.

'I will just sleep. I can put my nightdress on myself. Go to your mother. Tell her she ... she was magnificent. The prinzessin suspected nothing. She will not bother us again.'

'Good,' said Violette. 'I do not suppose you would give me permission to kill her, so I am glad we do not see her again.'

'I am glad too,' whispered Sophie.

She lied. She knew she lied. Tonight she had lost Nigel. She had lost Miss Lily too. And she had lost Hannelore.

Chapter 60

There are two kinds of women: those who men see, who charm or alarm them, and those they do not see, the ones who serve them. Sometimes it is useful to be invisible.

Miss Lily, 1910

VIOLETTE

The clock below struck two am. The grey-streaked blonde head lay unmoving on the white linen pillow. Violette sat on the chair by the bed, listening, watchful, the room lit only by the streaked glow of the pink-tiled stove.

A knock at the door. She ignored it.

The knock came again, soft but insistent.

'Answer it,' whispered the figure in the bed.

Violette straightened her black serge dress and tried to look as servant-like as possible. She opened the door slightly.

Prinzessin Hannelore stood there. She had not changed her crumpled dress. Her eyes were red and swollen. 'May I see Miss Lily?'

'I'm sorry. She is not to be disturbed.'

The bewigged figure in the bed gave a muffled sob. Violette looked back, then turned eyes of true anger at the prinzessin. 'Go away.'

'I ... I must talk to her. Please.' The prinzessin's voice rose slightly. 'Miss Lily, please let me speak with you. I must explain. I am sorry. I cannot tell you how sorry I am.'

Violette thrust her body further out of the room, effectively blocking it from view. 'Have you not done enough? To all of us? You think I am just a maid, that I have no feelings either?'

'I ... I didn't think —'

'No, *Prinzessin*.' The words were a hiss. 'You did not think. And so she lies there sobbing and nothing you can say can change that. And I may not sob, not yet. But I can tell you this: go away.'

'Please, ask Miss Lily if she will see me tomorrow. I know there is nothing I can do to make this better, but I must explain —'

Violette reached under her skirt and drew her knife from its sheath in her garter. The prinzessin stared at it.

'Do you know where the earl found me?' Violette asked. 'An orphan, who had been singing in the snow, prey for men. And yet he took me in, made me a maid and now I tend Miss Lily and I will tell you this,' Violette lowered her voice to a whisper, 'if you try to see Miss Lily again tonight I will take this knife and carve *Traitor* on your forehead, for that is what you have been to those who loved you, trusted you. Now go away.'

Did she imagine the prinzessin looked almost longingly at the knife? But she turned and left as instructed.

Violette shut the door.

'Violette.' The figure on the bed sat up and straightened her wig. 'We need to pack. We need to leave, now.' Green slid out of bed, shrugged off her nightdress and pulled out a travelling suit of soft blue tweed.

'Where do we go?'

'Your father made the arrangements with England yesterday. Two cars are waiting down the road to take us to the airport. We will fly back to England at first light.' Green sat suddenly as if her legs no longer supported her. 'And the coffin will be taken there too.'

Suddenly she began to cry, not the neat sobs she had pretended before, but snorts, as if she had no practice in sobbing, no idea how to do it well. Her whole body began to shake. 'He is gone,' she whispered. 'Nigel is gone, forever.'

Violette sat beside her. It was only then she saw the handle of a pistol protruding from under the pillow. She looked at the pistol, at the sobbing woman, then put her knife back in its sheath.

'Maman?' she enquired softly.

'I don't know how to be your mother. I never did! If I had known how then you would not have been alone. If I knew how I would try to be your mother now.'

Violette put her arms about her. 'I do not know how to be the daughter of a mother, even of a mother like you. But I promise you this,' she kissed the faintly powdered cheek, 'as long as I live I will make sure that no one kills you except if it is me.'

The woman who was her mother — yes, truly was her mother — looked up at her. Violette held out a handkerchief so her mother could blow her nose.

'Fair enough,' said Green.

Chapter 61

Friendship lasts. Remember that, my dears. If it does not last it was a temporary convenience, not friendship.

Miss Lily, 1913

'Soapie? Soapie, lass, it's me.'

'What!' Sophie removed the chair she had put under the handle and opened the door. She had already refused to open it overnight for Hannelore, and for Elizabat.

She did not feel real, though the nausea and the strange desire to sleep had passed. But Ethel *was* there, massive and comforting in a purple dust-coat and a hat like a dead purple rat.

Dead. Nigel was dead ...

'Oh, lass.' Ethel held her. Just held her, held her, held her. At last she said, 'I can't say it will get better, love. I never loved anyone that way, so how can I know? But you know, I know, that life goes on.'

Sophie nodded. It was all that she could manage.

'Our George is in a car outside. Your Mr Jones called me when ... when it looked like things ... anyway, we flew here. The plane is at Tempelhof. George is ready to fly you all back at first light.'

'I ... I haven't told the children yet. I don't know ...'

Ethel's arms were so wonderfully solid. 'No need to tell them yet, lass. Mr Jones said Nigel's sister needs to leave, and leave quickly, and her maid too. That right?'

'Of course. Yes, yes, they have to go too.'

If they left Berlin now Hannelore would never see Green, as

340

herself or as Miss Lily. If they left now then for Hannelore Miss Lily would still be alive, and Nigel dead.

Dead. Nigel was dead.

'We need to get you and the ...' even Ethel hesitated at the word '... coffin back to England. Don't want you to be held up here with an inquest. If we leave now we'll be gone before any officials start asking questions.'

Sophie hadn't even thought of an inquest, or a police investigation. Nigel had been murdered. The Earl of Shillings, murdered. Of course the police would ask questions, as would a coroner. There might even be a trial, if they found the men concerned. She would need to be a witness.

A trial would also mean a public admission of where he had been killed. And yes, he had been there decorously with his wife, but there might still be whispers.

No. She could not face questions, an investigation, much less a trial. She would not have Nigel's memory stained by it, nor newspaper reports the children might find when they grew older.

'Don't worry, lass. George and I will take care of it all,' said Ethel.

'Thank you.' She had been drowning in elegance, in aristocracy, in assumed and inherited power. None of that could withstand Ethel's solid Yorkshire strength. She could cope, with Ethel there.

She found that she was crying again.

'Cry away, lass,' said Ethel, taking out a plain cotton hanky the size of a bath towel. 'Best thing you can do now is cry. And then we'll have a cup of cocoa.'

'The prinzessin does not allow cocoa. There's none here.'

'There is now,' said Ethel.

Chapter 62

Sometimes I have wished I could have entered a silent order, as a nun, praying, trying to glimpse the face of God, or been the mother of six children, laughing and hearty, and sturdy grandchildren. But I never wanted those enough and nor, I suspect, will you. You will triumph, my dears. But that loss of simplicity will be a tiny tragedy as well.

Miss Lily, 1913

Two cars waited in the dimness of the streetlights as they crept down the stairs, Jones carrying Rose and Sophie cradling Danny, both children heavily asleep. Green, still dressed and wigged as Miss Lily, carried nothing beyond a handbag. Miss Lily would not have been expected to lug baggage.

Violette held a single portmanteau, as did Amy and a bewildered Nanny, with eyes red from crying, though Sophie knew Nanny would have waited till the children were asleep before she indulged her grief. She hoped the children's portmanteaux carried the teddy bear and toy zebra, or there would soon be wails of protest. But of course Nanny was far too experienced to have left them behind.

She glanced at Hereward. He seemed to be trying to pretend that a midnight flit was nothing out of the ordinary for a well-trained butler. His remaining hand carried a bag that presumably held his own necessities. Lloyd lugged a larger suitcase.

The rest of their luggage could be sent on. Or not. Sophie didn't care if she never saw it again.

An owl hooted, sounding strangely normal, as they walked through the garden and slid into the cars. They started, motors coughing loudly in the silence. Jones drove the one with Violette, Green, Lloyd and Hereward, with Ethel at the wheel of the second car with Sophie and the children, Amy and Nanny. Sophie glanced behind them as the cars made their way down the road. But no other lights had come on at Elizabat's, nor had there been any car in wait to follow them, which she had feared, either police or the brown-shirted thugs.

She had left an apologetic note for Elizabat, telling her the truth, or some of it: she was sorry, she was endlessly grateful, but she desperately wanted to get her children home, and that her household was accompanying her. She left no note for Hannelore.

Ethel took the corners faster than Jones, with the experienced competence of a woman who has driven not just cars, but a motorcycle through the highlands.

There was little traffic, and that mostly horse drawn, carts delivering milk or vegetables or meat to market. The few cars seemed to belong to late night revellers. Tramps leaned wearily against buildings, where they'd have been moved on during the day, and even the ladies of the night seemed to have decided that the business of this night, at least, was over.

Tempelhof airport was quiet, grey planes on a grey tarmac in the growing grey of dawn.

No officials came to meet them. Perhaps it was too early; perhaps no one bothered to inspect the papers of those wealthy enough to fly.

The aeroplane was larger than the one Sophie had flown in from Paris to Shillings. They climbed the steps, Jones leading the way, Sophie behind him, the children still asleep, leaving the cars behind. Sophie wondered if Jones had arranged to have them picked up. She found she did not care about that, either.

A nest of blankets and pillows had been arranged for the children at the back of the plane. Rose muttered as they laid her down, opened her eyes, saw her mother's face, then slept again. Danny hardly stirred. Nanny and Amy settled in their seats on either side of them.

'Thank you,' said Sophie quietly.

Amy said nothing, obviously torn between grief for her employer, and excitement at flying. Nanny looked terrified, with the set lips of a woman who refused to show her fear.

Sophie pressed her hand. 'It's safe,' she assured the older woman. 'I wouldn't risk anything that might hurt the children.'

'Yes, your ladyship,' said Nanny stiffly.

And yet I brought my children to Berlin and to political intrigue, and their father died, thought Sophie. Nanny is right not to trust my judgement now. Nor, of course, was flying entirely safe — every week, it seemed, there was a report of an aviator crashing their plane. But just now it was the best option.

Sophie turned to find Hereward behind her. 'I will reassure Nanny and the children, your ladyship. It is not my place to say so, but I would give my life to protect his lordship.'

'But —' Sophie stopped. She had been about to say that Nigel was dead. Hereward meant Danny.

The butler looked anguished. 'No one but his lordship's father would have given a man with only one hand the position of butler. All of us — the entire staff of Shillings, and every tenant too — knows how much we owe the family.'

'Thank you, Hereward,' whispered Sophie. She would have liked to say more, but words had left her. Nor could one hug a butler, at least not without embarrassing him.

Jones and Violette sat a few seats in front of the children. Green sat by herself, still dressed as Miss Lily. Neither Nanny nor Hereward had asked where Green was. Did they not want to intrude on Sophie's grief? Or did they, who knew Green well, recognise her? Both were estate-bred. Whatever they knew, suspected or wondered, they would be discreet, even to members of their own family, their greater loyalty to 'the big house' now. Sophie wondered how long the charade must go on for. Till after the funeral, she supposed. The older tenants who had known about Miss Lily's annual visits before the war would expect her to attend.

Ethel sat on the other side of the aisle from her. She took Sophie's hand as she passed. 'It will come right, Soapie lass,' she said quietly. 'Try to get some sleep if you can.'

Sophie sat in a seat at the front, where hopefully no one would see her cry. The plane already vibrated. Slowly it began to move, strangely like a car, for so long that Sophie wondered if they were going to drive all the way to the Channel. Suddenly the aircraft picked up speed. Its nose lifted, and then they were flying.

Nanny gave a cry, abruptly choked off, as her world tilted upwards, and bumped slightly, as if on a potholed road. The aircraft kept rising.

Sophie looked out the window. Berlin lay below her, enormous, peaceful, with its tree-lined streets, well-tended parks and gardens, with no sign of the turmoil and restlessness at its heart.

'I am going home,' she thought. Home to Shillings, home to Thuringa. Home with her children, her friends, with people who liked her and loved her. She had survived most of her life without Nigel. She would survive without him now. Just for a short time though, she did not want to.

She shut her eyes as the aircraft bumped a little more into the clouds, amateur clouds, wispy clouds, that had not yet learned how to grow into dangerous purple castles.

At last she slept.

She woke to yells of wonder: two small children bounced at the back of the plane. She turned to see Ethel presenting Nanny with a couple of Thermoses and a small picnic basket. The other occupants of the aircraft seemed to be eating and drinking already.

The plane still bumped, sometimes deeply, but already her body was used to it. She watched Ethel make her way up the aisle. She said something quietly to Jones, nodding to Sophie, then walked forward again, stopping to retrieve yet another small basket from an otherwise empty seat.

I have spent my life in the moments between picnic baskets, thought Sophie vaguely, suddenly longing for coffee, vast amounts of it, without whipped cream.

And then remembered. Nigel was dead. How long must her brain keep shocking her with the news? When would her body know it, accept it?

Ethel plonked herself in the seat next to her. 'How are you feeling, old thing?'

'As if I lost myself somewhere and haven't quite caught up again.'

'Well, you've seen enough loss to know what you need.'

'Time, more time, and home?'

'That's it, lass. How about some cocoa?'

'Is that what the others are drinking?'

'Milk with a cinnamon stick for the littlies, cocoa with a good slug of brandy for Nanny, and the rest are having tea or coffee, courtesy of Carryman Airlines.'

'Coffee sounds wonderful. Do all passengers get this treatment now?'

'Well, we can't always arrange a moonlit flit, or a dawn flit anyway. But we serve "refreshments".' Ethel's Yorkshire accent became refined at the word. She burrowed in the basket, and handed Sophie a Thermos with a lid that unscrewed to become a mug. 'Milk and sugar?'

'Neither, thanks.'

Ethel rummaged in the basket again. 'We can do you cheese sandwiches, cucumber sandwiches, currant buns, plum cake or Bath biscuits if your tummy is wobbly. Rose and Danny got buns,' she added. 'There's apples too.'

Suddenly Sophie was hungry, or rather, aware her body needed fuel, and was now capable of absorbing it. 'Sandwiches. Thank you.' She undid the lid of the Thermos and breathed in the wonderful scent of plain coffee.

She sipped, hoping it would remove the strangeness still buzzing in her head.

Things did not fit. The world was crooked with the death of Nigel, and yet it was more than that. Nothing mattered, of course, nothing compared to Life Without Nigel, Rose and Danny Without Nigel, Caring for Shillings Till Danny Turned Twenty-one Without Nigel.

But despite that, something else vibrated, a wisp of not-quite thought that would not leave. She drank more coffee, then ate a cheese sandwich, and found her puzzlement had grown, not lessened. Only one of the events of the past twenty-four hours truly mattered, the loss of Nigel. But now the first shock was over, questions were taking its place.

She turned to Ethel, and found her watching her. 'How did you get here?'

'By plane.'

'You know what I mean.'

'I've got a letter for you,' said Ethel abruptly. 'Nigel gave it to me before you left England. Said I was to give it to you at the right time. Reckon that time is now. With a bit of luck it'll give you all the answers you need for a bit, then maybe you can sleep again.'

'I don't understand.' How often had she said that? I am Sophie Higgs, she thought. I am the Countess of Shillings (or am I the Dowager? I must find out. Jones or Green will know ...) but all my life I have had a *need* to understand.

She took the letter, which was sealed in an envelope, and closed with the wax of the Vaile seal too.

'I'll go and sit with George in the cockpit for a bit. Might even let me take the controls,' said Ethel. 'Don't worry. He'll be there if I head towards the ground or Ethiopia and, anyway, I've been taking flying lessons.' Somehow the plane stayed steady as her bulk moved down the aisle.

Sophie broke the seal, then opened the letter, careful not to tear the envelope. This would — probably — be the kind of letter one kept, even if it had to be hidden in an 1890s encyclopaedia, Volume V–W, that no one would ever read.

The paper was good Shillings stock, thick and linen based, with the Vaile crest. The handwriting was Nigel's, which was not the same as Miss Lily's. She had never known if that was deliberate, or cultivated to keep their identities discrete. I will never know now, she thought.

She shut her eyes briefly. She had been mourning Nigel. Suddenly the loss of Miss Lily as well was too much to bear.

Except, of course, one did bear things, and went on.

Jones and Violette were playing horsey with the children at the back of the plane. '*This is the way a gentleman rides,*' Nigel had sung. This was not the time to tell them their father would never sing it again.

She glanced out the window, trying to put off the anguish of reading, but still only grey cloud was visible. She looked back at the pages in her hand.

My darling Sophie,

I am writing this at Shillings. We leave for Germany in a week's time, and you are picking roses in the garden. I think that was where I first fell in love with you, as Lily gazed out the window at that impossible colonial, Miss Sophie Higgs, walking before breakfast in the Shillings garden, a girl who could take on anything and who has, including the most impossible of husbands.

I am impossible, my darling, I know it. For a while, after the war and then when you flew back so dramatically to Shillings, I thought my love for you might make Nigel Vaile real, forever. But he is not.

Always, while Nigel Vaile lives, he will be a potential scandal, one I will not have my wife and children face. Do not blame Hannelore too much for this, or for what I am fairly sure is going to happen next, if the plans James and I concocted come to fruition. If it hadn't been for Hannelore we might have had a few more years … but I cannot write of that because I cannot think of it, nor fool myself any longer. I must both think and write this: that the time has come for Nigel Vaile to die, as he should have died, had not Sophie Higgs delayed it.

So this is the plan that has been carefully wound about you, without your knowing. James wishes to keep His Royal Highness out of the web of fascism for as long as possible. I doubt David has bothered to read Mein Kampf, *except a few pieces here and there, but there is much in it that will appeal to him, including casting the blame for the war on a convenient, non-existent, conspiracy of Jewish bankers, and the blame for the poverty and flightiness that has blighted the decade since the war on Jewish propagandists.*

It may seem ridiculous to you and me, but if this man Herr Hitler has managed to snare Hannelore — who has twice the intelligence and ten times the wisdom and integrity of His Royal Highness — then he is quite capable of capturing a man as uncertain, resentful and, to be honest though disloyal, as dull-witted as the Prince of Wales.

If you are reading this, then the plan has worked. Nigel Vaile has died in Berlin, carrying out the request of his prince, but you and the children are safe. Hopefully, David will feel enough guilt to stay away from National Socialism for a few years yet, though his attention span is never long; nor does he like feeling guilty. I predict he will not even be free to come to my funeral, but will send regrets.

If all goes as we have so carefully organised, you and I and Hannelore have seen Herr Hitler. I have insulted him, threatened to turn the prince from his cause, then we three have gone to a location we shall have chosen in time to let James know about, so the assassins know where and when to find me. I will be killed by hired thugs dressed in the fascist uniform. One can hire anything, it seems, in Berlin these days. But they will have strict instructions not to hurt you, or any others. I deeply hope that you are safely reading this, and did not fly to my aid — or that if you did, Jones prevented you.

So it will not have been Hannelore's friends who killed me, though she may think so. Hopefully, perhaps, she may not even believe the party's denials when they say they had nothing to do with it. I do not know. It would be good to think this might make Hannelore look more closely at those she has allied herself with. If possible — if you can bear it — stay in contact with her, and keep at least the tatters of a friendship which may be useful to England in times to come. But if you cannot do this, James and I entirely understand.

The admirable Miss Ethel Carryman will do as her name suggests. She and her nephew will have you all safely out of Elizabat's house that night and away from Germany by first light. James will use his considerable influence to deny any requests for you to return to Germany to answer questions.

349

There will be publicity. This, I am afraid, was James's price. The death of the Earl of Shillings at the hands of storm troopers while his young wife looked on is what I must pay for his cooperation. My murder will alienate potential fascist supporters in England. I am glad that, at last, Nigel Vaile has been of some use politically.

But you are the one who is going to have to endure the avid interest from the press and public until another scandal takes its place. I hope this will be weeks, not months, and that the journey to Australia will give you some respite as soon as you can resume it. I have left my affairs in as much order as possible without causing suspicion, but there is still going to be an inordinate amount of work for you to cope with. I so deeply wish I could help you. I wish, even more passionately, that I could be alive to do so.

I do not want to die. Never, at any time, think that. The past four years have been the happiest I have ever known.

How does one apologise to the woman you love for dying? For so carefully arranging one's death? For not warning you, because your shock and rage had to be real for Hannelore to believe it was her associates, not mine, who arranged for my death?

I have faced this last adventure without your knowledge, and that is perhaps the most unforgivable of all. Please believe that, of all things, I wished I could have shared this with you; that I could have had no better companion by my side; that my love for you is almost all of who I am, so much so that writing this I find I almost cannot face what I am about to do. But only 'almost'. This must be done not just for my country, so that Lily's, Green's and Jones's achievements and networks will continue untarnished by doubt or scandal, but so that you, Rose, Danny, even Shillings, will not bear a scandal that would be laughed at and whispered about for a hundred years, at Rose's debut, when Danny takes his seat in the House of Lords: 'You know about his father of course? And (sniggering) Miss Lily?'

I know this too: there is a part of you that holds duty as sacred as I do. I ask for your forgiveness, but I know the woman I was privileged to marry, to know, will not just forgive me, but also understand. No man has ever been so blessed.

I love you, I love you, I love you. I believe in the afterlife too.
What will remain of me, after the coffin rests under the soft grass
of Shillings, is my love: for you, for Rose, for Danny, for Shillings
and my country. The heart of me, since that morning you damply
wandered in the garden, that still heart within this spinning world,
is you.

Please — tear up this letter, and burn the pieces as soon as you
can. After that, the last evidence of the scandal I might bring to
those I treasure will be gone.

I love you. I am sorry. I love you.
N

She read it again, more slowly, and then once more. She
wondered if she should ask Jones for a lighter now, but a fire on
a plane probably was not a good idea. She slowly tore each page
to shreds instead. How dare he? How could he?

He had no right to give his life! His life was hers! To love and
to cherish until death us do part ...

But there was nothing in the marriage service about dying
without your wife's permission. There should have been, but
there was not. If she had even guessed that something like this
might happen, she would have demanded it was there. 'I, Nigel
Vaile, do solemnly swear not to die without the permission of my
wife ...'

If only this letter could seal off her love for him. But it did not.

It wasn't worth it, she told him in her mind. We could have
lived in Australia all our lives. Jones would have cared for
Shillings. Rose needn't ever have a debut, Danny need never take
up the title, or if he did, need not mingle in British society ...

But of course those were not her choices to make, nor even
Nigel's. He had freed his children. He had freed her.

And yet ...

Nigel had given her nearly four years. Four years, two children
(the image of Daniel flashed before her but she shoved it out of
sight). Nigel Vaile might have vanished to Japan once more and
been Miss Lily. 'Did you hear the Earl of Shillings has left his

wife? Much younger than him, and a colonial. Not One of Us, really. They say he's travelling in the East, no doubt to stay away from her ...'

Nigel had not done that, for her.

Because he loved her. No more than that. No less. Even in her loss, she knew she had been blessed.

Chapter 63

You will accept many duties in your lives, my dears. Remember this one above all: the deepest duty of humanity is towards our children. We build the world, maintain the world, for them. I have no children of my body. But every child is a child of my heart.

Miss Lily, 1913

They landed at an airport, a green paddock, a wind sock, a corrugated-iron hut, and autumn green fields hedged with hawthorn.

Three cars waited for them.

Sophie walked from the plane first, hugged Ethel, whispered, 'Thank you,' then waited for Nanny to bring the children down the stairs. She smiled at them and took their hands, then turned to Jones.

'Jones, would you mind driving me and Rose and Danny to a beach somewhere? The rest of the household should go home.' She realised she had no clear idea of where they were, nor where the nearest beach might be. But they had flown over the coast only twenty minutes before, so there must be one in reach.

'Of course, your ladyship.' He never called her Sophie in public. She wished he did. Wished he could. One day perhaps. But this was not the time to begin.

For this was mid-performance. Nigel had done his part. Now it was time for hers: the weeping widow, the Dowager(?) Countess of Shillings, arranging the funeral, accepting the condolences, settling the estate. Public duties.

But first a private one.

Jones drove. Sophie held the children in the back seat, Rose on one side, Danny on the other. Only three years old and the most intelligent, beautiful children in the world. She looked down at Danny, cuddling into her, holding his zebra tightly in his hands. Please, she prayed, let Danny at least be Nigel's. Let Nigel live in his son and his grandchildren.

She looked about her. This was England. Ten years ago she would have seen little difference between it and Germany, equally alien to Australian eyes. Now the slow munch of cattle, smaller, black and white or jersey instead of pale brown and cream, the paddocks of mangold wurzels, that scarecrow with the battered top hat, even the cry of the seagulls, told her where she was.

The car stopped. A line of shingle, rocks and grey water, small waves that lapped the land. And, miraculously — no, not a miracle, just Jones — an ice-cream cart on the boardwalk, with a small ice-cream seller shivering in the salt autumn breeze, that anywhere but England would be called 'a freezing wind'.

Jones retrieved a lap rug from the back seat, then took Rose's hand, while Sophie held Danny's. They walked down to the beach. Jones spread the rug on the shingle.

'I'll get the ices,' he said.

'Ice cream!' said Rose. Danny was silent. Both children had been too quiet since they landed, and were obviously confused, despite their joy in the wonder of flying and seeing the world toy-sized below them.

Sophie gathered them both onto her lap. 'We are going back home,' she said. It was only one of their homes and soon she intended them to go to the other. But that could be explained another time.

'Where is Daddy?' It was the first time Danny had spoken since they left the airfield. Rose still gazed at Jones, now at the ice-cream stand.

'Daddy can't be with us, darling.'

Rose turned at that. Her frown turned stormy. 'I want my daddy!'

'Daddy has died, darlings. That means ... that means we can't see him again. But his love for you will always be there. Always.'

'I want my daddy,' said Rose again, but less mutinously now.

Danny clung to Sophie, looking frightened. 'Daddy,' he said again.

'I want Daddy too,' said Sophie. 'I ... I want him so much. But we can't have him. Dying means he has gone forever. Like Pusscat in the kitchen died.'

Danny looked up at her, his forehead wrinkling as he worked it out. 'Daddy buried?'

'Yes. He will be. Like Pusscat.'

'No!' yelled Rose. She struggled in Sophie's arms, then suddenly grew still. She began to cry in ragged wails.

Danny did not cry. Sophie wished he would. Maybe if she cried, her son could too. She let the tears fall, roping sobs back, because sobs would frighten them. She wanted to scream, to lie in the shingle and beat her fists and feet against the rocks, to yell at the sea 'Bring him back to me!' and see him walk out of the waves towards them.

Just tears, and suddenly Danny was crying too. Did he even understand, or was he crying because his mother was upset?

She realised Jones was standing above them, holding four ice-cream cones. She nodded, and he sat on the blanket next to them, then handed Sophie her cone and licked his own. Rose looked up and grabbed another cone, still crying, but licking ice cream too. Danny sat back and watched the others then, at last, the tears still falling, took the cone and licked.

They ate in silence. It was good ice cream. Made, probably, by the vendor's wife or mother.

'One hand and a hook,' said Jones at last.

Sophie looked at him.

'The ice-cream chap. Don't suppose he could find a job, but he says he's doing well.'

You are telling us that ours is not the only tragedy in the world, thought Sophie. She ate the last of the cone, the best bit where the ice cream had melted into a puddle, then began to wipe the faces of her children with her handkerchief, a mix of tears and stickiness and inevitable toddler grime.

'Time to go home,' she said, lifting Danny, while Jones carried Rose.

'More ice cream?' Rose, naturally.

'No,' said Sophie.

'Want more ice cream!'

'No more,' said Sophie, beginning to walk towards the car. She glanced at Rose and saw her daughter's face relax. The world still had rules, like 'no more' and 'no'.

'Daddy,' said Danny softly and Sophie saw Jones was weeping too. Together they carried the children back to the car and settled them in the back seat. Within minutes both were asleep.

Chapter 64

People cope, my dears. They say, 'It can't be done.' But, mostly, then they do it. We really are a somewhat amazing species.

Miss Lily, 1913

Shillings lay like a painting, clothed in the golds and reds of early autumn. The haws on the hawthorn hedges were fat and scarlet. The first chill had come early. But the air was still as they drove through the gates, not a leaf moving.

Hereward stood at the head of the staff, all lined up to meet them, dressed either in black, or with black mourning bands on their arms. Sophie felt reality quiver again. Hereward must have reached there only an hour earlier, but already he was in charge. The household had been informed of Nigel's death, of Danny's ascension to the title, and whatever else Hereward felt they needed to know.

A good butler could perform miracles. It would not be polite to ask how he had managed this one. Despite the glimpse of builders' carts, a small pile of debris, and an unpainted shed that must contain the batteries, all indicating that the electrification of Shillings and its new bathrooms were still in progress, she knew that the family rooms would be immaculate, the sheets aired, their beds warmed. There would probably even be cherry cake …

She stepped from the car, realising for the first time the significance of her black dress, the one Violette had put out for her back in Berlin. She was in mourning, would remain in mourning, in black dresses, for a year.

And there was Green, herself again. Miss Lily might appear for the funeral, heavily veiled. If anyone asked — but possibly no one would — she was tactfully staying with close friends, an illegitimate sister keeping discreetly out of the way.

It was Green who must be present now, so that it would seem she had been herself the whole time, in her black serge dress. And if some of the staff and tenants suspected or even knew about Miss Lily, they would be discreet about Green, too, from duty and from love. Violette wore white, a child's dress, and had even assumed a child's look of innocent grief, which, quite possibly, was what she felt, though with Violette one never knew.

Mrs Goodenough was crying, tears coursing down her face as she stood steadfast in the line, till Sophie stopped, and put her hand on her shoulder. The older woman collapsed into her arms. 'Oh, your ladyship. I loved him like a son. Pardon me, your ladyship, I didn't mean to presume.'

'He loved you like a mother,' said Sophie quietly. Which had enough truth in it for her to say it easily.

Mrs Goodenough wiped her eyes. 'I'm sorry, your ladyship, the house is a trifle ... upset. Only one of the bathrooms is installed but I have told the builders they must now wait until ... that they must wait to do the rest. But the electric stove is in and —'

Sophie stopped her with a touch to her shoulder. 'You have done miracles, Mrs Goodenough and will keep doing miracles. Thank you, not just for ...' She found she could not speak. The two women gazed at each other. Mrs Goodenough gave a nod, which Sophie copied. She moved on to Ackland then Malachi the head gardener, to every one of the Shillings staff, there to see their family home.

And the new earl, staring at it all, confused but secure in Jones's arms.

The new bathroom next to her bedroom was all mahogany and brass and the smell of fresh paint. Its plumbing, miraculously, also worked. Her bedroom now had an electric-light switch, even though the hall still had loose wires carefully tucked up, almost out of sight.

Violette helped Sophie bathe and dress. Her demeanour was not exactly maid-like, though Green had trained her well.

Green herself did not appear. Sophie assumed she and Jones were together, sharing both their grief and shock, and, possibly, finalising whatever else needed to be done. Sophie no longer resented her exclusion, but was grateful for it. Her world had narrowed to her children, and must stay like that, till they had absorbed the change and smiled again.

As soon as she was dressed — black linen, low waisted, exactly the correct length below the knees — she helped Nanny and Amy give the children an early dinner: stewed chicken and vegetables, carefully cut into tiny pieces by Mrs Goodenough, for surely no hands but hers would have prepared the first dinner back at Shillings for the new earl and his sister, followed by semolina pudding with blackberry jam.

'Ice cream?' asked Rose hopefully, as Sophie tucked her into bed, a real bed now, not a cot. All her other carefully acquired words seemed to have gone.

'No,' said Sophie, kissing the petal of her cheek. She stepped over to Danny's bed. He clutched the sheet, looking very small and very scared and as if he dimly realised the weight of all he had inherited.

Sophie sat on the bed and took one of his hands. 'We will look after you,' she promised him. 'We will look after everything. You have so many, many people who love you. Never think that you are alone. Never.'

The boy said nothing. Surely he couldn't understand what she had said, but she felt he had understood the tone. Sophie turned off the new electric light, and smiled at Amy and Nanny, sitting either side of the fire, knitting, identical poses, in identical guardianship, the old woman and the young, their faces glowing in the firelight.

She walked down the stairs, wondering why it felt so odd. But of course there was no Nigel waiting for her, and no Miss Lily. Even in the brief period when she had looked after Shillings for Nigel while he was still in the army, she had known he waited for her somewhere, or that Miss Lily did.

Now she was alone. Or not. She opened the library door and they were there for her: Jones standing, as befitted a gentleman when a lady entered a room; Green toasting her stockinged feet at the fire, unthinkable in a maid or guest, and surely a declaration: 'I am home. I am your friend. None of that has changed with Nigel's death'; and Violette in a slightly too sophisticated black mourning dinner dress, sitting in the armchair, unaware it was where Nigel had always sat. But that was perfect too, for Sophie could not have borne an empty chair.

Hereward brought in a tray, followed by Samuel, also holding a tray. Both most deliberately did not notice Green's stockinged feet. It was impossible to read Green's emotion, now or on the journey home. Shock, at losing her oldest friend and mentor? Or perhaps she did not even know what she felt, except the impossibility of playing social roles tonight, in shoes or sitting at a table.

No soup. Blessed Mrs Goodenough, for soup was invalid food and when your soul was damaged but you had to carry on you could not afford to feel like an invalid. Instead there was roast lamb, from the Shillings estate of course, and roast potatoes, and peas and glazed carrots and two gravy boats and mint sauce, and it was perfect — the four of them, eating an English meal that this soil had produced.

Hereward and Samuel reappeared, at the exact time the plates needed to be cleared, two of the kitchen maids (Hereward must have debated this informality, but chosen it quite correctly) following with a bowl of fresh peaches, another of the mottled yellow and red apples only found at Shillings, which went floury two days after picking but which Sophie loved, a blackberry tart, a bowl of strawberries and another of clotted cream and a dish of sugar. The Shillings plates, hundreds of years old, the silver knives to eat the fruits with, the spoons and forks for strawberries and cream.

They helped themselves. They ate. And finally they talked.

'The necessary conversation,' Sophie began.

Jones didn't look up from his strawberries. 'Of course we are staying.'

'With me, or with Shillings? And Violette too.'

'I am your family,' said Violette indignantly, clanging her spoon against her plate. 'I will be where you are.'

'Of course you will. But if you want to … to learn to fly or something —'

'You need me now,' said Violette flatly.

'Yes,' said Sophie. 'I do.'

'When you need me, I am here. That is what family does.'

Green sniffed, refusing to shed a tear.

Sophie leaned over and hugged Violette. Violette endured it. 'Yes,' said Sophie. 'That is what family does.'

'And when I am twenty-one I shall have pearls like yours, and a party —'

'But we need not discuss that now,' said Jones quietly. 'Green and I are going to Australia with you. I cancelled the other arrangements, but will book again as soon as you think it suitable.'

'You will stay in Australia with me? I may have to be there some time.' She crossed to the desk, where Nigel's and Miss Lily's newspapers were left each morning after they had been glanced at in the breakfast room, and brought over that day's edition of *The Times*. 'It's begun,' she said flatly, displaying the front-page headlines.

'Something about Nigel?' asked Green. She looked at the headlines with relief and then asked, 'A stock market crash?'

'It's not going to be this London crash,' said Sophie sombrely. I'm betting America's will be soon, and even worse. 'It's going to be a long, irregular slide and it will go on for years, or even decades. This is what I've been warning everyone about for the past year, though I didn't expect it to happen now. But then I have been … preoccupied. America has been balancing on hope and delusion for years now, lending money they don't have to the rest of the world, including to Germany. And now it topples.'

'Will that affect us?' asked Jones.

'Us, as in our family? Very little — you did sell those shares, didn't you?'

Jones nodded.

'Good. The greatest change for us will be that I will have business decisions to make for the next few years, ones that probably can only be made by me.' She smiled wearily. 'Excuse my lack of modesty, but this financial crisis is beyond Mr Slithersole and Cousin Oswald and my other managers.'

'How much will the crash affect Australia?' asked Green. 'It is a long way away, after all.'

'It will affect us enormously, if not at once.' She shook her head. 'I have been saying this for over a year too, but no one has really listened. Others have said it and also been ignored. This will have as great an effect as the war. American investment overseas is going to stop abruptly. American investment and massive war loans will need to be repaid. Too many in Great Britain and even Australia have been tempted to make fortunes by investing in American stocks. They will lose everything, or almost everything.'

'That bad?' asked Jones quietly.

'Yes. England is going to need the loans it made to Australia to fight the war repaid, no matter how bad things are in Australia. Factories will close — though no Higgs factories. People will lose their jobs; without their jobs they will not be able to buy food or clothing or even pay their rent, so other jobs will go. We are in for a very bad few years indeed. But when times are hard people need the cheapest luxuries of life, like canned corned beef and tinned fruit salad that is half choko and so costs only sixpence, though I must work out how we can make it even cheaper. Higgs Industries will do as well from this as it did in the Great War.'

Sophie did not need to say that Higgs Industries would use the profits for good, as they had done during the war. There would be no new cars, no jewels bought — if Violette insisted on pearls she could have Sophie's, or borrow them at least.

'And Shillings?' asked Jones quietly.

Sophie shrugged. 'Shillings will remain insulated by the Higgs money, as it has been since Nigel financed my father's first factory. There is no need to sell the Shillings trees for timber to pay the death duties. No jobs will be lost, and every person will be guaranteed a job on the estate, if they wish for one.'

Jones smiled. 'I should not even have asked.'

'By the way,' said Green, 'we are Mrs and Mr Jones now, though of course in my capacity as maid I will still be Green. Too confusing to have two Joneses.'

'And I am their daughter and your ward, not your maid,' said Violette, just in case Sophie needed reminding. 'But a ward helps her Aunt Sophie, does she not?'

'She does indeed,' said the newly minted Aunt Sophie.

'You know the contents of Nigel's will?' asked Jones.

Sophie nodded. 'I'm the children's guardian, of course. If anything happens to me, it's you and Dr Greenman. Bequests for all the staff, which includes you — yes, you too Violette; he made the change before we left for Germany. Everything entailed goes to Danny, in trust till he is twenty-one. Everything else goes to me, which includes much of the Shillings estate, which Nigel,' yes, she could say that word now, at last, 'bought after his father had sold it. I need to update my own will. But we can discuss that after the funeral.'

The fire snickered in the silence.

'When will that be?' asked Green at last.

'Monday,' said Sophie. 'The vicar suggested we wait a week, so that the Ladies' Guild could decorate the church prettily, and the verger make sure the churchyard looks its best. But only family and the servants and the estate tenants will be at the service and then here afterwards.' She managed another smile. 'Even if it does make Hereward a little uncomfortable to eat crab puffs in the dining room, and not in the servants' hall.'

'Do you think the Prince of Wales will come?' asked Green. For of course no restrictions applied to the heir to the throne.

'I am pretty sure he won't,' said Sophie. 'I've asked Ethel to be here, though, and James Lorrimer is invited, but he has had to fly to Berlin to deal with matters there.'

'And the prinzessin?' asked Green. 'Will she be here?'

'She would not dare!' said Violette.

'I think she would dare,' said Sophie gently. 'But that is not why she won't come. She knows it would hurt us to see her.'

It was strange, but for some reason she wished Hannelore *could* be with them. She had been so much a part of this, both as instigator and unwitting pawn. Nigel had been right to ask her to try to keep their friendship, or at least rebuild it a little.

If Hannelore came then Sophie might possibly explain to her that the stock market crashes would create the very conditions she and Herr Hitler needed to control Germany. The loans to Germany from the United States must now be repaid urgently; nor would there be any more American investment. America would be licking its own wounds, not trying to solve problems or find business opportunities in Europe. With no money from the United States it would be impossible for the Weimar Republic to continue paying reparations to France.

The German economy was going to crumble more completely than any other nation's, and faster too. Herr Hitler would probably do very nicely with his country shouldering despair that could be channelled into a longing for revenge.

She must write to James about this. He had probably already foreseen the ramifications for Germany, but English gentlemen were sometimes so appallingly ignorant of the business world, which after all was what life floated on, not the artificial titles they bestowed upon each other.

'How long do you think we must stay in England?' asked Jones.

'I won't know for a while. We won't have to wait until probate is granted, at least, as so much is in my name, and I will give Mr Slithersole power of attorney. But there'll be bequests, and some long-term decisions to be made, if we are not going to be here for a year or more and conditions are to change so much.'

She looked around the room. 'I think it best if we stay away until the young earl and his father's death are no longer a novelty. There's that to think of, as well as the needs of Higgs Industries.'

'Will I make a tentative booking for mid-December?'

'Perfect.' Because that would mean they would have Christmas on the ship. The children — and Violette, and Nanny and Amy, who would almost certainly want to accompany them — deserved a proper Christmas, even if she felt incapable of providing one. 'A first-class stateroom as usual for each of us, adjoining if possible, though that may not be possible at this late date.' She managed a smile. 'Use whatever bribery is necessary though.'

'I am extremely good at bribery,' said Jones smoothly.

'My father is very good at many things,' said Violette proudly. 'And my maman too. Have you ever seen her shoot?'

'Actually, I have,' said Sophie. 'She was saving my life at the time.'

Violette looked enviously at her mother. 'I would like to save your life some time, your ladyship. Properly, with a gun.'

'You are doing pretty well saving my life just now,' said Sophie gently.

Violette frowned. 'I do not understand.'

'One day you will,' said Green. She smiled at her scowling daughter. 'I will take you out to the pistol range for a lesson tomorrow. Do you mind?' she asked Sophie.

'I can think of no better occupation,' said Sophie.

'Packing for Australia,' said Green. 'Ordering what we will need for the voyage, and summer there.'

'Well, there is that. But there is time for pistol practice too.' Sophie let her head fall back in the armchair and shut her eyes. 'I'm tired. I will sleep tonight finally, I think. And without the need for morphia in my tea. I did finally realise that you drugged me at the clinic,' she added to Jones.

'My apologies,' said Jones.

'I still don't understand why I had to be drugged.'

'Just to make it easier for you,' said Jones, a little too calmly.

Sophie opened her eyes. Jones was poking the fire, carefully not looking at her. And a small seed of hope blossomed, so improbable, so wonderful, it was hard to bear.

But she would not mention it. Not now. Not yet.

Chapter 65

Letters cannot press your hand, nor hug you. But one can re-read them, which makes them satisfying communication even when your heart longs so for a presence, not just a sheet of paper. Never underestimate letters, my dears.

Miss Lily, 1913

Letters came. A tide of letters, many of the envelopes edged in black; letters from the 'people like us' who had met the Earl of Shillings once at the House of Lords and felt a duty among the nuisances of life to write a letter of conventional condolence to his wife. Letters from officers or enlisted men Nigel had served with, some conventional, others that left Sophie weeping: 'He bought me a cherry cake when I was wounded. What officer would do that, eh? He was the best chap we ever served under and I wish the world was made of men like him.'

So many letters and among them, these two.

My dear Sophie,

There are no words, of course, so I shall not insult us both by wasting time with the conventional ones. I may, perhaps, however, be of use. The enclosed card gives the contact details of Miss Muriel Ermington, a reliable social secretary who will do all that needs doing in answering condolence cards, fending off attempted visits, and even responding to letters, including this one.

Miss Ermington will not expect continued employment, as she cares for an invalid brother (Ypres, 1917), but three months will help her both financially and mentally, as a break from

constant care and, if you wish, she may find you someone more
permanent. But I can vouch for her in every respect and she will
await your call.

I am so sorry, Sophie.

Yours, always,

Emily

Dear Lady Nigel,

His Royal Highness the Prince of Wales wishes me to extend
his deepest sympathy and also his regrets that he will be unable
to attend the service for your husband, due to the pressure of his
official duties. He asks me to extend his utmost sympathy and his
gratitude for the sterling service your husband gave for his country,
during the Great War and in the House of Lords ...

So you have abandoned us, Your Royal Highness, rather than
admit you might have had any part to play in ... unpleasantness.
You are a cad, David, thought Sophie. Rumour had it that the
Prince of Wales already had a new mistress and was preoccupied
by novel devotion. He had probably carefully forgotten his
request to Nigel.

I liked him once, she remembered. Did she still like him,
despite everything? Was it even appropriate to consider whether
one liked the heir to the throne? Surely loyalty outweighed mere
liking. But she was only an ignorant colonial.

Yes, she liked him, the way one might a spaniel with a weak
bladder who left damp patches every morning on the rug. He
was not much of a man, but some of what he was was good. An
incontinent spaniel had been made that way, and so David had
been constructed too, partly by his inbred genes (had there ever
been a monarch quite as silly as his godfather, the last tsar?) and
partly by the uncritical adoration of newspapers and the public
and the far too critical assessments of his parents.

And the war, she thought. That nightmare made flesh — and
shreds of flesh, and rotting flesh, the stench of which would stay
with all who knew it forever — must have caught the Prince of

Wales too, impotent to stop it, or even play a man's part in it. All of us who survived it, she thought, were reborn to some extent within its flames.

Poor David. But she was glad he would not be there. He might even have insisted on playing a pibroch for Nigel on the bagpipes and she would have cried at that, remembering David's bagpipes and the zebra who committed lèse-majesté by biting him the afternoon she flew to Shillings to save Nigel by marrying him.

And if that marriage had in some small way contributed to his death, she was rational enough to accept that, without her intervention, Nigel would not have survived the surgery in any case, emotionally not caring if he lived or died, and physically, without the hygiene and care her expertise had ensured.

She would not say, 'His death was my fault.' It was not Hannelore's fault either, nor even poor, ineffectual David's — and God help England (a prayer, not blasphemy) when he became king, and may that not happen for a long, long time, beyond the era of Mr Hitler, almost certainly already gleefully plotting the downfall of the debt-ridden Weimar Republic.

Nigel was dead. Asking why or casting fault now was not just fruitless, but a waste of time during which she could be remembering his love.

She resealed the royal envelope and placed it with the others in the study desk.

Chapter 66

A good woman works from her heart. A great woman works from the heart of humanity.

Miss Lily, 1912

This was their funeral. Not Nigel's: a funeral does not belong to the dead, but those they leave behind. This was for his closest family, the friends that had become like family too, his staff, his tenants.

Sophie sat in the front pew of the church, veiled, Rose on one side of her, Danny on the other. Jones sat next to Rose, with Violette next to him. The earl's half-sister, Lily, also veiled, sat next to Danny, his small hand in her gloved one. There had been a little murmuring as she entered, this half-sister who had not been seen at Shillings since before the war. Those who remembered her would be telling the youngsters all about her, about the 'lovely ladies' who used to visit Shillings before the season, each year.

Ethel sat next to Lily in a dress curiously resembling the elongated shape of a submarine and a hat that was ... a hat, with nothing more that could be said about it, except perhaps that it was black.

No one remarked on the absence of Sophie's maid, Green.

The coffin stood on an ancient wooden bench, where the coffins of Vailes had rested for at least three hundred years, if woodworm had not possibly necessitated its renewal in that time. It was impossible to tell, for a cloth of snow covered half of it, its white edges embroidered with the Vaile crest, repeated a hundred times, a gift from the Ladies' Guild, fashioned in the impossibly swift time of a week.

The British flag was draped across the other half of the coffin. Nigel had served his country in two wars, and was entitled to a full military funeral, though Sophie had refused that as tactfully as she was able. The flag was enough.

Goldenrod decorated each pew, great autumnal swathes of it, and white lilies from the Shillings greenhouses, another small miracle Sophie did not seek to question. Lilies had been needed and so were produced.

'*I vow to thee my country*,' sang the choir.

Sophie had chosen two modern hymns, created for and because of the cataclysmic war that had changed them all. But this, surely, was the hymn for Nigel.

'*The love that never falters ...*
The love that pays the price ...
... the final sacrifice ...'

The homily then. Sophie had left the reading to the vicar and the words too. He had chosen the unexceptional Psalm 23, beginning 'The Lord is my shepherd', but seemed to hesitate before giving his own words about the deceased. Sophie had never known how much the vicar understood about the relationship between Nigel and Lily, nor had he come to offer condolences to the woman who sat as Lily, despite dining with her many times.

At last he spoke.

'Nigel Vaile was a kind man. It is, perhaps, more usual at a funeral to speak of a man's title, his honoured position in the world, including his army rank and sterling service to his country. But I had the privilege of knowing Nigel Vaile, and I know that rank was not what he held important. Indeed, it was a burden he had to carry. But carry it he did, because his heart was great.

'Nigel Vaile cared for each person here, each child on his estate, each nook of England. He cared for humanity, and gave his life for it, for his death in Germany came about because of the express wish of his government for him to travel to Berlin to assess matters there. Nigel Vaile died in the service of his country, as much as if he had died in the Great War.'

Whispers at this; heads nodding. The newspapers had already said as much, though with no details. Nigel had been their earl, and none had any doubt that theirs had been the best aristocrat in England. And kind. Always, without hesitation, kind. They would be recounting his many kindnesses to each other for weeks.

The vicar gazed across the congregation. A single journalist lingered at the back, accompanied by a photographer, tripod and all, as if this were a wedding where all would pose outside. Jones had raised an eyebrow when they spotted him, as if to say, 'Should we get rid of him?'

But Nigel had said that publicity was necessary. As long as the journalist did not intrude, he could stay.

'You may expect me to give you great words about so great a life,' the vicar continued. 'But there are so few I need to give you. Each person here knows the life and history of Nigel Vaile. Each person here had reason to admire him, even to love him, perhaps, returning some of the love he gave to all of you.

'And now he is with God, and God is love. Nigel Vaile has his due rest at last.'

A moment's puzzlement, whispers, as the congregation tried to work that last bit out. The organ pealed again. The choir stood.

Another new hymn, 'Jerusalem', as Jones, with Danny in his arms, moved to the coffin, Hereward, Samuel, Mr Daley the estate manager, the vicar and Lloyd taking the other positions. Unconventional, but this was *their* funeral. This would be played exactly as they wished, and the journalist could publish and be damned.

'... *And we will build Jerusalem*
In England's green and pleasant land.'

You tried to build Jerusalem, my darling Nigel, she thought. We will never know how much of what you did succeeded. But this song, surely, is for you.

Sophie had decreed that the 'funeral baked meats' be more than the conventional sherry and biscuits served for People Like Us, though less than a cottager's 'ham funeral' where a sustaining meal needed to be given to those who would have a hard journey home.

This was also her chance to say what was needed to the people of Shillings before her departure. And this would give Mrs Goodenough an opportunity to farewell the boy, youth and man she had loved using all her skill and devotion. Sophie had left the choice of food to her, with the proviso that it could be left, buffet style, for all to help themselves, so the servants too could mingle with the tenants, to whom all were related. Even the drinks, to Hereward's mild anguish, were on a sideboard.

Crab puffs sat next to crustless sandwiches of cream cheese and watercress, egg and lettuce, cheese and pickle, ham and mustard; a platter of blini with caviar and sour cream flanked a plate of small egg and ham pies; slices of smoked salmon roulade nudged small rolls thick with roast beef and horseradish, sausage rolls and lobster in puff pastry, so that all here would have the familiar as well as the 'gentry' food expected at the 'big house'.

But the apple tarts, the apricot dumplings, the jam rolls, the sponge cake piled with strawberries and cream, the cream buns and buttered scones with raspberry jam belonged to every class, even if few could afford them often, and the cherry cake, thought Sophie, tears springing again, had been made for her alone. The cherry cake she had loved on that first glorious and bewildering day at Shillings, and made for her now, in her last months here.

No, not her last. Just her last for a while. And that needed to be made clear. She waited till everyone had eaten (and a few children filled their pockets too), till glasses of beer, cider, fruit cup, lemonade and yes, sherry, had been drunk, and the crowd was slowly moving back and forth to the tea and coffee urns manned by the Ladies' Guild, the only servers at today's event, and ones even Sophie hesitated to command to mingle.

Sophie struck her sherry glass with a teaspoon. The crystal sang. The room filled with silence and expectation, and the sound of a small voice demanding cake. Rose, of course.

'Ladies and gentlemen, dear friends.' Her voice broke, for they were dear friends, even young Tommy Rodgers with jam on his face and pockets bulging with apple dumplings. 'As you all know, I am leaving on a visit to Australia in December, the visit that has long been planned. But nothing has changed,' she managed a smile, 'or rather of course everything has changed. However, his lordship made certain arrangements more than four years ago, before his surgery.

'It is not polite to discuss money in society. Luckily we are not society today, just friends.' She waited for the murmurs of laughter, and sympathy too. These people like me, she thought wonderingly, and then no, these people love me. And that was a gift from Nigel as well.

'Higgs's Corned Beef is not just the best canned meat on the market, and a snip at sixpence a can,' more laughter, 'but means that death duties will not be a problem. Unlike many estates these days, no farms or other property need be sold to pay the taxes. All arrangements will continue as before. It is my hope that Shillings will continue to provide ever more jobs for its sons and daughters, not fewer.'

She waited for more whispers, for men to grab a glass of ale and down it in relief, for women to sip their tea and keep the depth of their gratitude from their faces. Of course the earl would have seen them right. Of course. They never doubted it. Except, perhaps, when the owl hooted and the foxes howled at two am.

'The household staff, of course, will remain as always, and I hope the renovations will not be too wearying for you. No matter how long my stay in Australia needs to be, there will be no reduction in staff, and no half wages. The house will be kept in readiness for visitors, and once the builders and electricians depart, there will be visitors, close friends who need the comfort, beauty and perfect service that is Shillings.

'Danny is too young yet to begin to learn his role here, but I know each of you will help guide him when we return. In the meantime, Mr Daley,' she smiled at the estate manager, 'Mrs Goodenough and Mr Hereward will continue as superbly as ever. But if, at any time, any one of you needs to contact me about a problem, or even advice,' she made laughing eye contact with Tommy Rodgers, managing to stuff a bun with the cream licked out into a bulging pocket, '*any* of you, please, do write to me, or send a telegram paid for by the estate, and I will attend to it, on behalf of my son, who is now your earl.

'That's it, I think, except to say please keep eating and drinking till all of this is gone. And thank you, from the bottom of my heart, for all you have given my husband, myself and Shillings.'

Did one clap at funerals? She could feel the indecision. Then Ethel began it, with a 'hear hear' too, and suddenly the room was full of clapping and chatter and relief, and hands reaching for yet another jam tart in celebration.

See? I did it right, she said silently to Nigel.

She could not stay inside after that. Emotion choked her; memory overwhelmed her; loss once more made the world grow dim. She slipped into the hall, as if she were heading for the lavatory, and then out the French windows in the study, the ones she had climbed through to inform Nigel she was going to marry him.

It was cool in the orchard. Yellow apple leaves fell like snow. Nigel had promised she would miss the next English snow. She still might, unless there was an early fall this year. Nigel ...

She looked back at Shillings, the mellow stone, the grass kept carefully the correct length to be a carpet but to let the lawn daisies grow. But not even Constable could paint its beauty, she thought, for part of the loveliness of Shillings was that it was moving, from the smoke drifting up from its eighteen chimneys to the snowdrops that would carpet this land beneath the trees as the snow itself melted. And then there would be bluebells, and the drifts of apple blossom, butterflies soft as the cheeks of her children, and as bright ...

Love is greatest when we accept that all that we love is transitory, she thought. But Nigel and I deserved just a few more years. His children should have had a father for a while longer …

'Mind if I join you, lass?' Ethel had donned a ginger cardigan, too small across the shoulders, too long in the sleeves, and almost certainly knitted by a friend. (You should always have at least two garments made with love to wear, Miss Lily's stylist had told her, in that world that was going to last forever, that perfect year before the war.)

'I can't see myself pushing you out of the orchard if I say no,' said Sophie.

Ethel laughed. 'Nay, it would take a good-sized prince charming to carry me off. I like your James Lorrimer though. He took me to the Ritz.'

Sophie stared. James and Ethel? No and no and no!

Ethel clapped her on the shoulder. 'Wish I had a camera to catch your face. First time a man has ever asked me out to dinner. We had oysters too, and he didn't mind when I asked for a second dozen. Nothing in an oyster. Twelve of them hardly wet the sides. Had a super time. I reckon he enjoyed it too. But it weren't romance, so you can stop looking like a stunned mullet. James wants me to do another job or two for him. Think I will too.'

And she'd be good at it, thought Sophie, looking at her friend with pleasure. Ethel was not a lovely lady, but women who were neither ladies nor lovely could play important roles in the world today, and even more so when steered by a master player like James. And Ethel was as strong, warm and unstoppable as the sun.

'We're going to have dinner again next week. He says he likes a holiday from being proper. Can't blame him, neither. I could never be bothered with all that grace and etiquette stuff, no matter how much they tried to teach me at that school. But it means I won't be coming to Australia with you, old thing. Not for a while yet, at any rate.'

'Midge will be disappointed.'

'I've been disappointing Midge on that score for years. But I'll make it out there one day, cross my heart. By the way, what you said back there, about guests staying at Shillings ... don't suppose you'd let Anne and her husband stay here for a while? They can only dig in winter in Mesopotamia, because of the heat, and they've been living with Anne's family during summer. Each penny they can scrounge goes on their digs. But she's breeding again now, due in February, so they'll be back early. Anne's family are a stuffy lot — she could do with a place away from them.'

'I'd love to have them stay here. And not just when we're away, either.' Sophie gestured at the many-chimneyed house. 'It's not as if we don't have room. Will you come down and stay here too now and then?'

Ethel nodded. She stroked a lichened tree trunk. 'I'd like to. Something about this place gets to you, doesn't it?'

'Yes,' said Sophie softly, 'it does.'

'So you really will be back?'

'Yes, I'll be back, though it will probably be a year or more, at least.' Torn between two homes, as Nigel had been wrenched in two — though her duality was socially acceptable: two homes, two countries, the same Empire. No such tolerance for Nigel and Lily.

Would that ever change? A hundred years earlier votes for women had been unthinkable. Would the world in a hundred years' time accept Lily and Nigel?

Even if it did it would be too late for Nigel. It was too late now.

Chapter 67

A life richly spent on doing good will cost you tears, emotional honesty, years of self-doubt. But the rewards will be impossible to quantify.

Miss Lily, 1913

Decisions. The horses would remain as breeding stock, even without master and mistress to ride them. So many horses had been killed in the war that they fetched incredible prices now, though Sophie expected that would change with what she saw as the inevitable deepening of the financial crisis. The financial situation might seem like a crisis now. In another two or three years, she thought, it will feel like normality.

But horses should still bring good prices. She asked Emily to recommend a stablemaster: Colonel Sevenoaks was a renowned judge of horses, and those who bred them. And diversifying Shillings would keep the estate viable, without subsidy from Higgs Industries.

They must plant more trees too: so useful, timber, for it could be sold as needed. And if — when — the simmering of the last war broke out into another, timber would be essential.

The building and electrification were put on hold till they left. For a brief time the household fell back to its old rhythms: she played with the children, watched Nanny bathe them, dined in the library with Green, Jones and Violette. And, in each of those pursuits, Nigel's absence ached like a lost limb.

Letters were piled neatly by one of the footmen at her place at the breakfast table each morning for her to read as she forked her (perfect) kedgeree, sorted into ones she should, or would want to, read by the invaluable and almost invisible Miss Ermington. The letters were a comfort, and a promise that there was still good life to come.

Wooten Abbey

(An unfamiliar hand, written for the ancient woman who had been one of Miss Lily's first English friends, from the home that had been the first hospital Sophie had organised, and where she had lived for three years.)

My Dearest Sophie,

I would say my heart goes out to you, but that unreliable organ is not a gift to send, so you have my love, as you have always had it.

At my age and decrepitude I need give no excuses for my absence at Nigel's funeral, but you will have known I was there in spirit, as I was at your wedding and the Christening celebrations of your children. I am blessed, however, to have seen you together in your visits to Wooten in the past four years. The joining of two of the people I love most in the world gave me so much joy.

I should be able to say that in old age you get used to the loss of friends. I can't, for if they were friends of the heart the scar remains forever, even if the pain lessens. Nor can I assure you that you ever truly recover from the loss of a beloved husband.

But I can promise you that, in a year perhaps, the tears with which you remember him will contain as much joy at having had him as sorrow at his loss, and that your memories of him will increasingly be of the happiness you had together, not the circumstances of his death. I can also promise that life and joy slowly seep in to the empty places the loved have left.

Write to me from Australia, my dear, and send me photographs of you and Rose and Danny. I will treasure them, for they will speak of the future to one who now mostly has only her past.

With love always, I remain yours,
Isobel, Dowager Duchess of Wooten

She would treasure this letter always, in the scented sandalwood chest that kept correspondence safe from silverfish. She would keep the next one too.

Macquarie Street
Sydney
Australia
Dear Sophie,

Nigel was a good man and a great man. The two are not the same, but he was both. I deeply regret the tragedy this has been for you, and please believe me when I say that I truly am immeasurably sorry he and I did not walk the river at Thuringa together, and watch your children play along the sandy banks.

There will, I know, be many who say, 'I am sorry for your loss.' I say it too. Please, even though it is a cliché, accept the words from all who offer them. We humans are rarely good with words. A cliché is no less meaningful because it has been said so many times before.

I do not know if this is presumption. If so, please say so, or simply order it removed: I am carving a cross for Nigel and will place it at the head of the others that I carved, in memory, in admiration, in respect and loss, and so all who pass through the Thuringa gate will see the memorial for Nigel Vaile, just as those who visit the Shillings cemetery will.

I like to think of Nigel Vaile's children knowing their father has a memorial in the land that is theirs too. But again, if this is a presumption or too painful or horribly inappropriate, please do not hesitate to have it removed.

Yes, 'I am sorry for your loss' is inadequate. I would offer my anguish for your loss, and hope that is not a presumption too.

Yours, always,
Daniel Greenman

A good letter. She was not sure what emotions it conjured up — perhaps was carefully not examining those emotions — but it left her smiling as well as sad, which she was sure was the writer's intention.

She picked up the next letter. The handwriting was becoming familiar to her, as were the postmark and choice of stationery. She smiled again at the expected comfort as she opened it.

Burrawinga
Via Warrnambool
Victoria
Dear Sophie,

John and I are deeply sorry for your loss. It seems so unfair that you, who reunited us, should be parted, and so soon.

Our lives now are a gift from you and Nigel. I am sure that Nigel has many memorials to his life, but our happiness is yet another. John is walking more easily and for longer each week. Long Tom the blacksmith here has modified a steering wheel so he can drive about the property: only two small arguments with trees so far, which John counts as a major success.

I hope Thuringa has been getting the rains, as we have. So much of New South Wales seems to have missed out. Our year has been perfect: fat lambs and no footrot.

Daniel tells us that you still plan to return to Australia this summer. If it is no intrusion, we would so love to see you, here, or at Thuringa, or even in Sydney.

There is one other piece of news I would like to share. Perhaps it has no place in a letter of condolence. It is very early to be sure, but we hope for a new arrival late next winter. If it is a boy, with your permission, we will call him Nigel. This too we owe to both of you.

Yours always,
Harriet

The next letter was in a familiar hand too.

Moura
Via Bald Hill
New South Wales
Australia
Darling Sophie,

Come home. You may already be on your way here but if you are not, gather your family and get on the next suitable ship, and Ethel too if she will come. Tell her you need her and she probably will come. Tell her I need her too.

We have so loved the fairy-tale of your romance with an English earl, but the sorrow in not meeting him is because we love you and wanted to love the man you loved as well.

Please come home, my dear. I know you, you see, and whatever duties you may feel keep you in England, I believe this truly is your home, and the place you need to be to heal. So come, even if you must return.

Please kiss Rose and Danny for me, and feel the kiss from me for you winging across the ocean. You cannot know how much I grieve for you, or how I wish to simply hug you.

Love and all the sympathy it is possible to send,
Midge

Sophie placed the letter back in its envelope. She would keep that one as well.

There was one more letter, and again in a familiar hand. She even knew the paper, thick and cream coloured, with dark blue ink and the Arnenberg crest at one corner.

Hannelore had not written before. There had been no flowers from her at the funeral, for which Sophie had been grateful. She would like to throw this in the fire, watch it shiver into blackness. But she suspected that whatever was in this single, slender communication after so long needed to be read, and possibly passed on to James.

She called for fresh coffee, drank half a cup, re-read the other letters to fortify herself, then put down the coffee cup and took up the letter opener.

There was no address at the top. It began simply:

Liebe Sophie,
*   It is impossible to express my sorrow for what I have done. Please believe that even if I cannot find the words, the guilt, regret*

381

and horror at the results of my actions are there.

    I give you my word I will not contact your family again, including Miss Lily. I owe her so much, and that is only a small fraction of what I owe you. The only repayment possible now is to ensure you do not have to meet me as you go about your lives in England or elsewhere.

    Herr Hitler assures me he knew nothing of those brutal actions that night. I believe him, and still feel he is the man to lead Germany through the troubled times ahead. But those men wore brown, and even if Herr Hitler cannot admit it, the National Socialist Party was responsible. While privately supporting Herr Hitler, I will not seek wider support for a party capable of that atrocity.

    I do not say 'accept my sorrow'. I no longer have that right. But know that I sign myself always,

    With all my love,
    Hannelore

So, she thought, Nigel has won. This, as well as safety from scandal for his family, and Lily's decades of work, was what he wanted. He had gained it all. Colonel Nigel Vaile's final victory. She would need to transcribe this letter for James, even the most personal parts of it, so he could judge the sincerity, and like her, find it real.

She looked out the window, at the grey lowering the sky till it seemed she might even touch it, if she wished to feel anything so cold and unsubstantial. The roses stood with bare thorny legs. Only the orchard was still beautiful, the lichened tree trunks as lovely as any sculpture.

Even as she watched, a faint white feather floated past the window, and then another, though they melted before they reached the ground.

'Your ladyship, it is snowing!' Violette erupted into the breakfast room. She began to lift the covers on the sideboard, filling her plate with kidneys, scrambled eggs and bacon. Hereward arrived with fresh toast and the milk coffee with a hint of chicory that Violette preferred, then departed.

Sophie remembered her joy at the first snow she had ever seen; how she and Hannelore had made a snowman; how Miss Lily had looked through this very window, and laughed. 'If there's more snow would you like to make a snowman, Violette?'

Violette snorted. 'Why should I do that, your ladyship? Snow is cold and wet.'

'True. But it is romantic,' said Sophie.

Violette shrugged at the idea of romance. She took a mouthful of kidney, then looked at Sophie speculatively. 'If I am your ward, should I address you as Aunt Sophie?'

'Do you like having me as your aunt?'

Violette nodded. 'You are rich, and capable, and I like you.'

Sophie laughed. 'Thank you for your honesty.'

'I will always be honest to you, unless it is not good for you. I would also like you to be my aunt even if you were not rich, or a ladyship. But I am glad you are.'

'I'm glad I am rich and a ladyship too. But though I will always be your Aunt Sophie, there may be times when it will not be ... tactful ... to use the term.'

'When we are on adventures for Mr Lorrimer?'

'I was thinking more of when we are moving among people in society, who might not understand the relationship. But on second thoughts, society can go jump in the sea. I am your Aunt Sophie always, except when — or if — we are working for Mr Lorrimer.'

'I am looking forward to the next adventure,' said Violette, reaching for toast.

And I am not, thought Sophie. I have given many years, my youth and a husband to the Empire and its battles. The snow was falling more thickly now, a world of fluttering white, though the ground was merely wet.

It was time for sunlight, the song of cicadas, the pounding of roos' feet at night, the noisy tide of emus as they swarmed towards the river.

It was time for hope, not grief. Time to see, perhaps, if a dimly seen possibility might just be true.

It was time to leave.

Chapter 68

I do not like books that have 'The End' on the last page. Life goes on, even if a chapter of life finishes. All we have given to life continues when we are gone.

Miss Lily, 1902

Seagulls shrieked, tearing the air with their sharp wings. The sea slapped against the pilings, as if saying, 'Follow me, and I will take you to the end of the earth, where you will find Australia.'

There had been no problem obtaining adjoining suites. The first London stock market crash had been followed by an even larger Wall Street disaster, a short rally, and then another crash. Businessmen leaped from the tops of their office blocks. Financiers shot themselves, with a maximum of publicity. Others jumped from windows. Even those who had not been wiped out, or 'badly bitten', were playing cautious now, staying home, not travelling expensively for pleasure.

It was odd to hear upper-crust English accents again as they crossed the gangplank, after so long in Germany and among the rural accents of Shillings.

'... she is heartbroken of course, but without money it's impossible. He's off to try and find another heiress ...'

'... has even had to sell his hunters, by Jove. Terribly hard on them ...'

'... the Cape Town climate is so restorative. I don't think his lungs would take another English winter ...'

'Crosswords, my dear. I've brought enough to last the entire voyage. I say, what, do you mean you've never tried them?'

The ship was ... big, and far too perfect, every chandelier gleaming, every staircase massive, carpeted, as if trying to combine the most opulent features of every baronial hall in England, with none of their shabbiness or quirks, with the shiny splendour of a Regent Street department store. This ship was beyond quirk. And it would take them almost directly to Sydney, via Madeira, South Africa, Perth and Melbourne ...

Six weeks to home, to sunlight on the harbour, to gum-tree trunk dapples and light that went gold as it was filtered through a million twisting, heat-narrowed leaves.

Midge and Maria would be waiting for her, surely, at the wharf, and Harry too and 'the brats', and possibly, probably, Daniel Greenman, about whom she would not think, could not think. She would let the sea wind wash away the knotted thoughts infesting her mind now and bring the clarity she lacked in its salty sharpness ...

Nanny, Amy and the twins occupied a double stateroom next to Violette's. Jones and Greenie shared a suite, for a wonder. Possibly this marriage that legally existed, even if it had never actually been celebrated, might actually work.

Their cabin was next to Sophie's, and yet Sophie was not surprised when Green paused at the cabin door and said, 'I'll leave you to settle in. Knock on the wall if you need me, or use the ship's telephone.'

Of course the stewardess would have unpacked for her; nor did Sophie need to change into yet another black dress for dinner for another two hours, but still it was never done for a maid to leave her mistress unattended when she entered her cabin.

And yet ... unless ...

Sophie closed her eyes, prayed, found her nails digging into her palms through her gloves. Impossible to mend those holes invisibly, she thought vaguely, then opened the cabin door.

'Hello, Sophie,' said Miss Lily.

A heartbeat later. An hour later. A century perhaps. She didn't know. She stood, not knowing what to do.

For this was not her husband. Nigel Vaile was dead, and this woman had planned that death, and executed it. But Miss Lily always knew the perfect way to effect a meeting, even such a one as this.

She held out her hands. Gloved hands, long cream kid gloves that reached to her elbows; the gloves matched a cream shantung suit with a multitude of thin black stripes, for she was in mourning for her brother. Sophie stepped forward, took the gloved hands, bent to kiss the cheek, felt herself held, and held with love, by Miss Lily.

A minute of wordlessness. One enormous sob of relief. At last she broke free, her cheeks still warm with tears, and sat beside Miss Lily on the bed.

'I wondered if you might faint,' said Miss Lily.

'I never faint, except when drugged by Jones. It was his drugging me which gave me the first clue.'

'You expected this?'

'I hoped. A tiny crumb of hope. But Green had told me I must be surprised, and so I didn't let my hopes fly too high. But why else should Jones drug me, instead of leaving me to sit with Nigel's body? He would know what a comfort that would be. They know?' Sophie smiled at her own question, 'Of course they know. Violette knows too, I imagine.'

'Yes,' said Miss Lily.

'And so I was left out yet again,' said Sophie, trying to keep her tone light. 'The first few decades of ignorance I forgive, as I wasn't born or was far too young. But if the four of you plan anything else without me I will be seriously annoyed.'

'I promise that we won't.'

Sophie examined her. The beloved face, the blonde and grey hair in a chignon, which must surely be a wig, though she imagined Miss Lily's real hair was growing underneath. Lines of grief that had not been there before.

Lily too, it seemed, was mourning Nigel.

'I could have asked you,' said Miss Lily apologetically, 'who do you want more, Nigel or Lily, if you couldn't have both? But it wasn't fair to make you choose.'

'Or to hurt Nigel by not choosing him? I don't know what I would have said,' admitted Sophie honestly. 'And I cannot say now I wouldn't have chosen him. But I'm speaking as if you are two people. You're not, are you? That was just how you presented to the world.'

Miss Lily nodded wordlessly.

'If we were on a desert island forever,' said Sophie, 'with Jones and Greenie and the children, of course ... who would you be?'

'Lily-Nigel Vaile,' said Miss Lily softly. 'Who is not an earl, nor a leader of men into battle. Who dresses in silk beach pyjamas and chiffon evening dresses, but sometimes, just sometimes, would wear trousers to go tree climbing or fishing with my wife and my children.'

'We would need a couturier on our island,' said Sophie lightly.

'Of course. And a library and telephone, for Sophie Higgs-Vaile to run her business empire.'

'Thuringa will give privacy,' said Sophie quietly. 'But it's not a desert island. Gossip spreads faster than a plague of grasshoppers.'

'I know. It's enough that you understand who I am, who I have always been through our marriage. Who I will be, even now.' Miss Lily suddenly looked as if she might cry, too. 'I ... I could have become Miss Lily permanently at any time. Left Nigel living on a Himalayan mountain, and run Shillings with a competent agent. I might even have adopted a child heir the Vailes would have found difficult to renounce. But I was Nigel too, I wanted to be able to be Nigel sometimes, until for the sake of all that we had worked for, I could no longer be. But I didn't know if you knew that Lily never wished that Nigel did not exist.'

'I think I did know, even if I wasn't sure. And I know what I feel now. I have you in my life again, and if you ever try to leave me I will chain you by the ankle. I love you and I am glad.'

'Thank you.' For the first time Miss Lily did not seem quite in control. 'That ... that means ... everything. The children?'

'Will have their Aunt Lily. Forever.'

'I am not quite sure I can last for eternity. But I will do my best. Should we ever tell them?'

'No. But they are my offspring and yours and thus extraordinarily intelligent in their different ways, and stubborn too. If they suspect and ask, we must tell them.'

'Yes,' said Miss Lily slowly. 'That will be best. And Dr Greenman?'

Sophie sat very still. 'What about him?'

'Do you love him?'

'Yes. But you always knew that.'

'Nigel always knew it, and knew too that you had chosen to marry him, and to stay with him. This is ... not quite the same.'

'Why not?'

'Because you are a widow now,' said Miss Lily gently.

'But I'm not —'

'The law says you are. James Lorrimer has been extremely thorough. Lillian Vaile, who at times used the name Shillings, sister of the late earl, now has a birth certificate, baptismal register, a bank account, investments, and sundry other proofs of her existence which we did not realise were necessary before. She is not even illegitimate — my father made an unfortunate early marriage that ended in divorce and mild disgrace. Which serves his memory right. I am honourably an Honourable. As for Nigel — if ever anyone tries to claim to be Nigel Vaile, Earl of Shillings, or that I am he, they will probably be locked up in an insane asylum. Or in comfort and security on the top floor of a very private clinic, for Nigel Vaile has a family who will be compassionate even to those who wish to discredit him. Nigel Vaile is dead, Sophie, and must remain so.'

'Yes,' said Sophie honestly. 'I accept that legally I am a widow. Having you sitting here does not make me less legally a widow. But the person I love is alive, Lily.'

'As a friend?'

'Is that what you want? We have never discussed this, but we should. Do you desire me ... now?'

'Yes. But I thought ...'

Sophie found it possible to both laugh and cry. 'I am not sapphic. But to me you will always be the ... the person I love, physically and in every way possible.'

'Sophie ...'

'But sex of any sort pains you.'

Miss Lily smiled. 'I think as I age I become androgenous. I have had little sexual desire the past year — even when close to you. And yes, there is pain. You deserve freedom.'

'That was why you chose to die?' The anger she had never admitted rose to the surface. 'You had no right to decide for me ...'

'Sophie darling, no, that was never part of it.'

'Oh,' said Sophie. She leaned against the person she loved, arms around each other now. What did she want? Just now, she realised, she did not want to even think of 'wants'. 'Widows are expected to have a year of mourning before they begin to consider life ahead. I need that before I can even work out what this may mean. But we can be together?'

'Always, or for as long as you may wish,' said Miss Lily.

'Then it will be "always".' Sophie glanced out the porthole, still showing the bustle of the docks, then back at Miss Lily. 'One day, in a year or maybe more, I might ... just might ... think ... what next? And even how. But not till then.'

'You were always wise,' murmured Miss Lily. 'The impetuous Cyclone Sophie, but wise within it all. What will you wear for dinner?'

Dinner dress was not worn the first night at sea. 'Black silk, with long strips of jet beads from shoulder to hem. Black netting with jet beads for my hair too, on this night at least. And we will not sit at the captain's table, not while in mourning.'

'Poor Violette,' said Miss Lily. 'She was so looking forward to that. And to the birthday party she couldn't have in a house of mourning.'

'We will make up for that with her Christmas presents. And she will have won the heart of every officer by the time we reach Madeira.'

'And if she hasn't, then we must teach her how. The two of us,' added Miss Lily. 'I will enjoy the challenge.' She stood. 'My cabin is next door. Green will come and help me dress, then come to you.'

For a moment Sophie's heart clenched tight once more. I cannot bear this. Cannot bear it. Because despite the promise of 'together forever' it would always be the cabin or the room next door, or down the hall, never in the bed beside her. Only Nigel had ever shared her bed. Miss Lily would not change that now. Nor did Sophie want her to, not if it meant pain for Nigel, or rumours that might hurt their children.

Nigel, she thought. I love you. Will always love you, always miss you. You have taken so much from me, yet given me so much. And there are still a million tears to shed for you, and maybe more.

Miss Lily looked at her with perfect understanding. She always had. 'Perhaps, some time,' she said quietly, 'we will cry for Nigel together.'

Chapter 69

'Every journey is a new beginning' is perhaps the truest cliché that I know. Every second may be a new beginning. Know that, my dear young ladies, and you will be truly mine. Miss Lily's lovely ladies, who will conquer worlds …

Miss Lily, 1913

SOPHIE

The table was discreetly in a corner, set for the five of them, with lush potted plants giving privacy even in a dining room whose expanse rivalled the playing fields of Eton. The room shrilled with the locust buzz of upper-class England.

'… it was a simply thrilling party, darling, with the most divine new cocktails, absinthe, pineapple juice and rum. You will never guess who the Prince of Wales appeared with …'

'… a score of ninety-eight not out. A jolly good show all round, what?'

'… says it is a favourite for the Derby. Clear soup, old chap, don't you think?'

'… the purser says it will be a calm crossing, but of course one never knows. Monty is a martyr to seasickness, aren't you, sweetie?'

Sophie took a small bite of her lobster thermidor. Tonight, perhaps as the ship ploughed the ocean, she would mourn her lost marriage. But this was a time to let joy return, too. 'You will find Thuringa strange at first,' she said to Violette, who was clad in a black silk dress of total elegance and suitability, with

391

just enough lace, embroidery and jet beading to make the girl content. 'But you will love it too. The sky goes on forever.'

Violette made a small gesture that meant she needed to swallow her mouthful before replying.

Miss Lily leaned forward. Sophie noticed for the first time that the wedding ring was on her right hand, not her left. She didn't know if she felt joy or pain at the sight. Both, perhaps. 'Take small mouthfuls,' Miss Lily instructed Violette quietly, 'then if you wish to speak, you can tuck them between your back teeth and your cheek. Try it.'

Violette took a minute portion of scallop mornay. 'Like this?'

'Ah, yes, excellent tucking,' approved Miss Lily.

'When the waiter comes again, look up at him, but count to five before you smile,' advised Sophie.

'Why must I do that?'

'Because it works,' said Green. She looked at Jones, then slowly, very slowly, smiled.

'Oh, yes, it works,' said Jones. 'Though I am not sure our daughter needs to know that yet. Nor other things ...'

'Of course she does,' said Miss Lily. 'Violette will be a charming "lovely lady".'

'I already charm men,' declared Violette.

'Only needy ones, my dear,' said Miss Lily. 'Men who wish to believe that a person with youth and beauty like yours can desire them. Do you really wish to attract men like that?'

Violette considered. 'No,' she decided. 'Not now I am the ward of a rich woman. Unless, of course, it might be useful. What should I call you?' she asked Miss Lily. 'Are you my aunt, as her ladyship is?'

'You will call me Miss Lily.'

Sophie smiled, the ten-second kind of smile that grew into a gleeful grin. That kind of smile worked as well. She caught Miss Lily's eye, and felt warmth and joy flow through her. 'This is going to be a most instructive voyage,' she murmured.

'Indeed,' said Miss Lily, spooning up her chicken consommé with pleasure, and the grace no other could achieve.

And at the end of the voyage, wondered Sophie? Not just this journey upon the ocean, but the expedition that would be her life from this moment on?

She did not know the details; nor was her mind free enough yet of the anguish and confusion of the last months to even try to think of details now.

But she knew there would be love. Love in many flavours, a thousand tastes of love: love of children, friends, a lover perhaps, even if she automatically stopped that thought then placed a wall around it. But not a stone wall. A wall of strips of stringybark, perhaps, like the roof of 'John's' old hut.

There'd be the love of colleagues and comrades, and each of those had a thousand different tangs and savours too. Each person in the world was capable of infinite varieties of love.

Nor could love die. Nigel's love still clothed her, and she would always welcome it. Nigel Vaile, beloved husband, father, friend.

Green lifted her glass, the champagne sparkling almost as brightly as the chandeliers. 'To Nigel,' she said.

'To Nigel,' said Miss Lily, her voice soft with grief for the man who'd ceased to be.

'To my darling Nigel,' whispered Sophie, knowing that Miss Lily's tears matched her own.

MEET MISS LILY
AND HER LOVELY LADIES . . .

BOOK 1 — Out now

**A tale of espionage,
love and passionate heroism**

Inspired by true events, this is the story of how society's 'lovely ladies' won a war.

Each year at secluded Shillings Hall, in the snow-crisped English countryside, the mysterious Miss Lily draws around her young women selected from Europe's royal and most influential families. Her girls are taught how to captivate a man — and find a potential husband — at a dinner, in a salon, or at a grouse shoot, and in ways that would surprise outsiders. For in 1914, persuading and charming men is the only true power a woman has.

Sophie Higgs is the daughter of Australia's king of corned beef and the only 'colonial' brought to Shillings Hall. Of all Miss Lily's lovely ladies, however, she is also the only one who suspects Miss Lily's true purpose.

As the chaos of war spreads, women across Europe shrug off etiquette.

The lovely ladies and their less privileged sisters become the unacknowledged backbone of the war, creating hospitals, canteens and transport systems where bungling officials fail to cope. And when tens of thousands can die in a single day's battle, Sophie must use the skills Miss Lily taught her to prevent war's most devastating weapon yet.

'The story is equal parts Downton Abbey and wartime action, with enough romance and intrigue to make it 100% not-put-down-able.'
Australian Women's Weekly on *Miss Lily's Lovely Ladies*

THE WAR IS OVER, BUT CAN THERE EVER TRULY BE PEACE?

BOOK 2 — Out now

Australian heiress Sophie Higgs was 'a rose of no-man's land', founding hospitals across war-torn Europe during the horror that was WW1.

Now, in the 1920s, Sophie's wartime work must be erased so that the men who returned can find some kind of 'normality'.

Sophie is, however, a graduate of the mysterious Miss Lily's school of charm and intrigue, and once more she risks her own life as she attempts to save others still trapped in the turmoil and aftermath of war.

But in this new world, nothing is clear, in politics or in love. For the role of men has changed too. Torn between the love of three very different men, Sophie will face her greatest danger yet as she attempts an impossible journey across the world to save Nigel, Earl of Shillings — and her beloved Miss Lily.

In this sequel to the bestselling *Miss Lily's Lovely Ladies*, Jackie French draws us further into a compelling story that celebrates the passion and adventure of an unstoppable army of women who changed the world.

'If you've sped your way through The Crown and are looking for another historical drama fix to sink your teeth into, *The Lily and the Rose* is going to fast become your next obsession.'

New Idea on *Miss Lily and the Rose*

Jackie French AM is an award-winning writer, wombat negotiator, the 2014–2015 Australian Children's Laureate and the 2015 Senior Australian of the Year. In 2016 Jackie became a Member of the Order of Australia for her contribution to children's literature and her advocacy for youth literacy. She is regarded as one of Australia's most popular authors and writes across all genres — from picture books, history, fantasy, ecology and sci-fi to her much loved historical fiction for many different age groups. 'Share a Story' was the primary philosophy behind Jackie's two-year term as Laureate.

jackiefrench.com
facebook.com/authorjackiefrench